Gerhard Roth

The Odyssey of Michael Aldrian

A Novel

Gerhard Roth

The Odyssey of Michael Aldrian

A Novel

Translated and with an Afterword
by Todd C. Hanlin

Ariadne Press
Riverside, CA

The Odyssey of Michael Aldrian
By Gerhard Roth

Translated and with an Afterword
by Todd C. Hanlin
reprinted with kind permission by the author
© 2022 Todd C. Hanlin

Gerhard Roth: *Die Irrfahrt des Michael Aldrian*
© S. Fischer Verlag GmbH, Frankfurt am Main, 2017.
All rights reserved by S. Fischer Verlag GmbH.
(ISBN 978-3-10-066069-5)

Front cover photo © E.M. Rose 2021

Image credits, in order of appearance:
P. 31. Giorgio de Chirico: *Mystery and Melancholy of a Street*.
From: Maurizio Faggiolo dell'Arco: *L'opera completa di de Chirico 1908–1924*. Milan 1984 (1999).
P. 123. Image from: Cesare Ruggieri: *Selbstkreuzigung. Der Fall Matteo Lovat*. Rudolsstadt 1807 (New edition 1984).
P. 159. Jacopo Tintoretto: *The Paradise*. Doge's Palace, Venice.
P. 186. Vitore Carpaccio: *Two Venetian Ladies*. Museo Correr, Venice.
P. 187. Vittore Carpaccio: *Hunting in the Lagoon*. J. Paul Getty Museum (Villa Malibu), Los Angeles.
P. 189. See images on pages 186 and 187.
P. 191. Vittore Carpaccio: *Hunting in the Lagoon* (painted back side), see image on p. 187.

Publisher's Cataloging-in-Publication data

Names: Roth, Gerhard, 1942 June 24-2022, author. | Hanlin, Todd C., translator.
Title: The odyssey of Michael Aldrian : a novel / Gerhard Roth; translated and with an afterword by Todd C. Hanlin.
Description: Riverside CA: Ariadne Press, 2023.
Identifiers: LCCN: 2023920266 | ISBN: 978-1-57241-234-7 (paperback) | 978-1-57241-231-6 (ebook)
Subjects: LCSH Venice (Italy)--Fiction. | Crime--Fiction. | Murder--Fiction. | BISAC FICTION / World Literature / Austria / 21st Century
Classification: LCC PT2678.O79613 O39 2023 | DDC 813.6--dc23

In either hand the hastening Angel caught
Our lingering Parents, and to the eastern gate
Led them direct, and down the cliff as fast
To the subjected plain—then disappeared.
They, looking back, all the eastern side beheld
Of Paradise, so late their happy seat,
Waved over by that flaming brand; the gate
With dreadful faces thronged and fiery arms.

John Milton, *Paradise Lost*

FIRST BOOK

Journey to the Continent of Memory

I was a child prodigy, now I am a nobody, Michael Aldrian thought, late at night, as he rode past the Vienna State Opera to the train station and glanced out the side window of the taxi.

He remembered that as a child he could learn every note, every melody, every libretto after hearing it only once—and everyone had been amazed. Back then his favorite activity had been attending opera productions at the Salzburg Festival. Over time a large collection of operas had become established in his head so that—along with the particular costumes of the singers, faces of the conductors and musicians in the orchestra pit—he could recall them in minute detail and see each one in his mind's eye.

The State Opera was brightly lit and now seemed to him like some ancient spaceship, the people streaming inside to become acquainted with a distant other world. He had spent 25 years as the *Maestro Suggeritore*, the souffleur, the prompter, in the small box under the stage until a sudden hearing loss forced him to leave the spaceship and return to the outside world. In the State Opera, the cover of the prompter's box had offered him protection like a giant helmet. Now he led the life of an insect, like some solitary wasp that hides and tries to avoid making any mistakes. From the perspective of a dust mite on the floor, it had been his job to correct or help the singers and conductors avoid mistakes. The more he thought about it, the more one-sidedly he saw himself now as someone who had been abandoned, because overnight he had had to rid himself of the illusion of being indispensable. If he had been brilliant in overcoming insecurities in the singers or lack of effort on the part of the conductors—as they reassured him during rehearsals or after the performance of an opera—, he now suddenly got the bitter feeling of being insignificant, because as soon as he had returned from the hospital, they suggested that he should be looking for some other profession.

Initially he had studied conducting and singing and had eventually landed in the prompter's box, but he was hesitant only in the beginning—he had soon become an ardent Maestro Suggeritore. And now they had replaced him like a tiny worn-out screw on some gigantic machine.

The fog was so thick that the State Opera disappeared behind him like some ghostly apparition. What remained was a feeling of worthlessness that made him angry. This anger that he had only rarely indulged had been dreaded in the State Opera since he could blow up like an unexpected thunderstorm. Sometimes it took two or three days until he finally calmed down.

In Vienna it had snowed the entire month of February, it had been foggy and cold, the reason Aldrian decided to leave earlier than planned for Venice where he had a studio apartment in his brother Jakob's home. In the past several years he had always gone to Venice for Christmas and had celebrated Christmas Eve and New Year's Eve with Jakob. But this time his sister-in-law was sick.

While he was still dredging up his angry memories, it occurred to him that he might have forgotten to secure the door bar at his apartment Am Heumarkt, and as the cab driver rushed him to the train station, he tried to remember his every movement before he left. First of all he had run into the writer Philipp Artner who lived above him and was just coming down the stairs.

"Are you off to Venice again?" Artner had asked, and when Aldrian replied "Yes," the writer added: "I'm working on a novel that is set in Venice, and you are in it. That will finally give me an excuse to write about your exploits in the Opera and perhaps about your encounters with the most famous singers and conductors." Before he said goodbye, he added: "You told me so much about the State Opera in the Café Heumarkt, do you remember?"

Michael Aldrian was a virtuoso storyteller of wicked anecdotes that he had witnessed from his perspective in the prompter's box as a so-to-speak forgotten or hidden observer. He had been obsessed with his work, as they say, he had been absorbed by it like nitrogen by the air. He had always hated "vacation days," because a return to normal everyday life threw him for a loss. And so for many years he had accepted an engagement at the Salzburg Festival where his work as a souffleur had begun almost thirty years before. Because of his capabilities as Maestro Suggeritore at the Vienna State Opera, they had called him a "Mephistopheles" who influenced the world of the living from his post in the netherworld and who dominated every situation because of his apparent omniscience and verbal dexterity— because along with his amazing feats of memory, he also knew the artists' weaknesses, their poor memory and insecurities, also their fears and aversions about working with him. Some singers, both male and female, said they didn't want to surrender themselves to him, and he politely made note of that fact. Needless to say, it then gave him great satisfaction when he helped them when they forgot their lines or forgot when to come in, and he politely accepted their reluctant but often lavish praise after the performance. Another silent triumph for him was his appearance as a magician at opening-night galas and among friends.

He had been interested in magic tricks since adolescence, and later, when he was forced to take time away from music, he practiced every slight of hand until he could hold his own with professional magicians. It wasn't surprising that his marriage to a makeup artist at the State Opera didn't last long, because he would wear disguises at home and practice tricks for his magic shows. Looking back, his enthusiasm for magic tricks had been his good fortune because as a magician he could improve his financial situation and even enjoy the anticipation of an evening performance. He always wore a mask onstage. Sometimes he dressed up as a rabbit, other times as a dog or a bird. As a farewell present, he had received appropriate masks and costumes from the State Opera storeroom. At first the props were like some silent insult, but then, when the opera singer Hesse got him a booking in a hotel in Spotorno and his brother got him another gig at a Christmas party in the Belmond Hotel Cipriani in Venice, he began to enjoy the transformations. His best number was calling up people from the audience and then picking their pockets in broad daylight so to speak; no one could say how he did it and none of the victims ever noticed the theft. He had been doing this trick for over twenty years now. He realized that none of his tricks entertained the audience as much as when he picked their pockets. Sometimes he even whistled the overture to Rossini's *The Thieving Magpie* as he was picking the pocket of some unsuspecting target, thus further distracting his audience and his "victim." His next engagement was booked for that coming summer in the Miramar Hotel in Opatija—he still called it Abbazia—on the Croatian coast.

Again Aldrian tried to focus on whether he had secured the door bar before he left. In any event he had put his camera bag and the framed print of Adalbert Stifter's painting *View of the Beatrixgasse in Vienna*, a present for his brother and his wife, on the windowsill in the hallway. He had held his notebooks in his other hand—for more than ten years he had been making notes and taking photographs in Venice because he planned to publish an unconventional travel guide to the city someday. At that point he had locked the door: he now definitely remembered that he had secured the door bar. The taxi came to a jarring stop at the West Station, and after he paid, Aldrian hauled his luggage up the escalator to the sleeping car compartment that—like the taxi—was not much larger than his prompter's box at the State Opera. Softly cursing from the effort, he stowed his suitcase and sat down on the lower bunk. I hope no one comes so I don't have to share the compartment, he thought, just as the sliding door opened and a huge man stepped in. He was wearing a black coat, a black hat, and had two suitcases that he barely managed to squeeze into the compartment. Sweating and puffing, with alcohol on his breath, he sat down beside Aldrian and asked if he didn't want the upper bunk—he was afraid the flimsy ladder might collapse under his weight. Aldrian shook his head and replied that he got dizzy easily.

"Aha," the fat man responded. "Just like me. It makes me throw up," he added in a threatening tone of voice. Since Aldrian made no attempt to reply, the man abruptly introduced himself as Gottlieb Heinzl, an optometrist from Zwettl. He explained that he was going to Mestre to "get rid" of some optical instruments, such as a "lensometer" and a "handheld refractometer," as he called them, and to buy eyeglass frames.

"You can see how bad I'm sweating," he added.

And since Aldrian still didn't say anything, the man asked him petulantly: "And with whom am I speaking?" Herr Heinzl reached into his breast pocket, pulled out a flask, and offered his counterpart a drink.

"Quince schnapps," he explained.

Since Aldrian only shook his head, the man took a healthy swig and began to undress.

At first Aldrian didn't understand what Herr Heinzl was doing and watched with interest as the passenger removed his overcoat and sport coat which he then threw down on Aldrian's bed, then took off his shoes, loosened his tie, and, last of all, slipped off his shirt, pants, black socks, and stood there in only his white undershorts. When Herr Heinzl was about to take them off, too, Aldrian lay down on the bed, facing the wall.

"My overcoat," he heard the optometrist protest, "and my sport coat! Where am I going to put them?" He wheezed, but must have found a solution, because Aldrian heard him take another swig from his flask and then, breathing heavily, climb the ladder and stretch out on the creaking upper bunk. He farted loudly and snorted, and a few seconds later didn't make another peep. A horrible stench slowly filled the compartment, so Aldrian opened the door to the corridor and then the window. He felt a jolt as the train started to move and watched as the platform went past and the rails fanned out before him. The compartment light was still on, and before Aldrian turned it off, he closed the door and the window and took a 10mg. Valium tablet with some sparkling mineral water from one of the two bottles that the sleeping car porter had placed on the folding table under the window. He only took off his sport coat and his shoes and stretched out on the narrow bed that, in relation to the upper bunk, again reminded him of his prompter's box. It occurred to him that "Falstaff" was lying up there above him, and he related this thought to Giuseppe Verdi's marvelous music. He could feel himself falling asleep, but just as he was dozing off, Herr Heinzl began to snore, loudly and unevenly. It sounded as if he were choking. Aldrian got up, turned on the light, saw that Heinzl was sleeping deeply, almost passed out, and out of curiosity watched the man as he snored away. Then he went back to bed. Under normal circumstances he never slept well on trains, and though he had taken the tablet, he didn't feel sleepy. Heinzl's snoring reminded him of his grandfather who had had a house and a barbershop in St. Gilgen am Wolfgangsee. His wife was a wigmaker for the Salzburg Opera and the Festival. Both were vibrant, active people and had one son, Aldrian's father, who continued the tradition. His mother had been born in nearby Bad Aussee where his grandfather had been employed managing the salt mine and in 1945 had joined in preventing the Nazi district leader from dynamiting the mine and the huge number of treasures from the Museum of Fine Arts in Vienna that were hidden in the galleries. His grandfather, together with several farmers and members of management, had joined in this dangerous undertaking. He had frequently taken his grandsons Michael and Jakob down into the interior of the salt mine and shown them where the "artwork" of Rembrandt and Pieter Brueghel the Elder, of Velázquez and Dürer, of Caravaggio and Vermeer had been located. Employing thick art books that he had bought over the years, he had first explained who Parmigianino had been, and then went on to Arcimboldo, Holbein or Gainsborough, Frans Hals, Ruisdael, Hieronymus Bosch or Raphael, Titian, Tintoretto, Giorgione or Giovanni Bellini. His brother Jakob had been so excited by the paintings and the lives of the painters that he had asked their grandfather time and again

14

to show him the painters and their works in the art books, while Michael himself had been more fascinated by the elevator ride down into the galleries, into the underworld. Eventually their grandfather had taken them to the Museum of Fine Arts in Vienna, led them through halls with countless large and small paintings. From that point on, Michael had associated the oil paintings, especially the hall with Pieter Brueghel the Elder, with the galleries in the salt mine, and later with Sigmund Freud's *Theory of the Unconscious,* and even later with his own profession as souffleur. In his imagination, he realized, he had felt that his prompter's box in the Salzburg Festival or at the Vienna State Opera was comparable to a gallery in the Bad Aussee salt mine. The costumed singers onstage were the hidden paintings that had come to life. He also compared them to his dreams. Jakob, on the other hand, had begun to copy the pictures in Grandfather's books and had developed an amazing dexterity. Due to Grandfather's connections at the Museum of Fine Arts, he had even gotten Jakob permission to copy paintings on certain days during the summer vacation. Michael, however, had started piano and violin lessons at an early age, and as a result of his unusual retentiveness had soon been playing compositions by Mozart, Hummel, and Bach from memory. But both he and his brother had remained only copyists in their artistic endeavors. They both lacked any creative powers, their own distinctive styles—one, a personal sound, the other, an original brushstroke: Michael was unable to create a distinctive musical style on his instruments, and his brother was unable to produce original drawings. Later Jakob greatly enlarged copies of cloud moods and fabric patterns from paintings and as a result began to paint abstract pictures, while Michael could only vary the compositions he had memorized. Nevertheless, their father was so delighted with his two sons that he could see them as a future director or stage designer at the Salzburg Festival where he himself, like his parents before him, created hairstyles and wove wigs, the reason why he also owned a barbershop with a workshop in Salzburg. Their mother, a teacher at the Salzburg elementary school, had ambitions for her children similar to those of their father.

The loud farting and snoring jolted Aldrian awake. The images in his mind disappeared. Half-asleep, he tumbled over to the window and yanked it down. Only now, as he stuck his head out into the darkness of night, did the fragments of his memories arrange themselves in chronological order. And when sufficient ice-cold fresh air had filled the compartment, he closed the window and shook Gottlieb Heinzl until he woke up. The optometrist, stinking of alcohol and perspiration, sat bolt upright. When Aldrian angrily started to explain that he was loudly snoring and farting, the man fell back on his pillow and soon resumed his uneven snoring.

Since Aldrian still couldn't get to sleep, random memories raced through his head. He stopped depending on memory to flood him with images in any random order, but asked himself—at the moment an impression appeared before him—what had happened next. That prevented the events from no longer being kaleidoscopically intermingled, but instead formed series of smaller narratives, much like murals or depictions found on Romanesque tapestries.

Lying on the narrow bed with his eyes closed, he could now envision his own fingers as he played the piano and his brother's adolescent hands as he was drawing with his crayons.

The first operatic production he had seen at the Salzburg Festival was Mozart's *The Marriage of Figaro*, and he recalled how he, as a six-year-old, had reconstructed the entire opera, including its distinct vocal parts and extensive libretto passages, for his enthusiastic parents in their living room the following evening.

From that point on, they had treated him like a young saint, just like his older brother. But it was often disconcerting the way they bragged about the abilities of their children to their acquaintances.

On a summer day they had spent in St. Gilgen am Wolfgangsee—by then he and his brother were fourteen and sixteen years old respectively—their father reported that he had cut the hair of the venerable Nobel Prize laureate Karl von Frisch. He had told the gentleman about his sons, and von Frisch—probably out of curiosity—had subsequently invited them to visit him in Brunnwinkl on the Wolfgangsee. Von Frisch had studied the language of honeybees, and in the next couple of days their father had read the Nobel laureate's book *The Dancing Bees* and every evening after dinner would give his children a simplified version of its contents.

On the following Sunday morning they parked their car at the entrance to the pedestrian zone and walked down to Brunnwinkl. Not one of them said a word. Brunnwinkl was a charming place. Michael and Jakob had come back several times since then and had read Karl von Frisch's memoir *Five Houses on the Lake*.

Meanwhile the sleeping compartment had become a quaking prompter's box. While Falstaff was snoring on the stage up above him, Aldrian, down below, continued to scroll through the musical score of his memories . . . Except for the second house, the Fisherman's House, the other four buildings in Brunnwikl were eventually acquired by Karl von Frisch's grandparents and parents. The little settlement was situated in a secluded area on a wooded inlet of the lake. In the rear building—previously a mill, separated from the woods by a meadow—, the bee researcher spent almost every summer of his long life; the rest of the year he pursued his profession as a biologist at the University of Munich. From 1945 to 1950—since the University of Munich had been bombed out during the Second World War—he lectured at the University of Graz in Austria. As Aldrian recalled, Jakob had been especially curious about the man who had deciphered the language of the honeybees. Jakob especially wanted to see the meadow where von Frisch had conducted the bulk of his bee experiments, while Aldrian was worried that the visit would be boring.

Brunnwinkl was a hotbed of activity in July. The buildings had been newly whitewashed, some—like the second, the Fisherman's House, as Michael's father had learned from the professor—had been furnished with a second story made of wood. Each of the houses had at least one balcony. Behind the second house stood a huge linden tree with a bench that circled the trunk. That was where—my father whispered, awestruck—Karl von Frisch was sitting, waiting for them. He was wearing lederhosen, glasses, and a white shirt. As he stood up to greet them, Aldrian realized that the man wasn't much taller than he himself.

"Are these the two child prodigies?" he asked, smiling and shaking the boys' hands. His silvery white hair shimmered in the sunlight. Aldrian's father always had an umbrella with him, opened it slightly and pulled out a piece of paper that he quickly gave to Jakob, and the boy in turn shyly handed it to the famous old man. Von Frisch glanced at the pencil drawing and then said: "You made that from one of my photographs, didn't you? I know that picture."

Jakob was so excited that he couldn't answer.

"And the bees ... You've copied them from a book about insects." He studied the drawing and then said: "Not a single mistake!" and held it up to the light. Aldrian hadn't really noticed at home that his brother had drawn a portrait of the professor, and now he saw the amazing result: the professor and a dozen bees that adorned the picture. A year later Jakob had painted a second portrait of Karl von Frisch with a swarm of bees encircling his head like a halo. He had given it to Michael for his birthday and it had hung in his apartment ever since. But Karl von Frisch had become a guiding figure for Jakob, and for Michael, too, but for other reasons ...

At first they had gone over to the mill where they drank raspberry lemonade and eaten honey bread. Then the professor had led him into a rustic furnished room with chairs whose backrests had heart-shaped cutouts—as was customary in these parts—and a large table where the family probably ate lunch together. Von Frisch put Giuseppe Verdi's *La forza del destino* on the record player—at an unbearably loud volume since the biologist, as it turned out, had become hard of hearing—and together they followed the first act. The opera was new to Michael because, although they did have a record player at home, they didn't have a recording of *La forza del destino*, so he listened with utmost concentration. And since he had been taking Italian lessons for the past three years from a neighbor lady in Salzburg, he was able to perform the opera, singing long portions of the text or—when he couldn't remember the words—singing only "lalala". When he had finished, von Frisch was astonished, and asked him: "Do you also see colors when you sing?"

"Yes," Michael answered truthfully. "C is yellow, D is green . . ."—he related the correlation between notes and sounds with colors, and the professor took notes the whole time.

Then the old man leaned back and said: "Music is continually changing. It is in a constant state of transformation. Metamorphosis is the vital principle of Nature. The process of transformation sometimes proceeds slowly, at other times more rapidly, but it has its effect on us, even when we think we have reached stasis. An insect first comes into being as an egg, then turns into a larva, pupates, and lastly hatches as an imago in the form that we all recognize. You can best see the beauty and variety of these transformations by studying the butterfly. What a surprise when the adult appears in the most striking colors: the common brimstone, the cabbage white, the small tortoiseshell, the large tortoiseshell, the swallowtail." Michael was enchanted. No one had ever spoken with him like that. And when the professor then outlined the metamorphosis of human beings—from child to adult to geriatric, from pupil to teacher, artist, or murderer—Michael realized that he had heard something new that he paradoxically had always known, but without knowing that he knew it. From then on he saw all further developments in his life like melodies in music, as continuing processes of transformation. Later, when Aldrian was a grownup, he no longer doubted that the professor's words had made such a lasting impression just because he was a boy, that special time when people try to salvage at least something of their existence so they don't perish before their actual death.

The professor praised him when they went back out on the veranda. He enthusiastically described the "experiment," as he called it, to Michael's parents and said he was looking forward to a future meeting—that unfortunately never took place. He then turned to Jakob and asked the lad to follow him. They were gone more than an hour before they came back out. The Nobel laureate exultantly showed them the drawing that Jakob had done in the meantime. From a zoological textbook he had copied a chameleon in two stages of its coloration, enlarged and in exquisite detail, and partially colored with crayons. "Here we can see something entirely different from the transformation, the metamorphosis that I discussed with Michael. The chameleon is a master of mimicry, of disguise. Since Darwin, we know that human beings have their origins from the remarkable monkeys. But I believe that we come from chameleons." He laughed, and the rest of us laughed, too—probably from tension and over-excitement. That was the second valuable lesson that Aldrian gained from the meeting. Karl von Frisch's words were never forgotten—such as the terms "metamorphosis," "mimicry," and the comparison of humans with chameleons.

The children and youngsters in Brunnwinkl had a sailboat, a rowboat, and a bathing beach at the shoreline where they could swim out into the water. Michael, too, secretly wished he could be like them, but the discoverer of the language of the bees was already on his way up into the attic of the front house where they saw hundreds of stuffed and mounted animals that had all been caught and killed by him and his extended family: foxes, badgers, groundhogs or rabbits, deer as well as snakes, salamanders or owls. In addition, there were glass cases with butterflies, moths, dragonflies, honeybees, beetles, grasshoppers, crickets, and other insects. Everything was labeled by hand, and when they were finished, the professor invited Jakob to spend the rest of the day with him and draw.

While Aldrian was having lunch with his parents in a nearby restaurant, Jakob, as they learned later that evening, was eating with the professor and his family in Brunnwinkl. As Jakob told them, the professor kept encouraging him to speak up, since the old man was hard of hearing. Jakob spoke softly, as was his nature, in contrast to his brother Michael. Sometimes Jakob only whispered so that Michael could barely understand him, and it made him angry.

That afternoon Karl von Frisch took his visitors out in the meadow behind the old millhouse where there were several beehives. To give them a treat, he briefly explained how he investigated the language of the bees, and finally the two brothers were also permitted to swim at the beach.

Meanwhile Aldrian must have fallen asleep, because when

he opened his eyes, awakened by especially loud snoring, he first thought he had been dreaming. Falstaff in the upper bunk suddenly sat upright, clumsily came down the ladder, turned on the light, and went out into the corridor in his underpants. So the ludicrous drama that Aldrian sullenly observed from his rolling, jolting, swaying prompter's box was going to continue. In the weak overhead light, the days from his past seemed so long ago. He thought about his brother, the way Jakob looked back then, as best he could remember, and about how Jakob himself had begun to study biology and to collect insects, following the example of Karl von Frisch. He had always been a marvelous illustrator of nature. Aldrian also recalled how his brother had made field trips to meadows and woods, while he himself had preferred to spend his time in the water. In his limited spare time, Aldrian had gotten certified for motorboats and sailboats, and, while studying to become a conductor, his love for the water even led him to become qualified as navigator for the local excursion boat. He would occasionally sit on the bridge with his friend, the boat's operator, and be allowed to pilot the ship across the Wolfgangsee.

But then came the fateful evening at the Salzburg Festival when the frantic director of the Festival Hall begged him to fill in for a prompter who had become ill . . .

The door to the compartment was yanked open and Herr Heinzl returned with a painful expression. As the man climbed back up the ladder to the upper bunk, Aldrian could hear him cursing and groaning until all was quiet again.

Aldrian thought he might now be able to doze for a couple of hours, but Falstaff started snoring again, and Michael fled back into his world of memories.

He remembered that his brother had later become an assistant in the Department of Entomology in Vienna and had published a guide to insects, the first of his illustrated books. Subsequently Jakob had used watercolors to illustrate a guide to birds, a botanical work about orchids, and an atlas of seashells. In his drowsy state, Aldrian could see the pictures that Jakob had given him and that now hung in his apartment . . . They were very beautiful, in his opinion. If you looked at them long enough, they emanated something magical; he felt an unusual affinity to the organisms and even to the plants. The visits to the galleries of the salt mine in Aussee had awakened a lasting curiosity about caves in Jakob and himself, and he recalled how they had met Jakob's future wife during a tour of the giant ice cave in Werfen. As it turned out, she was three years older than Jakob, tall, dark-haired, elegant, and her name was Elena. Jakob had already approached her during their hike through the extensive labyrinth of galleries, and after the three of them had come out of the cave exhausted, they learned over a glass of wine that she was a restorer at the Tate Gallery, having worked in the Louvre for two years. Her parents owned a store in Venice selling large seashells and mollusks, fossils, jewelry, and especially pearls; they were, as it turned out, extremely wealthy. Aldrian had also fallen in love with Elena, but since Jakob had already drawn some mollusks, birds, and butterflies for her before Michael had even had the chance to impress her with his piano playing in the bar of their hotel, and, besides, since he was younger than his brother, he resumed the planned hike into the limestone and river caves in Dorfgastein and Lamprechtsofen alone. He now remembered that when he had stepped out from the darkness of the caves and into the daylight, he had been blinded by the glaring sun.

But this time it was the porter who was shining a flashlight in his face . . . At first Aldrian was disoriented, but then saw that Falstaff had left the stage and the opera was over. He said to himself that in this quaking prompter's box he had finally fallen asleep—probably from exhaustion. The porter explained that the train had just stopped in Mestre and would continue on to Venice in twenty minutes. It was still dark outside, and his memories flew off to wherever they had come from.

SECOND BOOK

In Atlantis

For almost 25 years now, whenever he was in Venice, he stayed in an attic room with a kitchenette in his brother's home. On his usually brief visits, he normally went to the opera, the Teatro La Fenice, where he knew one of the Maestri Suggeritori, Lorenzo Verra.

His brother had often taken him on trips—to the Lido or to Murano, Burano and Torcello—so that they could hike around and seek out the most celebrated cafés and local taverns, the *ostarias*. Jakob enjoyed telling him about the history of the city, had given him books about Venice, and persuaded him to frequent churches and to look at paintings in the Accademia. As a result, Aldrian had also become familiar with St. Mark's Basilica, the Campanile, and the Doge's Palace. But his brother couldn't have suspected that Michael found religious Renaissance paintings and churches to be depressing. He equated them with catacombs and nightmares. He was satisfied with life in the art world as Maestro Suggeritore at the Opera where music suspended time and space and thus gave the proceedings something incomparable. From his vantage point in the prompter's box he saw legs, bellies, breasts and, above them, faces, like autonomous alien beings. On the other hand, for him the religious Renaissance pictures were to be understood as evidence of facts, as proof that whatever he saw couldn't be refuted. The sacral paintings reproduced in his brother's books truly haunted him even in his sleep. As far as he was concerned, the faithful suffered from a kind of persecution complex, since they continuously felt themselves observed and exposed before God who saw and knew everything.

He said to himself that they lived in a secret surveillance state, without seeing, hearing, or even knowing the observer. But since the Opera had been taken from him, he now wanted to confront these pictures, yes, he wanted to get to the bottom of this "watertown," as he jokingly called it. For the next several days, among other things, he had an appointment in the Doge's Palace, a place he knew inside out, but he wanted to see its "secret passages" again. The first thing he needed to do was keep his appointment in the Archivio di Stato di Venezia that the Director of the Austrian State Archives in Vienna, Dr. Mikoletzky, had arranged for him; in addition, a psychiatrist interested in the arts, Dr. Feilacher, had provided the opportunity to visit the former insane asylum on the island of San Servolo; and, last but not least, Dr. Rachinger, the Director of the National Library, had gotten him access to the Biblioteca Marciana on the Piazza San Marco. His brother and sister-in-law had also obtained various permissions for tours that they had sent him in the mail.

He carried his suitcase down the steps from the sleeping car to the platform and then, pulling his suitcase behind him and with the framed print by Adalbert Stifter under his arm, he went through the station lobby where people approached him with yellow plastic bags on their legs. He knew right away that it meant *acqua alta,* high water. He had already experienced it once, and dramatically so, back in 2008 during Advent. He and his brother had taken a vaporetto, a waterbus, to St. Mark's Square wearing rubber boots up to their hips. They had waded through the water to Caffè Florian and drunk a spritz cocktail in the marvelous accommodations. He couldn't remember how they had gotten home.

To his surprise, the acqua alta was even worse this time. On his way to the kiosks that sell tickets for the vaporetti, Aldrian had to wade through ankle-deep water, and on the steps to the station there were peddlers offering provisional boots—two yellow plastic bags with soles and heels. As he was waiting for the next vaporetto, he pulled on a pair—they went up to his knees—and walked over to the landing. Standing there, he called his brother's number on his smartphone, but no one answered. And he couldn't get ahold of Jakob's wife, Elena, either. But since he had already told them that he would be staying longer this time, perhaps they weren't in any great hurry to greet him.

The next vaporetto was almost empty, just an old married couple with their white lapdog were sitting amidships: the man was decked out in a wig and black three-cornered hat, his wife with a huge plume hat and lorgnon. With her face powdered white, her bright red lipstick made her teeth look dark yellow. The two in their costumes looked as if they had escaped from some museum. When he stepped into their compartment, they stared at him until he rested the picture on the floor; their lapdog briefly yapped, then, bored, they resumed staring out the window. Although Aldrian felt tired, he remained standing and gazed at the *palazzi* along the Grand Canal that he had seen so many times now. Before, they had always been romantic stage settings, but this time they seemed like a new home. As they passed by, even the Palazzo Vendramin, where Richard Wagner had died and that was now the Venice casino, was no longer just another tourist attraction; he associated the building with a production of *Tristan und Isolde* with its set design and music that spontaneously came to mind—but since he told himself that he had to start a new life, the recollection immediately disappeared. He turned back to the costumed couple that now seemed to him like two confused members of the State Opera chorus who had lost their way to the stage, and he realized that the man holding the white lapdog had left his seat and sat down one row in front of his wife so that he could also sit at a window. Aldrian noticed that the man was also wearing yellow provisional boots that made his Carnivalesque appearance a little more peculiar. His wife must also have been wearing provisional boots, he decided, and it made Aldrian think of two poisonous flowers in yellow porcelain vases. Each of the palazzos had a romantic flair that made him wish he could overcome time. He briefly had a feeling he was simultaneously in the present and in the past. Since he had come to the lagoon city this time with a specific purpose and had certain expectations, he was also dealing with the future. The palazzos that also represented the past and present and would also exist into the future, at least as long as the city existed, seemed to him confirmation of his thoughts. As a child he had sought the feeling of timelessness and sensed it first in puppet theater, then in the theater itself, and finally in opera. In a vague way—that was so ridiculous he felt ashamed—his own life had become an endless opera, with a sub-stage, fly space, audience, conductors, cast, and, not least, his prompter's box that could also be a taxi, a sleeping car compartment, a vaporetto, or a room. But he was afraid that someday he would become an object of ridicule if he didn't fight this mental image. He smiled. When he was a part of a vast opera performance, than it was more like an invisible atom of oxygen within the air, he said to himself. The gondolas on the waterfront were floating in the acqua alta like oversize forgotten toys, and there was little traffic on the Grand Canal.

At the next station two men with plastic boots up to their hips got on. They were wearing anoraks, jeans, and carrying briefcases that gave the trip a touch of everyday reality. Their expressions betrayed their indifference, as if everything going on around them was basically something they had seen many times before, and when one of them sat down and took a newspaper out of his case and started to read, it made Aldrian think of the fish market that he had to traverse to get to his brother's house and his store "Jurassic Park." The display windows of the store were decorated with animal skulls—recently with a crocodile, a swordfish, and a monkey—as well as the shells of marine snails, mussels, and expensive pearl jewelry. They looked bizarre, but in a sophisticated way elegant and respectable. Of course Jakob also sold the skulls, mussels, and even rare and expensive butterflies and crystals, but he made his biggest profit with pearls from China. That's what his brother had often told him. Aldrian had no idea how the business was doing. He rarely saw customers in the shop, usually just curious folks who were only browsing. In the distance he could see the Rialto Bridge and several gondolas with Asian visitors who were photographing every square inch of the city. Like all tourists, Aldrian hated the other tourists, especially the ones who, in search of romance, were rowed through the canals in gondolas. They probably thought they were experiencing the real Venice. But there was no "real Venice" anymore, Aldrian thought with schadenfreude.

There was no one in sight on the Rialto Bridge, and elsewhere everything seemed to be slowly sinking under the seawater. From his vantage point on the vaporetto he could only see the backs of the stores on the Rialto Bridge and couldn't be sure that the shops were even open. The high-water catwalks, benches placed end to end, had mostly been submerged under the darkly shimmering surface of the acqua alta, and he could only identify individual sections. He got off at the Rialto Mercato station and immediately found himself in knee-deep floodwater from the Canal. The fish market was apparently closed. And he couldn't see any activity at the vegetable market either. There was only a lone vendor offering his wares at a booth with a cloth top. A solitary old pedestrian—also in rubber boots and a narrow-brimmed rain hat on his head—was just having four or five oranges weighed. Aldrian could see onions, arugula salad, and eggplants in the old man's shopping bag. The fish market, normally a lively place with its large yellow retail gallery, was empty. As always, the red tarps that served as protection from sun and wind hung down from the arcades. Even on Sundays and Mondays the smell of dead marine creatures was noticeable, and today as well. As he crossed the gallery, the water was only up to his shins. All of a sudden, just two steps in front of him, he saw something just below the water's surface, a stingray, as he discovered. He paused and noticed that it was dead. The fish was floating above the floor with its yellow-grey belly up, and it moved slightly whenever Aldrian moved. It had obviously been left behind after the last market and been washed up by the acqua alta. Heavy-duty carts for the wares, tables, and equipment had been stored behind one pillar. The water level receded gradually as he approached the building with the sign "Jurassic Park," and the entrance was actually dry. From a distance the shop with the two display windows seemed to Aldrian to be deserted, but that had often been the case, even when his brother was at home. The shop was usually dimly lit: only the glass sales counter was illuminated from below and the ceiling lights were only turned on when a customer wanted to see better. His brother did this to discourage curiosity-seekers from coming in.

After he had unlocked the front door, picked up several pieces of mail, letters, brochures, and a newspaper from the floor and put them on a table by the coat rack, he took off his provisional rain boots. He was amazed at how quiet it was in the house and he asked himself where his brother might be. Then he took a deep breath before climbing the steep three flights of stairs to the top floor with his suitcase and the framed picture in the plastic bag. He noticed that the door to his brother's residence wasn't shut. He called inside that he had just arrived, but got no response. Jakob had probably just gone out somewhere . . . and Elena was traveling, he reassured himself . . . Still, it was strange . . . Exhausted and sweating, he climbed the stairs, put his suitcase down on the floor, and opened the door to his studio apartment. Inside it was ice-cold, as it always was on his winter visits, while it was generally unbearably hot in summer. Before he arrived, Elena had always heated the place or opened the windows, depending on the season. But this time, with the help of a nearby instruction booklet, he laboriously turned on the heating and the boiler, an activity that infuriated him more and more, because he didn't know the first thing about owner's manuals. Either he misunderstood or didn't understand at all. As Maestro Suggeritore at the State Opera, whenever he purchased some technical gizmo, he would always consult one of the stagehands and the man would put it together in his apartment and, as he assumed, laugh at him behind his back. He paid the man generously, so at least the fellow didn't make fun of him, Aldrian thought, but respected him for his musical and linguistic talents. This time, however, with the instructions all in Italian, he could tell how obtuse he really was. Of course he accepted that fact, but his impatience, his aversion to appliances, and his failed attempts finally drove him to the point where he pitched everything aside and left the alcove in the kitchen enraged, pulled his own hip-high boots out from behind the wardrobe, slipped on his anorak, and, without unpacking his suitcase, was about to leave the house when he noticed that the heater was running. At first he couldn't believe it, but it gradually got warm in the studio apartment.

After he had hidden his passport with the debit card and the bulk of his money, as usual under the brown paper that lined the wardrobe, he glanced out the window at the empty fish gallery that reminded him of the loneliness in de Chirico's paintings. So he went down to the piazza, first stepping inside his brother's residence and calling his name, but there was no answer. Once outside, he tried to peer through the unlit display window and into the store. But it

was dark and silent behind the glass, and Aldrian now realized that the lights beneath the sales counter also weren't on. He pulled his phone out of his raincoat and tried once more to reach his brother and then Elena, but, again, neither of them answered. He considered calling their son Emilio who was studying art in England. Or Elena's sister? But he put the phone back in his pocket and decided to wait until evening. He was thinking that now he was free—without any duties and without being attached to anyone. He strolled over to the Rialto Bridge with the sloshing sound of the water beneath his boots, first through the empty fish gallery, between the deserted fruit and vegetable stands and past the butcher's shop specializing in horsemeat that left a sweetish stench of death in his nostrils. It pulled him away from the Grand Canal into the confusing alleys where the water had collected in shallow puddles. But as he turned toward the Rialto Bridge, he again stumbled onto the acqua alta that suddenly was up to the top of his boots. The benches that were pushed together for pedestrians during high water were submerged, as he had noticed from the vaporetto. He stumbled, but was able to regain his balance. There wasn't a single person around. Usually a mass of tourists from the train station marched to the Rialto Bridge all day long, and from there to St. Mark's Square. But now everything was dead. A cat looked down at him from its window. Then, from far off, he could hear a vaporetto approaching. Meanwhile a barge with old furniture and three men in orange-colored jackets swept past on the Grand Canal. It occurred to him that he was possibly seeing Venice sink into the sea. He had already tried several times to visit the Museo Fortuny, but each time it had been closed for restorations. Fortuny, the son of a Spanish salon painter, had been a world-famous fashion designer. He acquired the Palazzo Pesaro degli Orfei where he received his female clients—actresses, princesses, and the wives of millionaires. But, more than anything else, Fortuny had been a set designer, photographer and painter, and an admirer of Richard Wagner. At the State Opera, Aldrian had prompted the entire *Nibelungen* cycle and knew the composer's other operas by heart. He liked *Tristan und Isolde* best. And it was precisely the illustrations of Fortuny's textile designs that he had seen and admired in Jakob's books that reminded him of this opera. When he arrived at the steps of the Rialto Bridge, he felt the wind and a fine spray of invisible water droplets on his face. As he climbed the steps, his legs felt noticeably lighter and gave him a feeling of weightlessness. He imagined he had never climbed the bridge so quickly before. He didn't see a soul and the majority of the shops had closed. The stores still blocked his sight of the Canal on both sides. If he wanted to have a view, he would have to take one of the side staircases. Just then he saw a pigeon in the clouded sky above his head, but the wind hampered its flight, so it landed with fluttering wings on the roof of a cottage-style shop. In the store below, all kinds of masks were on display. He had long been familiar with the "Plague Doctors" who in their costume—a beak-like nose, black hat and capes—looked like grieving ravens, or the long-nosed "Pierrots," and the women's masks that looked like dolls from the time of the Rococo. As a child, he had been entranced by masks and disguises, and during his vocal studies he had often found opportunities to make himself up as various historical personages. At the same time he wasn't happy that his whole life long he had been such a "dreamer"—as his ex-wife had called him.

He went into the shop, bought a plain comedic mask with a long nose, and asked to have it put in a relatively large plastic bag because he knew that the acqua alta could suddenly recede and then he would look ridiculous in his tall boots. Most Venetians carried around a large plastic bag during high water where they could also stow their boots when necessary. The water on the other side of the Rialto Bridge was just as deep, and the usual souvenir booths were gone from the piazza before he came to the first steps. The Grand Canal was strangely deserted. Aldrian felt the desire to go back and look down onto the Canal, but since he wanted to visit the Museo Fortuny, he slogged on to the Campo Manin that was covered with placid ankle-deep acqua alta that reflected the surrounding buildings like a mirror. The scene made him pause and glance around. It wasn't until a dog ran across the piazza and disturbed a portion of the mirror images so they then dissolved into strips of color and distorted reflections that he crossed the Rio di San Luca that had overflowed its banks and finally reached the Campo San Beneto where the water was calf-deep. He walked as fast as he could to the entrance of the museum at the backside of the magnificent Palazzo Pesaro. It was made of wood and had an exterior staircase. This gave the Palazzo a rustic appearance, while the front that faced the Grand Canal looked like an oriental palace. The Pesaros had been an influential family and had even contributed a doge. In the 17th century the building had been a theater, and in the 18th even a concert hall that had the name *Palazzo Pesaro degli Orfei,* The Palace of Orpheus, a name that had impressed Aldrian the first time he heard it. Just as he was climbing the wooden staircase, it occurred to him that the Museum might also be closed due to the acqua alta. The garden, the potted plants and shrubs, the tile floor and the small fountain were all under water that formed a small pond between the brick walls surrounding the garden. On every floor above him Aldrian recognized loggias with wooden pillars that allowed him to estimate the unusual height of the halls in the building's interior. A black-and-white photograph of a veiled woman hung in a glass frame as a poster at the front door. Just inside the Palazzo he realized that he was probably the only visitor. The attendant was sitting at a desk, seemingly preoccupied with cash register receipts, and didn't react to the sound of Aldrian's footsteps. Aldrian sat down at a table that was apparently one of the objects in the exhibit. The walls of the large hall were papered in various floral patterns—a type of pastiche composed of colorful theater curtains—and above that, the walls were decorated with gold-framed oil paintings in the Symbolist style. The ambience of the halls that he could see from the vantage point of his chair gave an oriental impression, similar to the front of the building. Hat-shaped lamp shades as big as wagon wheels and made from richly patterned fabrics hung from the wooden rafters on the ceiling. He stood up and took a few steps toward a cloudy mirror in a gilt frame to see how he looked. He thought he looked like a ghost. When he briefly closed his eyes, he heard in the back of his head Isolde's exaltation: "Are these waves of soft airs? Are these billows of delightful fragrances? How they swell, how they sigh around me, shall I breathe, shall I listen? Shall I drink, immerse? Sweetly in fragrances melt away? In the billowing torrent, in the resonating sound, in the wafting universe of the World's breath—drown—be engulfed—unconscious—supreme delight!" Then he imagined himself in a silent film, sitting alone in the hall of the Museum where he had found refuge as the lone survivor of a catastrophic flood.

He found himself in an enchanting universe that consisted of art. There were old photograph albums with brown-tinted pictures, framed textiles with patterns that seemed to him like microscopic slivers from *The Arabian Nights*, there were the hat-shaped lamp shades that transformed light into a maelstrom of revolving Chinese ideographs, and stage sets like rooms in dollhouses, drafts in the language of fragments, effusive gold-framed oil paintings of naked women, old black-and-white photographs with Venetian motifs that were taken from a boat or a gondola that reminded him of the perspective from his prompter's box, as well as pictures of a car race that Fortuny must have seen. The black-and-white photo showed an avenue of poplars where an open sports car had suddenly appeared, trailing a cloud of dust, with men in caps along the roadside observing the car with obvious curiosity. He glanced at the date, 1902. In addition, there were painted self-portraits, along with depictions of nude models, male and female, and a painting of Fortuny's wife Henriette; furthermore, skeletons of gazelle, ram, and ox skulls, the bust of an African male, death masks, plaster casts of hands, a giant seashell, and a piece of fabric with flamboyant ornaments that had been casually tossed into the mix. It seemed to Aldrian that Fortuny had tried to capture the flow of time and prospect gold nuggets from its riverbed. He wasn't concerned about capturing his present day and displaying that, he would rather distill from it a nucleus of beauty and make it visible for all time. Aldrian stopped before a display case that exhibited a dark-green vestment of silk and velvet, and studied its golden pattern, consisting of a jug, a circle, and imaginary plants. Seen from afar, the robe had something pompous-regal about it, but close up, something of Merlin's magic. He scrutinized the ornamentation and material as living microscopic tissue. A dress of silk and velvet displayed a pattern of scales as if it had been stripped from some large fish, but on the side in the darkness it more reminded him of the representation of a cemetery with tombstones rounded at their top. Another fabric, at first glance, seemed to be covered with footprints of some unknown creature—double circles that contained monochrome flower petals and long-stemmed buds. In another display, silk and velvet produced imaginary purple bouquets or revealed delicate botanical creations seemingly concealed in drops of blood. Snakes with poppy-seed heads were lying on light brown earth. It gave him the impression that Fortuny had succeeded in peeking into Paradise through a tiny crack and grasping atoms and molecules from the Creation. Fortuny had transferred his visions onto fabrics that he then fabricated with the aid of printing machines on the island of Giudecca. The next thing Aldrian saw was a large dark-brown decoration that was mathematically calculated in minute detail and he was amazed all over again. It was set on a gold background that was itself decorated with patterns of pale plants. For Aldrian it was like a oracular symbol that contained all the alphabets in the world, including the language of plants and birds, fish and insects, of dogs, cats, frogs, and rhinoceroses. The other cryptic and symmetrical creations struck Aldrian like fairytales of geometry. On dark-green, dark-red, dark-blue, and dark-brown textiles he detected grapes, pineapples, frolicking dogs, ocean waves, flowers like black blobs, symmetrical thorn bushes, vases, or birds with long tongues hanging from their beaks. He also saw that Fortuny had designed colorful pillows on a sofa, white Grecian sculptures, torsos of young boys. Fortuny's photographic equipment—a wooden box with a lens—was in another display case. Aldrian was lost in thought when the attendant came over and pleasantly asked if he also wanted to see the second floor that was presently closed. Aldrian saw that the man was half-bald, had a beard and false teeth. He happily pulled off his rubber boots, put them down with his mask in the plastic bag beside the attendant's desk, and followed him up the stairs.

Later on he could only remember isolated details from the artist's studio: the small sink with the brass faucet and, above that, like a lush colorful bouquet, the brushstrokes from color samples that Fortuny had left behind on this part of the wall. The attendant went on ahead, opened a door, turned on the light, and showed him the library, a room painted dark-red, bookcases with white busts in Grecian style, the painted trim on the wall above embellished with symbols. Beside the large desk was a printing press with a star-shaped swivel rod. In among the books he saw framed panels in Arabian calligraphy, but even the attendant didn't know what they meant. As on the ground level, the floor was stone, folios were lying on the table: an ancient anatomical atlas, a thick photo album, and the blueprint for a theater or an opera house of the future, as the sign said. He also noticed a still camera of light-brown wood with its front protected by a brass plate and, in the desk between the Arabic panels and the books, a drawer with hundreds of small drill bits. In addition there were other tools, cans, glass containers with dye powder, test tubes, pipettes, boxes full of little doll parts, and a yellow collapsible metric tape. Grey daylight was visible through the tall crown glass windows. The attendant opened a small hidden door in the bookcase behind Fortuny's desk; it led to a narrow antechamber with a wooden staircase to the roof. Here, too, Aldrian discovered yet another chaotic hodgepodge of the most diverse objects—three walking canes, corked dark-green bottles, things wrapped in paper, brushes, paintbrushes, cans and boxes, little prescription bottles with chemicals and paints, drawers with new and old colored pencils, old glass vases, white light bulbs, custom-cut flat boards. He realized that he was standing in the secret core of Mariano Fortuny's world.

When they returned to the hall on the ground floor, he put his green boots back on, and since there was no catalogue on sale, he quickly left the building. His head was full of impressions that intermingled with memories of the State Opera, of workshops, props, the storeroom for costumes, and the open musical scores in his office. He pushed on through the almost clear water, and it occurred to him that the Venetian opera house, the Teatro La Fenice, was on the way to St. Mark's Square. On every prior trip to Venice he had always gotten together with one of the souffleurs, Lorenzo Verra. He had a sudden impulse to call his friend, but he immediately dismissed the thought. He couldn't say why, but here in the deserted quarter, in the midst of the acqua alta, he felt strangely liberated from his own ego. The only thing he wanted to do now was write his guidebook on Venice, he told himself, analyzing the city like a pathologist. First, the head, the brain: the Archivio di Stato di Venezia; but San Servolo, too, the little island where the insane asylum had been located; and then the Doge's Palace, and the Biblioteca Marciana. The eyes of Venice were the museums and the ears were the Teatro La Fenice. His next step would be to examine the digestive organs, the ostarias, restaurants, the foods and beverages. Besides, he would get to know them automatically everyday, whenever he ate or drank. And finally the veins, arteries, and neural pathways in the city's limbs, the narrow streets, the canals, and the beach at the Lido. As a part of the head, the Museo Fortuny had fit nicely into his concept, he thought. Venice itself was a time capsule, and Mariano Fortuny with his salon, study, library, his secret room and the factory on La Giudecca was one of its internal images.

He stopped, waited until the water at his feet had calmed, and then studied his reflection: above him, the cloudy sky; and around him, buildings, windows, and colors. When he looked up again, he realized that he was standing in front of the Palazzo Contarini del Bovolo. He could look over the low iron fence and into the courtyard with its "Snail Tower" staircase, the "Bovolo." It seemed like a lucky break, because he had actually wanted to start with the Campanile, the bell tower at St. Mark's. But the view from the much smaller Bovolo now seemed more unique. The architecture of the Palazzo's Snail Tower resembled the Leaning Tower of Pisa: it was five stories tall, and the most notable parts were the loggias that became larger and taller in one part of the Palazzo, and the white stone railings in front of the staircase with its arcades, white columns, and Roman arches. He thought it looked like sets of false teeth, piled one on top of the other. The round cupola of the tower was covered with a brass sheet roof that was green from verdigris. The acqua alta was now up to his calves, and Aldrian saw a rat . . . and then more rats swimming behind it, from one side of the Palazzo to the other, and then they all hastily disappeared into a hole. Curious, he pushed open the garden gate, sloshed to a gatehouse at the entrance to the tower, and peered in through a window. An older woman in knee-high rubber boots was resting on a recliner. She was sound asleep, her head on one shoulder. A sign announced that he would have to pay an admission fee, but he didn't want to disturb the woman, so he counted out the money and put it on the counter before he began to climb the pleasantly level steps of the stone Snail Tower. As he passed each loggia, he stopped and glanced down, until he finally reached the tower's upper-most platform where he could look out on the rooftops and church steeples in the city below. The nearby streets were all flooded from the acqua alta that reflected the buildings and clouds, resulting in unexpected optical illusions. He didn't see a soul. He took a foldout map from the pocket of his anorak and determined that the Palazzo was at the intersection of two canals, the Rio di San Luca that flowed into the Rio dei Barcaroli and the Rio de la Verona. Comparing the water level to the height of the front doors, he discovered that the acqua alta was deeper at some spots and shallower at others.

It was lovely being in the tower. There was nothing claustrophobic or scary about it. It seemed to Aldrian as if the building wanted to transport its visitors up into the skies with its upward circular movement and the countless arches and pillars that allowed them a view of the sky, the land, and the water. The structure's lightness and mass were combined in a playful manner so that he enjoyed standing there, gazing out onto the city. He was overcome by a rare feeling of satisfied curiosity.

The old woman in the gatehouse was still sleeping.

Aldrian left the courtyard, stepped into the street making splashing noises, and was standing not far from the Palazzo at the display window of a shop featuring gilded frames for pictures and mirrors. Stepping closer, he could see through the window the dim contours of a small workshop. The entrance to the store was protected from the high water by a metal barrier, and a young man, alerted by Aldrian's knocking, brisky opened the door and asked him to climb over the obstruction and come right in.

The shop was dark and cold, at least as cold as it was outside. From a framed plaque on the wall he read: Giuseppe Barutti, Costello 5990, 30122 Venice, and the telephone number. An old man with thick white hair was sitting at a table in the workshop, sketching. It turned out that he was the owner of the store and the young man was his son. The old man, pleased to be speaking with a potential customer, told Aldrian that his grandfather had run the business and painted pictures himself. Without saying a word the son laid a thick book about Venice on the table; it had the grandfather's photographs and some of his watercolors—primarily of canals and buildings. But before Aldrian could read what was in the book, the old man got up from his chair and whispered, not without pride, that he wanted to show Aldrian something. It was an ancient mirror, as it turned out, with a gilded frame. The reflecting glass was composed of various large rectangular pieces so that it fit together like a puzzle, but appeared to be lopsided. He was immediately fascinated by the strange "showpiece," as Giuseppe Barutti called it. But when Aldrian heard the price, he asked to see a different mirror that might be missing some of its facing. It made him think of the Museo Fortuny and its own "apparitions," in his silent formulation. Giuseppe Barutti shook his head. "Then you need to go to an antique store. Who needs a broken mirror . . . I only use the frames." The old man was visibly disappointed, turned on a small portable radio that was playing a rap song, bent over and tried to find a different station while Aldrian climbed back over the metal barrier and stepped out onto the street.

It wasn't far to the Teatro La Fenice to judge from the city map he had consulted while up on the Snail Tower. The depth of the acqua alta gradually receded, but it became deeper as he approached the opera house; the high-water catwalks there were especially large. The closer he came to the theater, the more display windows he noticed for antiques and masks. He knew that he had to be careful of his footing and watch where he stepped, but he enjoyed walking above the water on the catwalks. He stopped in front of the Teatro La Fenice. Since there were steps leading up to the building, the columns and the entrance were dry. He made note of that fact with the relief of an aficionado. He immediately thought of two operas by Vincenzo Bellini, *Norma* and *I Capuleti e i Montecchi*. He had seen and heard them here with his brother. Afterwards they had gone to a restaurant across the way, and, as always, his brother wouldn't let him pick up the tab. The memory prompted him to pull out his smartphone. He climbed the steps to the columns at the entrance, paused, and tried once again to reach Jakob and his wife Elena, but there was no answer. Where were they? He had a hard time suppressing his anger, put the smartphone back in his pocket, came back down the steps and went over to the restaurant that was also protected by a metal barrier. The green awning was in place as usual, though the canvas with its transparent plastic walls for the protection of the guests who were sitting outside had been removed along with the tables and chairs. The large dining room was empty. He glanced at his watch, it was 11:45, still very early, and the acqua alta in the city was presumably quite deep. The waiter let him decide which table he would prefer, and when he took off his boots, he pulled the mask out of the plastic bag and stuffed his boots back inside. As he sat there, the white mask with its Pinocchio-like long nose lying on the table where he had placed it, it must have looked peculiar, like some occult session. He knew the menu by heart, scanned it, and ordered spaghetti with clams, fried bass with vegetables, and a bottle of pinot grigio. It was remarkably quiet, as if he were a private patient sitting in some doctor's waiting room. From his seat at the window he could even see the entrance to the Teatro La Fenice. The opera house had first burned down in 1774, and since there were disagreements concerning its reconstruction, they had rebuilt it as it had been, but in another location, and called it "Phoenix," "La Fenice," in reference to the fire. Forty years later the Teatro La Fenice was also damaged in a fire, but that time it

41

was restored within a year. Aldrian could remember how the theater had almost burned to the ground on 29 January 1996 when two electricians had started a fire. He had talked with his brother on the phone the very next morning and asked to hear all the catastrophic details. At the beginning of February he even came to Venice for a couple of days to see the scene of the fire because he hadn't wanted to believe Jakob's account. And even more incredible, he had gazed at the ruins through pocket binoculars because the site was still cordoned off by the police. Every time he came to Venice after that he checked on the progress of the reconstruction, and every time he was pleased to see that the building, brick by brick—as slow as molasses, it seemed to him—was assuming its former appearance. It took seven years until everything—every chair, every bit of stucco, every chandelier—had been replicated to look the way it originally had. He hadn't been able to participate in the opening ceremony for the resurrected opera house. And he also didn't want to participate since they were only featuring an orchestra concert. But on the 12th of November 2004 they staged the first opera—Verdi's *La Traviata*. He had made sure that he could attend. As he always did when he went to other opera houses, he first noticed the mistakes during the performance, but eventually the singers aroused his enthusiasm. He was a perfectionist who easily lost any enjoyment due to his pedantry, but as an event receded in time, the more his "carping," as he himself called it, dissipated. In the end he often had only positive memories.

The spaghetti with clams was delicious, the fried bass as well, and he had grown tired after the pinot grigio. The waiter brought him the check, he paid, pulled on his boots, put the mask back in the plastic bag, and left the restaurant, heading for the opera house. A group of tourists was standing between the columns, and since he assumed that they were waiting for a guided tour through the building, he climbed the steps and reached the top just as the group started to move. He followed them into the foyer where a guide began her spiel. But Aldrian kept going to the auditorium entrance, was able to catch a glimpse of the closed velvet curtain, the immense chandelier on the ceiling, the red upholstered seats, the gilded stucco and the loges before someone inside closed the door. At that moment he thought about his deafness, and for an instant had the thought of looking into his own ear where all the music was stored.

As he walked along the catwalk over the water—without knowing where he was headed—he could still see every detail of the Teatro La Fenice auditorium, no longer as a view into his inner ear, but as an encounter with a fairytale world. That was how Neptune's Palace might look beneath the sea, he thought, a splendid edifice where the musical notes, like transparent fish, were waiting to be played, so that they could assume their characteristic colors. There were no more benches for the catwalk and he had to slog through the water as he was bombarded with thoughts, so when he saw a stationery store, he climbed over the metal barrier in hopes of purchasing a notebook where he could record his impressions and ideas. He preferred black moleskin notebooks because they fit so nicely in his jacket pocket; just the look of them stimulated his urge to write, but he hadn't been able to find a single one in all of Venice. The Venetians produced marvelous diaries, financial planners or pocket calendars, but they just didn't meet his specifications. The paper was too thick, the size was problematic, and most of all they were too expensive. When he mentioned what he was looking for, a handsome gentleman in a rain slicker placed a dark-grey model on the counter. Although it was the right size, Aldrian didn't like the paper's stiffness and, since it was bound in leather, it cost 45 euros. Then the salesman showed him others, smaller and larger ones, thicker and thinner ones, all of them much too expensive, and by this time Aldrian wasn't even sure he wanted to make any notes at all. Disappointed, he mumbled something and quickly left the shop. Just two streets further on, where he encountered several people rushing by, he discovered the corner store of yet another bookbinder. The notebook they showed him had the right kind of paper, the booklet was marbled light-brown and violet—the problem was that every page had the day of the week, and that wasn't what he was looking for. While he was back walking the catwalk over the high water, he imagined that it might be stimulating to write something in such a notebook. Still, it seemed unpleasant to have the calendar in his coat because it had stiff square corners and, besides, was too thick. His jacket pockets would be more liable to bulge or wear out. Besides, he didn't want to keep shopping, so he was willing to put up with the obvious disadvantages. Fortunately, he realized, he had gotten out of the habit of immediately writing down his impressions following an evening at the opera or at a concert because his companions hadn't appreciated waiting on bridges and street corners or—like now—in high water until he had made all his notations. Or he had taken breaks, sat down in cafés or restaurants, in churches or on park benches, and jotted down his thoughts, unresponsive to anyone else. Even if it didn't take long, the frequency of his breaks had caused his friends and acquaintances to become impatient and, finally, angry. It was better to wait until evening when he was in bed, and only then begin to put into words whatever he thought was important for his work.

He just kept walking, past many stores with their shutters down, over small stone bridges with stair steps, or along canals that had overflowed their banks. Then on, beneath arcades and passsages under buildings, without knowing where he would end up. There was something canal-like and subterranean about the flooded little streets. At one point he stopped in front of a nearly empty display window where the only thing to see was a dusty model of an old sailing vessel. He stared at it for a long time, without thinking of anything in particular. Then he crossed a bridge as a man holding a small dog approached. The animal looked at him warily and the man avoided eye contact. At the Campo Santa Maria Formosa that looked like a giant puddle, he finally realized where he was. Children in yellow and red rubber boots were jumping and whooping and splashing in the water, others were running around, one even had an inflated swan under his arm. Aldrian wanted to visit the large church at the end of the piazza and, while he was walking, continued to observe the children out of the corner of his eye.

Two children were just being baptized in the Santa Maria

church. Aldrian noticed that the relatives were sitting in chairs that were gathered in a circle, and a girl about five years old—dressed completely in white—had a small white wreath in her hair. The bald baby, resting on a pillow, was just being held over the baptismal font. The priest in a dalmatic wore sandals on his bare feet and carefully shook the consecrated water over the tiny head. The baby slept through the procedure, and since it didn't cry, the relatives applauded and shouted "Brava! Brava!" The priest, too, praised the child before it was returned to its mother.

As Aldrian was leaving the church, he was approached by an African wearing a brown corduroy sport coat, knee-high boots, and carrying a gym bag. He quickly opened the bag, showed Aldrian some little boxes, took one out and held it up in front of Aldrian's face.

"Look! Look!" he pleaded, as Aldrian read the label: "The Vatican Library Collection."

"From the Vatican," the stranger enthused.

Aldrian opened the box and looked inside—on green cardboard with the same gold inscription as on the label—a gilded little chain with a Jerusalem cross. When Aldrian hesitated—the man was annoying but at the same time sympathetic—the African rapidly pulled out more little boxes that all had the same label: silver tie tacks, silver and gold cufflinks embellished with crosses, also silver- and gold-plated money clips. Aldrian shook his head and was about to walk on, when he noticed in one of the boxes a small gilded dove that the vendor claimed was "The Holy Ghost." The pin was no bigger than two thumbnails and had a polished glass splinter on its back.

"This? You want this?" the man pressured him, holding up elaborately adorned glass earrings with a silver filament.

Without really intending to, Aldrian pointed to the dove. They dickered briefly and he paid for the box. He was embarrassed and tried to act as if he weren't embarrassed, pulled down the zipper of his black anorak and attached the "Holy Ghost" dove to the back of his sport coat lapel so that only the fastener was visible from the outside.

Then he looked up, but the African had already disappeared. The water near the church was over his ankles and he could feel how cold it was. Quickly, and without a further glance at the playing children, he turned into the next street, the Calle Lunga Santa Maria, as he read on a house plaque. It occurred to him that the Teatro La Fenice also had a golden bird, a phoenix, as its symbol and was embossed on all the programs and its letterhead. Just the thought of it made him feel better.

Since he didn't encounter anyone and the water now was up to his calves, he momentarily considered whether he should turn back, and he paused in the deserted street in front of one of the few display windows that wasn't shuttered. A sign said: "No photographing allowed." Primarily animal figures in fired and painted clay were on display: heads of pugs and schnauzers, caricatures of miniature plastic spaniels and dachshunds. Too, various owl figures, the mask of an obese idiot, and, inside the shop, a huge Pinocchio figure. As a child he had read the book by Carlo Collodi and also the comic book, and had seen the animated movie by Walt Disney. Since that time he knew the entire film by heart and—by playing the various parts and mimicking the voices of the characters—had performed it for his friends from school who had heartily laughed at him.

To the left of the building that housed the store with the display window was a paved courtyard that sloped down to another shop. The metal barrier was still keeping the water out. Several stands with picture postcards were protruding from the water. A bunch of tattered books were lying out on a table with long legs with a cardboard sign on top that bore the handwritten notice: "WELCOME TO THE MOST BEAUTIFUL BOOKSHOP IN THE WORLD." According to a sign, the bookstore was called "ACQUA ALTA." Curious, he opened the door. In the semi-darkness he recognized the prow of a gondola that was packed with partially arranged books and two display mannequins that represented the gondolier and a female passenger. There was no one here, and he didn't hear a sound. Aldrian's eyes became accustomed to the poor light and he could see details within the chaotic mess. Among the books in the gondola was a pole, painted in a blue and white spiral, the kind they use to tie up motorboats, and the two mannequins were dressed for Carnival with whimsical headgear and masks that completely covered their faces. Two chairs in the gondola were covered with books, located behind various small costumed dolls that looked like they were part of a fairy-tale comedy. Two tiger cats with white blotches were sleeping on the table where the owner or an employee might normally sit. At the back of the room a glass door with a Roman arch and wrought-iron bars led outside. He crossed the shop and noticed that the closer he came to the backdoor, the more water there was on the floor. Finally it came up to his shins. He suddenly had the feeling of being watched. He turned around and determined that the two tiger cats were still sleeping. Outside the glass door the water was almost to Aldrian's knees. Various plastic chairs were standing in front of a hedge of second-hand books that were piled up before a brick wall. This section of books was probably twenty or twenty-five feet long and ten feet tall, and the adjacent brick wall surpassed that by another three feet. More books were stacked on both sides of the wall as stair steps. Since the riverbed of the canal behind the brick wall was higher than the piazza where the bookstore was located, in spite of all precautions the high water inundated the shop's rooms. Two gondola steering oars were leaning up against the wall with a sign above them that read: "FOLLOW THE BOOKSTEPS, CLIMB, GO UP." A white arrow pointed in the direction of "up." He discovered yet another sign above the wall of books, this time in blue: "WONDERFUL VIEW." He noticed the books that formed the stairs were old encyclopedias and coffee-table books with spines in all colors as he climbed them so that he could look out over the canal. An old rowboat that was tied to the opposite house wall with a rope was gently swaying in the high-water current. Aldrian's instincts cautioned him about this strange stairway. He awkwardly climbed back down into the water that gave a splashing sound. When he finally opened the glass door to the shop, he found out that there was a second room where books were piled up on bookshelves just as they were in front of the wall overlooking the canal. Moreover it wasn't really a room, but simply a passageway with no roof, and the floor was made of cobblestones. Three more cats were sleeping on several of the six or seven stools and chairs and on an old iron garden table. He spied a gum tree with drooping leaves. On the floor the outlines of shoe soles were painted yellow, leading from an open door to the next passageway. Behind that was a narrow dark alley where the acqua alta was knee-high and had flooded half the passageway and the books on the lower shelves. Curious, Aldrian slogged out into the narrow alley and into the neighboring building, discovering six more rooms with bathtubs and rowboats—all of them full of books—and overflowing bookcases along the walls. But the further he got from the alley, the less water there was in the rooms. The last three rooms, whether larger or smaller, were dry, while tables, cabinets, boxes, and a recliner were positioned in front of the bookcases. A fluorescent light flickered. In the next to the last room various old chandeliers were hanging from the ceiling, and in the last room pictures were hung between the bookcases on the few available spaces or they were lying in small stacks on a red carpet that covered the floor. A wall of windows looked out on the flooded inner courtyard. Wherever he looked, groups of smaller pictures were leaning against books. Or there were rolls of maps lying in front of a window that was covered by a sheet. On his return, Aldrian discovered a cloth rocking horse, porcelain figurines, a pendulum clock, a copper Oriental serving tray with a mason jar that held wadded paper and a cigarette butt. White masks and souvenir plates were scattered here and there between piles of books, small tacky mirrors with glass frames were hung in a corner . . . The word "FUTURE" was written on a red sign that was set aside near plastic baskets and partially covered by water. As he learned, it was the section for science-fiction novels. Still, the dominant feature were the books themselves—thousands, tens of thousands that, like refugees in a desolate detention center, were awaiting their fate.

Despite his calls no one appeared, so he left the shop—also because he began to feel that the bookstore had become creepy.

By now he had had enough of wandering around, enough of the

dead streets and districts, and, until evening came, he just wanted to find a table in the warm dry Caffè Florian and let someone in a white jacket wait on him. He knew it would cost an arm and a leg, but his longing for the red golden salons was stronger than his reservations. Passing countless souvenir shops and mask stores, he came to St. Mark's Square that, to his surprise, was full of life. Even in the streets near the piazza he ran into excited tourists taking pictures of each other in the acqua alta. A swarm of people, some in costumes, had congregated beneath the flooded arcades and regarded the acqua alta as a tourist attraction. High-water benches hadn't been set up to form a catwalk; besides, they wouldn't have been high enough, and all the shops that were open had their own metal barriers. He was immediately attracted by the atmosphere, the combination of illusion and reality. The red stage curtains on the tent for the small orchestra by the Caffè Florian were closed off facing the Square, while two women and two men on the side toward the arcades were playing *The Blue Danube* waltz with mild disdain, or so it seemed to Aldrian. Large numbers of patrons, sitting on dark-brown padded chairs and benches at the small marble tables, listened, chatted, ordered drinks or indulged in a cappuccino. Aldrian glanced in the open illuminated windows. He determined that the Caffè was occupied predominantly by customers wearing masks. The waiters in their white tuxedos looked like officers on a cruise ship. In the last of the—as he knew—eight salons, the murals had been exchanged for others: unfurled screens, like huge maps, had been weighted at the bottom with wooden rods and now covered the places where the murals had previously been. A large angel, painted in a modern style, now hung above the wall behind the tables and benches. It was using a Morse telegraph that was connected to telegraph cables. On the floor in front of it, a paper tape meandered about. In its left hand, the angel was holding a triangle; at its feet, a putty head; in the background, tiny ships. The image tried to combine technology and religion, Aldrian thought—forming some type of magical entity. Aldrian recalled that this innovation was replacing the old image of the angel that also held a triangle in its left hand and kept watch over a naked child. He knew all the rooms by heart: the Sala degli Uomini illustri with portraits of Goldoni, Marco Polo, Titian or Palladio; the Sala di Senato with paintings devoted to science and progress; the Grecian and also the Persian salon—an Oriental room—the Sala Liberty as well as the Sala delle stagioni, a salon devoted to the four seasons. He sat down at a free table, took off his boots, put them in the plastic bag, and placed the white mask on the chair next to him. All of the rooms were decorated with ceiling frescos, stucco, and other decorations, and the paintings on the walls, in round Baroque gold frames or behind glass between gold ornaments, displayed a world immersed in itself: women playing harps, Chinese couples, ladies from antiquity and the Baroque, birds and plants. He had come to the Caffè full of anticipation. Reflective mirrors in richly decorated gilt frames reproduced the interior: the customers in their costumes with large red and blue feathers on fancy hats or with down feathers on three-cornered hats, a black curtain, a curled wig atop a white-powdered face, the purple-velvet upholstered benches and chairs, the marble tabletops, and the waiters who quickly fluttered past like cabbage white butterflies and then disappeared. He ordered a spritz that was served with ice cubes and crispy cheese straws, along with a handful of olives in a porcelain cup. He quickly ordered a second and third glass, nibbled the cheese straws lost in thought, and studied the old red wallpaper, now almost black, that was made of some material that had been hand-painted like oil canvas: floral patterns that could have been designed by Fortuny, but were scarcely recognizable today. He assumed they had been blackened by tobacco smoke. The bench he was sitting on was as hard as a wooden one in a garden, and the parquet floor had obviously been trod by many thousands of shoes: a backdrop for the tourists who turned up here. The waiters, on the other hand, felt they were actors who—according to ritual—let each and every customer demote them to the role of supernumeraries and yet carried out their duties in elegant inconspicuousness. Like jugglers, they balanced their alpaca trays—frequently one in each hand, filled with bottles, plates, cups, and glasses—and proceeded to the tables with rapid decisive steps and buoyant elegance. Aldrian glanced through the glass windows at the doors. People with and without masks were staring into the salon or taking pictures of it with their camera flash and, as Aldrian was pleased to note, the only thing they would get would be a harsh light flare from the pane of glass. Seen from outside, the customers were ornamental fish in an opulent aquarium. Looking from the inside out, you could view the curious bystanders as if they were figures in some Carnival procession. For all of them St. Mark's Square was a gigantic, unfathomable, and apparently endless stage. He now saw a man in the salon who seemed to be watching him. Of course the man didn't look him squarely in the face, he was staring into one of the mirrors where their eyes briefly met. The stranger turned away, took a sip from his coffee cup, and yawned, his hand shielding his mouth. He was of medium height, brawny, was wearing a leather jacket and jeans, and had a beard. His eyebrows were black, as if they had been traced with charcoal. Aldrian glanced at his watch, but immediately forgot what time it was, because he had the impression that time didn't pass in the Caffè. He told himself that time only went by outside, while he in his salon, as if in a luxurious diving bell by Jules Verne, had advanced into a timeless dimension. Meanwhile he noticed that the stranger was watching him again—or still!—in the mirror. Among the costumed and masked people he looked like a stagehand, like an electrician or a prop man. Aldrian noticed by chance that the man, like the other customers, was wearing yellow rubber boots that made his appearance seem a bit strange. At that point a gentleman sat down at an unoccupied table; he was dressed like a noble before the French Revolution, with a three-pointed hat sumptuously embroidered with gold threads atop his grey wig and gold-colored vest. He had on red lipstick, and his rimless glasses didn't quite match his outfit. He was accompanied by three ladies, one was dressed in a costume similar to the man's; the colors of their clothes and their hats set the other two apart. The oldest woman was wearing a mammoth pirate hat, embroidered with countless gold stars as if in competition with the night sky, and a lofty gold shawl over her violet dress. The younger two had hidden their eyes, foreheads, and noses behind gold masks and feather creations nestled in their garish red wigs. Just then, a white-haired admiral in an opulent uniform and a costumed prince in a Rococo outfit, knee-high stockings and his own three-cornered hat with a white ivory cane in one hand, joined the group. After they had placed their orders, they began to discuss an opera performance of Mozart's *The Marriage of Figaro* and Rossini's *Barber of Seville*, and their opinions were such that Aldrian was tempted to intervene. But they soon changed topics and conversed about hairdressers in Florence and Milan. Aldrian tried not to listen, ordered another spritz, and realized that the man who had been watching him in the mirror had disappeared. By midnight there were only a few customers sitting at the small marble tables, generally in twos or threes—he was the only one sitting alone. He was drunk, but he restrained himself as best he could. He didn't care about the check that had been presented to him, just the opposite: he gave the waiter a generous tip and was pleased to have done so. Then he unpacked his boots and put the mask away, but as he stepped out onto the dimly-lit St. Mark's Square, he realized that the acqua alta had disappeared. His first impression was that somebody was trying to fool him, even though he knew that it was just in his imagination. Since he briefly felt dizzy, he turned toward one of the benches under the arcades that were placed in front of the Caffè, sat down and took off his boots, awkwardly pulled the mask out of the plastic bag, and put both boots and mask back in.

He didn't meet a soul until he arrived at the shelter for Line 1 that was swaying on the Grand Canal. His back hurt and his thoughts were muddled. The vaporetto finally came and when he went onboard, the stranger who had watched him in the mirror of the Caffè Florian got on behind him, along with another man. Like him, neither of them was still wearing boots. At first Aldrian couldn't imagine where they had come from so suddenly. But the vaporetto set off, and without any further concerns he opened the door to the seating compartment where a young nonchalant couple in everyday clothes—lost in their mutual affection—were snuggling. Since Aldrian didn't hear well, he scarcely understood the names of the stations as they were announced. He looked out at the two men on deck, but they had their backs to him. He saw nothing but darkness outside, even the water was part of the darkness. Occasionally the lighted windows of a palazzo appeared, a gleaming chandelier hanging from the ceiling gave Aldrian the impression of a jellyfish aglow in the water. One of those phosphorescent marine creatures was probably fifteen or sixteen feet long and floated motionless in the nocturnal silence that was broken only by the droning of the engine before the jellyfish disappeared behind him.

The vaporetto stopped at the San Silvestro station and he got off at the last second, before it moved on. He immediately looked back and saw the two men standing at the exit and the two lovers in the compartment who were just kissing until they disappeared into the darkness. After a low passageway that always reminded him of a cellar, he set off for the Campo San Silvestro and, from there, to the Rughetta del Ravano, part of the beaten path for the mass of tourists. He knew this area very well—it had the *Antico Dolo* where he often dined and the mask store owned by Diego Sarcia who had written him in winter that he absolutely had to see a performance in the State Opera, but then had to cancel at the last moment. And, not least of all, the Ostaria Dai Zemei where he had spent many evenings with his brother and Diego Sarcia. It was probably too late now to call Jakob and Elena. At a corner where he could see the Rialto Bridge, a man stood, urinating against the side of a building. So Aldrian took the Ruga dei Speziali, an alley with numerous small grocery stores and delicatessens, but their shutters were closed, so after a short distance he turned off to the Campo della Pescaria. In the meantime he briefly stopped and listened to see if he could make out any suspicious sounds, but all he could hear was his own breathing. As soon as he reached the weakly-lit front door to their building, he was relieved and searched for the key in his pants pocket. In the same instant he felt a sharp pain in his head and lost consciousness.

In the Mesocosm

It was still dark outside. He was lying in bed and discovered he was in his studio apartment. His head was exploding. Half-dazed, he carefully touched the painful spot under his hair with his fingers and felt a thick scab. He didn't know why, but he wasn't surprised. Just the opposite, it seemed logical that he was injured. He assumed he had probably fallen. But how had he gotten in bed? He turned on the light on his nightstand, sat up, and saw that the white pillowcase was covered in bloodstains. As he got out of bed, dizzy, and staggered to the bathroom, he also noticed that the door to his apartment was wide open, contrary to his usual practice. Now he checked the painful spot underneath his hair and saw that it was a gash. Astonished and puzzled, he sat down in the kitchen alcove. He had the impression that he was watching himself sit down. Naturally he asked himself what had happened. He had been in the Caffè Florian, had gotten drunk, that much was clear. And now he saw the face of the man who had watched him in the mirror and knew immediately that the stranger with his companion must have gotten off the vaporetto at the next station, Rialto Bridge, after he himself had gotten off at the San Silvestro station. He remembered the exact route he had taken, up to the moment when he held the key to the front door in his hand. From that point on, the only thing he could recall was a brief instant when two faces were bent over him, one was that of the stranger with the black eyebrows, the other was the red face of a man wearing a Carnival mask with little bells hanging from long points. He could hear the tinkling sound they made all over again. Once again he struggled to the bathroom, took a shower, and changed his clothes. The wound on his skull was bleeding again, so he cut off some tufts of hair around it and used the scissors to shorten the tape on the Band-Aid before he put it over the wound, then rearranged his hair as best he could so it wouldn't be visible. At first he couldn't believe he had been attacked, but how else to explain the fleeting memory of the two men's faces and the Carnival cap. He slipped into his pants, reached for the key ring but couldn't find it, it also wasn't in his sport coat or the black windbreaker he had worn. So he carefully went downstairs, past the door to his brother's apartment that, to his astonishment, was now closed. He knew that it had been ajar when he arrived and that he had leaned in to holler to them, but without hearing a reply. Confused, he hurried down to the front door and found it locked. He found himself transposed into a different world without any transition. The window by the front door had bars over it, so he could only break the window and call for help. As he looked at his watch, he saw that it was a few minutes before six and most of the vendors at the fish market were probably in the process of putting their wares on the sales counters. Then he remembered the side door to the shop. He had no expectations when he went to open the door, but to his surprise it wasn't locked. The showroom was immaculate, he determined, he didn't see anything suspicious. His head wound still hurt. He gradually understood that the disappearance of his brother and his wife must have something to do with the assault and the blow to his head. He instantly felt the urge to get out of the house, but the front door to the store was also locked and the telephone wire to the plug in the wall was missing. Then he tried to locate his smartphone, but it wasn't in his pants or in his sport coat. That leaves only the black windbreaker, he told himself. He ran upstairs to his apartment, again searched through all the pockets of the clothes he had worn, but the phone had disappeared. So someone had stolen it along with the keys . . . He sat down on the bed and suddenly felt as if he were in his prompter's box. There was a different reality surrounding him, a reality from which he was cut off in some incomprehensible way. He just had to concentrate on the libretto and the action onstage, and his job was to avoid mistakes. Agitated, he went back down to the store so that he could think in peace. Perhaps the mailman would come soon, or a customer . . . He tried to turn on the ceiling light, but apparently power to the store had been disconnected because it remained dim. So that he wouldn't lose his composure and panic, he decided to not let his pursuers drive him out of the building. He would find a solution, he persuaded himself. The dominant thought, however, was concern for his brother and his wife. Even in the Caffè Florian he had thought about his sister-in-law, because the management had consulted her several times in her capacity as an accomplished conservator. He still secretly loved her. He also was attracted to her sister Margherita who was married to the dentist Eugenio Bellucci, and not least of all to a girlfriend of Elena—Beatrice Stefanelli. She worked as a correspondent for a Milanese newspaper, was divorced, and traveled frequently.

He was amazed that he felt safer in the store than in the rest of the house. In the first of the two adjoining rooms stood the glass display cases with selected marine mussels and snails: larger ones and smaller ones, some plain, others white, and still others with dark patterns, stripes, dots, armed with spines, snail-shell-shaped, and others of silver mother-of-pearl. Pearl necklaces from China, pearl earrings and pearl rings were scattered above and in between. Cases filled with crocodile skulls, fossils of all types, crystals and other minerals occupied the second room. Amongst them were stunning pieces of jewelry, but also elephants carved from bone; the most colorful, most ample, and most mysterious butterflies and flying insects were framed and hung on the wall. But as far as Aldrian was concerned, the actual centerpiece were his brother's framed watercolors of insects, birds, and plants that were for sale together with old botanical and zoological engravings.

Aldrian had dozed off in his chair when a familiar voice woke him. He realized it was Margherita. So that he wouldn't startle her, he remained sitting and spoke her name loudly. The shouting stopped and an instant later she appeared, wide-eyed and with a perplexed look on her face. "You're here? Where are Jakob and Elena?"

"I lost my keys and my cellphone . . . I think they were stolen," Aldrian replied, distracted.

"How did you get into the house?" she asked, alarmed. "And what happened to your head."

Aldrian reflected that he didn't want to frighten her and was embarrassed by what had actually happened, so he made up a story that he had gone out last evening and had drunk too much. He went on, that at midnight he had gone home with two men, one was wearing a cap with points and little bells, the other had a beard and thick black hair and eyebrows; he wanted to share a bottle of wine he had bought in the store with them up in his apartment. They had spent two hours in a heated discussion about Venice, but when they left, they attacked him and took his keys and his phone.

"And your wallet?" she asked, horrified.

"They got it."

"Did they take your ATM card?"

"You mean my debit card?"

She nodded.

"No. When I'm in a foreign country, I always carry a second wallet where I keep just what I'll need for that day."

"And what about the rest of your money?"

"I withdraw funds every other day."

"But your ATM card?"

"The debit card is in my passport, and I've hidden the passport. Why?"

She paused.

"Perhaps something's been stolen from the store? Or from their apartment?"

"I've checked in the store—I didn't notice anything wrong."

He didn't tell her that the telephone wire was missing. "And I don't have a key to their apartment."

She was visibly upset.

"I don't understand you," she blurted in disapproval, then she pulled herself together and stood up. "We've got to change the locks and report this to the police."

He nodded.

"Are you coming?"

He shook his head and explained that he had an appointment in the Archivio di Stato di Venezia that couldn't be postponed. He he'd decided to write a guidebook about Venice.

"I'm worried about Jakob and Elena," Margherita interrupted.

"So am I," he responded. This time he was telling the truth.

"When did you get here?"

"Yesterday."

Suddenly her tone of voice changed, she demanded that he come with her to Jakob and Elena's apartment so that together they could make sure that everything was in order.

He agreed, of course, and a moment later Margherita found the spare key to Aldrian's studio apartment in the little key box by the kitchen door. Everything was in its proper place. And since Margherita knew that neither Elena nor Jakob kept large sums of money at home, she seemed somewhat relieved.

Aldrian thanked her for the key, and she went out into the hallway, dialed a number on her cellphone, closed the apartment door behind her, and spoke frantically with someone while he waited.

"You need to stay home," she said when she returned. "The police are coming right over."

He knew that he couldn't continue to lie, and that he couldn't tell a police detective the same fairytale he had told Margherita. They'd ask him the name of the restaurant where he had met the two men, and then question him about everything else. He considered that he would have to "confess" to Margherita that he hadn't wanted the incident to frighten her and that he was still dazed from the blow to his head.

He climbed the stairs to his apartment, and after he had entered his room, noticed a piece of paper that was sticking out under the bed. Cautiously he picked it up and read his name in red magic marker—it had been crossed out and had a cross after it. It took a minute for him to realize it was a threat. Presumably everything had been planned in advance, he thought. They had scouted him, followed him, and attacked him. It had to be connected to his brother and his wife. He wadded up the piece of paper and threw it in the garbage can. I'll tell the police everything I know, he whispered to himself. Then he remembered that his smartphone had been stolen, too. It had all of his contact numbers: telephone numbers for singers, stagehands, stage managers, conductors, the other two prompters, as well as his private contacts. Something had happened that had wiped out his past. He realized he would have to postpone his appointment in the Archivio di Stato di Venezia. At the same time he wondered if he should give the police the paper with his crossed-out name and the cross. It struck him that he was acting like a criminal, but he also didn't feel like a victim—more like a witness or, better, like a future perpetrator. He decided he would put up a fight. And he'd find his brother, just as soon as he had a clue, a lead . . . And he would work together with Margherita and the police, or else he would be in an untenable situation. After he had taken two aspirin from his dopp kit and made the bed, he went into the bathroom and glanced in the mirror, saw the Band-Aid, initially wanted to take it off, but then accepted the fact that he was wounded, and staggered downstairs.

The police still hadn't arrived. At the exact same time two uniformed policemen and a man in plain clothes were coming from the arcades in the fish market, heading right for the house. Aldrian concluded that they must have docked along the canal.

Margherita opened the shop, led the men through the two rooms, and then invited them into his brother's apartment. Aldrian, however, didn't want to correct his story in front of Elena's sister and asked if he could lie down on the bed in his attic apartment because he had a headache. Needless to say, he would be at their disposal.

The man in plain clothes—Commissario Galli—had introduced himself when he arrived, silently accompanied him, and sat down on a chair in Aldrian's room while Aldrian stretched out on the bed, fully dressed. The Commissario was a skinny man of medium height, completely bald and unshaven. He was wearing a sport coat, jeans with ankle-high black shoes and apparently felt at home wherever he was.

"You speak Italian very well," he said. "Where did you learn it?"

"I am *Maestro Suggeritore* at the State Opera in Vienna. Please speak a bit louder, I have a hearing loss," he added.

The Commissario subsequently posed his questions slowly and distinctly. "What's that pin on your coat?" he wanted to know. Aldrian didn't speak, flipped his lapel, and showed him the little gilded dove with the glass splinter. The Commissario nodded.

For an hour he spoke respectfully with Aldrian—every little detail was important to him.

"How long are you staying in Venice?" he asked in conclusion.

"Until summer," Aldrian replied.

"I'm surprised that we haven't found your brother's and his wife's laptops . . . But maybe they've taken their computers along on a trip . . . Did they usually do that?"

Aldrian nodded. "Yes," he responded.

The Commissario stood up and—puzzled, because Aldrian had just been complaining about a headache—, granted his request to go to the Archivio di Stato di Venezia.

"When you get a new phone, call me and give me the number," the Commissario added.

Aldrian promised to do so.

He glanced at the clock, it was quarter to ten. It had only been three hours, and it seemed to him that he had lost his identity in the meantime. He must have become somebody else, somebody whom he himself didn't know, he thought. From underneath the brown wrapping paper in the wardrobe he pulled out the wallet with his passport, took out some money, and put the wallet and the passport back in their hiding place. Before he left the house, he went looking for Margherita in his brother's apartment, but she had already gone back into the shop with the policemen.

"The telephone cable is missing," she said judgmentally, when he came in.

He just shook his head in disbelief, and felt like some opera singer who had lost his lines.

The Commissario, who had just been speaking with her, listened attentively.

She went on, claiming he hadn't told her the truth . . . Why not?

"I didn't want to frighten you," Aldrian answered, and again it was like a scene in an opera that had hit a snag.

He understood that she didn't want to discuss it further in the Commissario's presence when she informed him in a business-like tone that all the locks would be changed and new door bars would be installed. Aldrian would have to get his own phone . . . In response to his question she reluctantly gave him an address where he could "try," she said with exaggerated indifference.

"I hope you make it to your appointment on time," she said sarcastically as she dismissed him.

He didn't respond, but hurried to the shop near the Campo san Polo, hoping to find the same brand as his old smartphone. After a quick glance at his watch, he went on to the former Franciscan monastery by the Frari Church. A few costumed children crossed the street. He stopped to check that he had his ballpoint pen, but couldn't find it. Farther on, he came to a small stationary store and, glancing in the window, observed inside a fifty- to sixty-year old blonde woman who had just put a pair of knitting needles and some blue and red yarn on the sales counter. She adjusted her glasses, looked up, and saw him through the window. She gave the impression that she wasn't to be taken lightly. He entered the store, requested a certain ballpoint pen that was on display—the bottom part had a pattern of black and amber-colored spots and the top was black. The clip was of some chrome-colored material. On a similar chrome-colored band around the middle was a large slightly-convoluted letter "D." Aldrian was so taken by the somewhat old-fashioned writing utensil that he immediately bought two, along with some refills, which raised the older lady's eyebrows.

Out on the street, people in masks and costumes were standing or strolling and letting tourists take their picture. Aldrian felt dizzy again. He hadn't eaten breakfast, and the early-morning excitement had only brought more confusion. He took a deep breath, and the first chance he got, he bought a slice of pizza and a small bottle of sparkling mineral water that he emptied.

In the Archivio di Stato di Venezia

When he arrived at the former Franciscan monastery and glanced at his watch again, he was relieved that he wasn't too late. A flock of screeching seagulls flew up and landed on the church roof. He went through an archway to the right of the church and entered a small inner-courtyard that was bounded by the church wall and the monastery. Behind the glass doors the gatekeeper was sitting at a table where two women stood. One of them was wearing a thick white anorak. He guessed she was about 35 years old. She had long blond hair and was delighted that he spoke Italian. He could easily understand what she was saying, even though her voice was soft.

Despite his low spirits, he felt a little happiness coming on. He had left the reality in his brother's house behind, and now entered a new and different one in the hope of being swallowed up by it as Pinocchio was by the sea monster. The other woman, who spoke more distinctly and had a small mole on the right side of her upper lip, was cheerful. tall, had black hair and wore a black coat. They greeting him, laughing, introduced themselves, and led him down a long corridor containing old hand-written card catalogues to the Sala di Studio, the reading room, where they sat down at one of the long yellow wooden tables—at a distance from the glances of the students. To begin, the blond woman complained that the acqua alta had caused some damage in one of the archive rooms, but the other woman had already started her spiel. Aldrian reached for his notebook and one of the ballpoint pens in his coat pocket and started to take notes in Gabelsberger shorthand that he had mastered to perfection. In the back of his head, however, was the Commissario and Margherita, he saw himself in the bathroom mirror as he put the Band-Aid under his hair and visualized the slip of paper he had found under the bed with the cross and his name crossed-out. He hadn't told the Commissario about it because he didn't want them to possibly put him under surveillance. He believed that the two men who had stolen the keys and his smartphone just wanted to chase him out of his brother's house. He didn't know the reason why, and he was reluctant to try to find out. In any event, it would have been easy for them to kill him.

Meanwhile he noticed that he had automatically written down that the former Franciscan monastery has been used as the National Archives since 1815. The woman with black hair had explained that there were over 15 million books and manuscripts and 250,000 documents in the 300 rooms. The woman went on to recite that the monastery itself was laid out around two interior courtyards with cloisters—the first was "The Holy Trinity," the other was dedicated to "Saint Anthony." If all the items were placed end-to-end, they would stretch for 50 miles, the distance from Venice to Verona.

He looked up and tried to follow her presentation. But while the woman was speaking, his eyes wandered to the pointed barrel arch up above and to the six columns that supported it. He counted ten rows of tables with padded chairs, black halogen table lamps, and several laptops. The arched windows started at head-height in the two-story hall, he noticed, and almost reached the ceiling. There were wooden bookshelves of various heights, as well as more card catalogues.

In the meantime the two woman had stood up, and he followed them automatically.

"Do you have any more questions?" the dark-haired woman wanted to know.

He shook his head, and the woman with the soft voice explained that they were now on their way to the monastery's old kitchen. They went down several stone steps and the first thing he saw was a dead dove floating in the residual high water.

"I told you," the blond woman said, expressing her sorrow. She continued, saying that the kitchen was just recently uncovered by archeologists and pointed to a hole in the wall: "That's where the ice blocks were stored." Aldrian strained to pay attention. Only now did he feel the cold that permeated the room. He was freezing and silent. The blond also inhaled, softly hissing between her teeth before she went on: "They placed the meat and the fish on top to cool. The monks even served sorbet to prominent visitors for refreshment." Above the hole hung a small devotional picture of a small fat angel on a red background; half of the painting was gone. A man in orange overalls waved to them and they climbed up on a high water bench and walked until they came to a wrought-iron gate and the canal, the "waterway to the Dominican monastery on the other side," the woman with dark hair said.

"That's where the acqua alta comes from," the blond woman added. The walls of the kitchen were not plastered, and the tiles combined with the water on the floor to form a geometrical pattern. Here, too, there were pillars, but no daylight. Relieved, Aldrian followed the women up another flight of stairs with a round wooden bannister fastened to the wall by bronze fists and then back along the corridor into an old neglected archive. There were files piled on top of one another, here and there the boards of the bookcases had caved in and the files had fallen to the level below. Individual pages were floating on the surface of the shallow water that covered the floor; other piles of folders were sticking out, and several bookcases had completely collapsed, burying yet other folders and files under them. What was in these files, Aldrian wondered. What fates did they contain? What laws, decrees, prohibitions? What decrees?

"These are the archives from the time when Venice was ruled by the Dual Monarchy of Austria-Hungary," the dark-haired woman said in reply to his question.

They stood silently before the chaotic mess that appeared as if some natural catastrophe had occurred. For Aldrian it looked more like a helpless attempt to erase not just a certain time period but its universality. The hidden, destroyed, wet, torn, moldy letters of the alphabet that he saw on the pages of various documents—he couldn't make out any complete words—were, as far as he was concerned, an expression of impotence and revolt. In his mind he saw the torn yellowed dog-eared files that had been stuffed into undersize folders infested with insects that—like hornets—transformed archives of invisible letters and contents they had eaten, digested, and defecated into giant "jars" of paper that would eventually become their dwellings. It was the transformation of time into oblivion.

Without saying a word the women closed the doors and, due to the huge expanse of the building, Aldrian could no longer remember which rooms he had seen, in what order, and which he had left behind. A two-story hall with a gallery halfway up that was enclosed by a small bannister came to mind, and shelves stocked with diverse-colored file folders against the walls, white labels dated by year and hand-written summaries of their contents as well as worn and faded fascicles that were bound with loose archival knots and provided with a printed number. He had no idea what it all meant and didn't want to ask, he just wanted to keep moving. But the deeper into the archives they went, the more he became accustomed to the unimaginable mass of files that had been compiled in unimaginably many hours by unimaginably many nameless scribes on unimaginably many pages with unimaginable amounts of ink. They went higher, then down a floor, and then back up again, even higher, over wooden bridges as if crossing raging streams on a hike in the Alps. Without pausing they were already walking into the next dusky room with its crown glass windows, florescent lighting, and grey metal shelves. Then they hurried over to a bright window that at first seemed small, but as they got closer, became larger and larger until—still in semi-darkness—they climbed yet another stairway. The folders with their multi-colored bindings were amazing. All the ones he had seen since they left the messy room were well preserved and only marred by time, if at all. Brown leather spines alternated with black ones, in one room of the archives they were made of white leather, while other files had only been covered in wrapping paper.

The two women unexpectedly opened a door and led him out onto a terrace that fronted the arcade court. The sky above was overcast, with dark rainclouds. Beside the brick parapet stood stone statues of saints and angels. But in the middle of the courtyard that spread out before them he recognized a grave; with its vault supported by four pillars, it looked like a fountain. Standing in front of the grave was a clustered group of human figures in stone. Since the arcade hallways and the court were uninhabited and there wasn't a sound, time seemed to have disappeared entirely from the world. But why were they suddenly back on the second floor of the building, Aldrian wondered. According to his instincts, by now they should have been on the fourth floor or in the attic. Evidently he had lost his bearings at some point, he admitted. The two women were laughing at him—his confusion was apparently obvious. He shared their good humor before they really did go upstairs, then up a short but steep iron ladder until they finally reached the attic. From there he could see the second courtyard with its cloister, though he didn't really know which one was the first, which one the second. He repeatedly imagined he was just a thought in some vast brain that had gotten lost while looking for a missing memory.

He looked through the hatch at the red tile roofs of the former monastery, the domes and, farther away, the statues of saints at the Frari Church. The woman with dark hair called to him from the foot of the ladder, saying she had written her dissertation in a room on the third floor. As he climbed down and followed her, he was amazed that they hadn't continually gotten lost in the huge archives. On secondary stairways and through rooms jammed with files, through strings of smaller rooms that all warehoused inscribed paper and had the oldest wooden shelving, they finally reached the office that had a window overlooking the two courtyards and the cloisters. In spite of the chill in the building, at some point he had begun to sweat. The two women made coffee, got sweet pastries from a cupboard, set a water pitcher decorated with a blue grape on the table, and asked him if he had come with his wife and what he did professionally. While he was telling them about prompting, he took a coin out of his wallet and made it disappear in his fingers, found it in their hair, behind their ears, up their sleeves. Out of curiosity they wanted to know more and more about his magic tricks and about prompting; he almost told them about the events of that morning that were coursing through his mind, but he didn't. He said nothing. Filling the silence, the blond woman barely whispered a lecture about what they were still going to show him: "The center of the Archive is the Crociera, an enormous hall on the second floor. It is somewhat like the nave of a church. This nave has two side aisles—one each at the beginning and at the end—that, seen from the middle, form two crosses—one left and one right. All documentation about the life in the city is preserved here, from prostitution and ship construction in the Arsenal to the records of births and deaths." Aldrian thought, without irony, that the Crociera had become a sacred hall of memory. "There are two Crociere," the woman with dark hair clarified, "a small one and a large one. But first we are going to visit the Sala Regina Margherita, the archives for diplomatic affairs of the Serenissima. This is where all the treaties and documents are stored. Venice as a great power," she continued, "had cultivated contacts everywhere and collected the written communications. It is the city's political memory bank. In earlier times, monks' cells were located all around the Crociera. Now this is where you can find all the dispatches about those places where Venice had developed trade, chronologically arranged by each city. For example, records of the French Revolution, because Venice had trusted intermediaries or even spies in all the cities and countries with which it had developed contacts; these agents had provided exhaustive logs concerning all events." Recently she had visited a historian from France for assistance in locating the existing documents about which clothes Louis XVI was wearing at the time of his execution in Paris. "And, believe it or not, a Venetian diplomat had recorded every significant detail for posterity. Moreover there are also reports from envoys, civil servants, or delegations."

So then the monks' cells had become side chapels of memory, Aldrian thought. He took out his notebook and the ballpoint pen and made a sketch of the premises as best he could deduce from the blonde's remarks. She emphasized, however, that her explanations were only correct in principle, but in no way corresponded to a basically complicated reality. Since the woman had seen his sketches, she then wanted to know which language he used in his note-taking. He implied jokingly that it was a secret code, but the dark-haired woman contradicted him and stated that it was the Gabelsberger system that Enrico Carlo Noë had translated into Italian.

They all laughed and continued their excursion. From this point on, there was not a single wall that didn't have shelving. Aldrian noticed one with record books bound in grey leather, though he didn't ask about it. A few steps farther on, the women were pointing to a long hallway, the "Small Crociera," they said, with aluminum ladders on the bookcases and two rows of files with worn bindings and damaged yellowish paper in the middle of the room. An off-white side door opened and a woman in glasses with short hair entered, pushing a cart with several fascicles and in search of more. She calmly climbed one of the ladders, glanced at a slip of paper, and then reached for a file. The ladders had wheels, as Aldrian noticed, so that they could easily be moved to any part of the shelving. Metal piping had been installed from the base of the arches to the ceiling as support for the walls. There were also tall windows that separated the bookcases, but their blinds were down. Light from a three-part window at the end of the hallway fell on the stone floor and gave a bright and hazy reflection. The folders on one wall were numbered, extensively labeled by hand in black ink, and might be full of secrets, it seemed to Aldrian; then again, dark-brown files that seemed abstract and forbidding attracted his attention, and he learned that they were account books.

"From them we can reconstruct in great detail how people lived in earlier times," the woman with dark hair explained, and then added: "You can find out how much a parrot cost, a liter of wine, fruits, bread . . . the value of a chandelier, how much a construction worker or a manual laborer earned, or the amount Tintoretto received for a fresco." She randomly pulled out a volume and opened it. Aldrian saw that the pages were covered in a clear, neat, beautiful, and slowly fading script.

"Here they've recorded the amount they paid for the Plague Hospital, in another volume how much for the Archangel Gabriel on top of the Campanile."

They left the "Small Crociera" for the Sala Regina Margherita of Savoy where they saw a marble bust of the Queen in an adjoining room. Furnished with dark old wooden bookcases, some even with glass doors, the Sala itself gave an overall impression of being well-maintained. Aldrian was struck that everything was meticulously arranged, to this point it was the most elegant and most beautiful hall he had seen. The folders were bound in the finest leather—white and brown—and gave the impression of precious objects, yes, they seemed to Aldrian like sacred books. Repositories with white cardboard rolls up to six-feet tall were located in the center of the room containing, Aldrian assumed, especially significant covenants. "No," the two women countered. "There are approximately two-thousand maps in these rolls that painstakingly inventory every significant detail—because Napoleon had ordered the mapping of the entire city and every individual island for the Treasury Department. The repositories are filled with hundreds of pick-up sticks, enlarged to the point of absurdity, partially bundled together. The hall is the archive for Venice's diplomatic affairs," the blonde repeated. As she spoke, he glanced at a long bookcase with tall, narrow compartments. They held more cardboard rolls. The casings made him think of doctoral diplomas and shipping tubes for posters. The casings were marked with mysterious symbols on various-sized round labels. The dark-haired woman noticed he was interested in them, pulled out one of the rolls, opened it, and he could see that documents were rolled-up inside. "You are now standing before the diplomatic memory of an epoch that lasted for centuries," she explained solemnly and, after several seconds of silence, led him back out into the corridor and from there into several roomy and bright monks' cells that—like all the spaces, halls, and rooms—were chock full of more and more file folders. They were the previously mentioned documents with reports about the cities and countries with which Venice had undertaken trade relations at the time of the doges. It seemed like the files were jumbled together, with names like Petersburg, Monaco, Munich, Germania—everything beyond the Alps was lumped in this category, as he learned: Austria, Bavaria or Saxony, in addition to Florence, Milan or Istanbul, France and Spain. The merchants were also required to write down all perceptions and report them to the authorities. "Scholars from the above-mentioned cities and countries," the women said, "still came to the archives to resolve their issues."

As they entered the Large Crociera that was much like the small one, Aldrian's confusion was so great that he was afraid he wouldn't remember everything correctly. By now he had the feeling that he had gone non-stop through rooms where every detail was repeated ad infinitum. Time and again, more and more file-universes had spread out before him, up and down and down and up stairs. At one point the women had shown him tiny tightly-lettered papyruses, but he had forgotten what that was all about. While he was observing, he was forgetting, but, in spite of his waning attention span, he hoped that traces would still remain in the back of his head. The hall where they had stopped was almost twice the size of the Small Crociera that he had seen first. In the bookcases to the left and to the right were rows of thick bound volumes with documents and files, labeled according to subject area. Just the part that he could see was so incomprehensibly huge that it was impossible to gain an overview. It seemed he was in an oversized file crypt, a parallel world that preserved every trace of every person that ever existed. There was nothing left of all these people but the hand-writing of anonymous clerks on mottled disintegrating yellow paper that was stored on an endless highway of files, in folders and portfolios of various colors and labels as well as in special cabinets and drawers. Too, of the clerks who had constructed this parallel world in hundreds of thousands of hours, there was nothing left but their handwriting.

By now it was so cold that Aldrian struggled to keep his teeth from chattering. He no longer tried to revive his original curiosity, but the two women, who were better protected from the cold in their winter clothing, hardly noticed. They put thick folios and files on a table and thumbed through them or took out copper engravings that they spread out before him. First there were pages with illustrations of General Domenico Gasparoni's soldiers with their small artillery standing in head-high trenches from which they could see tents with flags in the distance —apparently the camp of the enemy army. Then, behind a wall of stakes, cannons aimed at a city. Next, several soldiers preparing to load an artillery piece, while one of the gunners was already aiming at the charging enemy. Again, tents of the enemy army in the background, and on the next page, too. There were dead soldiers lying on the ground, nearby a cavalry waiting to be deployed while under fire from cannons in the distance. Several pages showed cannon barrels, and one depicted the Venice Arsenal as seen from above. The last copper engraving was devoted to a naval battle. Fifteen frigates, not far from shore, were firing their cannons at each other, the flight paths of the shells indicated by a line of dashes.

Without completely unrelated out of the blue, the two women opened one of the city's death records, a narrow black volume with the title *Necrologica* in sequential years. Each person's name, address, and date of death were entered, and, lastly, the cause of death. The scribe had frequently made sketches, too, for example a dog, which meant—as the two women explained—that the person in question had died from a dog bite. A gallows stood for the type of execution. Or a knife signified the weapon that had killed the victim. A woman throwing herself off a balcony indicated that she committed suicide. A burning house revealed that a person had perished in a fire. A bullet, a rifle, or a pistol meant that someone had been shot. Or a plague doctor indicated that the person had died from an epidemic. An occasional sun, on the other hand, was the symbol for someone who had lived a hundred years or more. This type of entry was proportionately rare.

In conclusion the two women pulled down several thick volumes in black paperboard with hand-written labels and explained that these were books listing the plague victims. In all these records, four times as thick as the general obituaries, there were no sketches, simply a long series of names and dates that were documented in green ink.

"From June 1575 until February 1576, 3,500 people died of the plague, during the second epidemic in the following year over 4,600—more than a third of the population. The city pledged," she continued, "to build a votive church when the plague was over. The sickness actually did disappear then in 1577. In memory of their salvation the city had Andrea Palladio build the Il Redentore church on the island of Giudecca. At the end of the third epidemic that afflicted Venice from 1630 to 1631 they built another church, Santa Maria della Salute; again, one-third of the city's inhabitants perished during this last great plague. Why the plague disappeared from that point on has not been resolved, while Europe was ravished by the plague until 1720."

There were also books that dealt with the plague infestation in animals, and others about the plague in other countries, such as Germany, Austria or France.

The two women put the documents back on the shelves and led him down a tall white corridor and over a marble staircase to their offices. He caught a glimpse of desks with computers, furniture, and more shelving through the open doors.

"If you want to know more about the plague, we will introduce you to Dr. Dr. Galotti, our specialist for the history of medicine," the blond woman said, pointing to an administrator sitting at a desk. Aldrian wanted to thank them and leave, but the woman with dark hair was already introducing him to the short, overweight, grey-haired man with a beard who was wearing over-sized eyeglasses with a gold frame and a black suit. Aldrian said a hurried good-bye to the two women. Dr. Dr. Galotti, who had doctorates in both medicine and philosophy, the women explained in parting, bustled ahead of him, snatched his coat from the coatrack, scurried out the building, always a step ahead of Aldrian, out to the forecourt and, without pausing, over the canal bridge into the nearby Caffè Frari that had four or five small tables, up a winding staircase to the second floor, took off his coat and sat down at a window seat. He wheezed and ordered from the owner—apparently they were well-acquainted—a Campari rosso and two pieces of toast. Aldrian had the same thing.

"I know you . . . Wait . . ." Dr. Dr. Galotti now addressed him . . . "You look like Jakob Aldrian. Are you his brother?"

"Yes."

"From Vienna? The Maestro Suggeritore?"

"Yes."

"That is marvelous . . . Your brother has told me about you. He frequently comes to our archives. I had to show him the old illustrated books about Venice's flora and fauna, and he consulted them time and time again . . . By the way, you really do resemble your brother. Are you twins?"

"My brother's disappeared," Aldrian said earnestly. "I'm trying to find him."

"Leave that to the police. You might put yourself in danger. I can't tell you any more than that." He paused briefly and then continued: "So, you want to know something about the plague in Venice . . . Do you have something to write with?"

Aldrian nodded, perplexed, and took out his notebook and one of the two new ballpoint pens, while Dr. Dr. Galotti hurried to the men's room.

When he returned and finally sat down across from Aldrian, the owner had already brought their order and the Doctor immediately began to eat. As he spoke, he devoured the two pieces of toast, inadvertently spitting out tiny half-chewed morsels, and paid no attention to whether or not Aldrian could keep up with his notetaking. Dictating with his mouth full, he ordered a second Campari and more toast, while Aldrian maintained a disinterested expression.

After some time the man absent-mindedly glanced at his wristwatch, arched his eyebrows, leaped up, and shook Aldrian's hand before he clattered down the staircase.

Aldrian ate the two pieces of toast the man had ordered, drank a Campari, another, then a third as he read through his notes on

Venice and the plague. That wasn't easy, since he hadn't understood everything in the archives due to his hearing loss, so he had to piece everything together. Moreover he couldn't forget Dr. Dr. Galotti's warning about putting himself in danger. The archivist, he discovered, had already paid for their meals, and so he only had to cover the Camparis he had ordered afterwards. He was sleepy and exhausted. As he made his way to his brother's house, dazed by the exertion and the alcohol, he again thought about Dr. Dr. Galotti's suggestions, spit out during the meal, and his words and sentences about the plague in Venice and its history.

The Plague in Venice

As best Aldrian could remember from Dr. Dr. Galotti's dictation, in 1347 traders from Genoa and Venice had been besieged by Mongols in the city of Kaffa on the Crimean Peninsula. The Mongols had catapulted blackened human corpses over the city walls. Dr. Dr. Galotti had paused before he added that the bodies were plague victims. Subsequently a Venetian galley had carried back infested rats and fleas. The fleas had conveyed the plague bacillus to the crew and later to the city's inhabitants. From there, the epidemic had spread over the entire continent. In just four years—from 1348 to 1352— the plague claimed a total of 25 million victims. That would be roughly one-third of Europe's population at the time. In Venice alone, less than half of the inhabitants survived. Aside from the fact that the illness was spread from one person to another, no one knew what caused it. It wasn't until a half-century later that a law was passed requiring that the crew of every ship be placed under quarantine for forty days after entering the Venetian harbor before they were allowed to come ashore. But since the Venetians didn't know about the infestation from fleas and rats, the measures didn't serve their purpose. There were two types of plague, according to Dr. Dr. Galotti: boils and lung plague. In the case of boil plague, following fleabites, pathogens of the illness penetrated the lymph nodes and—together with acute fever and headaches—infected the groin, the armpits, and behind the ears, causing tumors up to 4 inches in size that burst and oozed bloody pus. However, if the pathogens got into the blood stream, they caused lung plague. Recovery was perhaps possible only if the boils burst or were opened by a plague doctor—which threatened the patient's life. Lung plague exhibited a bluish coloration of the skin as a result of extensive bleeding of small blood vessels, difficulty breathing, and a bloody black expectoration; the patient would die within a few days. In addition, Dr. Dr. Galotti explained while nibbling his toast, there was a manageable form of the plague that infected people could survive and which gave them immunity for an extended period. But usually no diagnoses were made. Between 1348 and 1630, in intervals of 25 years, there were further plague epidemics. The pestilence continued to break out and, for reasons that are still unclear today, would suddenly disappear again.

Dr. Dr. Galotti had reflected for a moment. "In 1575, the year of the second great plague epidemic," he had continued, "the physicians, the *medici*, at first were uncertain which type of plague they were dealing with, and the merchants had totally denied any resurgence of cases of plague-type illnesses so as not to jeopardize their business dealings. This time the plague had been brought by someone on the continent, a man from Trento by the name of Matthias Tridentinus. According to reports it was the boil plague. We have precise records of the events in the files at the Archivio di Stato di Venezia. Even before the physicians had made the correct diagnosis, the public health authority had already begun to isolate infected people. As soon as the pestilence had assumed epidemic proportions, sickbays were built. A portion of the infected was isolated in homes, and only caregivers and plague doctors were allowed admittance. At the same time the medici were ordered to wear protective clothing: a black coat that reached to the floor, the face covered by a bird mask, its long beak filled with aromatic herbs because the stench from the victims was horrific, and, furthermore, they ascribed a protective influence to the dried and processed plants. Incidentally, there were sufficient plague doctors the entire time," as Dr. Dr. Galotti added. "The dying and mortally ill were transported on boats to the small island of Lazzaretto Vecchio, near the Lido, and housed in a hundred rooms.

No one infected lived longer than seventy hours. The *Picegamorti*, men with little bells on their sleeves, then rowed the dead to the funeral island and buried them in mass graves five feet deep. The name 'lazarette' comes from the term *lazzari*, the expression for lepers who were later treated in the same building, though this time by the Order of Saint Lazarus. Plague houses were marked by filth, stench, and the capriciousness of caregivers recruited from prisoners who were promised subsequent release. Furthermore, the government sent prostitutes to the lazarettes. The Picegamorti were also responsible for the caregiving. They also carried out the incineration of all property of the dead in the city and were responsible for maintaining the isolation of the afflicted in their homes. But still, the men and woman who provided care had to assume that they would not survive their term of duty. The consequences were corruption, vice, and sadism. It was also obvious that they could steal from the deceased. In addition to the prisoners and prostitutes, poor people were also enlisted as manpower with the prospect of high wages. The Venetians themselves called the Lazzaretto Vecchio an 'inferno' and 'hell.' There were large numbers of suicides and insanities," Dr. Dr. Galotti lectured in a monotone. "The other lazarette, the Lazzaretto Nuovo, had been nicknamed 'limbo' and 'purgatory.' They housed patients who were not completely afflicted with the plague and who still had some hope. The Lazzaretto Nuovo was located on the island Sant' Erasmo. A jetty led to the complex of buildings. Almost ten thousand people were evacuated to the island, and at that time the waterways to Venice were clogged with hundreds of ships and boats."

"When there was no more room in the two lazarettes, they established sickbays on the water that were overseen by the national guard. Mostly wealthy people lived on the ships. They were supervised by physicians and priests, and relatives were permitted to provide them with abundant foodstuffs from nearby boats. There were descriptions in the archives of the ships as 'buoyant' islands in a sea of misery and death. In the evening people in the city could hear the songs and prayers of people on deck. Convalescents on board had organized noisy farewell parties, even though there were sick people who had gone mad. Normal everyday life in the city had almost completely collapsed—there were only funerals and mourners. People fled the city whenever possible, left behind were primarily the indigent and the infected whose only consolation was their religion. In the second great epidemic in August 1576, the famous painter Titian died of the plague. It wasn't until 1894 that they were able to identify the plague bacteria *Yersinia pestis* and its path of infection and, with Alexander Fleming's discovery of penicillin in 1928, to combat it." Dr. Dr. Galotti concluded his lecture and then rushed off.

Beatrice

Dazed, Aldrian stopped several times before display windows and stared at the merchandise to calm his brain. Perhaps he was also reluctant to return to his brother's house, not knowing what was awaiting him there. He glanced in a shop window at the tawdry green and blue gondolas that were being sold as ashtrays. In the next window were flamboyantly spotted neckties, and at one of the many market stalls he happened upon a basket with colorful Carnival masks that had points with little bells like the disguise that one of them men wore who had assaulted him at the front door. A shop right beside it was offering various types of masks. They were intended for women and decorated with colors and patterns like butterfly wings. There were bird masks and harlequin masks, masks of cats and coquettes. It occurred to him that he wanted to pay a visit to Diego Sarcia who had always wanted to attend a production in the Vienna State Opera but had never gotten around to it; his mask store in the Rughetta del Ravano was on his way and was located not far from their favorite restaurant, the Ostaria Dai Semei. So Aldrian paused at the mask store and saw Diego through the window. He was sitting on a high stool at a lectern-like small table in his tiny workspace and was in the process of painting a mask black. The small shop distinguished itself from all the others by the strange dolls that hung from the ceiling, on the walls, and in the display window: a plague doctor, a fat priest with a pudgy face, an Odysseus and a Cyclops, Giuseppe Verdi, Rigoletto, and Richard

Wagner, or a mouse chef and a frog with a stovepipe hat. Along with the dolls there were the usual masks, for example, ugly people with exaggerated grimaces or something you might see in classic Greek tragedies or Japanese masks with white makeup as in kabuki theater. Every time Aldrian came to Sarcia's shop it made him think of the "puppet master Fire-Eater" who took Pinocchio into his traveling theater. Time and time again the masks disappeared from the walls, from the table and the ceiling because they were sold, while new and different ones took their places so that a complete turnover occurred in the jam-packed store. Diego had worked in a large circus where he learned the art of maskmaking. Aldrian and his brother had coincidentally spent several days in Tuscany once and had quickly gotten to know Diego's wife Carla and his two children who studied in Mestre and lived with his in-laws. Diego was of medium height, half-bald, had a long beard, wore glasses and at work an apron that went from his chest to his thighs and was covered with an abundance of paint smudges. He was a hot-tempered oddball. His expression had something fierce, something penetrating about it, and in his past he had been a scrapper, as he liked to admit. He raised his head as Aldrian entered, looked up, and then quickly came to meet him as he always did.

"Mikey!" he roared, and hugged Aldrian.

"Jakob and Elena have disappeared," Aldrian said softly.

"I know," he answered sadly, as he embraced Aldrian. "The police were at your place today and the locks have been changed." They stepped back, and Aldrian asked in astonishment how he knew that.

"It gets around pretty quickly. You were mugged and your keys were stolen," Diego, uneasy and also reproachful, went on: "Let me take a look at your head."

Aldrian waved him off. The whole time he had been looking at the theater in the background, and it seemed as if he were in a puppet theater for children.

"Don't you want to go to the Ostaria Dai Zemei?" Diego suggested in a tone that didn't leave room for dissent.

Aldrian shook his head. "Some other time."

"Is it true that you woke up in your own bed even though you were attacked out on the street?" It sounded like an interrogation.

"Yes," Aldrian responded unwillingly.

"And that you were locked inside the house?"

"Yes, it was a shitty morning."

"It was probably a warning," Diego said. They were still standing in the middle of the shop. "At least a warning." He paused briefly and looked Aldrian squarely in the eye.

"You're in trouble, Mikey," Diego calmly continued.

He turned around, pulled something out of his desk drawer and handed Aldrian a small pistol. "A Röhm RG 70 caliber, six shot," he added matter-of-factly.

Aldrian tried to decline the weapon, but Diego cut him off with the argument that it only shot gas cartridges. He locked the door, let down the blinds, and without further ado explained the mechanism. "What a strange reunion," Aldrian thought, and made reluctant head gestures.

"What'sa matter?" Diego asked and looked up.

"Nothing. I was just thinking that this was a strange reunion."

Diego didn't lose his train of thought, but asked Aldrian to practice loading, putting the safety off and on, and pulling the trigger—and waited until the pistol disappeared in his friend's sport coat pocket. Only then did he pull up the blinds and unlock the shop door. His instructions had taken less than five minutes.

Aldrian had to smile, because he suddenly had a feeling of being protected. He realized that it was silly, but he didn't fight it.

When he left the shop, he still felt relieved, though nothing had changed. He intentionally went back the same way as last night and looked in the store windows on the Ruga del Speziali to dull his memories with new impressions, and at the end of the narrow street turned off to his brother's house. The fish market had closed long ago, the hall was deserted, and his brother's store was still dark. He used the big brass doorknocker hanging from the mouth of a lion, could hear a window opening up above him, and saw Margherita looking down at him.

A moment later his sister-in-law's sister greeted him with concern.

Once again Aldrian felt relief, and even something like joy that he wasn't alone and that she had been waiting for him.

"I had gone to meet with someone who familiarized me with the plague years in Venice . . ." he mumbled in apology as they entered Elena and Jakob's apartment. In the meantime all the locks in the house had actually been changed and replaced with door bars. Sitting at the kitchen table, he learned that the police had searched the rooms and wanted to have him repeat the precise course of events, so Commissario Galli would come over around ten o'clock tomorrow, Margherita said. She gave him the new keys for the front door, the shop door, for his brother's apartment and his own room. Then, since she wanted to cook supper for her husband and her friend Beatrice, she asked him to gut four sea bass because, according to her, the fish dealer hadn't had time to do it. Aldrian was wondering why she had specifically chosen his brother's apartment for the invitation, and asked her about it. She was superstitious, she replied and, as she washed two lemons in cold water, told him that her sister and Jakob hadn't even told their son Emilio that they were leaving.

Aldrian raised his eyebrows in amazement while he put the money for his share of the bill for the new keys on the table.

That was why she hadn't told Emilio about the incident during their phone conversation, Margherita continued without looking up, since she didn't want to upset him. Moreover she informed him that his parents had changed the locks.

Aldrian hadn't seen his nephew in a long long time because he was studying art in London. He cleaned the first two fish and cut open the other two, while Margherita began to stuff the bellies of the sea bass with herbs and lemon slices. Before Aldrian went up to his apartment, he washed his hands and gave her a kiss on the cheek.

Up in his room he plugged the power cord for his new smartphone in the wall socket and tried to memorize the new phone number. The door bars had turned the house into a fortress, he thought. Suddenly he became angry with his brother and Elena who had vanished somewhere. When he thought about it again, he became worried and afraid. It was possible that the assault on him had nothing to do with Jakob and Elena's disappearance. The two events, he felt, could also have occurred independently of each other. But if that was the case, why had Jakob and Elena disappeared? Possibly for financial reasons . . .? Or had they gone to China to straighten out something related to the wholesaling of pearls? But if the attack on him and the disappearance of the two were connected, he thought, then he knew even less . . . What could be the cause, and who could be behind it? Someone had wanted to frighten him and drive him off—that much was clear. But what if he stuck around, what then? And what could it mean that they didn't want him in the house? He closed his eyes and, exhausted, fell asleep until Margherita woke him up.

"Are you coming?" she called through the crack in the door, and when he didn't respond right away: "Are you sleeping?"

He cleared his throat and answered in a hoarse voice that he was awake now. The door slowly closed. He took a shower, changed his clothes, put one of the two ballpoint pens on his nightstand and left the other one, along with the notebook and the gas pistol, in the coat he had worn earlier.

The table had been set in his brother's living room. Margherita, Eugenio, and Beatrice were sitting together, drinking Prosecco, and they poured him a glass. Aldrian could tell that they felt sorry for him because Eugenio asked if he didn't want to stay at their place for the next few days. But Aldrian didn't like to sleep in a strange apartment as someone's guest. It seemed indiscrete to mention it in front of his hosts, and he also avoided telling them anything—an old habit, an idiosyncrasy—about himself.

Margherita purposely hadn't removed the scales from the bass so that they were crispy and firm; now she removed the skin and broke the fish up into filets. He watched her at work because he had come into the kitchen to help, but she had already prepared the salad, so together they served the meal.

Just as he had suspected, the conversation revolved around the disappearance of Jakob and Elena. Now Margherita was also upset that their two laptops hadn't turned up in the apartment or in the store.

"Maybe the two men took them, the guys who stole my telephone and keys," Aldrian said, trying to calm her. But then Margherita began to cry and couldn't calm down until Eugenio stood up and took her home.

Apart from his remark Aldrian hadn't said a word the entire time and noticed that Beatrice had secretly been casting stolen glances in his direction. On his last visit to Venice he had already noticed that she enjoyed his company. The two of them now sat silently side by side, and he poured a glass of white wine for her from a half-empty bottle of Merlot. Since nothing else occurred to him, he awkwardly reached for her hand, and, to his delight, she let him take it. Margherita's crying had made her sad, while it had only frightened him. He didn't want to imagine what could have happened to his brother and his wife before there were any leads. And besides, he was superstitious and was afraid that he might have caused the entire ordeal himself.

He told her what he was thinking, invited her to join him on the couch and have another glass of wine, and she leaned on him. In that moment he became aware of the silence that prevailed in the house and out on the street. She got up, shook her hair, and when she said that she wanted to go, he kissed her and begged her to stay.

It had been six months since he had last hugged a woman. His few visits to brothels had never provided what he had hoped to find. And his fleeting relationships were generally limited to hurried embraces in some hotel room. He had frequently heard someone's remarks—partly in amazement and yet disparaging—that he was crazy or had to be crazy, and gradually he also became aware of his behavior: his phenomenal memory for music, his passion for opera, his dubious magic tricks had taken up so much of his time that he wasn't able to talk about anything else.

For several years now he had seen Beatrice Stefanelli at Margherita's and was impressed by her looks, her knowledge, and her judgment. From the beginning it was clear that he wouldn't have a brief fling with her, and on the other hand he wanted to avoid saying something wrong that would cost him her affection. But this time it had simply happened, and they were embracing.

At the Fish Market

Beatrice woke him early the next morning and kissed him on the cheek. After breakfast in the kitchen he promised he would come over to her place that evening. He was still entranced by the warmth of her body and last night. As he locked the front door behind her, he already missed her and admitted to himself that he was happy—in any event, as long as he could still hope that his brother and Elena were safe. And if they weren't?

He dismissed the thought, and it occurred to him that they could have come home while he and Beatrice were making love in their living room.

He climbed the stairs to his apartment and laid down on the bed. Half-asleep, he thought about his time with Beatrice.

He woke up around 8 o'clock. His smartphone was charged, he had memorized the number and written down the PIN and first called Beatrice to tell her that she could reach him at this number and how much he was looking forward to that evening. Next, he gave his number to Margherita who apologized for her breakdown last evening, but she was inconsolable.

"Don't cry," he said, about to hang up, but that made her start crying all over again.

When he called Galli about their prearranged meeting, the Commissario acted as if his mind was elsewhere. Without saying a word he apparently made note of the telephone number Aldrian gave him.

"No," he said, "I think I have enough for now. I'll be in touch if there's something new."

Since his visit in San Servolo wasn't scheduled until Sunday, he had plenty of time. He slipped into his clothes and carried the picture by Adalbert Stifter that he had brought from Vienna down to Jakob's and Elena's apartment, unpacked it, and put it below the framed pictures that Jakob had painted. He put the glasses, cooking utensils, and dishes in the dishwasher, tossed the wine bottles and paper napkins along with the wadded death threat from the wastebasket in the garbage bag, aired the place out, vacuumed the rug, removed the table cloth, and straightened up the couch. Last of all he called Beatrice and asked if he should pick up something from the market for dinner. She thought that was a good idea. He closed the windows, emptied the dishwasher, put the garbage bag out in front of the house, then locked the apartment and took a shower. He put on fresh underwear, a long-sleeved black polo shirt, jeans, and a windbreaker, got two shopping bags from the kitchen pantry, and pocketed some cash and his ATM card.

By now the fish market was busy. He noticed that there was small, colorful, round and square confetti like some children's star-spangled sky lying on the ground outside the hall. In winter the hall was darker than usual since the sun didn't shine on it. Silver-blue swordfish were for sale at several counters. The heads of the smaller fish had been cut off; their big round dark eyes and swords were lying in a sea of other dead fish, mussels, crabs, and scampi. From a distance he had the impression that the swords were broomsticks that had choked the creatures. He gazed at the largest specimen that had a clipped horn and eyes like ink. One of the side fins hung limply from the counter like the arm of a child. The seafood for sale was marked with hand-written price tags. A man with a rubber apron, white work gloves, a heavy turtleneck pullover and a woolen cap hosed off the headless body of a swordfish and began to cut it in slabs. In the center of each oval chunk he could see the cartilage of the spine. The man handled the knife deftly, and in no time at all there were swordfish steaks on a bed of ice. Something similar happened with the head, until only black eyes, the open mouth, and the bone sword were left. They looked like the remains of some big decapitated bird. At the next booth a stingray was lying on a dolly with a white plastic crate. The large caudal fin reached all the way to the ground, the head was propped up, and the tail with its pointed serrated stinger resembled the long beak of some prehistoric monster. He walked on past the booths while all around him marine life was being gutted, cut up, and descaled. He also saw small sharks at the market for the first time, their gills made him think of eyes with the lids closed, the barely closed mouth reminded him of the letter "C." Turbots were stacked beside them, large flat fossil-like creatures with fins all around, as if they were old dried sunflowers from unknown gardens in the sea. Spotlights that highlighted the wares were mounted above the closely aligned sales tables. The fish stench mingled with sewer gases and the sweetish fragrance from booths of flowers and fruits, forming a cloud of odors that the merchants and customers were forced to breathe. Dead black eels shimmered in a green tin bowl. Huge crabs that reminded him of turtles with spider legs were lying next to red and white scampi. Octopi and their black liquid covered almost the entire surface of another sales counter, and polyps with white tentacles were tossed on another table. Their button-like suction cups looked like the pearl keyboard of a rustic accordion. Moving on, he noticed a slimy deep-sea creature dappled with brown and white spots whose lifeless light-grey eyes, like those of a blind person, saw right through him and made him think of some strange giant snail that had survived for centuries beneath the sand. The black-gold eyes of the dead polyps and the sight of the monkfish with pointed teeth in their gaping mouths of their dragonheads recalled nightmares of his childhood. Every sales booth had a round weighing scale with a large white dial and an indicator.

He selected two tuna fish steaks, bought a bouquet of white roses outside the hall, and since he was thinking of cooking risotto, he got saffron, rice, lettuce, tomatoes, potatoes, onions, lemons, and mandarin oranges in a grocery store across the street. He also had a melancholy butcher in a white work coat cut a slice of roast beef for him. Beside his cutting board the grey-haired man had three knives, a large one like a short sword, one with a pointed narrow blade, and a sturdy one for everyday tasks. Various types of sausages were hanging from the ceiling, and in the display case, alongside innards and a sheep's head, he saw a boiled ham with little fat, so he also had the man cut him a large slice of that. Since his shopping bags were full and he had to carry the fruit in a net sack, he went back to the house, climbed the stairs panting, put the bags and the net sack on the kitchen table and laid down on the bed for a moment to rest up from his exertion. As soon as he had put everything away, he went back down to the market. This time he took a backpack for the drinks. He chose the route via the narrow street with the gourmet shops and bought mineral water, butter, cheese, olives, balsamic vinegar, peppermint, eggs, orange marmalade, and white bread with a nice crust from a nearby bakery. Even though he was very familiar with the fish market and vicinity, every shopping expedition was still an adventure that he loved. In a side street he went to find his favorite store for pasta and wine. The quiet older woman didn't recognize him—as she never did after a protracted absence—but handed him the requested spaghetti, bottles of Merlot, Cabernet Franc, and Prosecco that he stowed in the backpack and in the bags. After Aldrian had lugged the food and drinks back to the house and put them in their rightful places, he grabbed the backpack and made one last round, as he always did, just to make sure he hadn't forgotten anything. He didn't go to the fish market this time. A young man was standing at the flower piazza with tubs of yellow bouquets that Aldrian thought might be a certain type of chrysanthemum. He thought it was pretty how they were reflected in the tinfoil in which they were wrapped. At the fruit and vegetable booths he examined heads of red endives that seemed like wine-red plant organs with thick white veins from the darkness of the earth, the orange-red pomodori—the literal translation for these tomatoes is "golden apples,"—scaly artichokes and shiny black and smoothly shaved eggplants. All the while he was thinking about the beauty and the cruelty of creation, about the opera house with its wonderful music that first breathed life into the tragic libretti, and most of all about Elena and Jakob who came this way almost every day and could see the fish market from their windows. He sighed and pushed open the door to the candy store that was filled to the ceiling with large glass containers with brass fasteners and were stocked with bonbons in every conceivable color. On each of his trips to Venice he paid a visit to this shop. The glass containers had tags with just numbers on them. Every time he came in the door, it reminded him of a magic pharmacy that he had invented for himself as a child. In his imagination there weren't just all sorts of candies, but each one had a different effect. He could make himself invisible with a blue bonbon, could transform someone into an animal with a green one—into a fly that he could squash or into a cat that he could snuggle—he could fly away like a swallow with a red candy, could read somebody's thoughts with a silver one, walk through walls with a yellow bonbon, and so on. For every metamorphosis there was a special sweet, and he now realized that he had forgotten many colors and shapes and their consequences. He had the friendly lady who owned the store make an assortment of bonbons in all the colors he could remember, realizing that it was positively childish of him, and he secretly smiled at himself. The next shop, the Macelleria Equina, as he had read so many times on the sign in the display window, was a butcher shop specializing in horsemeat. Two magnificent horseheads were painted below the inscription. He always stopped out front with a mixture of displeasure, disgust, and curiosity. In any event he had never gone in, just glanced in the store window. The place didn't have floor tiles, but cork flooring and walls that gave it the appearance of a cardboard box. A long display case featured meat products that looked the same as those from other animals. Next door, of course, was the shop where he had just bought the roast beef: on one of the tile walls—as he still could recall—hung half a pig minus its head, it was red with white ribs and vertebrae; yellow plucked chickens that also were headless. The shop window reflected him as well as the fruit and vegetable stands across the street with customers gathered outside. He heard his telephone ring and answered. Margherita excitedly informed him that the trace on Jakob and Elena's mobile phones turned up nothing new. She had just found that out from Commissario Galli.

"We know as much and as little as before," she said, disappointed.

Aldrian was relieved that it wasn't something worse, but refrained from saying that and instead consoled Margherita.

"I've got a bad feeling," she said. "I'm afraid . . . also afraid for you . . . Why did they attack you? Who put you in bed, took your telephone and keys, and locked you in the house? Do you know something you're not telling me?"

"It's as much a mystery to me as it is to you," he responded.

"Aren't you afraid? It's obvious they're threatening you so you'll leave. The Commissario thinks so, too!"

Aldrian thought about the gas pistol in his sport coat pocket and about the sack with the multi-colored bonbons in his windbreaker.

"I don't want to leave just yet, and most of all I want to know what's happened to Elena and Jakob."

"Emilio called. Now he's worried." She fell silent, but then continued: "The laptops haven't turned up either,"

"We've got to be patient," Aldrian answered, using a phrase that he had often heard as a prompter or had used himself.

"You're right," she said bewildered, and hung up.

Nearby he bought a slice of Pizza Margherita and realized the name's similarity to that of his sister-in-law's sister. Nevertheless he bought a second slice and drank a bottle of beer with it.

What does it mean that he's devouring this pizza, he wondered . . . He suppressed any thoughts, just as he did with his cares and fears, because, in truth, it wasn't the colorful bonbons from the candy store and it wasn't the gas pistol that gave him strength—it was the night of love with Beatrice. Margherita wouldn't know about that . . . Or would she?

He thought about calling Beatrice, but didn't. When he looked out at the canal, he saw a ferry with passengers going from one waterfront to the other. On the opposite bank was the Ca' d'Oro that he always visited when he wanted to be alone, but since he knew that the palazzo was loveliest in sunlight because the light coming through the windows cast unusual shadow patterns on the mosaic floor and on the walls of the halls, he postponed his visit for more favorable weather.

Back at home, he collected the mail, newspapers, and flyers from behind the front door and put them on the small table. Up in his room he shook off the thoughts that had come to him while he was picking up the delivered items and then read in his notebook what he had retained from the Archive. In the back of his mind he saw the rooms and shelving again, the two women and Dr. Dr. Galotti. He paused and then wrote with his new ballpoint pen that the cold Venice archives store tiny remains of fossils that hold the flora and fauna of past ages—similar to ice core samples that are unearthed in climate surveys at the poles—and pieces of the puzzle of everyday life or other traces of past ages are stored in the file fragments. And like scientists who use these artifacts to reconstruct the climate of past centuries and even millennia, historians in the archives can take these files—that are piled on top of each other or wedged together like the ice floes in Caspar David Friedrich's painting—and eventually make the lives of people in the past accessible.

He fell asleep for a short time, and when he awoke, he made notes of his impressions at the fish market before he suddenly decided to call the Commissario.

When Galli answered, Aldrian could hear voices in the background, possibly from a bar, he suspected. Without hesitation he asked what it meant that they weren't able to track the two mobile phones. The Commissario thought for a moment, and in the meantime Aldrian could hear only the voices in the background.

"We started the initial trace while I was with you at the house. There was nothing. Since then, we've tried several times, but had no luck. Signora Margherita Belluchi, the sister of your sister-in-law, phoned me today and asked me about it . . . I told her everything I know."

"And what does it mean that you've had no luck."

"Perhaps your brother and his wife have disposed of their phones, perhaps the phones have been destroyed—either intentionally or by accident."

Aldrian became anxious and felt like he was going to faint.

"There are cell phones that are impossible to track," Galli added, as if in consolation. "They operate with a protective case on the principle of the Faraday shield. Otherwise we're able to listen in on conversations or even inconspicuously take photos and retrieve them. It works the moment we have the telephone number, even when the device is turned off. In any case we're taking the matter very seriously," the Commissario concluded.

Automatically Aldrian turned on the TV and saw a report of yesterday's news on the acqua alta. They repeatedly showed the flood at St. Mark's Square and people in masks standing in calf-high water. When the program was over, he turned the set off and knew that he couldn't tell Margherita about his conversation with the Commissario without precipitating a new crisis. He closed his eyes and envisioned his brother and Elena sitting here in their living room. Unresponsive, they gazed across at him. He couldn't tell from their expressions what they wanted him to do, so he tried to have a mental conversation with them, but it was futile. In his imagination they just sat there and gazed at him.

As a distraction, he thought about getting his iPad out of his suitcase, but he remembered that he had left it in Vienna because he wanted to concentrate totally on his work. In retrospect he was glad, because he knew that the two men who attacked and robbed him would have taken his computer, too, as they had perhaps done with Jakob's and Elena's laptops. He was slightly encouraged by the fact that Elena always took her laptop on trips and for her restoration work, and Jakob, too, took his for business dealings and, even more, because of his passion for painting.

Then he went downstairs to the small side room in Jakob and Elena's apartment where they had their electronic devices, but he only found cables lying on the floor. Jakob had a cabinet for his DVDs that reached the ceiling. It was so jam-packed that Aldrian couldn't make heads or tails of it. Most of all there were portraits of painters and their works, operas, and the couple's favorite directors. Jakob had movies by Pasolini, Visconti, Buñuel, Fellini, Peter Greenaway, Ingmar Bergman, Michael Haneke, and documentaries about birds, insects—primarily bees and ants—beetles and butterflies, but also amphibians and plants. Elena's favorites were Alfred Hitchcock, David Lynch, Stanley Kubrick, the Coen brothers, David Fincher, and Martin Scorsese. For their mutual pleasure, the two of them would always watch each other's favorite movies together.

Out of curiosity Aldrian pressed the "Open" button on the DVD player and saw a computer game; it was *Grand Theft Auto* that Emilio loved to play with his friends while he was still in junior high school. How many times had Aldrian taken the boy by surprise while he was playing—connected with his friends in junior high via smartphone—shouting out loud, especially the American phrase "Oh, my God!" The PlayStation, a small black plastic box, was lying with its controller under the TV table, which surprised him since Emilio was in England. Maybe he had come for a visit at Christmastime and no one had watched any DVDs after he left. Still, that wasn't very likely, because Emilio had his own room and kept his equipment in there.

Aldrian had never liked *Grand Theft Auto* because it reinforced his "paranoid predisposition," as he called it—incidentally, like religions with their god who knew everything about you down to the smallest detail. Even when he went to the toilet or slept with a woman, this god was watching. It was a train of thought that automatically formed in his head at the slightest mention of religion. For that reason, whenever possible he had avoided visiting the Schole synagogues, the art galleries of the Accademia or of churches in Venice because they conveyed the impression that God's eye was watching him from out of one of his likenesses, as if through a hidden peephole. He felt they were ideological propaganda pictures that were trying, silently but eloquently, to convince him of a parallel but invisible world of faith without rationality. On the other hand, he loved to listen to the Masses by Johann Sebastian Bach, Anton Bruckner or Wolfgang Amadeus Mozart and the music of Arvo Pärt or Sofia Gubaidulina. But he generally hurried past images of the saints, scenes from the Bible that combined the metaphysical with reality, though he was fascinated by depictions of hell in churches or by Hieronymus Bosch because they revealed the innermost fears in people's minds and their willingness to commit gruesome crimes. In spite of his aversion to *Grand Theft Auto* he was in the process of loading it and playing it. For his contests with Emilio he had even bought a second PlayStation that must also be somewhere in his room. Emilio won most of their matches, and eventually his nephew became bored playing against him, much to Aldrian's relief. The boy found his uncle's clumsiness driving the virtual vehicles or shooting the virtual targets to be tiresome and all he could do was laugh at him until one day he no longer asked Aldrian to play with him. Emilio had always chosen a muscular athlete as his alter ego, frequently an African-American. For his part, Aldrian had always taken whatever was available. Aldrian plugged in the devices, loaded the program, and chose the option that Emilio preferred. The animated character raced a stolen sports car down the highway through a driving rain, inadvertently sawed off telephone poles and trees, slammed into another car and flipped. The athlete got out of the wreck uninjured and, at Aldrian's command, stopped a semi. When the driver opened the door, Aldrian's character yanked him out, leaped up behind the steering wheel, and sped off. The point was to rise within a criminal hierarchy and make money by carrying out contract killings, robbing banks, or committing larceny. It was even possible for the perpetrators to steal tanks, helicopters, or jet fighters from a military base. The city and the surrounding area were real in an unusual way, like in a dream. Although Aldrian had played the game often and watched Emilio play even more often, time after time new and surprising landscapes appeared on the screen. Basically there were no ground rules. The police, who were controlled by the program, were just as aggressive and bloodthirsty as the bad guys.

If Jakob and Elena could see him now, they would probably think he was insane. But he had the impression that the game was helping him at this moment. On the one hand it diverted him from his own situation; on the other, it also intensified his anger that there were only questions and uncertainty.

All of a sudden he felt ridiculous. He turned off the PlayStation and the TV and went back to his room. If at least Emilio were here, he thought, but then didn't want his nephew to be worried. He closed his eyes and rode with his athletic game figure in desert landscapes, through forests and around street corners, he broke into strange apartments, ran along a beach, and finally came to the house in Venice where he was staying. Just as the athlete was opening the front door, Aldrian woke up, leaped out of bed, opened the door to the stairwell and listened. It was dark and quiet outside.

A Long Night

Beatrice Stefanelli was happy when he hugged her and that he had brought flowers and the tuna fish steaks.

"I've missed you all day," he said shyly.

"I've missed you, too," she replied to his delight.

He got right to work in the kitchen.

"Tell me about your ex-husband," he suggested. He needed rosemary that Beatrice had in a pot on the windowsill outside the door in the hallway, peppercorns and bay leaves, ground them in a mortar, tossed them in olive oil, and salted them.

All of a sudden Beatrice stood up and kissed him. He kissed her back and remembered that he still had his apron on . . .

When they got dressed again and went back into the kitchen, he was enchanted by her affection. He secretly doubted, as he always did in affairs of the heart, that his impressions were correct. He picked up where he had left off with the preparations, tied his apron back on, and began to heat the pan before he browned the tuna fish filets on both sides.

In the meantime Beatrice had put a glass bowl with tomato salad on the table. They worked together as if they had been doing it forever. Lastly he opened the bottle of Pinot Grigio. The flowers were already in a glass vase when they sat down, squeezed hands, and gazed in each other's eyes before they started to eat.

Afterward he gazed out the window of her apartment at the

Campo San Polo that was dimly lit. A man in a hat was standing beside a small dog that was just lifting its leg.

They talked about Aldrian's scheduled Sunday visit to the island of San Servolo where the old insane asylum for Venice had been located. Aldrian was familiar with the island and its buildings. The asylum had closed in the 1970s and been converted into a university where, among other subjects, traditional restoration techniques were offered. Aldrian began to tell about Elena, the lectures and seminars she offered there; he had accompanied her a few times and was amazed by her knowledge and her skills. Perhaps she had been trying to show him, as he later suspected, that she was also capable, because on their visits together with Jakob to the Teatro La Fenice and afterwards in some restaurant, he had impressed all their friends with his own knowledge and his recitation of memorized examples from the opera in question. Occasionally he would wander around alone on the island of San Servolo that was ringed with a high wall. One time he had a map from the 1970s that showed where a cemetery was located, and out of curiosity he set off to find it. He encountered numerous students—men and women from Japan, England, Germany (whose accents he recognized), and particularly from Italy—professors in suit and tie and female faculty with fashionable jewelry and nice shoes who were bantering back and forth in the halls while the students unfailingly wore green or beige jeans, sneakers, pullovers and windbreakers and sat in the café or on a bench outdoors. The buildings looked out on the choppy sea and the town in the distance; they had been restored at their original location in the large park with the tall trees, high brick walls, 21 window slots—he counted them!—and wrought-iron bars. Everything attested to their efforts to eradicate the past, that historical time when the entire complex had been an insane asylum. He peeked into several buildings, but nothing hinted at the pain and fear that must still reside within the walls, he thought, even though he knew it wasn't true. Any references to the past had also been removed by the conversion work, he believed. When he saw a cleaning lady with her bucket and mop scurrying down the deserted corridor, he whispered sarcastically: "You've really tidied everything up!"

Aldrian went on with his reminiscence. He had taken the park's main path all the way to the end of the island, maybe 1/3 of a mile, until he came to the spot where he thought the cemetery might be. Here the park was overgrown. Tall grass, bushes, poppies—quite romantic, he decided. He tentatively started to look for remnants, but didn't find any. Not even a cross, a tombstone, or any kind of relic. The trees seemed taller and nature undisturbed. The only thing he found in the tall grass was construction material, trash, and an upholstered swivel chair. "A shabby trash dump," he concluded. The paved path went to a builders' shed with a bicycle leaning against the doorway. A middle-aged man was sitting in the shed, filling out a form in the twilight.

Aldrian called to him: "*Scusi!*" and asked him where he could find the cemetery.

"The cemetery?"

"Yes." Aldrian took out the old city map and showed him the green rectangle with the small black crosses.

"The madhouse cemetery? My God! Everybody's forgotten all about it. That was a long time ago. There's no cemetery here anymore."

Once again Aldrian silently pointed to the map.

"No, no!" the man contradicted, annoyed that Aldrian was confronting him with some old map and asking about the nuthouse cemetery in the midst of the beautiful renovated building complex, and he turned his back on Aldrian.

Building materials were piled behind the shack. A workman in a blue floppy hat was carting bricks in a wheel borrow to a building site and had suddenly disappeared in the tall grass between the trees and bushes. Aldrian waited for several minutes without knowing why, but the workman didn't return. Finally he himself went off into the tall grass to look for graves. He was convinced that the dead were resting beneath the ground he was walking on. Who would have removed them? And why? And where?

He now saw that his map had a drawing of a Marian chapel, and when he looked more closely, he discovered it further on in the park. On its open side he recognized a waving Madonna with the baby Jesus on her arm. A tiny lizard scampered from an exterior stairway that spiraled up to the roof. He slowly climbed the stairs and gradually could see farther and farther into the distance. Now he could look out over the surrounding walls and see a distant luxury cruise ship and the sky with ponderous white clouds. And from up above he then discovered several small gravestones in the grass, just tall enough so that he could make them out. Sometimes a second stone was of a similar height so that he could imagine how the row of graves must have been laid out. Near the chapel two green-yellow lizards were sunning themselves and apparently felt safe in their solitude. Aldrian recalled that on the roof he finally saw a flat white stone with a relief that depicted a dead person. It looked like a gravestone for a bishop interred in his vestments with pointed hat, but it was much too small for all that. It was probably a memorial stone that came from the wall of the church, he thought. It probably came from the chapel roof, to cover a hole or to weigh down the tiles so that they wouldn't be blown away in a storm. Aldrian climbed back down and set off for the vaporetto station. On the way he sat down on a stone bench beside an ancient tree so that he could think. A chunk of the tree roughly the size of a man's ribcage and another small piece had broken off from the trunk and were lying on the fragrant new-mown lawn. Aldrian imagined that the tree had a gaping wound, and the chunks of wood lying in the grass, rotting and riddled with zillions of holes, had turned into something else a long time ago: into sculptures from the sun, the rain, and the dampness of the earth. He also thought of the wreckage of ships that had sunk and were drifting in the ocean. And he remained seated until the trees began to speak about the patients on San Servolo who were only allowed to see their city from a distance as a mirage at sea . . .

They were drinking the second bottle of wine when Beatrice remembered that as a child she had visited the island with her aunt at the time when the renovations were almost finished. Her aunt was a friend with one of the gardeners who had invited her to visit him.

"This isn't for you," her aunt had said, and led her to a bench where she was to sit until the aunt returned. With that, Beatrice went on, her aunt disappeared into a building with the gardener.

She was left alone in the park, listening to the construction noise and watching workmen who ignored her. There were two huge agave plants in front of the main building, and they may still be there today. Oleander bushes had blossomed and the trees had cast large shadows on the lawn. The window slots in the wall seemed to her like moving pictures. The ocean with its small bounding waves, seagulls, the island opposite with its buildings, and the clouds together with the bare bricks of the wall gave off something surreal, though she couldn't have formulated it so succinctly back then. She also noticed the variety of bright green leaves on the trees that swayed in the wind like poisonous alien algae. She felt like Alice in Wonderland. But the things that impressed her most were the buildings. They were a combination of schools, a college, a hospital, and military barracks. Truly she found herself in a painting.

Beatrice suddenly began to laugh, and Aldrian laughed, too, until they finally kissed. Aldrian got his sport coat that had been draped over an armchair and folded the lapel back so she could see the pin with the gilded dove. He told her how he had acquired it.

"It's strange," he said. "Up to now I've always thought I was prone to paranoia, and now, when I've got a good reason for it, I'm only worried about Jakob and Elena." They tried to draw some conclusions from what little they knew, but Aldrian couldn't even say whether the assault on him was in any way connected to the disappearance of his brother and sister-in-law.

"It feels weird," Beatrice was saying, "and I'm afraid for you when you sleep in your brother's house. If you want, you can move in with me until everything is cleared up."

She laid her head on his shoulder and closed her eyes.

When they woke up together the next morning and looked out the window, it was snowing heavily.

Snow

Aldrian found Beatrice desirable, whether in high heels or barefoot, her hair done up or let down, her toe- and fingernails painted or not, he was fascinated by her intelligence, her kindness and her vulnerability. He had always eaten breakfast alone, though it had never made him feel lonely. His ex-wife wouldn't wait for him to wake up the next morning, even when they both hadn't had to work the night before—tired, the music from last night or the previous day still in his head, or the rehearsals for operas that were already in preparation. Usually he would fix something before he did his personal hygiene: peppermint tea, white bread or toast with butter and honey. At breakfast he began by reading the daily paper, one that he had subscribed to for over twenty years and thus knew as well as a musical score from one of his favorite composers. He knew where articles were located, he was familiar with the thoughts of the journalists that he had never seen or met, the style of the cartoonists, and most of all the layout of the culture section. He almost never watched television, with the exception of the noon news. In his spare time he usually slept, listened to various renditions of the same opera, studied scores or practiced magic tricks, and was bored listening to his wife from whom he became increasingly more estranged.

So when Beatrice spoiled him—with orange marmalade, fruit juices and Russian tea that he watered down—it was something special. She went on to tell him about her ex-husband since Aldrian had asked the night before who he was. She told Aldrian that he was still working as a pathologist at the Medical University in Bologna and had given her a paperweight with a slice of a brain that was then sealed in a clear plastic cube. The brain specimen had come from a world-famous conductor who had frequently performed in Milan's La Scala. In the middle of the night Aldrian asked if he could see the paperweight. It was on the top shelf of a bookcase in the living room, hidden behind other things, and when Beatrice noticed his interest, she had given him the gruesome relic as a present. To tell the truth, she had always found it weird, she now admitted. In addition she also owned a whole collection of antique paperweights of Murano glass in the millefiori technique and several from Bohemia that were especially lovely. The millefiori paperweights, as she indicated, had mostly colored abstract designs, and their effect derived from the combination of colors, symmetry, and uniqueness. They evolve from the bottom up to the dome, usually the lower 1/3 is missing—because, obviously, you view them from above. On the other hand colorful glass flowers were usually encased in the Bohemian paperweights that resembled rock crystal. For each paperweight Beatrice knew when and where she had found it, the store where she bought it, and the price she paid for it.

Then Aldrian showed her the gas pistol Diego Sarcia had lent him. Thoughtful and silent, she studied the weapon and then pulled a revolver and ammunition out of the desk drawer. Her ex-husband had left it there so he wouldn't "commit suicide," as he told her at the divorce proceedings. He then went on to say he would come and get it "later." Aldrian learned that Beatrice had actually left her husband for a younger married co-worker who then ended the relationship two years later. Beatrice didn't want to divulge any more about the affair and also wouldn't comment on her silence.

"Do you still see him?" Aldrian wanted to know. She shook her head, but he didn't believe her.

"I'm going to Padua and will be back in the evening," she said after breakfast. "Will we see each other?"

At that moment Aldrian's phone rang. Commissario Galli was on the other end. He was calling, he began, "just to fill you in." The last time they were in his brother's house, they were searching for the business records, but had no luck. "Not a checkbook, not a receipt, nothing." And the cash register was empty. His sister-in-law had given them the name and address of their tax accountant. "With his help we've gone over the books, but found nothing suspicious. Everything seems to be in perfect order. But that they've disappeared without a trace is still a mystery . . . We have no clues, no leads and can only speculate. Have you ever spoken with your brother or your sister-in-law about their finances? Or had they ever mentioned them?"

"No."

"If anything should occur to you, please call me. We'll talk with Margherita Bellucci later. We've left her a voicemail."

After he told Beatrice about the call, she thought for a long time.

"If you want, you can go to Milan," she then said. "I've got a company apartment there," she went on, "where I can stay on weekends. Also, my brother lives in Milan."

She reached for her smartphone, but Aldrian declined. He didn't know why.

"I'm not afraid," he said. "And you know that I'm working on my travel guide."

She didn't say anything, stood up, walked over to the window and watched the snowflakes falling from the sky. "The last time it snowed like this I was still in grade school," she said without turning around. "Everything seems so peaceful . . . I can't say exactly say why I'm so worried about Jakob's and Elena's disappearance, and I don't want to upset you, but I've got a bad feeling. Why did the two men who attacked you drag you into this?"

"It probably has nothing to do with the disappearance of Jakob and Elena," he disagreed.

"If they're watching you, they now know that you spent the night here with me," Beatrice continued. "And if they don't already know, they'll soon find out, the next time you stay."

Aldrian didn't speak while he was deliberating. She's right, he thought.

"I'll go back to sleeping at my brother's house," he said.

"If I come visit you there, they'll find out about that, too."

As he put the paperweight with the thin slice of brain tissue from the famous conductor in his pocket, he could feel the gas pistol.

"Can I leave the pistol and the specimen here with you until I come back?"

"Yes."

"I've got to go now," he heard himself say, and he had the felling he was being a stubborn child. He turned around and saw her still staring out the window at the heavy snowfall.

"What should I do?" he asked. "I can't go to Milan." He said "can't," and not "won't," so that he wouldn't upset her.

"I know," she replied, and turned to face him. In the semi-darkness of the room he couldn't see her face. When he got closer and was about to hug her, he noticed that she was distracted, thinking about something.

A little later he was hurrying over the Campo San Polo.

It's probably best that I sleep in my apartment and we meet every time in a different hotel, he thought. It's also important that I inform Commissario Galli. Aldrian checked to see if anyone was following him, stopped at the front door to a building, and dialed the number of police headquarters. Everything around him was peaceful, the people who were out on the piazza and in the streets reinforced each other's joy at the snowfall.

The Commissario answered the phone, listened to Aldrian, and explained that at the moment there was nothing he could do for him and Margherita. As long as there was no trace of his brother and his wife, it wasn't possible for the police to get involved. Besides, he had no policemen he could spare. "In the meantime, however," he went on, "we've established contact with the appropriate Chinese authorities. They've inquired at the companies that did business with your relatives Jakob and Elena. Just a half-hour ago I heard from the Chinese authorities," the Commissario explained, "that in recent weeks neither one of them had entered or left the country, and at this time there has been no contact between them and the companies.

Representatives of the companies have stated that for the last three days all Internet traffic has been disrupted and, in cooperation with the respective companies, the authorities are investigating. They have confirmed that we're talking about pearl necklaces, jewelry, fossils, animal skeletons, and minerals. Call me if you suspect you're being followed," the Commissario concluded.

Aldrian took a picture of the Campo San Polo with his smartphone as the snow was falling and, lost in thought, headed for the Rialto Bridge instead of his usual route to the vaporetto station San Silvestro. He looked back again and decided that he wasn't being followed.

To him the Rialto Bridge with the surrounding buildings in the snowstorm seemed like a roughly scanned black-and-white photograph where the white dots suddenly begin to dance . . . In the driving snow the Grand Canal toward St. Mark's disappeared before the bend.

He climbed the steps to the bridge and observed everything from up above: passengers in the gondolas shielded themselves from the wet snow with umbrellas, vaporettos and barges emerged from under the bridge vault or disappeared beneath it. It seemed like he was staring at a video installation. The gondolas that were moored to poles in front of the palazzi were covered with snow, as were the small store awnings. First the shopkeepers swept the snow off with long mops and then rolled up the awnings. He climbed back down from the Rialto Bridge and bought a tube of toothpaste in the "Farmacia." The neighboring baker's child, a girl in tights with a bright-blue vest, ran down the street, whooping for joy; a photographer who was going to take her picture was just setting up his tripod, his camera stored in a transparent nylon bag. In no time at all Aldrian's hair and clothes were wet, and he had to clean his glasses off with a tissue. He thought it would be best if he changed clothes before he went to San Servolo. The fish market was always closed on Sundays and Mondays. He passed the covered fruit and vegetable stands and the shop window for the horse butcher, and to get out of the snow he headed for the fish hall—its smell immediately enveloped him. Outside, by the arcade arch, the snowflakes were still coming down. No one passed by, no one was standing on a corner reading a newspaper, just two pugs were crossing the forecourt, panting and barking, and then they, too, disappeared. He hurried over to the house, opened the front door, and then locked it behind him. Then he checked that his brother's second-floor apartment was locked. Up in his room he opened a window to get rid of a musty odor. The toilet stunk and the air in his room smelled the way it did just before it was going to rain. He put the tube of toothpaste down on the sink, changed his wet clothes, got a black wool cap and jeans from the wardrobe, and then closed the window. It was snowing and blowing. The flakes were falling diagonally from a milky grey sky. He had never seen it snow in Venice before, his brother had only told him about it. The thought of Jakob and Elena was so powerful that he had to close his eyes. When he opened them, he was hypnotized by the driving snowfall outside the window. He stared into the flurries to forget himself, and all he saw was a white rain that fell faster or in slow motion, depending on the direction of the wind. The rooftops he could see from his window were also white. Religious thoughts raced through his head, but gave way to the delight of this new experience and the muffled silence. He was slowly overcome by fatigue. But he kept staring at the snow falling before his eyes and made a mental note of the varying speeds of the snowflakes through the air. He was still fascinated by the spectacle— they seemed to hover in the air for fractions of a second and then just be whisked away. Occasionally the two speeds intermingled and made him think about wind turbulence, like when a helicopter starts up. When he stood up and gazed out the window, he recognized isolated tracks in the snow. Two women with flowery umbrellas were just slipping into an apartment house. A passerby, an open Knirps pocket-umbrella in his fist, was smoking a cigarette. No one cared about his concerns, Aldrian observed, amazed at his own naiveté. When he turned on the TV, he watched a documentary about fly maggots that far exceeded his tolerance for nauseating disgust. Fly eggs in a film canister were placed on a rotting pig's liver. You could also see the maggots under a microscope and, lastly, on a woman's ulcerous leg—living surgeons, so to speak.

Before he left, he looked out the window one more time. The television antennas wobbled and gently nodded in the wind, like plants made of wire.

He headed back to the vaporetto station at the Rialto Bridge and on the way passed a market stall for embroidered wares from the island of Burano—most of the vendors had already left the small forecourt—and paused. The man who owned the stand on wheels was also in the process of shutting down, and in the falling snow the fine embroidered merchandise looked like precious frost patterns that had been lifted from a windowpane. Some people in masks seemed to be enjoying the snowfall and were boisterously dancing and laughing. In the vaporetto it seemed to Aldrian that he was in a Venetian snow globe that had just been shaken so that white dots fell on the boat he was taking down the Grand Canal to St. Mark's Square. In the passenger cabin all the seats were taken, so he hung on to a handrail. Only a small number of the passengers wore masks. They traveled on together like statues, silent and unmoving: an old nobleman, a woman dressed as a dark-gold plant, a drunken gondolier with a clown nose and glasses. When passengers got off at the next station, he took one of the available seats before the remaining ones were claimed. Outside, under the Venetian snow globe, the palazzi went by in pale colors, and their mirror images on the water, fragmented in tiny particles, were continuously erased and then for a brief moment became visible again. He glanced around, determined that the man who had followed him and assaulted him was nowhere in sight, and he recalled how many times he had taken this vaporetto route together with Jakob and Elena. The porous snow curtain also seemed to close silently around the boat and to dissolve the past behind it. But unlike a curtain in the opera house, it didn't separate imaginary reality on the stage from the reality in the audience. But precisely due to its transparency it fostered the osmotic infiltration of memories. Aldrian's thoughts depressed him.

They overwhelmed him even when he was doing research for his guidebook or humming an opera excerpt, and he felt that something horrible must have happened to his brother and his sister-in-law. Perhaps they had taken off for a cave trek in the dark and that's why he couldn't reach them. He was reluctant to talk about it because he had read in the cabbalistic Book of Creation, *Sefer Yetzirah*, that God first created the ten numbers and the twenty-two letters of the Hebrew alphabet that then formed the world with all its stones, plants, animals, the four elements, and finally mankind. He was convinced that words could thus become reality, and numbers facts. Wasn't this the way music was captured in musical scores? He thought of Hieronymus Bosch's *Garden of Earthly Delights* and its two outer panels that depict a moment in the creation; Hieronymus Bosch was one of those painters he especially appreciated. There was even a time when he prized Bosch above all others because—according to Aldrian—the painter realized people in their most abject misery. He now felt that he would have to awaken within himself something of this evil, this hate, this brutality in order to survive the insanity that confronted him. Till now he had only felt it was important not to be afraid, and he had been able to do that in spite of his anxious thoughts. Without transition he now thought that Lorenzo Verra, the retired Maestro Suggeritore in the Teatro La Fenice, was probably sitting in the Caffè Florian, waiting for him as they had previously arranged. He glanced at the clock and was relieved to see he still had fifteen minutes. After shopping at the fish market he had called Lorenzo and told him basically what had happened. Lorenzo liked and respected him, not least of all for his musical memory. He had spontaneously offered his help and wanted to know exactly what had happened. They had agreed to go to San Servolo together where the Vice-director, Dr. Calzea—as Aldrian had learned from Dr. Feilacher—was expecting him. Since Lorenzo was a bachelor, he liked to sleep late and have breakfast around noon in the Caffè Florian. His two-room kitchen apartment was close by, but he didn't encourage visitors. Aldrian suspected the place was probably a mess, but avoided asking about it.

After the vaporetto had docked, Aldrian hurried to the Piazzetta, stopped and looked up at the sky and the falling snowflakes ... And for the first time he dared to run between the two pillars—the one with the St. Mark lion on top and the other with Saint Theodore posing on a small crocodile-like dragon. He had learned from his brother that on this spot the condemned were beheaded, hanged or quartered—the reason Venetians avoid this route even today. He turned around and gazed out at the lagoon, the Bacino di San Marco, the Santa Maria della Salute church, and the bell tower on the island of San Giorgio Maggiore that was vanishing in the grey atmosphere. He passed the Caffè Chioggia where, beneath the arcades, a piano player in a black coat was playing excerpts from Donizetti's *Elixir of Love*. In the driving snow the colonnade of the Doge's Palace across the way gave him the impression of an optical illusion.

When he looked at the Square, he saw a figure coming his way, wearing a colorful Carnival hat with bells, and in the first instant thought he recognized one of the two men who had assaulted him. Right behind him, at the same pace, came a bearded government official from the 15th century. The man in the Carnival hat was—as it immediately became obvious—a teenager, and his companion's beard was part of the costume he was wearing. Nevertheless his heart was pounding in his chest. He pressed on to the Caffè Florian amidst female tourist guides holding an unopened umbrella while leading a procession of tourists, fluttering swarms of pigeons, tourists taking pictures with photoflash, and passersby costumed as noblemen and ladies-in-waiting, as an American president and a German chancellor, as Stan Laurel and Oliver Hardy, or outfitted with masks from the surrounding stores. All of them were absorbed into the crowd as the falling snow resembled a never-ending white rain of confetti.

Lorenzo Verra wasn't yet sitting at his spot in the corner of the Moorish Room—he hated window seats—as Aldrian was relieved to see. He sat down at a table that had just become available, ordered peppermint tea that was called "Infuso di Menta" in the Caffè Florian, and gazed out the glass entrance. The small orchestra in front of the Caffè Florian was just taking a break. The musicians were relaxing in a corner near the front door, drinking coffee. Aldrian had the impression that someone outside was playing Giuseppe Verdi's *Un ballo in maschera*, and his head was instantly filled with music. He could hear the beginning of the third scene in the third act, the "Large Ballroom." It dealt with the planned assassination. Cautiously he glanced around, looking for the bearded man, but the room with the portraits of voluptuous Oriental women was mainly occupied by old women who weren't wearing masks and by several elegant gentlemen reading newspapers. Watching the snowfall outside the window inspired memories of his childhood when he had longed to be a grownup. Back then it seemed to promise a new life where he was free. And he also recalled Fat Tuesdays during elementary school and the first years in middle school because those were days when he and his classmates were allowed to dress up: as Mickey Mouses, as princesses, as Cowboys or Indians, Chinamen and sorcerers. Aiming out the window, he took several pictures with his smartphone of pedestrians in the snow and masked people, then captured the Moorish Room with flash. But when the older ladies and gentlemen gave him an irritated look or put down their newspapers, he quickly checked the display to see the snowflakes and the people in their masks, then put the phone back in his pocket. A waiter discretely served the peppermint tea. Aldrian scarcely noticed. It's horrible to live in uncertainty from one minute to the next, he said to himself, when he once again thought about his brother and his sister-in-law. He took out his notebook and the new ballpoint and began to write down his observations. At the same time the small orchestra beneath the arcades began to play again, and he noted: "Caffè Florian, red upholstered furniture, old glassed murals, 'Biedermeier-like,' with Oriental, Chinese, and Italian figures, including mythological ones—like windows onto the past. Parquet flooring, little round marble tables, older women sitting with a cup of hot chocolate and small carafes of water. Just now pigeons are flying past the 'train compartment windows.' Pedestrians strolling under the arcades of the Procuratie, men dressed as women. Muffled music in the room:

violin, clarinet, piano, a concertina. The waiters act like pigeons on the square—they briefly gather together, coo, mutter something to each other, split up, and then regroup again. The customers in the Caffè usually stay longer than normal. Japanese with surgical facemasks: they first walk on by the Caffè, come back, enter, sit down at some small table, and look like surgeons before they take off their facemasks."

"Scusi, scusi!" Lorenzo Verra hugged him from behind as he always did, and, wearing a quilted jacket and a scarf, sat down before he took off his elegant hat, displaying grey hair that was combed back severely. He was remarkably short, almost the size of a child, wore light- and dark-brown flecked custom-made tortoise shell glasses, and his thin white eyebrows were dyed black. His teeth were *too* perfectly crowned—all together an oddly youthful and yet mature charisma. Whenever Aldrian thought about it, it seemed to him that Lorenzo looked less like his alleged forty-five years and more like a ninety-year-old because his speech and gestures didn't correspond to his actual age. To tell the truth, he wasn't a sympathetic figure, and it took Aldrian some time before his original impression had settled and he realized that this was a chaotic insecure human being who frequently changed his opinions when challenged so that, as he said, everything would remain in harmony. Yet he wasn't an opportunist. He was satisfied, as he explained to Aldrian, to give people something to think about. But he definitely didn't want to provoke them. As Maestro Suggeritore he had admittedly been a dictator. In his official position there was no trace of a conciliatory Lorenzo Verra, instead he had been transformed into a "defense attorney for the notes and words" in the musical score. Ever since Aldrian found out about that, he had forgiven Lorenzo any quirks and had become his friend.

Lorenzo was just about to order his usual breakfast when Aldrian insistently told him that they had to be at the San Zaccaria vaporetto station on time, since he had a 1 p.m. appointment with the vice-director, Dr. Calzea.

He slid the Infuso di Menta, that he hadn't even sipped, over to

Lorenzo along with the equally scrumptious cookies in a bowl.

While Lorenzo quickly drank the tea and wolfed down the cookies, Aldrian paid and went out onto St. Mark's Square. Everything looked so bizarre that he could have stood for a long time, gazing at St. Mark's Basilica and the many thousands of snowflakes falling on it. But a couple of seconds later Lornzo shot out of the Caffè, briefly stumbling, but catching himself.

"Why did you go?" he asked excitedly. "Did you mean to leave me sitting there all alone in the Caffè?"

Lorenzo had never been to San Servolo. He was apprehensive, and Aldrian suspected that he was perhaps hoping to start an argument so that he could duck out. "I was thinking of Jakob," Aldrian lied for his excuse and instantly felt he was being mean.

They kept walking beyond the arcades in the snowfall.

"Oh, no," Lorenzo interrupted him. "How could I forget . . . Are you even up to going to San Servolo?"

That was probably yet another attempt by Lorenzo to put off the trip, Aldrian thought, and saw his brother before him and how he would throw snowballs at Jakob when they were children.

"Yes, I know you have a one o'clock appointment with Dr. Calzea," Lorenzo went on, after a brief pause, "and you absolutely have to go to the island, and I can stay in Venice if I want and you won't be mad at me. But I'm definitely coming along, Michael!"

They must have looked like a strange pair, Aldrian thought. When Lorenzo had his hat on, from a distance they looked like father and son.

In the snowstorm several people in costumes from the Commedia dell'arte had set up shop in front of St. Mark's so that tourists could photograph them. Lorenzo knew all their roles: Pantaloon was wearing the mask of an old man with wrinkles, a pointed nose, a goatee, and wearing a black cloak, yellow slippers, and red tights—he represented the caricature of a greedy Venetian merchant. To keep warm, *Arlecchini*, Harlequins who had the ability to travel to the afterlife and back, repeatedly leaped up into the air and, following the laws of gravity, landed back on St. Mark's

Square. A *Colombina*—"little dove"—enthusiastically clapped her hands, and the bumpkin *Pulcinello*—"little rooster"—a buffoon in a white costume with broad sleeves, a black half-mask and a pointed hat tried to lure Colombina with pigeon feed, all the while loudly commenting on his actions. Then the Arlecchini symbolically thrashed the buffoon to the amusement of the spectators. "Revenge is something we all dream about," Lorenzo pontificated. "Many go to war because they are pressed to avenge their fate and they are inspired by a reason. We spin things so that in the end people will take revenge for something completely contrived if their position is validated by just a few idiots." Appalled, Lorenzo stopped, as if he just realized that Aldrian could misunderstand his remarks. But Aldrian wasn't interested in revenge at that moment, he didn't know for sure what had really happened and on whom he should seek revenge. About all he could do would be to kick the wall of a building or spit in the Grand Canal.

Lorenzo changed the topic without changing his tone. "Thanks for the fantastic breakfast. I never eat more than a couple of cookies, but I always drink coffee, never tea. Still, I must admit that the peppermint tea was excellent."

As they walked through the turbulent snowstorm, he talked and talked until they climbed into the small vaporetto for the trip to San Servolo. But once on board, after the boat had set off, he resumed talking once again.

"Have you asked yourself why the two men beat you up, carried you into the house, and put you in bed? I've been thinking about that the whole time, but as a Venetian I can only whisper one thing to you"—he lowered his voice and breathed into Aldrian's ear: "M."

"M?" Aldrian asked in a normal tone of voice.

Lorenzo then did something he had never done before: though no one could see him, he punched Aldrian in the ribs and then turned to the window, miffed.

"M?" Just then Aldrian realized that he could have meant the Mafia, but he felt Lorenzo's behavior was exaggerated and shook his head.

"You didn't believe me about the fire at the Teatro La Fenice either," Lorenzo whispered sullenly.

"And what was the conclusion? It was two electricians!" Aldrian fired back irritably. He simultaneously noticed that the seats in front and behind them were taken. But Aldrian hadn't whispered out of fear of the "M," but because he was ashamed to be having a conversation with Lorenzo that other people would consider ridiculous. When Lorenzo didn't reply and just kept looking out the window, insulted, Aldrian now whispered the question: "And why? Why would they want to do that?"

Lorenzo turned to face him, enraged, and hissed: "Why? You have to ask that?—They don't want you nosing around! They want you to disappear! They know all about you! Even that we're going to San Servolo—because you're being watched day and night!"

The snowstorm and the sea surrounding them made it impossible to make out the city behind them, they only saw an elongated white building emerging from the water ahead of them. Aldrian thought it fit in nicely with Lorenzo's exasperated and fearful whispering.

He turned away from Lorenzo and gazed ahead, because he really wanted to stop all the whispering. But that just made Lorenzo even more determined to give his opinion: "What do you know about La Fenice? *I* was their Maestro Suggeritore, not you! *I* saw the theater burning on 29 January 1996 with my very own eyes."

Aldrian was no stranger to Lorenzo's outbursts and had already heard his version of the fire many times, so now he tried to calm him down.

"I know, you've told me the story before. We'll talk more on San Servolo," he whispered into Lorenzo's ear.

"You don't know anything," Lorenzo hissed back. He leaped up and apparently didn't want to sit beside him anymore, so Aldrian also had to get up to let him pass. Lorenzo wildly pushed his way out and scampered up the two steps to the deck where he froze into a statue staring out at the sea.

But the confrontation had also left its traces in Aldrian's brain. Lorenzo was possibly right, he thought. But he now wondered how his brother and his sister-in-law could have been involved with the "M"? As far as he knew, the couple's business was the only possibility, most likely the pearl trade. But that seemed preposterous, and he would have loved to get up and resume his argument with Lorenzo. Jakob and Elena loved the good, the true, and the beautiful, as the saying goes, they contributed to charities and were devout Catholics. But that wasn't proof of anything, he instantly objected.

Now he could vaguely make out the lighted pilings that led to the elongated white building. Two church towers loomed above it, but due to the low grey sky and the falling snow you could only make out a shadowy silhouette. The closer they came, the more it reminded him of a monastery.

Suddenly a gondola appeared. One man at the prow and one at the stern, each with his own oar, were rowing and steering.

Any sound was drowned out by the noise of the vaporetto's engine.

He noticed that there wasn't a single light in the entire white building, except for a mysterious glimmer behind the wrought-iron gate that led to the sea. They had just landed and, to his relief, Lorenzo had gotten off first and was waiting for him. He came over to him and whispered: "Scusi, scusi . . . *You* are the one in danger, and *I* am an idiot"—and glanced around apprehensively, probably because he had said the one word that was taboo here. "And *I* am an ass," he corrected himself.

"No," Aldrian contradicted him, "at first I didn't understand what you meant . . ."

"Yes, 'M.'" Suddenly they both laughed and then went on speaking in a normal tone of voice.

San Servolo

There was snow on the palm tree in the corner of the entrance building, on the path, the lawn, the balcony railing on the second floor, and on the roof. Like the other visitors, they entered the foyer and followed a directional sign into a large high-ceilinged room where a buxomly secretary behind a console alternated telephoning and working on her laptop.

Aldrian explained to her that he had an appointment with Dr. Calzea and received the message that the Vice-director had a twenty-minute delay.

Aldrian didn't want to sit in the waiting room, so he suggested to Lorenzo that they go for a walk.

"It's snowing," his difficult friend argued and seemed to want to be upset at Aldrian's suggestion, but before it came to that, he added: "Wonderful. When it snows in Venice, you've got to do something special, because it almost never snows."

Aldrian nodded.

"Where shall we go?" Lorenzo asked, polite yet anxious. "In the snow a park looks like a cemetery."

The park had changed completely since Aldrian's first visit. All the plants, from tall trees and lance-shaped cypresses to forsythia bushes and ball-shaped hedges, was covered in snow that seemed to have fallen more heavily here than in the city that they could no longer see through the rectangular openings in the brick wall that surrounded the island. Almost all the buildings were painted yellow, and the facility now looked less like a monastery than a detention center or an administrative fortress.

"I'm cold!" Lorenzo whispered, sucking in air between his clenched teeth, and he stopped dead in his tracks. Since Aldrian didn't respond and just kept going, Lorenzo ran after him and asked if he was trying to freeze to death.

The buildings' windows were tall and had Roman arches, and when they came to the chapel where a stone Madonna figure beckoned, Lorenzo finally fell silent and crossed himself. The chapel was smaller than Aldrian had remembered. It stood in the snow like a Lego toy on a white tablecloth. At the location of the former cemetery they had now erected an open hall on pilings that presumably was used by students and staff in the summer so they could eat outdoors. Nearby were a fenced-in soccer field and a basketball court. It was almost certain that the dead were reposing beneath the two structures, Aldrian mused. In one corner he discovered a trash dump with blocks of stone, fragments of old pillars, and construction materials. Since everything was covered with snow, Aldrian couldn't determine whether there were gravestones underneath.

On the way back, they stumbled upon a basket with pinecones. Lorenzo explained that each one had up to three thousand ovules.

They arrived back at the entrance to the main building and, seeing the church towers looming behind it in the dreary sky, Lorenzo crossed himself again. The high-ceilinged hall was empty. The secretary smiled, and they sat down on a bench where Aldrian immediately began to take notes in shorthand. Lorenzo watched him out of curiosity at first, and finally asked him what his notes were about.

"About our walk," Aldrian explained.

"Really? But we didn't actually see anything!"

Dr. Calzea appeared at last, a sweating fat man in an elegant grey suit with a white shirt and tie. His parted hair thinly covered his evident baldness.

"When did they build over the old cemetery?" Aldrian greeted him politely.

"Which cemetery? There is no cemetery here," Dr. Calzea replied decisively.

"Oh, yes—" Aldrian differed, "I've got a very old map of Venice that shows where it was located."

"Show me the map."

"I don't have it with me," Aldrian responded in an annoyed tone, "but there was a cemetery."

The Vice-director turned to the secretary who had been listening attentively and instructed her to call a friend in the office of the police commissioner who had been involved in the renovations on the island of San Servolo. Then he shook hands with the two guests. Lorenzo took the opportunity to tell about the discovery of the basket with the pinecones, and Dr. Calzea had the secretary retrieve them.

The secretary had just put down the phone when the Vice-director asked her impatiently if there had actually been a cemetery. With a crisp "si," the secretary let him know that he had been wrong, and she went back to her work.

Embarrassed, Dr. Calzea stuttered that the cemetery could have come from a time when the island had first housed a Benedictine monastery and later a convent. He hurried on ahead and only stopped when he reached a framed picture with eighty small oval black-and-white photographs of distinguished gentlemen. He explained that these men were students of the famous Cesare Lombroso, a Turin professor of forensic medicine and psychiatry. Lombroso founded the scientific branch of criminology—so-called criminal anthropology—that eventually developed into criminal biology.

"In the beginning there were two occupational groups vulnerable to paranoia: criminals and investigators. Both were engaged in putting the other in a state of fear and thus outwitting them," Dr. Calzea continued. "Usually the criminals were a step ahead—especially the Mafia who enjoyed collaboration with spies and traitors, with people who could be blackmailed and those who were frightened. They developed deceptions and disguises that the police first uncovered with the aid of science. In San Servolo the pathological human spirit was 'x-rayed,' so-to-speak. You know what I mean."

In the meantime Aldrian had looked at each of the individual portraits of these criminal anthropologists from the end of the 19th century. They were exclusively men who had probably disappeared from human memory by now.

"In San Servolo," the Vice-director went on, "they employed the old concept of normality as defined by one's behavior in society. The scientists and the nursing staff were basically baffled. They had just discovered a new continent, a new planet, no, a new universe: insanity, schizophrenia, depression, mania, paranoia. More than anything else, they recoiled when faced with paranoia—because every individual had some of the following traits: false suspicions, jealousy, envy, hate—these create false concepts in the human brain. The result was fanatics, troublemakers, conspiracy theorists, serial killers, hypochondriacs. In his textbook on psychiatry in 1899 the German psychiatrist Emil Kraepelin described paranoia as a delusional system that accompanies complete retention of clarity and order in thought, volition, and conduct. There was also the viewpoint that paranoiacs could not be part of a "we," as it was called, and they couldn't tolerate others. So a paranoiac unintentionally built a bridge to them by seeing himself at least as persecuted. Are you familiar with the saying: 'Just because you're paranoid, doesn't mean there isn't someone following you'?" He laughed. "If we could read the thoughts in each other's minds, we would be shocked by the distorted notions and concepts that predominate, and in the end we would become paranoid ourselves. So we don't retire to some chamber of horrors, but to a dream world that we can influence—in contrast to the patients."

He turned on his heels and off he went. Lorenzo shrugged his shoulders, pointed his index finger at his temple, and made a face like a police detective who's heard it all before.

They proceeded silently down a long hallway with a checkerboard floor and several chandeliers hanging from the ceiling to a staircase leading to the second floor and the Museo del Manicomio, the museum of the onetime insane asylum. Right at the start Dr. Calzea showed them the memorial tablet for the most famous patient, Matteo Lovat, "who crucified himself," as Dr. Calzea observed. A drawing depicted Lovat in the act.

"As a child, Matteo Lovat wanted to become a priest—perhaps one reason was because as such he would live better than poor people," he explained. "But his parents didn't have any money to send him to an appropriate school, so he became a cobbler. A strict master forced him to sit all day long and silently do his work. As a result of insufficient nourishment consisting only of millet gruel and polenta, he came down with pellagra, a symptom of deficiency that produces inflammation of the skin with a lichenous peeling rash, especially on the face and hands—the parts of the body that are exposed to sunlight—and can initially cause diarrhea and later even dementia. Four years before his death at the age of 47, here in San Servolo, he was conspicuous only for his exaggerated piety, as the physician Cesare Ruggieri wrote in his clinical history. The only things Lovat talked about were the days of fasting and high holy days, of sermons and saints. One day in July 1802 Matteo Lovat locked himself in his room and cut off his genitals that he then tossed out the window. Dr. Ruggieri writes further that Lovat's fear of the sins of the flesh drove him to this decision. Furthermore Lovat had obtained pressed and chopped up herbs that peasants in his native village used to staunch bleeding, and he prepared strips of old linen so that the wound in his groin would heal quickly. When the villagers mocked him, he went to live with his brother in Venice where he found work in a cobbler's shop. One year later, in 1803, marks the first time he wanted to crucify himself, in the middle of the street. When he was about to drive a stake through one foot," Dr. Calzea continued, "passersby prevented it. When asked why he wanted to crucify himself, he gave no answer. He only admitted to his brother that that day had been the feast of Saint Matteo, his namesake. And that was all he would say. Not long after, he found work in another cobbler's shop and moved to the fourth floor of a building in the Via delle Monache, number 2888, as we learn from Cesare Ruggieri's account. Once again he had prepared a self-crucifixion, acquiring spikes, a crown of thorns, strips and bands. He used these to make a broad net of ropes that were to maintain him in an upright position. You can see the sequence of the self-crucifixion in the illustration," Dr. Calzea said, pointing to the picture on the wall. Aldrian recognized Matteo Lovat, standing in his net like in some upturned umbrella, his feet and his left hand nailed to a homemade wooden cross, the left hand also nailed to a beam, while his right hand was pierced by a spike

and hung over the net, his head with the crown of thorns had fallen to one side. In a complicated manner he had fastened the cross with ropes to a beam below the ceiling of his living room with a large rectangular window so that it—with his bleeding body—ultimately hung outside on the brick wall of the apartment building. Dr. Calzea continued: "Cesare Ruggieri described Lovat's entire torture in minute detail: first the nailing of his own body to the cross, and then slipping into the prepared net—procedures that he had undertaken in his room—, then the agonizing process that allowed him to successfully hang himself with the cross, visible beneath the open window on the fourth floor, and thus complete his work of suffering. 'After they had laboriously taken him down from the cross, he was taken by boat to the Santi Giovanni e Paolo hospital.

His hands were scarcely able to hold a pound of weight when he took his prayer book and read it the whole day,' Rugieri writes. At the end of August 1805, he was brought to San Servolo," Dr. Calzea went on, "where he began to fast a week later and would not even take a sip of water. Another patient was able to convince him to break his fast and begin eating, but fifteen days later he refused to eat again. Just as the first time, he was treated with daily nourishment enemas. But this time his fasting lasted eleven days, and then continued on and on. In the meantime he steadfastly exposed himself to the burning rays of the sun at every opportunity, and they had to use force to bring him into the shade. In January 1806 they discovered the first symptoms of consumption. And on 10 April he 'gave up the ghost,' according to Ruggieri's account." Dr. Calzea paused briefly while Aldrian and Lorenzo silently viewed the picture.

"The consequence being," he then concluded, "that faith also borders on the world of delusion and that this border is fluid. I find it remarkable that for centuries Benedictine monks and later nuns lived here in San Servolo—in monasteries they built themselves where they could dwell in their imagined-religious world and then spread the word that their invisible world was the only true one, and the real world was a work of the devil. But science, too, the physicians, live in their own minds, so to speak, according to their state of knowledge that presumably will seem like a helpless groping in the dark to people living a hundred years from now."

While he was speaking, they had moved on and entered the first hall.

Everywhere you looked, there were grey plaques with white captions in English and Italian that described the development of the insane asylum and the methods of treatment employed.

"You can see," Dr. Calzea said, "all the barbarities we humans can dream up that stem from our helplessness. The main cause is our incapacity to put ourselves in the minds of people who are different than we are—if it should ever happen, then without respect and curiosity. In those days they only wanted to confirm illness, the so-called abnormal, and then remove it or even destroy it. Most people today still are not able to discover the unfamiliar universe within someone else. A notable exception here is religion that is spoon-fed to us as children and is exemplified in our environment. A religious person believes in the miraculous, whereas a so-called deranged person experiences the miraculous from within himself. But above all, so-called lunatics have lost the ability to deceive, especially when they survive a crisis situation commonly called a seizure. Then they overperform or underperform normative thinking, if I may call it that. I would like to leave you alone now with your thoughts and impressions. If you have any questions, please wait until the end of the tour. Otherwise you run the risk of considering San Servolo a sunken ship at the bottom of the sea. To tell the truth, it is a mirror image in which we can see ourselves."

First they viewed a cylindrical machine consisting of numerous frames filled with index cards. The arrangement in alphabetical order allowed quick access to patient information. It made Aldrian think of the Archivio di Stato with its hundreds of thousands of records and, seeing this monstrous file-card drum, how important it has always been for people to have everything under control—whether vital, as in this case, or not.

In the large exhibition hall with its stone floor that must have previously been a hallway because there were no windows, various objects were on display in glass cases. The room was lit by floodlights mounted on wooden beams that had been subsequently built into the ceiling. From the beginning of the tour to its end Lorenzo continued to talk in a whisper as if he were at some sacred place, but it was really the impact of the macabre, as Aldrian knew, to which he was susceptible.

"His explanations about paranoia were nonsense and the comparison with the Church inappropriate. Most people believe in God. What's so terrible about that?" he erupted.

"On this earth there is no single truth that is unique and covers everything," Aldrian answered in his normal voice, which just annoyed Lorenzo.

They were standing in an alcove with red wallpaper. A showerhead was encased in a brass cage-like construction; a control panel, managing more than a dozen valves with a round dial for a manometer, regulated the water temperature and pressure. From the illustrations—partly black-and-white photographs, but also etchings—you could see treatment in San Servolo that might include hoses or baths in bathtubs. For example, they might spray a patient's head with cold water or prescribe warm twelve-hour baths.

On display cases on the right side of the alcove were signs reading "Contenzione," "straightjackets," with an impressive collection of long chain cords to which manacles or ankle cuffs could be fastened, along with the corresponding keys; also leather wristbands to immobilize knee- and elbow joints, neck and chest straps for better restraint, two straightjackets and a wooden suitcase full of copper enemas whose individual parts were described in hand-written notes and instructions. One display showed a raging woman with disheveled hair in a straightjacket and beside it, the same young woman, this time shyly gazing at the floor, once again leading a normal life. Yet another picture showed a female patient shackled to a bed. Aldrian read from the inscription that she was being taken to "hydrotherapy." Lorenzo had only briefly glanced at the objects and then moved on to the next section of the hall that, as Aldrian immediately observed, displayed works by inmates at the time—to be sure, there were very few items. Aldrian noticed that Dr. Calzea had slipped away, so he asked Lorenzo why he was so upset.

"The Vice-director is so cynical," he whispered insistently, as he usually did. "I pray, I go to Mass now and then, I celebrate Christmas and Easter—does that make me crazy?"

Since Aldrian didn't respond, he flared up again, hissing and screaming in a whisper: "I much prefer living in a world with an imaginary God than just muddling through life without Him!" It was obvious that he had lost all interest in the tour. As he was speaking, Aldrian read that out of four hundred patients, two-thirds had done manual labor: in the bakery, in the kitchen, in the park, in the photo studio, in the printing shop, as barbers, tailors and cobblers, but some also worked brass or other metals. Furthermore, primitive paintings, woven baskets, and small wooden boats were on display—for example, a realistic model of a gondola—window shutters, various types of shoes, a small cask or some wooden object that Aldrian couldn't define; it resembled a human head with impact marks on its "skull" and its face was painted which made Aldrian think of a ghost. A piano for music therapy stood in one corner, and Aldrian played a few bars of the *Moonlight Sonata* on the out-of-tune instrument. Lorenzo immediately came running over, shook his head, rolled his eyes, and blatantly held his hands over his ears. A sign said that the patients, together with the staff, made music twice a week, and on one day someone played the piano at an open window in the immediate vicinity of the park. There was also a photograph that showed patients together with people in uniforms and caps—perhaps nurses—while several men with black derby hats on their heads were standing behind them.

In the next hall Aldrian viewed devices for electrotherapy— the impersonal and drab-looking electroshock machines—which could induce controlled epileptic seizures in patients. According to the explanation, these would be employed in serious schizophrenic conditions or in the event of depressive disorders that could lead to suicide. But what immediately attracted Aldrian's attention were the eighty black-and-white prints from a book labeled "Album

Comparativo" that were displayed individually on a long window ledge in the adjacent room. The oval black-and-white comparison photographs depicted people at their admission and then after treatment, as "Guariti" or "cured." The overwhelming majority were men. You could recognize confusion on the faces of those who had just been admitted, the "Malati." They looked squalid and their hair was disheveled. Some wore dirty torn clothing or uniform jackets and military caps. Their expressions were distant, frightened, introverted, weepy, praying, aggressive, contemptuous, surprised, full of sadness, and always wary. In the pictures of two women there were also relatives who held the patients' heads by propping one hand against the females' foreheads—Aldrian concluded that the women didn't want to be photographed. The second oval photograph showed the same patients at discharge, now groomed, coiffed, ready to go, shy, cheerful, offended, skeptical, serious, amused, timid, indifferent, but in rare cases even more alarming than when they were admitted. There were strange "grave photographs" that Aldrian imagined at the invisible cemetery of the forgotten, and there were presumably heartbreaking destinies hidden behind the depicted faces. Along with the photographs were individual diagnoses, in neat handwriting: "Mania con furore" beneath the portrait of a reckless looking soldier, "Monomania intellectuale" beneath a defiant man with a mustache who is staring to one side of the camera, "drunkard" for someone whom Aldrian thought he could envision launching loud diatribes in some bar. He glanced out the window and saw it was still snowing. Later he studied the old plate camera in a wooden box, half-covered with a blue cloth, displayed on a tripod in the opposite corner. He turned to the other side of the hall, passed six enlarged black-and-white photographs of a diseased brain that had been dissected—"a fading Milky Way," he thought, before he paused. It was impossible to imagine what had transpired in that convoluted, wrinkled undulating hunk of flesh. All the feelings, images, words and thoughts were now gone. Then he stood in front of more—this time color photographs—that showed old brain sections, stained black, red, and yellow. One was covered in small white dots as if the memory of snowflakes was stored there, but it was only the effect of some minor chemical process on this slowly oxidizing sample. But Aldrian panicked when he thought of Beatrice's paperweight with its own brain sections of the famous conductor—a molecule from his musical memory?

Dr. Calzea and Lorenzo were waiting for him in the adjoining room with seating accommodations. Neither one seemed to notice the other, because Lorenzo was listening to Verdi's *Requiem* on his smartphone, as he later admitted to Aldrian, and the psychiatrist was holding an open paperback. As he stood up, Dr. Calzea announced, without so much as glancing at Aldrian or his colleague: "In conclusion, I want to read you a footnote from Cesare Ruggieri's report about Matteo Lovat's self-crucifixion. Ruggieri writes in connection with Lovat's obsession to expose himself to direct sunlight: 'Unusual beneficial results from the influence of the sun's intense rays, as we are frequently able to observe with the employment of the Brenncylinder in cases of nagging insanity, insensitivity, and apathy, were claimed by the Benedictine monks in the Ossiach monastery which I visited in Upper Carinthia, from crystalline balls the size of a bitter orange that Mother Mary placed on the altar during the Holy Mass in the year 1300. They employed these balls to heal the possessed, the apoplectic, the deaf, the dumb, the blind, and those with debilitating headaches. The afflicted had to sit before the church, bound to a chair, in direct sunlight. A priest took one of these balls, held it toward the sun, and burned the seated man until he began to scream, and then he was relieved of his illness. The only relapses were suffered by those who made sacrificial offerings to Bacchus or Venus.'" Dr. Calzea laughed, put the paperback in his pocket, and abruptly said quite solemnly: "Take a moment and rest a bit, I am at your disposal." Then he went back to the staircase and silently hurried off

"I told you he's crazy. Let's get out of here!" Lorenzo whispered as loud as he could, and Aldrian, who also felt Dr. Calzea's behavior had been a bit strange, followed him.

Outside, Aldrian paused for a moment and considered what he

should do, since he didn't want to leave without saying goodbye. Meanwhile Lorenzo kept shouting: "Let's get going!"

But before Aldrian could agree, Dr. Calzea appeared out of the snowstorm from the other side of the building and breathlessly asked them why they didn't want to wait for him. He had just gone to the lavatory, he apologized, and sounded slightly miffed. He scurried on ahead and, after they had passed yet another building, waited, opened a door, and invited them to come in.

Aldrian recognized a large stone autopsy table with a honeycomb-like drain in the middle of the tiny room and white glass cabinets containing surgical instruments: hammers, saws, surgical knives, scissors, forceps, retractors, along with round glass washbasins—everything neatly arranged as if a post-mortem examination could take place in the next instant. The white sink with two rusty black spigots was set in one corner. Only then did Aldrian notice the collection of brain casts and skulls in the display cases across the room. If they didn't donate the dead to the university for anatomical classes, if there were no living relatives, where did they put them? In the abandoned and subsequently built-over cemetery?

The brain casts were yellow in color, only one was dark-grey, and they just lay there like huge nuts that the ocean had washed ashore. The skulls were predominantly from old people—he determined that from the many missing teeth. The tops of the skulls were all open and the brains had been removed; a skullcap, turned inside out, was lying beside its owner's head. Dr. Calzea shown his flashlight on the last, lowest section of the display case and two horribly deformed heads that made Aldrian think of the skulls of prehistoric beasts.

When Aldrian stepped outside and looked for Lorenzo, he noticed that the Maestro Suggeritore had taken refuge some time ago beneath the entrance of the adjacent church.

Meanwhile, Dr. Calzea had hurried on ahead. They opened the large door and saw him just turning on the lights. The high church nave was modestly furnished, and, as a result of the snowfall, very little light penetrated the interior from the windows behind the altar.

"Come in!" he invited Aldrian, and then left the two so they could view the meager furnishings.

After a prolonged silence he continued in his usual tone of voice: "I would like to show you the historic apothecary, it is the oldest in all of Italy." Again he scurried on ahead, the two prompters following a few steps behind. In the meantime Lorenzo had become so angry that he began to clack his teeth rhythmically, something he always did prior to a temper tantrum, as Aldrian knew from experience. At this point one wrong word would be enough to make him lose his composure.

But when Dr. Calzea turned to him and asked with concern if he was freezing, Lorenzo just shook his head amicably and stopped clacking his teeth.

Once inside the historic apothecary, Lorenzo was able to calm down. The room had wooden Corinthian columns with gilded capitals and brown shelving on all sides. The shelves displayed Majolica jars with two handles in a dense blue leaf pattern on a white background, crucibles, tins, and earthenware jars. Together with the apothecary's instruments that were displayed in a glass case, they created the impression of a botanical experimental chamber with hand-painted vases.

Suspicion

On their way back, Lorenzo said: "Visiting the mental hospital was a waste of time."

But Aldrian was lost in thought, far, far away. He stared at the snow falling in the vaporetto's headlights and imagined that seconds, minutes, hours, years were falling from the sky as tiny frozen crystals. The past dissolved, as did the future, only the present existed, this moment that was nothing but a transparent bit of glass in a kaleidoscope that continually changed its patterns or suddenly froze and completely disappeared in the darkness. You could hardly recognize anything outside. It wasn't until they approached St. Mark's that Aldrian saw a white illuminated luxury steamer slowly and silently glide past like some floating skyscraper. As they disembarked, people with umbrellas were bustling about. The pair plodded to the landing at the other end of the piazza among the crowd of masked and unmasked folks. Aldrian thought the snow looked like clouds of dandelion seeds flying toward the city to cover it under a white coating. And as if these seeds would keep falling from the clouds forever, he imagined. Or white swarms of insects that silently fell from the sky on rooftops, streets, and roads that were already covered with tiny larvae, small as raindrops, weightless organisms whose chitinous exoskeletons made a crunching sound when passersby stepped on them.

Lorenzo seemed relieved and insisted on accompanying Aldrian home.

"Because of the 'M.'?" Aldrian asked with veiled sarcasm. But Lorenzo preferred to ignore the remark.

The vaporetto to San Silvestro was so full of passengers that it was impossible to find a seat, so the two of them stood on the platform in a crowd, squeezed between: a bald old gentleman with a large black eye-mask that covered half his face and an artificial rose in the buttonhole of his Burberry coat; a young man in a gold helmet with red ostrich feathers, a gold embroidered red vest and a regal cape; a princess in a white silk bridal gown; and a lady whose eye-mask reached from her lips to her blond wig, artfully crowned by a tall, even taller open treasure chest that was enhanced with two candlesticks—Aldrian had the impression she had just sprung up from some "Alice-in-Wonderland Pop-up Book." Since the wig and the treasure chest reached the ceiling, she had to stand with her head lowered, and the conductor asked her to find a seat outside the cabin. She became upset since she didn't have a coat in the nighttime cold and pointed out the driving snow. The others laughed, taunted or defended her, but she didn't budge from the spot. In the midst of the uproar Aldrian's phone rang. Because of the tight quarters he had to struggle to get the smartphone out of his jacket pocket and read Beatrice's number on the display. Twice he shouted "I can't understand you!" into the microphone, inciting others to join in and loudly repeat the sentence. A young woman, dressed like a court jester in a magnificent old costume, provided him a momentary respite with one word, "Silenzio!" which first provoked laughter from the crowd. But the passengers' chatter and the vaporetto's din and roar before the next landing were still too loud, and Aldrian couldn't understand what Beatrice was saying, so he ended the conversation that hadn't even begun. Lorenzo was just about to point something out when a man in a "bauta"—the classic Venetian masquerade with a black three-cornered hat and black coat—simulated a pistol with his thumb and index finger and pointed it at Aldrian, subsequently turned away, and then hurriedly leaped off at the next station. Yet at the passenger shelter he turned once again to face the vaporetto and the people crowded on deck, aimed, simulated another "shot," and then disappeared in the driving snow. Though none of the other passengers paid any attention to him, Lorenzo exploded. In spite of his small physical stature, he had seen everything and hissed: "Did you see that?"

Aldrian had seen it, but didn't think it had anything to do with him.

"That was all about you!" Lorenzo prompted with a frightened expression.

"No," Aldrian contradicted, also in a whisper, "knock it off!"

"I told you so!" Lorenzo countered.

Peering between the other people on deck, Aldrian saw the colorfully striped "paline" go past, the "poles" where noble Venetians moored their private boats, and did not get off as usual at the San Silvestro station, but only when they had reached the Rialto Bridge stop.

"Now what's wrong?" Lorenzo had excitedly inquired when Aldrian didn't get up. "We have to be careful," the latter had responded, without looking at his friend.

He then found a spot near the Bridge with an overhanging roof, stopped, and dialed Beatrice's number. Lorenzo kept his distance, he even turned his back on Aldrian, gazing in the shop window of a CD-store. Aldrian was relieved. When Beatrice finally answered, he asked her if they could meet in the Ostaria Dai Zemei. It was the Ostaria where he used to meet his brother and drink an "ombra" or, in the evening, a spritz and eat a creamed salt cod sandwich.

"I'm still tired . . . I'll call you back."

"Fine. I'm out with Lorenzo Verra. You know him."

"The souffleur at the Teatro La Fenice, a short older gentleman?"

"Yes, he went to San Servolo with me. I'll be at your place in an hour. I love you, Beatrice."

"I love you, too."

When he had ended the call, Lorenzo came over, beaming, and shouted: "You're in love!"

"You were eavesdropping!" Aldrian angrily retorted.

"I wasn't eavesdropping," Lorenzo answered, still laughing. "You forget that I have excellent hearing. I didn't want to listen in, but you were speaking so loudly, probably because you're hard of hearing—"

"Asshole!"

Aldrian now hurried to get to the restaurant. In winter it had always been closed because it was small and narrow and consisted basically of a bar, which was the reason Jakob usually went to the Antico Dolo across the street and only a few steps farther on. The rest of the year the customers in the Ostaria Dai Zemei could sit outside underneath a canvas awning and the owners could at least make a profit. In the meantime they had rented the apartment next door and expanded their place.

The new dining area was furnished with metal wicker armchairs and small tables, and the two owners, Ettore and Giacomo, were hard at work making sandwiches. They had previously been musicians at the Teatro La Fenice, but had been laid off following the fire in 1996. During the reconstruction of the opera house, they had made the restaurant at the corner of Rughetta del Ravano and Rio Terrà San Silvestro into such a popular hangout for locals and an insider's tip for tourists that they never went back to the orchestra. Primarily members of the chorus and their musician friends, along with stagehands, now frequented their place instead.

Aldrian and Lorenzo were welcomed as long-lost sons. They quickly found a free table and in no time their customary spritz was on the table.

Aldrian went straight to the restroom. On his way back to the table he overheard snatches of conversation coming from the dining area, but initially paid no attention to them. But then he paused and tried to comprehend what the man was so excited about. "Where are they? With the fishies!" he said.

"But why?"

"Why? Why? Everybody's got a secret!"

"What about you?" a woman's voice was asking, and then everyone laughed, but that changed into a cordial greeting for apparently an old friend had arrived. Aldrian could hear the newcomer join the table, and the first man continued: "Whadda you think, Sergio? You're a diver . . . Whadda you think happened to the Aldrian couple? I think they're with the fishies."

"I'm not gonna say," the voice answered.

"Why not?"

"Cause I don't know nothin'!"

"But they just disappeared?"

"So what?"

"You think somebody tossed 'em in the canal?"

"That's just gossip!"

"Where'd you guys pull out most of the dead bodies for the cops?"

"In the lagoon."

With that, Aldrian entered the room, went right to his table and sat down.

"They're talking about the disappearance of my brother and his wife," he said quietly to Lorenzo who immediately tried to make out what they were saying.

"I know Venice inside and out. I know what the giant forest of tree trunks underwater looks like and what's above water," Lorenzo quietly translated the man called Sergio.

But Sergio changed topics, and Lorenzo whispered to Aldrian: "Everybody in your district is talking about it. Nobody says it was the 'M.,' but I know it was."

"How do you know?"

"Do you want my advice?"

"No."

"Wait in Vienna until this whole thing is over . . ."

Just the very thought seemed to Aldrian a betrayal. He hated the thought of sitting at home, while in Venice he could be following every step of the investigation. He also thought he couldn't just abandon his brother and his wife, although it was obvious that that was nonsense.

To his surprise the man named Sergio got up from his table in the corner and came over to them, to briefly introduce himself and, as it turned out, to apologize. His name was Sergio Celi and *had known* Jakob Aldrian. But in the same breath he corrected himself, that he *knew* Jakob Aldrian. "I assume you're his brother Michael. He's told me a lot about you. In any case you look like him. I think it's terrific that you're staying here and waiting until everything's straightened out." He made a slight bow though he didn't return to his table, but answered Lorenzo's questions about the "M."

"Do you think that it's something to do with the . . . You know . . .?"

"You don't seriously expect an answer."

"What would you think if you were Herr Aldrian?"

"I guess I'd try to figure it out, and at the same time believe that my relative would be back soon."

Aldrian asked for the check and prepared to leave.

"I'll come along with you!" Lorenzo whispered, and also got up.

They were just out on the street—the snow was still falling in large flakes—when Beatrice called. She was on her way to the fish market, and he agreed to meet her at the Rialto Bridge. He put his phone away, and Lorenzo blurted out: "This Sergio Celi . . . smooth as an eel, you can't trust him, lots of people work for the 'M.'"

Aldrian suddenly felt dizzy. He stopped and took deep breaths.

"What's the matter? What's wrong?" Lorenzo asked anxiously.

"Nothing." He hurrried on, as Lorenzo resumed imploring him: "I'll go with you to the Rialto Bridge, and then I'll leave you alone . . . I'm sorry, but I heard that you have a date with a woman . . . The 'M.' is everywhere. Maybe you should consider getting a hotel room. God bless you."

Until they reached the Rialto Bridge—in a falling snow that spread peace—Aldrian was silent. Without another word, Lorenzo whispered "Adieu" and hugged him before he slipped away over the bridge, enveloped in snowflakes like in some Japanese woodcut.

Aldrian was still feeling dizzy. The words "Sergio Celi" and "M." had brought back the image of his pursuer that he had seen for the first time in the mirror at the Caffè Florian, and now he was positive that—without the beard and hair—it looked just like Sergio Celi.

The more he thought about it, the more he was convinced of this insight.

Lost in thought, he walked with Beatrice under her umbrella in the dark, through the arcades of the Fabbriche Nuove to the market. Beatrice had chosen this route, presumably to better take in the surroundings. Nevertheless he still felt uneasy, but since he imagined that he had to protect Beatrice, he conquered his fear and didn't let it show.

She told him about her trip to Padua and her conversation with a biologist about the flora and fauna in the lagoon. The fellow knew Jakob and liked him, especially on account of his—in the man's own words—"exceptional" illustrations in entomological textbooks, and he even compared Jakob with Maria Sibylla Merian. She laughed.

In the darkness they could look through the round archways at the Grand Canal and the falling snow that silently disappeared in the water.

"He also appreciated," she continued, "that you know most of the operas by heart . . . your brother told him . . ."

"He did?"

"Do you want to meet the man?"

"Not at the moment," Aldrian answered evasively, and his thoughts returned to Sergio Celi.

"Do you know Sergio Celi?" he asked abruptly.

"Who? No, I don't think so. Who is he?"

"I don't want to upset you."

"But you're doing it nevertheless."

At first he was silent, but then told her what had happened in the Ostaria.

She took her phone out of her purse and, without consulting Aldrian, called Ettore while they walked. She knew the number of the Ostaria by heart, since she met Jakob and Elena there frequently last summer.

Aldrian tried to stop her, but she had already reached Ettore and wanted to know if he knew a diver named Sergio Celi. She switched to loudspeaker and described his appearance, but Ettore was certain he had seen him that evening for the very first time. And he also didn't know anyone from the table where Sergio Celi first sat down. He apologized that the Ostaria had been so full and he had struggled to keep up with the sandwich orders. "Is there something going on with him?"

"I don't know."

"Wait a second!"

They could hear paper rustling and then Ettore talking with someone, but with all the noise in the restaurant, they couldn't understand a thing.

Ettore finally was back: "No," he said, "it's strange, but no one knows him."

"He works as a diver for some construction company."

"Yeah?"

"Try to imagine him with longer hair and a beard," Beatrice insisted.

Ettore laughed.

"Does that help?" she added.

"I only caught a glimpse of him, I haven't got a clue."

"If he comes back, ask him where he works, give him a real grilling."

"I can't promise anything."

"But it's very important. You know that Jakob and Elena have disappeared?"

"They're probably on a trip. They always take off somewhere."

"But there's not a trace of them."

Ettore was silent.

Then he said: "And you think that this diver—"

"Sergio Celi," Beatrice interrupted.

"—Sergio Celi's got something to do with that?"

"Yes."

"Good. I'll be glad to help."

Aldrian had a bad feeling when he opened the front door. It was deathly quiet. He turned on the lights, shook the snow off his clothes and stomped his feet to clean off the soles of his shoes. He

139

bent down to get the mail, put it on the table, and on his way upstairs to his apartment, he checked to see if the door to Elena's and Jakob's apartment was locked. Everything was just as he had left it. There was nothing unusual in his studio apartment, other than the fact that the heating was working.

They lay down on the bed and embraced.

At some point they made love.

In the kitchen they prepared supper from everything they could find in the refrigerator. At first Beatrice insisted that she cook for him and that they drink a glass of red wine together. But their usual enjoyment was missing.

Eventually Aldrian cooked by himself, and she drank the glass of red wine. He spontaneously did little magic tricks with the vegetables and cooking utensils, but he soon gave up when she didn't seem interested.

As they were starting to eat, her telephone rang. She got up, went into the bedroom, and spoke so softly that Aldrian couldn't understand what she was saying.

He was surprised by a vague feeling of jealousy. A bad day, he thought.

But Beatrice came back into the kitchen, laughing. She still had the phone in her hand and explained that Ettore had just called and connected her with Sergio Celi who had just come back unexpectedly. That's his real name. He first worked as a diver for the police, but then more recently for a construction company, and now works there as an expert and consultant—she recited the name and address of the company. Celi was also involved with archeological studies beneath the city. "He gave me his address and telephone number," she said. The people at the table where Sergio first sat down were his boss, the boss's secretary, and two other colleagues. And: "He's never had a beard or long hair, and he doesn't own a wig or a false beard. He's sorry," Beatrice concluded, "that he frightened you, but you can call him anytime."

"Did you tell him everything?" Aldrian asked, and his expression betrayed his anxiety.

"Yes. I also told him you have doubts."

She sat back down at the table, laughed once again, and announced: "Now, let's eat!"

But Aldrian was embarrassed because he had acted so panic-stricken—that was the last thing he wanted to do. But to his amazement, his panic had only seemed to inspire Beatrice's devotion. She joked and drank with him until they both happily fell into bed.

The next morning Aldrian had only a vague memory of the night before. His head was pounding, and on the bed beside him was a note Beatrice had written in capital letters, saying she loved him. "FOREVER," she had added, and then further on: "IT'S STOPPED SNOWING."

He got up and glanced out the window. Everything was as the day before, but the snow that covered the courtyard up to the arcades had numerous black footprints and no longer completely covered the rooftops. Then he remembered the tour of the Secret Itinerary in the Doge's Palace that he had taken several times. Even so, he had bought a ticket over the Internet while he was still in Vienna since he wanted to explore them again so he could take notes. But there was still time before he had to leave. He called Beatrice, told her how much he wanted to be with her, and she consoled him with promises for that evening. In the bedroom he discovered that last night she had brought along the gas pistol, the revolver, and the dopp kit with his toiletries along with the brain slice of the famous conductor and left them all in a nylon bag on the nightstand. He put the gas pistol on the nightstand and stored the revolver and brain slice in the wardrobe. Even though he knew it was macabre, in the back of his head he could hear—the plastic cube with the fragment of a genius's brain in his hand—the "Hallelujah Chorus" from Handel's *Messiah*. He couldn't get it out of his mind as he aired things out, made the bed, cleaned up the kitchen, arranged the dishes in the dishwasher, vacuumed the carpet, and put the garbage in one of the black plastic sacks that were folded in the kitchen. It persisted when he closed the window, put his dopp kit in the bathroom, showered and washed his hair, brushed his teeth, and preserved his hairstyle with a little wax. Several times he interrupted the "Hallelujah Chorus" and said to himself, half-out loud, "Idiot." He got dressed, took the gas pistol from the nightstand, put it in his pocket, and placed the garbage bag in front of the house where he knew a man in municipal grey work clothes would pick it up. When he gazed at the sky, he was surprised that there weren't any clouds and the snowy roofs were in bright sunlight. He also thought he could hear the gurgling and sloshing of melting snow, but couldn't be sure. He was taking deep breaths when a delivery boy arrived with a large package under his arm.

"Are you . . ."—it was an effort to decipher the name on the label—". . . Michael Aldrian?"

"Yes."

The young man gave him the parcel that was wrapped in a dark-grey plastic wrapper, and disappeared around the corner. The label, as Aldrian determined, was pre-printed, with his name as recipient but no sender. He was puzzled because the package was quite heavy and tied on top with a cross-shaped bow. He struggled to get the package into the house, used it to shove some newspapers off the table that then fell on the floor. He noticed the item had no stamp and no cancellation mark. So it had to have been delivered by a private company. But why didn't he have to acknowledge receipt with his signature? And why was the delivery boy in such a hurry that he didn't even stick around for a tip? While he was considering all this, his sister-in-law Margherita called and invited him for breakfast. At first he wondered if he should open the package first, but then he put it off until that afternoon after he'd been to the Doge's Palace.

Water Music

Elena's sister, Margherita Bellucci, lived with her husband Eugenio, a dentist, at the Campo San Tomà near the Archivio di Stato di Venezia. At that location were a vaporetto stop and the "Trattoria San Tomà", but best of all was a store owned by Carlo Fibonacci, a master glazier and dealer for old Venetian photographs, postcards and maps, posters and prints.

A narrow door opened onto the tiny shop that was stuffed with frames, tools, a small sales counter and a large red billboard for Campari Bitters, along with a portable radio and rolls of paper. In one of the two display cases was a sign: "Specchi e cornice," "mirrors and frames," with Fibonacci's name beneath it.

Since Aldrian had a travel pass for the week, he took the next vaporetto that morning and sailed in the sunshine just one station further, to the heights of the Archivio di Stato di Venezia. Carlo Fibonacci was a friend of Jakob, he had sold his brother the mirrors for his apartment, framed his pictures, and dredged up an old city map of Venice that he also framed and was now hanging in Jakob's office. Aldrian realized how familiar all these pictures had become in the meantime, and now that Jakob had disappeared, they suddenly seemed like mental images from his brother's mind.

He knew that Elena had brought back colored etchings from each of her trips, mostly pictures of insects, but also birds, a rhinoceros, chameleons, snakes, and blossoms. Once he had accidentally glimpsed a stack in their living room. Several times he had made jokes about his brother. "You're Noah," he had said to him, and Jakob had laughed and replied that Michael wasn't wrong—he had an ark in his study in the shape of a metal cabinet with drawers. He was collecting colored etchings of every animal, every plant, of worms, clams, fish and snails, as well as sea eagles, whales, orangutans, tigers, and elephants. He had a study? Aldrian mused—he'd never thought about that. He had no idea what Jakob had meant by that. Maybe Margherita or their son knew something about it. The thought of a study and the metal cabinet with its pull-out drawers, "Noah's Ark," and the comparison with the Biblical story haunted him while he gazed out the side window as the vaporetto passed a barge carrying a large metal cabinet. He couldn't take his eyes off the boat until it was out of sight. Was it a sign? he asked himself, disconcerted. In any case he would start searching for Jakob's study as soon as he talked to Margherita.

Before the vaporetto docked and he disembarked, he got a call from Commissario Galli.

"We can assume," he said, getting straight to the point, "that your brother and his wife didn't travel to China. They haven't applied for a visa at the embassy. Or for any other countries. We've checked. Their finances are in order, but your brother has an account in Switzerland. Did you know about that?"

"No."

"There are eight million Swiss francs in that account, and expensive jewelry in a safe. Not only that, but the two of them own property and a villa on the Greek island of Lesbos, in Skala Kalloni, a small fishing village on the Gulf of Kalloni, though they've apparently never been there. It is supposed to be a bird sanctuary. Everything was handled by a Greek lawyer who has also disappeared. The couple's assets, as far as we've been able to determine, cannot be explained solely by the income from the pearl transactions and their other business. Can you tell me where we go from here?"

"No . . . no," Aldrian stuttered as he got off the vaporetto.

"Do you have any leads, no matter how insignificant?"

"No." And it made him think of Dr. Dr. Galotti from the Archivio di Stato di Venezia who explained the plague to him and warned him not to investigate by himself, of the barge with the metal cabinet, of Jakob's study that he'd forgotten, of the two men who assaulted him, the masked man who pointed his finger and shot at him, and of Lorenzo Verra, his colleague from the Teatro La Fenice who had repeatedly whispered to him about the "M." He wasn't convinced that everything was connected to Elena's and Jakob's disappearance, but one or two things definitely were. He said nothing and stepped down the gangplank and into the street.

"What's more, your brother and your sister-in-law frequently went to Paris and London," the Commissario continued, "as far as we can tell, seventy or eighty times in the last couple of years. But they're also not there now. Normally, Signora Aldrian works in the Louvre or in the Tate Gallery. She's in great demand as an expert in her field. The last time she worked in these museums was in November and December. What could have caused her to just disappear? Her son Emilio knows nothing, your sister-in-law knows nothing, and you yourself know nothing." Without thinking, Aldrian turned his lapel over and saw the small gold-colored dove that he had bought on the Campo Formosa during the acqua alta. He heard the sound of melting snow, the gurgling in an eavestrough, the spattering of water drops on the ground. It occurred to him that the snowmelt was a musical event. It sounded like a spinet that was being played in the Grand Canal, a Water Music, and instantly he heard Handel's composition in his head, as Commissario Galli went on: "As always at the start, we have only bits and pieces, but we're patient puzzler solvers . . . Will you be staying on in Venice?"

"Yes."

"As you wish, Signor Aldrian. Of course we'll continue our investigation. Now more intensely in Venice, that means in the entire lagoon."

That sounded ominous, as if the police had already given up finding them alive. He was upset at the Commissario, and he imagined how the diver Sergio Celi would recover the bodies of his brother and Elena in the underwater forests of tree trunks.

He hung up without saying goodbye and hurried—the spattering, the lapping, the splashing, the gurgling of the thaw, the distant melody of Handel's *Water Music* still in his head—to the Campo San Tomà. He first glanced over at Carlo Fibonacci's mirror and frame shop and indistinctly saw the man behind the open door in his tiny room taking a frame down from the wall. With his long grey hair, his scraggly grey beard and the gold-frame glasses he looked like a hippie who had become a professor in his old age.

At first Aldrian stopped in front of the building where Margherita lived and suddenly felt something like a strength that emanated from a violent temper. He could still hear Commissario Galli's words: "Now in Venice . . . that means in the entire lagoon." His anger wasn't directed at him, but at whatever it was that lurked behind the void, at the invisible enemy who had played with his brother's and Elena's fate and now wanted to frighten him, too. He would stay in his brother's house until their disappearance was cleared up—and with child-like determination he was certain the gold-colored dove by its hidden presence alone would remind him of his decision.

Margherita and Eugenio's apartment on the third floor was spacious and bright. There was a small garden behind the building where the couple ate their meals together. Margherita's mother lived on the floor below them; she had owned the house before she transferred the title to Margherita. Aldrian had often been a guest here with Jakob and Elena, and he had always felt at home in the apartment furnished with expensive furniture, sofas, lamps, and carpets that he had jokingly called the Palazzo Piccolo on the Rio di San Tomà.

As in Aldrian's own apartment in Vienna, Jakob's watercolor of a chameleon, based on the prototype from an old textbook, was framed and hanging on the wall. When he saw it, he again felt enraged at whatever was behind the void, trying to control him.

Eugenio was already at his dental practice, so Aldrian was sitting opposite Margherita who, with teary red eyes, had made a small breakfast of white bread, butter, marmalade, honey, and tea. As always, Aldrian had decided on the butter and honey. He began to eat silently while Margherita tried to compose herself.

"Did the Commissario call you?" she asked.

Aldrian nodded.

"So?"

"We have to wait and see."

"Don't you want to go back to Vienna?"

"No."

"Elena and Jakob had their dreams," she continued after a brief pause. "They dreamed about the Garden of Eden . . . We all knew that."

"I didn't know." Aldrian answered. "But now, after talking with Commissario Galli, I understand. It's an idea that triggers other ideas, like a magnet attracting iron filings.

"It does?" She wiped her nose with a Kleenex.

"And the money?" she asked. "Where did it come from?"

"We'll find out."

"What do you think?"

"Nothing."

"You disappoint me!" she angrily shot back. "You're taking the easy way out."

"I don't want to presume something that only turns out to be speculation. At any rate, I'm trying not to."

"I understand," she snapped sullenly.

Aldrian ignored her reply. Margherita stood up, went into the kitchen, brought back a plate of oranges, and placed it in front of him. Her eyebrows were squinched together, which told Aldrian that she was looking for a fight.

"These are very sweet. Take some. Eugenio just bought them today."

"He did?"

She picked up the fruit knife and began to peel one of the oranges for him; she was extremely adept, as he knew. In fact she loved to show off her dexterity almost casually for guests and at the

147

dinner table, because no one could do it better and everyone admired her for it.

"Are you and Beatrice together?" she suddenly asked, and her expression revealed her misgivings.

"Who told you that?"

Now it was her turn to be silent, and she enjoyed letting him fidget. She put the yellow spiral orange peel she had just artistically finished on the empty plate and handed him the immaculate fruit.

"Beatrice called Ettore and Giacomo in the Ostaria yesterday and asked about a certain Sergio. I don't know him . . ."

Aldrian understood that she was apparently trying to make him jealous.

"I don't know him either . . . It was all just a mistake. Let's talk about something else—"

"I can only talk about things I'm thinking of . . . and I'm unhappy . . . I have a very bad feeling," and she started to cry. Aldrian knew that he had treated her coldly, possibly because he still felt his rage about whatever was hidden beyond the void and controlled their destiny.

Before Aldrian left for the Doge's Palace, he stopped in Carlo Fibonacci's tiny store.

"I just wanted to stop by and see if you were still alive . . ." he greeted the old man.

Carlo reluctantly looked up and asked Aldrian why he wouldn't be alive?

Just as he was searching for a witty reply, he saw on the small counter a drawing that undoubtedly had been done by Jakob. It depicted a bizarre beetle, its wings golden brown with a black shiny beak that consisted of a long curved horn and a shorter lower one. The insect seemed contrived to him, resembling a rhinoceros beetle, and was almost eight inches long in Aldrian's estimation. Fibonacci had tentatively selected a dark-brown frame that was lying nearby.

Aldrian now noticed that Fibonacci had been apprehensive ever since he entered the shop.

"Where did you get this drawing?" he asked anyway.

"Why?"

"Jakob's disappeared—"

"I know," Carlo hastily replied and quickly added: "He gave me the picture a short time ago. The *Dynastes hercules* is the largest beetle in the world," he continued and tried to change the subject, but Aldrian wasn't going to let him off so easily.

"I want to buy it!"

"Buy it?—No, it's not for sale."

"Why not?"

"I want to keep it."

"Think it over," Aldrian responded and, with a wave of his hand, left the shop. He assumed he had irritated Fibonacci, and just the thought made him happy.

Again he heard the gentle music of the melting snow, the rhythm and sound of the drops falling from the rooftops like the nervous beating on a child's drum or like short high notes from a glass clarinet. Also the sound of shoes sloshing through puddles, in his mind, cymbals of water. In retrospect he couldn't say why he wanted to put pressure on Fibonacci, but, he told himself, there must be a thread somewhere that, when tugged, would reveal the confusing asymmetrical configuration hiding the disappearance of Jakob and Elena. A poor comparison, he corrected himself, but at the moment he was expressing what he felt.

The shelter at the San Tomà vaporetto station, gently rocking on the water, was already full of passengers, mostly tourists with cameras, cellphones, and masks. A few locals, primarily women holding shopping bags, battled the foreigners by grimly shoving their way to the front of the line, and Aldrian joined them, pretending to be distracted. He made it to the middle of the shelter and now had a good chance of getting a seat on the next Line1vaporetto that he could already make out—overflowing with passengers—in the distance.

"Ah, Signore Aldrian," a short man murmured, smiling at him ironically in the throng. Aldrian recognized Dr. Dr. Galotti instantly.

Apparently he had come from his office in the Archivio di Stato di Venezzia to the closest station, that being the one at San Tomà.

"Still in Venice?"

"I live here," Aldrian replied.

"I know. I thought you would go back to Vienna."

Aldrian shook his head.

"I was afraid you might have begun to investigate by yourself?" Dr. Dr. Galotti asked out of curiosity.

Aldrian felt challenged by his question. Besides, he was upset that not only his sister-in-law and Carlo were talking about it. Now the archivist, too, was involved in conversations about his brother.

"I'm going to wait until Jakob and Elena return," he said in a dismissive tone.

Dr. Dr. Galotti squinted: "Did you know that your brother had asked me about an old book of magic, a grimoire? We were talking about Johannes Hartlieb's *Book of All Forbidden Arts*. Jakob wanted to get it for you, but I was not able to acquire it for him."

At that, Aldrian slapped him on the shoulder with one hand and with the other took Galotti's wallet out of his coat pocket and in one fluid movement deposited it into his own pocket. No one noticed.

"Really?" he had exclaimed at the same time.

The Line 1 vaporetto was just docking, and some passengers rushed off the boat, scrambling the cue waiting in line. Aldrian saw Dr. Dr. Galotti being swept away by the crowd, quickly took out the man's wallet, found lira banknotes, two IDs, and, as he was about to put everything back, a small black-and-white photograph of his brother Jakob with the archivist and a stranger, as best he could tell at a glance. He took out the small photo, discovered several phone numbers on the back, put the wallet back in his coat pocket, and barged ahead. It was a struggle, but he made it onto the vaporetto before the steel gate closed and the waterbus began to move. Aldrian—as he was forcing his way onboard—had already begun to look for Dr. Dr. Galotti and found him in the cabin, seated by two young women in fancy costumes and masks. This time Aldrian was polite, asked the standing passenger to let him through, please, and made his way over to the archivist. At the next station the masked young women got up and Dr. Dr. Galotti had to get up, too, to let them by. Aldrian deliberately stepped on the first women's foot and made her scream out in pain, allowing Aldrian to put the archivist's wallet back in the latter's coat pocket. He simultaneously apologized to the masked woman and her companion, which, together with the vaporetto's deceleration, only increased the confusion.

Aldrian squeezed into one of the two free seats and pretended to cough.

"I will be glad when Carnival is over," Dr. Dr. Galotti said. "This time of year there are lots of riffraff out and about."

Aldrian agreed and asked him how long he'd known his brother Jakob.

"I admire him very much, as you know," Dr. Dr. Galotti responded. "A mutual friend, an entomologist, introduced us . . . Jakob had only been in Venice a short time and was interested in the insect life in the lagoon . . . He had drawn them all, and I was supposed to provide some text . . . But I had just completed my second doctoral degree in the history of medicine and had no desire to start something new just at that point . . . We went out into the lagoon several times with a fisherman, a man from Chioggia who knew absolutely everything. Today he is the largest fish distributor . . . In any case, I kept procrastinating until the project deadline eventually expired."

"What a shame."

"Yes, a shame."

"Where could Jakob and Elena be staying, if they haven't left town?" Aldrian asked.

"Why would they be hiding? I am shocked that they have disappeared. I have been racking my brain ever since. You know that he is religious. That will not be news to you, but he is not like others who only follow the rituals and otherwise do not give a fig about what kind of life they live . . . He is no saint . . . And he does not want to be one . . . I do not know what to tell you . . . He loves the beautiful and the good—and that is it. In his lifetime he has never tried to change this concept . . . I mean, he enjoys drinking . . . He knows how to earn money, he loves women—of course, with discretion . . . He is independent and he promotes no social projects . . . He tries to see only the good in a person, in an event, and does not say a word in their absence . . . I do not want to exaggerate, but we all love him." Dr. Dr. Galotti continued speaking, hesitantly, with longer and longer pauses. And to Aldrian's amazement, the man fell asleep. Should he wake him up? Would he wake up by himself? Where was he going? On the other hand Aldrian was glad that the double doctor hadn't wanted to show him the photo in his wallet.

Aldrian, along with most all the other passengers, got off the vaporetto at the San Marco Giardinetti station. Before he crossed the gangway, he glanced back at the sleeping man to convince himself that Galotti hadn't pulled one over on him.

He took the shortest route to the Doge's Palace and this time avoided passing between the columns on the Piazzetta with the St. Mark lion and San Teodoro with the dragon, because he recalled how Jakob had described the executions that had taken place there: that around noon the condemned were shackled at the Piazzetta, forced to climb into a boat, and were brought via the Grand Canal to the Chiesa di Santa Croce church; how they were tortured with glowing tongs; their hands, tongue, or ears cut off and then hung around their necks. Aldrian also remembered that a physician would tie off their arm stumps with a pig's bladder so the criminals wouldn't bleed to death before they were hung or beheaded; and that they had to make their way back to St. Mark's on foot if they didn't want to be dragged over the road tied to a horse's tail. Following the execution, the corpses were quartered, the hacked-up remains skewered and often placed on display until they decomposed . . . Aldrian approached the Doge's Palace and tried to think of something else entirely. Since he had the ticket for the tour of the building's Secret Itinerary in his pocket, he didn't have to wait in line, but upon admission—they stuck a red paper dot on the lapel of his windbreaker as a sign that he was admitted to the tour—he could enter the large courtyard and sit down on a bench beneath the arcades. He read a nearby handwritten notice that the tour would form up at a designated column. There were still small mounds of snow in shady spots, and the stone floor was gleaming wet. Here an attentive listener could still hear the music of the melting snow, though only in isolated tones and with long pauses. The sides of the Doge's Palace with their columns and windows that surrounded the courtyard seemed to Aldrian like four mighty organs that transmitted the music of silence. In a mysterious way, they produced—at least in his imagination—the atomistic sounds that he thought he could hear at a barely audible volume.

The Doge's Palace

Time and time again he had visited the Doge's Palace, alone and with Jakob or Elena, and each time he had the desire to memorize the place like the music scores of operas. But he also felt it was delightful that he could never completely "understand" it—after all, it was a huge richly-decorated historical "toy box," both inside and out, from the Gothic period where Heaven and Hell had blended into one entity.

Once with Elena he had visited the "construction hut," the original workshop for the maintenance of the Palace with its reparation and restoration department, also the Museo dell' Opera with its brick walls—a total of six rooms, dominated by rows of columns that projected an atmosphere of a petrified labyrinth.

He now remembered that the feelings he originally had for Elena had transformed over the years to one of love for a sibling.

He unconsciously gazed again at the large gondola in the middle of the corridor—an inverted prompter's box from the Teatro La Fenice, he thought. That reminded him of the *Maestro Suggeritore* Lorenzo Verra, and he could imagine him standing in the inverted prompter's box, escaping the flames of the burning Teatro and gliding down the Rio della Fenice, aided by an equally strange and monstrous conductor's baton.

He leaned back and recalled the musical pieces he had once chosen for each of the halls and rooms in the Doge's Palace so that he could retain them in his memory. As a result, the splendid building had become an operatic potpourri with twenty-six scenes and various stage settings. At the beginning of the musical score there was always a clef. Aldrian always considered the clef for the Doge's Palace to be the so-called "Bocche di leone," the lion heads on the walls of the corridors and staircases. In earlier times people would toss anonymous denouncements and written accusations into the lions' mouths. For Aldrian they had the appearance of fat "eavesdroppers" who strained to look up and catch even the faintest sound. These complaint mailboxes at several different places in the Doge's Palace all bore the inscription *DENONTIE SECRETE CONTRO CHI OCCULTERA GRATIE ET OFFICH O COLLUDERA PER NASCONDER LA VERA RENDITA D'ESSI*, to encourage the Venetians to spy on each other and bring them to the jail that was also in this building, thus Hell behind the curtain of this Paradise, as it were. Thieves, murderers, sex offenders, people who ostensibly threatened the Venetian state or insulted its representatives could be put to death. Even blasphemy and curses could result in execution.

In his head he now heard Gluck's *Orpheus* overture that conjured up the first image—the arcade courtyard. He was now concentrating so intensely that in his imagination he practically floated through the Palace. A tremendous flood of paintings on the walls and frescos on the ceilings of the halls drew him ever deeper into the giant "toy box" and thus into another time.

To make it easier for him to remember them, he had associated all the paradisiacal halls with operas by Giuseppe Verdi, and the infernal courtrooms and jails with works by Gaetano Donizetti. If Verdi's chorus from *Nabucco* defined the magnificent halls, the mad scene from *Lucia di Lammermoor* portrayed the judicial wing. This way he could play back the rooms in his head as if with a computer, along with their acoustical accompaniment, or even shuffle them together like playing cards. If he got tired, the individual acts with their stage settings took on their own momentum, they overlapped and dissolved each other, and the music resembled the sounds of instruments in an orchestra pit tuning up before the actual performance. He had already loaded the program in his head as he imagined going up the Scala d'Oro, the Golden Staircase, to the Appartamento Ducale. The rooms, decorated with their stucco works and frescos on the ceiling, appeared in his mind's eye and he studied the details—always with Verdi playing in his ear, now *Otello*, then *Un ballo in maschera, Simon Boccanegra,* and later *La forza del destino*. The halls were equally grandiose, but completely different in size and decor. Each successive Doge provided his own private furniture to the so-called Appartamento, and after his death his heirs would carry off the valuable objects. For that reason the private rooms were empty except for one old mirror, and the only remaining trappings were coffered ceilings and silk tapestries. As always, he was enchanted by the Sala delle Mappe, a corridor with a globe and a celestial sphere and maps on the walls. And, as always, it was the terra incognita on the globe back then, the unknown and undiscovered fifth continent, Australia, and other lands that caused him, lost in thought, to take a seat on one of the extended wooden benches along the walls. When he imagined the globe as a brain, then the terra incognita was the temporal lobe, the part regarding time that was to come. After his retirement from the State Opera, Aldrian had the feeling he had left everything behind. He had sailed past elapsing time without noticing anything. But now, since he's been in Venice and been with Beatrice, he thought that there was much in store for him, even if it might be danger and adversity. He noticed pale constellations on the old celestial sphere—brown shadows on a lighter-brown, seemingly faded surface. He also loved the chandeliers of Murano glass that hung like holy spirits from the ceiling. The first things he noticed in the adjoining Sala Grimani were the three paintings of the winged St. Mark lion—one of them by Carpaccio. It reminded him of the painting of the two aristocratic ladies that hung in the Museo Correr and had always seemed to him to be Carpaccio's satire on the boredom of the upper classes.

The Sala dei Filosofi promised more than it delivered. For Aldrian it was only a connecting room. Previously the portraits of twelve ancient philosophers hung from the walls, but now they belonged to the Biblioteca Marciana, and the room with its splendid stucco works had become a bizarre "empty closet" of philosophy that attempted to fill this vacuum with inaudible and invisible words.

On the other hand, the Sala delle Quatro Porte and the Sala dell' Anticollegio were waiting rooms for ambassadors and delegations. Though their frescos and paintings were competent, he didn't care for them because they only served as self-aggrandizement and self-glorification of the mighty.

In the striking Sala del Collegio that followed, the large elegant clock attracted his attention; it had been provided for the assembly of the judicial authority. Aldrian also knew that the wooden seats and the tribunal were original. The clocks on the walls in the next room, the Sala del Senato, the meeting place of the Senate, were even more beautiful. All the rooms—with their Titians, Bellinis, Veroneses, Tintorettos, Tiepolos in gilded ornate frames, with their depictions of saints and mythological scenes in gleaming colors, their rampant stucco work and ceiling frescos that simulated the nearness of God and timelessness, with the terrazzo flooring that swarms with dot patterns and simultaneously reflects the light— invoked the exclusivity of the place and its Doges. They affected a symbiosis of divine omnipotence, Venetian worldly power, and their own majesty.

The clocks in the connecting Sala del Senato displayed the twelve signs of the zodiac on their dials and, moreover, paintings by Jacopo and Domenico Tintoretto and Veronese that were once again of religious or mythological nature. From previous tours that Aldrian had taken with his brother, he knew that in the 14th century, sixty senators ruled; by the 16th century, they had become three hundred. The Doge, who took part in the sessions, discussed everything from politics to declarations of war. Aldrian wasn't surprised that one Doge, Pasquale Cocogna, was depicted on the ceiling, in prayer during Holy Communion. Consequently Aldrian also knew there were additional painted homages to Doges who, as stated earlier, seemed to be in direct contact with the heavenly powers.

The next hall, the Sala del Consiglio dei Dieci, served the Council of Ten as their courtroom. The Council investigated any individuals who appeared to threaten the tranquility and security of the state. With its gold walls the hall seemed to be more of a showplace for weddings. It was no accident that the ceiling was decorated with Paolo Veronese's *Juno Showering Gifts on Venetia*.

Still mired in his thoughts, Aldrian reached the Sala dell'Armamento. It was a fancy arsenal that gave Aldrian little enjoyment since it reminded him of his own predicament. The space here was basically utilized as an armory for weapons and munitions: supply wagons, cannons and weapons such as halberds, pikes, lances, spears, crossbows, swords, and bludgeons. Originally there was a fresco on the walls portraying the coronation of the Virgin Mary, but it had been damaged or totally destroyed in a fire. The colors had partially faded or could at best be recognized as a delicate shimmer, while the figures, like everything else on the walls, could only be intuited. But it was precisely this heavily damaged representation that had always fascinated Aldrian. Time, fire, and dampness had almost completely obliterated everything. It now stood for the disappearance of religion, Aldrian thought, and showed it gradually fading away. Jakob had emphasized over and over that every particle in the entire universe was transitory, religions as well, though, paradoxically, they promised immortality. But in the frescos Aldrian also saw stains on the walls that had randomly evolved to a subjectively explicable form, similar to reading meaning into cloud formations. The once sumptuously painted pictures, only recognizable today in fragments, of angels and saints also had something archeological about them. He was now afraid that they could vanish if they were exposed to the light. Finally he looked out at St. Mark's Square through a window of crown glass that distorted reality.

When he saw the Sala del Maggior Consiglio ahead, the triumphal march from *Aida* resounded in his head, and in his imagination the ten members of the Great Council who regulated the government of Venice till the end of the 13th century were just filing in. It was the most impressive hall. Aldrian had seen it for the first time in his childhood, accompanied by his parents. But the one thing he remembered most were the vast dimensions that he equated back then with the world of grownups. For him, all the pictures in the hall were not so much paintings as facts, even though they had later completely disappeared from his memory. Most of all, he no longer knew what he had thought about the 74x30-foot mammoth painting *The Paradise* by Tintoretto.

Presumably it had so overwhelmed him that he had scarcely noticed it. Even during his last visit Aldrian hadn't been able to concentrate on the painting. For him it was a pond full of colorful human tadpoles, in Jakob's words a picture of an ant or bumblebee multitude, a painted cloud of hominid birds, a swarm of fish swimming every which way in the ocean. In any event, it had little to do with human beings, even though every individual in the crowd had a face. He had also had the feeling that he was being crushed by this powerful painting and could imagine that, at the end of his life, he would be one of these figures.

He didn't care for Tintoretto's idea of paradise, but he had visited the Doge's Palace once to study it. On the opposite wall of the same hall you could see images of all the Doges, but in place of one of the portraits was a painted black banner with a white inscription in Latin: "This space is reserved for Marin Falier, beheaded for his crimes," who had been executed on the steps of the Doge's Palace and his head impaled and displayed at the Piazzetta. Falier had been accused of conspiring against the state. Falier had been insulted by a young nobleman who supposedly accused his wife of infidelity. Since the taunter had been accused but acquitted, Falier mounted an insurrection—according to the legend—against the noble judges. The black banner in place of his portrait was the symbol for the *condemnatio memoriae*, the obliteration of his memory. But it secured the Doge unintended eternal life in the minds of many visitors, Aldrian thought—at least as long as this hall existed, while most of the other Doges portrayed here had soon been forgotten. But later, Aldrian couldn't recall even the expunged Doge, that is, his black blemish. The only thing he could remember, he reflected, were the splendid stairways, huge magnificent Jacob's ladders that he had climbed up and down until he felt that he himself was only a dried brushstroke of the gilded decorations that formed a confusing pattern. Aldrian was fascinated by the Doge's Palace, even if he only saw it as a labyrinth of pictures and halls: just gazing out the window, at no place else on earth could city and ocean be seen so near to each other, and nowhere else had stately rooms and jail cells—beauty and horror. But there was also no place else where reality seemed so illusive. It wasn't the mystery of this reality that made the Palace so special, but that the everyday had been overwhelmed, and the ornamentation and paintings of the pompous halls presented world history and religion as the true all-encompassing reality. The Doge was, as previously stated, God on earth who determined war and peace, the destiny of men, life and death, as his heavenly counterpart influenced the universe, all souls, heaven and hell.

In the Sala dello Scrutinio he saw massive paintings of battles, and the one that depicted galleys at war was his favorite. He recalled that this painting—together with the splendid stairways—had also impressed him in his youth. It was a panoramic picture like Tintoretto's *Paradise*, done by Andrea Vicentino, and portrayed the Battle of Lepanto where the Turks were defeated in their quest for supremacy in the Mediterranean Sea. In this oil painting hundreds of men tried to kill each other, as in Jacopo Tintoretto's rendition of *The Conquest of Zara* and others. One other wall was devoted to Jacopo

Palma the Younger's *The Last Judgment*. Everywhere you looked, masses of people were pushing their way through the heavenly gates or being thrust into hell.

The paintings vanished again from his thoughts, and in the arcade courtyard he glanced at the black gondola and the group of people who had gathered for the secret itinerary tour through the Doge's Palace. All of a sudden he no longer had any desire to take the tour, no desire to stride through the ceremonial rooms or to crawl around in narrow and damp passageways. He took off the red dot on his collar and waited until the group had set off. An odd lady appeared on the scene. She wore a fur coat and spoke in a stern voice, like a teacher in front of a class of students with disabilities. He heard her say that cameras and purses or backpacks had to be checked in. There were 24 participants—Aldrian had counted them—who then received further instructions: you can't take photos with your smartphone, you can't touch anything, you must stay with the tour group—before they disappeared, as he imagined her saying, into the "haunted house."

With the mad aria from Donizetti's *Lucia di Lammermoor* swirling in his head, he imagined himself entering the judicial wing. The furnishings gave a viewer the impression of being below decks in a large old sailing ship. First you came to a small room. It was somewhat like a captain's cabin, because even the floor was made out of wooden planks. At the end of the long and narrow room stood a small table, a cushioned chair, two other wooden chairs and a chest of drawers. This was the office of the Cancellier Grande, the highest official, appointed for life. He did his duty every day and was "force fed" money until he became a Croesus so he couldn't be bribed. In return, however, he was not to "propagate the charisma of power," according to his contract. Aldrian tried to imagine this austere man in his comparatively modest chamber as a split personality—a family man and a bureaucrat who, during office hours, was a merciless legal mechanic, an automatic recipient and administrator of orders. A door led from his captain's cabin to the archives of secret files whose fascicles would later land in the Archivio di Stato di Venezia. The entire construct was intended to monitor and police. The bare adjoining Sala della Cancelleria Superiore or "Segreta"—the Chamber of the Secret Chancellery—was the officers' mess on the ship, so to speak. In the back of his head Aldrian could hear Donizetti's opera *La lettera anonima*. With a marble balustrade at the front, this room had a wooden ceiling and a row of cabinets along the walls. Up to 24 clerks went about their work, each only allowed specific knowledge of one specialty that was at the disposal of the Cancellier Grande who then made decisions about any further course of action. Other official duties included making copies—the Doge, of course, required a duplicate of each fascicle—taking dictation or translating documents in foreign languages, and searching for files. "Top secret" papers were kept in wall cabinets with locks.

Another staircase at the opposite end of the archives led to a table with three chairs. This was where the Cancellier Grande sat when he had discussions with the clerks. You opened a door, went along a corridor with small windows of crown glass to get to the Sala della Tortura—the torture chamber. This room, too, was all wood and could have been a stall and slaughter room for cattle. Behind a table with three chairs he noticed four windows, again with crown glass. There was a candleholder on the table. In the middle of the room a hangman's noose hung from the ceiling. (For this location Aldrian had chosen Donizetti's *Roberto Devereux*, the Queen's aria as she signed the death sentence.) The interrogatee's hands were tied behind his back; he was then pulled up by the rope so he could be interrogated while hanging in midair. Four observers sat in each corner of the torture chamber and from there posed questions to the dangling offender. It usually didn't take long to get the prearranged confession, according to the account. The "criminals" served their time in the cellar, in the "pozzi," a well that was under water during acqua alta. On the other hand, "political prisoners" were taken to the "piombi," the lead chambers above the Sala degli Inquisitori and under the Palace attic with its lead-plated ceiling where they suffered to the fullest extent the cold of winter and the heat of summer.

Aldrian could see the narrow halls and steep stairways—everything was wood and stone—and the first of the two prisons for Giacomo Casanova. It was so low that the adventurer couldn't stand upright, so he was allowed to use a private chair. There was also a bed. The room was considerably smaller than the others he had seen in the Doge's Palace. A narrow window looked out on the lead roof of another part of the Palace edifice. With an iron doorhandle that he had found on his brief daily strolls in the attic, Casanova began to bore a hole in the Sala dei Tre Capi, the Hall of the Three Judges, just below However his cell so he could escape during the night. Before he could carry out his plan, however, he was transferred, to his horror, to a different cellblock. Casanova's futile digging, Aldrian had read, is still evident today; in any event, the ceiling frescos by Veronese and Ponchino in the Hall of the Three Judges were unscathed. Aldrian recalled the large attic where Casanova had found the iron doorhandle. This was above the Sala del Maggior Consiglio, the hall with the huge painting of Paradise by Tintoretto. Aldrian also remembered how he had stood on a catwalk and gazed around the judicial wing in the dusty hulk of his imaginary large sailing ship: pillars, struts, roof beams all about, the lead roof above, and through the dormers the lead roof of an adjacent part of the building. From there he had hiked over more stairs, catwalks, and passageways to the second prison cell where Casanove had been transferred.

The adventurer hadn't known why he had even been imprisoned. Supposedly someone had secretly denounced him for immoral conduct. It could have been initiated by a jealous husband or transpired for religious reasons. He had allegedly been involved in magic and given blasphemous speeches; in the end, two books about magic had been found in his apartment and were confiscated, according to the story. On top of all that, he had been accused of consorting with foreigners, the reason why they suspected him of espionage. His sentence—five years in prison—was for religious sacrilege.

Collaborating with another prisoner, Marino Balbi, he was able to burrow through the attic of this second cell and, after wandering around on the roof and in the halls of the Doge's Palace for a time, was finally able to escape.

Aldrian remembered how the guide had opened the door to Casanova's second lead chamber—the cells beside each other like cabins—and how he stared into the sparsely furnished void. He had tried to imagine what it must have been like to spend years in such a dismal place, but he couldn't. The actual nothingness he saw resembled the attic of his grandparents' house in Bad Aussee, at least that was exactly how he felt when he saw it as a child. Aldrian now recollected that the prison cells had barred windows looking out onto the passageway, the floors were wood, the doors extremely low so that only a dwarf could pass comfortably.

The next thing he remembered was the Sala dei Tre Capi. It was not very large and not especially resplendent, yet clearly distinguishable from the "Piombi," as if he had entered a luxurious room on the old sailing ship, reserved for its aristocratic owner: paintings on the walls, coffered ceilings of 24-carat gold, candelabras, and upholstered armchairs made of wood on one wall, and a sophisticated pattern on the marble floor where you could become lost and yet have the impression it consists of small black and white stair steps. When Aldrian concentrated, he could recall the pattern, but he forgot what he was thinking and suddenly found himself back on the bench in the arcade courtyard; in his mind the pattern of the marble floor kept vaguely unwinding. Still, it occurred to him that there was an easel with a painting of the three judges—two worldly judges dressed in black, the religious judge in red—and he heard the prologue to Donizetti's opera *Lucrezia Borgia* that is set in Venice during Carnival.

Aldrian stood up and took a couple of steps, but the urge to recapture his train of thought was so strong that he stopped by the black gondola and considered what he had seen after the Sala dei Tre Capi, but he was no longer able to conjure up the pertinent musical theme . . . Presumably, he thought, it was the Sala degli Inquisitori. He could see a large fireplace and a ceiling fresco by Tintoretto . . . The feared office dealt with the unauthorized dissemination of state secrets, in other words, with counter-espionage, and it operated in absolute secrecy . . . No matter how hard he tried, Aldrian wasn't able to recall anything else. He only knew that there had been the Signori della Notte al Criminal who had met by torchlight in a lofty room with no paintings and bare walls to immediately solve and punish any crimes that had taken place that night; a Sala dei Censori whose name was self-explanatory; as well as the Sala della Quarantia Criminal and the Sala dei Cuoi—all were further rooms in the so-called "judicial machinery." In addition there was the Esecutori contro la Bestemmia" and other similar "hovels for bloodhounds," he thought grimly. Finally he recalled the Bussola Hall, named for the three-part installation in the room that concealed two doors, one of which led to the jail cells. This door had two locks and therefore could be opened only by the two authorized officers working together, since they each had one key. The Bussola Hall served as a waiting room for the condemned, which reminded Aldrian of the appropriate music, the dungeon scene in the the third act of Donizitti's *Maria Stuarda* where Mary Stuart is plagued by hallucinations before her execution. In his mind he returned to the Sala dei Tre Capi and the confusing pattern on the marble floor, and then to the Sala del Magistrato alle Leggi that promoted compliance to the legal system and had the 16th century painting *The Mocking of Christ* and two triptychs by Hieronymus Bosch. Aldrian was very familiar with this painting by Bosch, but now he could only recall the part where several angels carry the deceased through a dark passage into a brilliantly illuminated heaven. The blindingly bright opening was perhaps, as Jakob always speculated, the eye of God through which departed souls could return to their home in the mind of their Creator. Aldrian shuddered, because even in his recollection he could hear his brother's voice.

He quickly visualized the dungeon and crossing the Bridge of Sighs to the new prison. But again he lost the thread, the music fell silent, and he found himself once again at the large black gondola under the arcades. Then he pictured himself climbing up and down stairs and through cold musty cells. Some jails were disguised with wooden beams so that the ten convicts in each cell had the impression they were lying in a large coffin. He recognized the tower with its rooms and prisoners' messages on the walls. In one particular prison you could see drawings and detached chunks of bricks with graffiti in glass cases. He could recognize women, heads, ships, even individual words—all things considered, a storybook of anguish, of pain and despair. In the Doge's Palace, grandeur, power, malevolence and impotence were side by side with violence, vanity, callousness, and brutality, papered over with the nightmares and visions of the greatest artists.

Pursuit

Aldrian tore up his ticket and threw the paper scraps into a wastebasket. Outside on St. Mark's Square, by now completely free of snow but sparkling with dampness, once again people and masks were swarming about. Flocks of doves flew up—they made Aldrian think of the pin on the back of his jacket lapel—, a balloon sailed upward, everyone was taking pictures of everyone else, and people in masks enjoyed being at the center of things. He felt the need to disappear in the crowd, to become part of the chaos. He thought of the physical law of entropy that states how every order inevitably transitions up to and including its complete dissolution in disorder. As he cautiously turned, he noticed a man in an eye mask and three-cornered hat. He turned again and determined that the man was still following him. Subsequent checking confirmed that he was still pursuing Aldrian, and without attempting to hide the fact. Aldrian abruptly doubled back, quickly passed his pursuer, and retraced the entire route back to the Doge's Palace and, finally—because the stranger was apparently still following him—to the San Marco Giardinetti vaporetto station, but without entering the waiting room. Instead he hid in the small park behind the Procuratie Nuove, the elongated building with it offices for construction and finance that enclosed the long side of St. Mark's Square. A homeless man was lying on a bench and turned his back to Aldrian. Grandmothers were taking their grandchildren for walks in the small park, and an old woman with a cane had just leaned her shopping cart against a bench so she could sit down and arduously tie her shoes. Aldrian felt for the gas pistol in his pocket, went up to the Canal at the back of the Procuratie Nuove and gazed into the dirty-green water where several boats lay on the waterfront. He briefly considered hiding in one of the boats, pulled out the gun and read the company name on the barrel: Röhm RG 70. After he had put the gas pistol away again, he abruptly swiveled around. He realized that his pursuer was standing at the entrance to the park and, apparently bored, gazing at the market booths with their souvenir trinkets. The man obviously had plenty of time. In an instant Aldrian decided to confront him. Without having anything specific in mind, Aldrian approached and watched in astonishment as the stranger—after casting a fleeting glance at Aldrian—turned and started to flee. At first his pursuer calmly strolled along the bank back to the Piazzetta and tried to pretend he was harmless, Aldrian thought. But Aldrian started walking faster, to catch up to him, but the masked man only began to walk faster himself. He realized that the stranger had the same build as the bearded man who had watched him in the Caffè Florian and later beaten him up. But this one didn't have a beard and also no hair on his head, as Aldrian could tell from his temples. In the meantime they were hurrying through the pillars of San Marco and Teodoro and past the gondolas covered in blue tarps, crossed the Ponte della Paglia where a group of tourists with their backs to the two men was photographing the Bridge of Sighs, and finally rushed to the waiting room of the vaporetto station in front of the Hotel Danieli. The man unexpectedly stopped at the landing area and screamed at Aldrian with a Slavic or Russian accent: "What do you want? Beat it!"

At first Aldrian couldn't answer, but he now believed he recognized the eyes of his antagonist from Caffè Florian. He knew he could be mistaken, but he was nevertheless convinced this was the right man. He said nothing and boldly looked the man right in the eyes—they appeared cold and revealed no fear.

"*You!*" Aldrian blurted out, angry but anxious. He suddenly felt a blow to his ribs, heard the din of the docking vaporetto, and considered knocking his opponent's hat off when the stranger scornfully called out in his strange accent: "For the last time: Beat it!" and, with exaggerated calmness, lifted his head, entered the passenger shelter in the wake of exiting passengers and joined those waiting for the boat who were crowding around. Why Aldrian didn't just take off, he himself didn't understand. Like all the others, he climbed aboard the vaporetto, stood on the front platform and looked around, but didn't see either a three-cornered hat or an eye-mask. Instead he read on the framed sign with the ship's route that he was on Line 4.2 via La Giudecca to the train station. As soon as the boat sailed out into the lagoon, he was relieved to feel safe. Once again he began to search for the man and suddenly discovered he was behind him. The stranger was still wearing the eye mask and the three-cornered hat, staring at Aldrian like a dog owner at his disobedient animal. His face displayed indifference, but his eyes had something unrelenting about them, and Aldrian realized that his adversary was only waiting for the next opportunity to get even with him. Aldrian held his gaze, but then turned to look at the sea and saw seagulls circling in the sunshine beneath a blue sky. He felt the gas pistol in his pocket and wondered if the stranger might have seen him draw the gun back in the small park where Aldrian had fled. Staring at the water and the bouncing waves, he decided that, if it came to an altercation, he would shoot his adversary in the face. He just shouldn't think about the consequences, he told himself. At the same time it occurred to him that the man behind his back could have a knife and could wound or even kill him. He moved a few feet away to be with the other passengers and could see in the reflection from a windowpane that the masked man was keeping an eye on him. That dispelled Aldrian's doubts that he was mistaken, because these were the same eyes, he was now convinced, that had watched him in the Caffè Florian. But the longer they sailed, the more he mistrusted his perception. Probably the best thing would be to let the man get off, while Aldrian stayed on board. Or, he wondered, should he get off himself and forget the man in the vaporetto.

By the time they had left San Giorgio Maggiore behind, he had become so despondent that he accused himself of being a fool because he was now stalking his pursuer. He located the stranger in the windowpane, as the other was also doing with him, and when the vaporetto docked at the Zitelle station on La Giudecca island, he observed the man quickly leaving the vaporetto with the other passengers. With little hesitation Aldrian followed him. He no longer asked himself why he was doing it, because he needed to concentrate on not letting the man get out of sight. The stop was in front of the Chiesa delle Zitelle, and he was surprised that his adversary was suddenly running away. Perhaps he had seen Aldrian fingering his pistol . . . Aldrian ran after him. He suspected this was a ploy, since the man didn't rush up the long Fondamenta, but fled across the piazza that ended before the narrow strip of land leading to the island of San Giorgio. While he was concentrating on the potholes in the road, the masked man suddenly appeared ahead, jumped up and quickly glanced back. Aldrian had made up some of the distance between them, but his adversary was faster: the stranger had barely crossed the piazza when he disappeared in a side street, and Aldrian, following blindly, saw when he reached the intersection that the man had turned off to the right. Aldrian followed him into another narrow alley and reached for the gas pistol in his pocket. Everything around him seemed dead, and he could sense the isolation of the seemingly deserted district. At the same instant—from a door that suddenly opened—the man leaped out with a knife, blocking his way. Aldrian briefly thought that he looked like a big kid, poorly dressed as a pirate. Aldrian hastily aimed at the man's face and pulled the trigger. The stranger dropped the knife and, with a roar, fell to the ground. He moaned loudly and covered his face with his hands. With the gun in his outstretched hand, stifling his own fear, Aldrian screamed at the man: "What's your name? Who are you?"

As if following the rules of some magic trick, Aldrian fired two more shots directly into the man's face, picked up the knife, snapped it shut, and pocketed it. He then yanked the three-cornered hat from the helpless man's head and put it on his own head so that he wouldn't be recognized. In doing so, he noticed that because he had shot at close range, his adversary's face was covered in blood, so he didn't bother to rip off his eye mask. He first searched the man for a phone, quickly took out the SIM card and put it in his pocket. He also found an ID with a photograph of the now unconscious man, made out to a Russian citizen by the name of Petrus Petrussjan. He put the papers in his coat pocket, thought of the phrase "beat a hasty retreat," and immediately took off running. But no matter in which direction he fled, he ran into one cul-de-sac after another—he had to turn around and ended up in yet another cul-de-sac. He panicked because he was afraid that his wounded adversary could call for help. After numerous trials and errors, he finally came to the Fondamenta Zitelle. He didn't dare stay in the passenger shelter, afraid that someone might remember him later, and instead hurried along the Canale della Giudecca until he reached the Chiesa Redentore. On the way he had to fight his guilty conscience that accused him of having committed a crime. What if his pursuer choked on his blood?—After all, he left him lying on his back. The longer Aldrian rushed along with the three-cornered hat on his head, the more insane his deed seemed. Ultimately his remorse paralyzed him to the degree that he couldn't go on. It was impossible to go back to the injured man, he told himself, because if the would-be Russian belonged to some organization, he would just be getting himself into even greater danger. And what if the stranger died? He had no answer for that. He finally realized he had to disappear and call Commissario Galli. He encountered few other people. They didn't pay any attention to him, as he realized to his relief. When he turned around, he recognized in the distance the next scheduled vaporetto and, further on, the Chiesa Redentore that he had once visited with his brother. He slipped into a side street to get rid of the hat, but he was also afraid that the police could find some clue that would lead them straight to him. The street was so narrow that two pedestrians couldn't walk side by side. From behind the church he saw that the structure was extended to an adjoining monastery. He looked around again, but no one was following him. "This isn't me!" he said to himself, and then kept repeating the sentence. At the end of the cul-de-sac he threw away the hat, ran back down the Calle delle

Cape, according to a wall sign, and just reached the passenger shelter as the Line 2 vaporetto was docking.

Angels and Demons
The Package

First he thought he would ride to the train station and then on to the Rialto Bridge, but after the first stop he realized—standing this time with only three other passengers on the platform—that the boat was heading to the opposite bank. He had a feeling that an iron ring was closing around his throat, felt strong pressure in his chest and that his heart was beating erratically. He painfully clung to a wooden handle, took deep breaths, and tried to think of something else and not stare as if in a trance at the passenger shelter they were approaching. His heart didn't calm down until he disembarked at the Zattere Ponte Lungo. Confused, he took a few steps and stopped in front of the Campo san Trovaso. He had passed this way many times and each time had stopped to watch what was happening at the gondola boatyard. This time there were five gondolas lying with their keels toward the water on the lot in front of the barracks-like sheds with the tall chimney. Just as on the first day after his arrival when he saw the Palazzo Fortuny, the boatyard made a rustic impression on Aldrian ... He thought about the mask-maker Diego Sarcia to whom he was "indebted" for the gas pistol, and about the prompter Lorenzo Verra who had warned him about the "M.", but also about Beatrice, about Jakob and Elena. Just then he noticed that a worker in a blue sweat suit was checking the dimensions of a gondola with a yellow tape measure ... From time to time Aldrian anxiously glanced back at the island of La Giudecca where the man he had shot in the face was probably still lying, unconscious. Since he had taken the man's SIM card from his smartphone, the stranger couldn't even notify EMS or the police . . . One of the sheds ahead had a long balcony where washing was hanging out to dry on the railing. He automatically counted the laundry, there were eleven items . . . And he knew that it took 280 individual pieces to construct a gondola. In addition, they used various kinds of wood. Only cherry, walnut, pine, and oak came to mind . . . Then three young men began to inspect the gondolas more closely. Aldrian had gradually calmed down and strolled aimlessly along the Rio di San Trovaso until he came to a street that led to the Grand Canal. Since he now knew where he was, he turned off to the Accademia Bridge where he boarded a vaporetto. The only thing he was aware of the whole trip was himself. Things no longer spoke to him. He noted their charm and told himself it was his own fault. Without a great deal of thought he got off at the San Tomà station, but no sooner was he at the Campo, then he headed off in the direction of the Rio della Fescada, thinking about Jakob and when the two of them had gone to the nearby Chiesa San Pantalon—against his wishes, so they had gone to a small pizzeria first and—when Aldrian finally gave in—found the church locked up tight. He went looking for it and in no time was standing before it. It was an inconspicuous brick structure and its exterior façade had never been completed. He recalled that his brother had told him everything about the ceiling painting that consisted of forty individual pictures. It could signify that Jakob's life also was composed of various parts, like a puzzle— no, it had to be that way, because that was the way life was—and that he, Aldrian, was one of these little pieces, and only his brother, if anyone, knew where he fit in. It reminded him of the mosaics in St. Mark's Basilica. They, too, were composite pictures that only made sense when each piece was in its proper place. As Aldrian was about to enter the church, he saw on a sign that tours were only from 8 to 10 a.m. and from 4 to 6 p.m. He glanced at his watch and was amazed to discover that it was 3:50 p.m., but he would have been equally surprised if it had been 10 a.m. or 2 p.m. He didn't want to recap these last few hours, from when to when he had been in the Doge's Palace, how long the mutual pursuit had lasted, and how long the trip on the vaporettos . . . He stumbled on the pizzeria that he and Jakob had visited back then and ordered a "focaccia alle olive" and a glass of wine. The focaccia was a type of bread made of yeast dough with olives, and he could still remember how good it tasted with wine. He drank a second glass before he returned to the church.

It was dark and empty. When he looked up, the fresco surprised him because the interior seemed to open up into vast heavenly dimensions. He then had the impression that he himself was flying, and from up above could watch the War in Heaven, the fall of the rebellious angels who are transformed by their fall into demons with dark wings, as in paintings by Pieter Brueghel or Hieronymus Bosch. There was such a throng among the holy figures that Aldrian thought of a swarm of locust that were drawn to the fires of hell. To the left and to the right of them arose the pillars of a throne room where the floor apparently had broken away. According to the painting, God had thrown the insurgents, as if through a trapdoor, down into the flames where they had burned, been consumed, incinerated, and finally reduced to ashes.

Between the pews at the main entrance Aldrian discovered a coin-operated apparatus that would illuminate the ceiling painting for sixty seconds. Aldrian searched for a coin and sat down in the nearest pew. As he sat in darkness, spotlights lit up the entire panorama. Looking up, he could see angelic bodies flying toward a gleaming light—following some law of nature, attracted like moths or hornets by a light bulb. They hovered overhead, motionless, weightless, for a long time, forever and ever. Then the spotlight went dark, and the ascension into heaven turned again into the fall from grace, and instead of looking upward, Aldrian gazed down into the depths as in the beginning. Tossing in more coins, he observed the positive and the negative of the same picture for some time. It was a marvelous magic trick, he thought. In the end he stretched out on the pew in the dark and, exhausted, fell fast asleep.

He woke up with the arrival of a class of school children. They occupied the benches at the rear while their teachers conferred up front, until one of them finally began to lecture. No one put a coin in the apparatus so they could see heaven, Aldrian told himself, instead of hell.

He straightened up with some effort and walked out while the children quietly laughed, apparently thinking he was homeless or crazy.

At first he didn't know what he should do next. Then he called Beatrice and asked her if they were going to get together that evening. Beatrice was startled by his question and replied with a question of her own: had he changed his mind? She laughed happily, and he was relieved.

"No, no," he countered. "Are we going to meet at your place or mine?"

"Where are you right now?"

Aldrian fibbed that he was at the gondola boatyard.

"Your place, around eight," Beatrice continued. "And this time I will bring something for us to eat."

The sun was still out, but a wind had come up that made the passenger shelter sway with a gentle bumping motion, which made the fragmented reflections of the buildings and the sky undulate on the water in every conceivable color. Gradually things began to speak to him, he noticed, and he felt his head was clearing. He still didn't know what he would do next. Maybe nothing. But what about the stranger's SIM card? And the telephone numbers on the back of the photo that he had swiped from Dr. Dr. Galotti? The gas pistol that had fired three shots? His pursuer's knife? The man's ID?

More and more people gathered in the passenger shelter, some discreetly pushed their way to the front. Lost in thought, he almost took the vaporetto going in the opposite direction when it docked and the waiting passengers slightly lost their equilibrium before they hurried to get onboard.

It was cold on the next boat and the seating area was overflowing, but he did find an empty seat between someone in a mask and someone in everyday clothing. A woman sat beside him with a box containing a frightened cat that scrutinized him. Aldrian thought that was probably the reason why the seat wasn't already taken. The animal didn't make a sound. The door to the vaporetto cabin hissed open and shut which irritated the people on the platform as well as the seated passengers. Aldrian figured out that one or another of the passengers in the throng was inadvertently bumping into the button that functioned to open and close the door.

After he had fought his way on land, Aldrian hurried to his brother's house. He again found mail behind the front door, and the package the mysterious delivery boy had delivered that morning was still lying on the table where he had put it. He set it down on the floor, collected the mail, and then took the package up the two flights of stairs to his apartment. There he took off his windbreaker and emptied his pockets of everything that he had with him since the incident. He also set aside the gas pistol before he went into the bathroom and deliberated as he always did when he went in there. Under no circumstances did he want to involve Beatrice in this affair. On the other hand he had to invent a story that was plausible. At any rate he wouldn't mention the gas pistol, it had to cease to exist, so he decided to tell Diego Sarcia he lost it . . . Or was it stolen? But where? At St. Mark's Square or in the crowded vaporetto? What should he do with the knife? He could claim that he had been followed and threatened, and that he had taken it from his adversary along with the ID and the SIM card during a scuffle on La Giudecca. It didn't matter if anyone believed him or not. "*Der springende Punkt*," he thought . . . what a strange expression, a point that springs. His brother had once told him where the sentence came from. The *punctum saliens*—Jakob had used the formulation frequently when they were younger—was a pulsing red dot that could be seen with the naked eye on the fourth day of incubation of a fertilized chicken egg. It signified the metamorphosis from plant to animal life. Aldrian had noted the entire story so that some day he could be a "smart ass," as he now told himself . . . Now *der springende Punkt* was the gas pistol. After he had left the bathroom and washed his hands, he got some scissors from a drawer in the built-in kitchen and opened the package. The cross-shaped bow and the dark-grey plastic wrapping gave Aldrian the impression that it was the remnant of some crime or other. He carefully and apprehensively opened it and found a letter inside, beneath that an antiquarian book with a mottled cover. And when he took these two objects out, on the bottom were countless small packs of hundred-euro bills, sorted and bound together with rubber bands. Stunned, he lay down on the bed and closed his eyes. He lay there for some time, then sat up and read the letter that had been composed on a computer. The first thing he saw was that it was signed by Jakob, thought not in his handwriting, but printed out. "Dear Michael," he read in Italian, "You will certainly be wondering about Elena's and my disappearance. For various reasons we are compelled to begin a new life. Please take care of our son Emilio for the time being. Three-fourths of the money is for him, the rest is for you. Please consider it your inheritance from me. And leave Venice, so that you are not exposed to even greater danger.—Your Jakob."

He determined there were 1,000 euro bills, and the first thing he did was to put the package under the bed. But he immediately pulled it right back out and reached for the mottled book. It was a chapter from Johannes Hartlieb's major work, *The Book of all Forbidden Arts*, and had the title *The Art of Chiromancy* that showed more than forty human palms in large format, male hands on the left side, female hands on the right. The illustrations were accompanied by text in old script that made Aldrian think about the magic handshakes that were depicted and described in magic handbooks, the only difference being that back then the future was foretold from open palms. He now recalled his last visit, when he and his brother had discussed magic for an entire evening. And he also remembered that Dr. Dr. Galotti, during their conversation on the vaporetto, had mentioned he had acquired a grimoire for Jakob. In his *Book of all Forbidden Arts*, Hartlieb described the *Liber Consecratus*, the sworn book, the *Picatrix*—an Arabic compilation of texts on magic, astrology, and talisman lore—and the Sepher Raziel, the book of the angel Raziel whom Noah had purportedly taken aboard his ark after the angel had taught him how to build the ship. Hartlieb had turned against all these publications and composed his work so that people would reject magic. Of course, to this point he himself had written magic books. Aldrian, for his part, had gotten involved through his interest in history. He opened the mottled volume and read the dedication: "For Michael from Jakob, Christmas Eve." Though he was confused, he deduced that Jakob had wanted to give the book to him for Christmas. In any event, the book wasn't proof that his brother was still alive, nor was the letter. And the money? No one who might have kidnapped or murdered Jakob would have walked away from such a large sum . . . And one more thing bothered him. He took out the letter again and read: "And leave Venice, so that you are not exposed to even greater danger—Your Jakob." Aldrian suspected that it was a veiled threat. And he remembered how his pursuer at St. Mark's Square hadn't let him out of his sight. Maybe he was one of those strangers who threatened him, had shadowed him to see if he would leave? He closed his eyes, shook his head, briefly considered whether his brother had wanted to outperform him with his own magic trick, and stowed the money, the book and the letter under the bed. The first thing he did was phone Diego Sarcia, the proprietor of the mask shop. "Mikey!" Sarcia greeted him enthusiastically, and when Aldrian told him that the pistol had been stolen in the crush at St. Mark's, Sarcia interrupted him, saying: "I gave it to you, but you didn't want it. Now I'm giving it to you again!"

Concerned, Sarcia even went so far as to suggest bringing Aldrian another "gun that fired blanks" that he had never used, but Aldrian promised to come over to his store. He resolutely put the gas pistol in his pocket, went down to the courtyard, crossed the deserted market hall, strolled along the canal, abruptly bent down and untied one shoe, tied it again, and inconspicuously pulled out the gun that he had stuck under his arm. After making sure that no one was watching, he dropped the gas pistol over the wall and into the water. It sank with a gently gurgling sound. He was able to pull it off so quickly and unobtrusively from doing his many magic tricks. Then he stood up, looked around, and went back to his apartment. He felt better, even though he wasn't actually relieved—at least he had gotten the gun out of the house. Things were still lying on the kitchen table. It probably would be best to call Commissario Galli . . . but there was no way he would tell him about the box with the money and the book about palm reading. He would hand over the ID, the Russian's SIM card and his knife, but he definitely wouldn't mention that he had shot his pursuer on La Giudecca. The story only worked if he admitted that he panicked and ran away. After the incident he had to flee on the vaporetto to the island of La Giudecca, and after the scuffle with the stranger had taken the waterbus to the San Silvestro station. He dialed the number, but it took a while before the Commissario answered.

"I was followed and attacked," Aldrian said.

Galli didn't ask many questions, just told him to stay home. And then he hung up.

Aldrian again intended not to mention the box with the money. He put the photo that he had taken from Dr. Dr. Galotti in his wallet, confirmed that you couldn't see the package with the banknotes under his bed, and then got a call from Beatrice that she was on her way. He still didn't tell her what had happened, nor that Commissario Galli was coming over; he only told her that he loved her. He also felt the need to give her something . . . A large lavishly expensive paperweight?

When they had finished their conversation, he thought of the mirror he had seen during the acqua alta in the shop near the Bovolo, the "Snail Tower." It was obviously a masterpiece that had made a great impression on him. Now he remembered all the many details. He also thought about the money, the fat bundles of 100-euro bills bound by rubber bands . . . He wouldn't touch them. He had always had the ability to solve problems, and gradually those powers were reawakened. He told himself that he must do everything to solve the disappearance of his brother and his wife. How often had he saved opera performances by his lightning-quick reactions, how often had he kept quiet about something that would otherwise have made enemies, and how often had he had to fib or make something up to avoid controversy—that gave him courage. Still, he doubted he was up to every conceivable situation. He opened the wardrobe, saw the revolver that Beatrice's husband had given her for safekeeping, and took it out. It was a snub-nose Rossi M33, so it would easily fit in his jacket pocket. The cylinder was loaded, and for the first time Aldrian was grateful that he had completed his military service. Meanwhile the doorbell rang, he put the revolver back in the wardrobe, went downstairs, and opened the door. But it wasn't Beatrice, as he had expected, it was Commissario Galli, accompanied by a policeman. Afraid that they might accidentally discover the box under his bed or the revolver in the wardrobe, Aldrian led them into Jakob's living room and invited them to sit down while he sent Beatrice a text message that the Commissario had come to see him. He then sat down at the table.

The Commissario wanted to know all the details surrounding the incident, but Aldrian didn't tell him—as was his intention— his actual role. Galli was most interested in the struggle between him and his pursuer, and Aldrian gave minimal responses to each question. Several times he insisted he couldn't remember exactly. He also didn't mention the three-cornered hat. Meanwhile the Commissario studied the photo on the ID that Aldrian had taken from his adversary, the knife, and especially the Russian's SIM card.

"You took the SIM card out of your pursuer's phone?" the Commissario asked, amazed.

Aldrian replied that as a magician he could do lots of tricks, and took the SIM card out of the Commissario's hand, rubbed his own hands together, and showed him that it had disappeared. The Commissario didn't react. Aldrian unobtrusively shook the SIM card out of his sleeve and gave it back to the Commissario.

Then Galli said that there had been no police reports that a man on La Giudecca had been beaten or injured or treated in a hospital, and then fell silent.

Meanwhile the policeman had collected the objects as evidence.

He did all this as if he were a robot.

The Commissario then wanted to know the make and model of the Russian's smartphone, and Aldrian answered his question.

"I think it would be better," Galli suddenly said, "if you went back to Vienna. In Venice they will certainly continue to follow you. Besides, there is also the danger that they may try to retaliate."

Aldrian turned to one side and noticed Beatrice who was standing speechless in the doorway—he didn't know for how long—and following the conversation.

"Here is Signora Stefanelli," Aldrian reluctantly introduced her. Since they were all staring at her, Beatrice said that she had seen a light from the piazza and had come right in. The front door wasn't locked.

"You didn't lock the front door behind you!" Aldrian remarked with irony, glancing at the Commissario, and smiled.

Galli stood up—the policeman jumped up, too—and looked him in the eyes. "Take some time and think about what I've told you. I'll keep you informed, and I'll try to request personal protection for you. Good night."

Aldrian heard them going down the stairs, and after the front door closed, he told Beatrice what had happened, but without telling her that he had withheld most of it from the Commissario.

"I don't believe you," Beatrice said dryly. "I can understand that you might lie to the police, but not why you won't tell me the truth."

"I did tell you the truth," Aldrian answered.

When Beatrice got up and walked to the door, he became worried and asked her if she was leaving?

She stood in the foyer where she had taken off her jacket and said nothing.

"I did tell you the truth!" Aldrian repeated.

"You did? The whole truth?"

"No," Aldrian responded, "not the whole truth."

"So, what is the whole truth?"

At first he didn't answer, but then blurted out: "A pile of shit."

They both sat down in the living room and didn't speak.

"I want us to go to my place. I wanted to cook for you anyway, but I didn't get around to it," Beatrice said after a while. "And bring the gas pistol with you."

"I threw it away."

"Why?"

"Because I shot the man in the face."

She thought for a minute and then asked why he hadn't told the Commissario.

"That just makes everything more complicated. Then I'd have to explain where I got the gas pistol," Aldrian clarified, "and then they'd start to doubt me and ask even more questions."

"What else aren't you telling me, Michael . . . Don't say anything else, it's bad enough."

Aldrian was relieved, but he knew that later he would also tell Beatrice about the package, the money, and the letter.

"Then take the revolver I gave you and come along," Beatrice said quietly. She went with him up to his apartment, made sure that he took the gun, dressed warmly, and locked his apartment and the house. The whole way through the Rughetta del Ravano to the Campo San Polo they took turns looking back and checking their surroundings, as if they were on the run.

Aldrian comforted her: "I'll do it . . . You'll see . . . I'll stay with you."

"I know," she responded in a calming tone of voice.

Before they reached the Campo San Polo they split up and met again in the darkened hallway where Beatrice was already waiting for him, and she kissed him.

"When are you planning to tell me everything?" she asked him.

But Aldrian didn't want to divulge anything more before he had decided what he was going to do with the money and when he would inform Emilio. As always, he wanted to wrap things up right, that's just the way he was.

"First I've got to think if there is something important that I haven't told you. I'm still confused and haven't been able to sort things out."

"You won't escape me!" she replied, and laughed.

He understood that she didn't believe him and that her cheerfulness was all an act. But at least he had created some breathing room.

Carpaccio

The evening went by quietly and calmly. Beatrice didn't ask him any more questions, and he tried to forget thoughts of his pursuer. Everything he had experienced from the trip to the Doge's Palace and in the courtyard was eradicated, and only brief fragments of his experiences came to mind.

Beatrice cooked spaghetti with meat sauce while he considered what kind of present he could get for her. He alternated between the paperweight and the mirror, but then decided on an especially lovely paperweight, because they could only shop for the mirror together or else the question of its significance would come up. In any case he knew a store in the Rughetta del Ravano where he—as best he could remember—had seen old paperweights from Murano, though he had never been interested in them before now.

During dinner they didn't say a word about Aldrian's situation, and his silence affected Beatrice. Not until they were drinking wine did the conversation revert to Jakob and Elena, and about how the couple loved art. Beatrice mentioned the painting that the two of them thought was the most magnificent of all: Vittore Carpaccio's *Two Venetian Ladies*. It was done at the end of the 15th century, and Aldrian remembered that he had seen it in the Museo Correr. Elena, he recalled, had repeatedly made enthusiastic comments about the painting and spoken about a second one. "But it wasn't a duplicate," Beatrice explained, as she took down a thick catalog from her bookshelf and opened it. Aldrian recognized the colorful illustration of the two women and read beneath the picture on page 237. "Why 237?" flashed through his brain. He realized he was about to lose his mind. Or did it have something to do with the left side, page 236? The sum of the digits of the first page was 12, his brain told him, and eventually 3; the second page, however, was 11, thus 2. Irritated, he picked up the catalog and looked at the two bored upper-class women sitting on a terrace, the one gazing absent-mindedly into the background, a white handkerchief in her hand; the other was concentrating on what was happening at her feet. Their hairstyles and clothing were impressive. In the foreground, on the floor of the terrace, was an opened letter. It was a magnificent painting, no doubt. Carpaccio, as the Impressionists to follow, had captured an ordinary scene. A small white dog had its paws in the elder woman's one hand, while in the other she held a riding crop which a larger

dog, only its head visible, was biting. The marble floor had a pattern of crosses, squares, and diamonds that formed a geometric figure. A green parrot and a peacock were perched in front of the woman in the background, and a young boy or an older child was just climbing through the columns of the balustrade. The balustrade itself was embellished by two dove-like white birds, a pomegranate, and a vase with the stem of a plant that perhaps was in blossom but wasn't shown in the painting. While Aldrian struggled to read the script on the letter in the foreground, Beatrice encouraged him to turn the page. He read the page numbers, 238 and 239, and his brain automatically calculated the sum of the digits 1 + 3 = 4 and 1 + 4 = 5. The right-hand page depicted a cormorant hunt: 26 men—he counted them all—were standing in 7 boats. The static picture, as if frozen in time, was called *Hunting on the Lagoon*. Two men were

rowing each of the boats, and an archer was bagging the cormorants swimming in the water or perched on scattered poles or, in the background, on a long fence that runs the width of the painting. Beyond the fence are three huts with cane roofs and a dark-green ring of reeds, a flock of fifteen birds—he took the time to count them—that were flushed out, with one lone bird on the left side of the painting attempting to escape. One large concentrated cloud and several smaller ones in pale-violet and pale-blue were spread out over a pallid sky. While Aldrian's brain was still working on the numbers and calculations, Beatrice showed him the left side. There the two pictures were suddenly united. The bored women in the foreground were awaiting the return of the men who were hunting cormorants in front of their balustrade.

"Do you know how they found out that the two paintings belonged together?" Beatrice asked.

Aldrian turned the page to the picture of the two ladies and then back to *Hunting in the Lagoon,* and to his surprise discovered the decisive evidence. The stem of the plant in the vase on the balustrade of the terrace picture is continued in the foreground of the hunting picture and displays three lily blossoms that people had previously considered to be wild plants on the shore. For Aldrian it was fantastic and yet grotesque, especially since *Two Venetian Ladies* was hanging in the Museo Correr in Venice and *Hunting in the Lagoon* was in the J. Paul Getty Museum in Los Angeles. Beatrice went on, saying they used recurve bows in the hunt for ducks and cormorants, also arrows with ball arrowheads of dried clay instead of an iron tip so they didn't damage the birds' plumage or meat. But, Aldrian wanted to know, how the painting came to be separated into two distinct parts. "We still don't have an explanation for that," Beatrice said. "In any event, it's obvious that the images belong together. The two were either decoration for a cupboard door or for a window shutter, because the wood grain is identical. The grain of the wood," she continued, "is like a dactyloscopic finger print. No two are identical. Actually, there must have been a second cupboard door or a second window shutter,

at least that's what the grooves and hinges on the panel with *Hunting on the Lagoon* indicate. Elena always felt that the panel must have been a window shutter," Beatrice said, "and would have been viewed from inside the room, and with the shutters closed—a likeness of the actual view of the terrace and the lagoon, as if the shutter weren't even closed, which must have produced a delightful effect."

At that moment Aldrian recollected what Commissario Galli had said to him on the telephone, specifically, that Jakob and Elena had purchased a house on the island of Lesbos . . . near the Gulf of Skala Kallonis and the village of the same name. "It is supposed to be a bird sanctuary," he could hear the Commissario's voice saying. The whole time they were engrossed in the paintings, the images had been like clues for him. He interrupted Beatrice and recounted all the details of his conversation with Galli. She was taken aback that the couple had property on Lesbos, apparently that had been a secret . . . They had frequently mentioned that they were on the lookout for their *paradiso* for the time when they were old. And now Aldrian remembered that as well. The two of them silently looked at the pictures until Beatrice said the two women could be the sisters, Elena and Margherita, and the boy on the terrace, Elena's and Jakob's son, Emilio. "It's an apparent idyll," she went on, "and the other world, the brutal one, is far far away. If you're looking for paradise, hunting is something evil, killing animals . . . The hunters are the colonialists of Nature that retreat in stages. The only riddle is the letter on the terrace . . . It gets even more mysterious when you look at the small painting of the back of the door or the window shutter." Aldrian now saw that it showed a painted doorframe supporting a "letter holder," in other words, a taut line bearing six letters. The whole thing was so wonderfully arranged that it gave the impression of being almost three-dimensional. Beatrice explained that Carpaccio's everyday scene was not only the first in the history of Italian painting, but his picture of the letters on the back of *Hunting in the Lagoon* was the first optical illusion, what artists call *trompe l'oeil*. Aldrian's thoughts returned to the letter lying on the depicted terrace with the two women, and since the younger one, as mentioned earlier, was

holding a white handkerchief in her hand, he now believed that the letter holder on the back had something to do with it. "Possibly the message lying on the terrace is a farewell letter from her lover, and the others on the line are his love letters," Aldrian said. "Or her lover told her the hunt would take longer because they would have to stay overnight in the small huts in the background . . . Or that he was going to leave for home when the hunt was over."

Other explanations immediately formed in Aldrian's mind, as Beatrice continued: "But that's not all. The letter holder Carpaccio painted is an enlarged copy from the painting *Saint Jerome in his Study* by Niccolò Antonio Colantonio that hangs in the Museo di Capodimonte in Naples. It portrays the patron saint of all translators in his study. Jerome had translated Cicero and Plato. Sitting on a chair, the scholar is holding the paw of a lion and using a quill to remove a thorn from the pad of its left front paw." In the meantime she had gotten out another book, opened it, and placed it before Aldrian. "You can see that there are no windows in his study," she resumed, "on the back wall is a wooden bookshelf with folios and rolls of paper . . . the archives of the translator. Jerome didn't want to be distracted by external reality, and the lion was supposed to protect him from it. Of course the saint had spent many years in the desert, and the lion is also a reference to that, since from that point on he was his savior's constant companion. Usually things end the other way around: the lion is relieved of the thorn and then eats his helper."

Aldrian wanted to go back and figure out the story of Jakob and Elena in the oil painting, but Beatrice interrupted him: "That won't help us get any farther," she said. "All these details are just confusing, like a dream. Maybe they themselves didn't even know how much their own fate was tied to this picture."

But many things went through Aldrian's mind that evening, and the wine had slowly intoxicated him so that he fell asleep in her living room.

Forged Realities

He awoke the next morning, alone on the couch in Beatrice's living room. Beside him lay an 8½ x 11-inch sheet of paper with her signature. He picked it up and read: "I know so much about Carpaccio's painting because Jakob and Elena took me to the exhibit 'The Renaissance in Venice and Painting in the North.' That was in 1999 or 2000. Elena in particular knew every detail about the painting, and Jakob, who had heard about it from her beforehand, had made references to it later."

As he was reading, Aldrian recollected a remark Jakob had made about one of Carpaccio's oil paintings in a "to be continued" technique that he compared with a revealed secret, and Aldrian thought of his pursuer, the box with the money, and Commissario Galli. He definitely had to find out what their house in the bay of Skala Kallonis looked like, the one Jakob and Elena had purchased and kept a secret.

"Don't think about it too much," he read, "it's a picture that spoke to them in its totality. I mean, the various levels of reality—the terrace that seems isolated and the bay, the hunters and the cormorants, and last but not least, the mysterious letters, more specifically, the picture of Jerome the translator with the lion and the bookshelves in the background that has a near copy of the letter holder by a different painter. Our arts editor had a completely different interpretation; according to him, the hunt beyond the terrace is only a thought in the women's minds while they are waiting for their men who are off hunting and had written them the letters. By the way, in Jakob and Elena's library you'll find a *History of Venetian Painting* with a thorough explanation. It's 6:30 a.m. and I've got to travel. I'll be back from Padua this afternoon. Please stay in the apartment till then: I've got books, a CD player, complete operas, and a TV. There is mineral water, beer, wine, butter, cheese, and ham in the refrigerator, and a sandwich from yesterday in the breadbox. Don't get your hopes up: You'll never get a 'Dear John' letter from me! I love you, Beatrice."

Aldrian straightened up and took a deep breath. No, now he did want to buy that paperweight, pay his promised visit to Diego Sarcia, check to make sure everything was in order in Jakob's and Elena's house, and—since the sun was shining, as he realized when he looked out the window—go see the Ca' d'Oro.

He dialed Commissario Galli's number. He answered abruptly and, without even saying hello, began to speak: "I was just going to call you," Aldrian heard him say. "Yesterday the police went to the house of your brother and his wife in Lesbos to see if it was occupied. As far as we can tell, they found nothing unusual. But last night the structure burned to the ground. There was an explosion that you could hear everywhere in Skala Kallonis, and following more explosions, everything was in flames. Where are you at the moment?"

"At home," Aldrian lied. "Is there a picture of their house in Greece?"

"Yes, we got one from the real estate agent who sold it. It was a large old building with a terrace directly looking out over the sea."

Aldrian considered whether he should ask the Commissario for a copy of the photo.

"One more thing—about your pursuer," the Commissario continued. "To date, no one with a similar injury or with that name from the ID has been taken to any hospital. And no death has been reported."

"That makes me feel better, thanks," Aldrian said. "Incidentally, could you send the photo of the house to my smartphone?"

Galli replied with a succinct "Yes." He again recommended that

Aldrian go back to Vienna, and, without waiting for a response, hung up.

Aldrian gazed out the window, slipped into his shoes, put on his windbreaker, and hurried down the stairs. From the front door he checked the piazza once more for any suspicious activity and then set out for his apartment as inconspicuously as possible. Most of the stores were still closed. And the display window of Diego Sarcia's mask shop wasn't lit either, just like the store that actually did sell paperweights. Aldrian peered in and found a large paper-weight in the millefiori technique. He pulled up his collar, glanced around, and turned off before the Fabbriche Vecchie, kept on through the Fabbriche Nuove arcade where he could more easily spot a tail, and on to the Campo della Pescaria, blended in with the crowd at the vegetable and fruit stands and smelled the fragrance of fruits and flowers. This early in the morning the shoppers were mostly elderly folks who couldn't sleep. On the Grand Canal he saw that a traghetto was just leaving, a wide gondola-type ferry where the passengers mostly had to stand while a man with an oar propelled the black boat along. He wandered among the market booths, not intending to buy anything, just wanting to enjoy the beauty of the fruits and vegetables. Because inside, in his brother's house with the now-lowered shutters at the Jurassic Park store, the cardboard box with the money and the many enigmas, another nightmarishly frightening world existed, he thought, that was just as real as the death market of plants and animals where he was now standing. He went on over to the fish market, as he always did, because even in the living creatures that were killed by human hands he could see the beauty of a hidden world with hidden destinies. Merchants were gutting octopi and calamari on long tables, and it was, as always, a grisly sight. Once again he saw the black liquid leak out, spatter the men's rubber gloves and the white bodies of the cephalopods, and leave behind marks on the countertops with the round hole where the scraps disappeared. At that point they took a small hose and washed off the animal that had now become food for the table, their rubber gloves, and the countertops, and subsequently the next marine creature was similarly transformed into food. He stood at the table for a long time and didn't really know why.

After he had determined that the small revolver was in his jacket pocket and he had looked around several times, he unlocked the front door and, once inside, immediately locked it again. He also locked the door to his apartment after he entered, and only then did he pull out the box with the money . . . He could dispense with it all and give the entire amount to Emilio, he reflected. It occurred to him that the house and his apartment could also be destroyed by fire, and his helplessness made him furious. He wanted to smash or destroy something, but at the same time he knew it was senseless. But if it was senseless, then he could also appropriate the senselessness for himself. The thought assuaged him. He would accept the senselessness, the emptiness that concealed the masterminds. He didn't have to act logically. In retrospect he was quite satisfied that he had shot his pursuer three times in the face with the gas pistol . . .

He showered, put on fresh clothes, found the day-old sandwich, spread butter and honey on a couple of slices of bread, made tea, and stuffed himself. The he took ten 100-euro bills from the box and put them in his pocket. He would stick it out here until he knew what had happened to his brother, he told himself. First he would find the *History of Venetian Painting* in Jakob and Elena's library and read what there was about Carpaccio's painting. When the telephone rang, he saw the name "Beatrice" on the display.

"Are you at my place?" she asked

"Yes," he lied. "I'm fine . . . I have to get something in the Rughetta, and then I promised to visit Diego Sarcia."

"I'm worried about you."

"We can move into a hotel."

"That doesn't change anything."

He didn't respond.

"I'll be back soon. Wait for me. Then we can deal with everything together."

"Fine."

"Promise me?"

"I love you," Aldrian replied, because he didn't want to lie to her.

He pocketed his phone and, preoccupied, went down to Jakob and Elena's apartment, unlocked the door, and searched the library for the book by its author Günter Brucher. It was in three volumes, and on the last pages of the second volume he stumbled on the painting by Carpaccio and a thorough description. The text was clear and insightful, revealing the meaning of every detail of the painting. The two doves were a sign for fidelity in marriage, he read, the white handkerchief in the younger woman's hand signified, like the lily, chastity, and the boy squeezing between the pillars of the balustrade on the terrace was possibly bringing yet another letter. Aldrian understood that every object in the picture had significance, every pose of the depicted people and animals, every item, no matter how seemingly insignificant. Everything in the explanation was coherent and yet only a sum total of speculations. But what he took from it for his own situation was that each and every thing could be important. He put the volume back on the shelf and turned off the heat in Jakob and Elena's apartment, his only thought being to save money. He decided he would buy the paperweight first and then go see Diego. Then, if he felt like it, he could go to the Ostaria Dai Zemei and drink a spritz or an ombra with Ettore and Massimo, and return to his apartment later. They probably wouldn't try to burn the house down during daylight . . . Besides, he couldn't go back to Beatrice's apartment—he didn't have a key. Or he might go tour the Ca' d'Oro. He had barely taken two steps when he stopped and looked around. There was more activity in the Rughetta now than in the morning, and the first masks were starting to appear. There were just a couple of days till Sunday, the culmination of Carnival activities in Venice. Then life would slowly return to normal, Aldrian thought.

Since the crowds continued to grow the further up the Rughetta he went, he hurried the last few yards before he entered his friend's shop.

Diego, as usual, was already seated at his table at the back of the store. Aldrian weaved carefully through the masks and other furnishings to get to the stool beside the table.

Diego, in a blue apron, had his glasses on and was concentrating on painting a fantasy mask.

"Speak," he welcomed Aldrian, distracted.

To his surprise, Aldrian wondered if he could trust Diego and then reluctantly told him basically what had happened. He just didn't mention the package with the money. Diego stopped working, and Aldrian could tell from his facial expression that he was stunned.

"You can't go back to Jakob's house, do you hear me? You have to leave right now. Get far far away from here. And wherever you end up, be quiet, if you don't want to be silenced for good!"

"No."

"No?"

"I have to know what's happened to my brother and his wife. I can't rest till I do."

"You idiot!"

"You're an idiot yourself!"

"Sorry."

After a pause, Diego got up and pulled open the desk drawer.

"Then you've got to have a gun!"

"No."

"What do you want from me?"

"I want to ask you something."

Diego looked at him sadly and suspiciously, and didn't say a word.

"If you were in my shoes, what would you do?"

Diego thought about his answer, scratched his head, coughed, turned his back on Aldrian, and then said: "There's lots of talk about this in our district, lots of speculation, but everybody agrees that you're in big trouble. I understand you, but I still think what you're doing is wrong. It's senseless."

There was that word again, and Diego had put into words what he had been thinking the whole time.

"Then I'll do something that doesn't make sense."

"Fine . . . Put on a mask when you leave the house. Here, take this plain white one."

It had a different look than the one Aldrian had bought at the Rialto Bridge on his arrival.

"And take another one, too, or else it won't take them long to figure out it's you," Diego continued. "You've got to be inconspicuous and maybe even silly. You can also take this Pierrot mask." Aldrian felt that Diego was now worried about him—much like his brother Jakob. And like an older brother, he wouldn't take any money.

"Have you got my telephone number?"

"No. But I'd really like to see your workshop in the other store."

"Sunday . . . around 8 a.m. . . . ." He wrote down his telephone number, and Aldrian copied it into his smartphone.

"You can call me anytime, and I'll put you up at my place in Mestre when you finally get smart and realize you're better off there," Diego went on.

At his urging, Aldrian tried on the white mask. He had barely stepped outside when he felt elated at the thought of being anonymous. And he immediately gave in to the idea of buying the paperweight while wearing the mask. It made him feel like a magician on stage. And Diego was right—it had to be the most common, the most inconspicuous mask. He had a sudden desire to forget the whole thing and go back to performing as a magician instead of having to deal with the box and the 100-euro notes. The chain of associations that ran through his head had helped him carry out his profession as souffleur with great precision during operatic rehearsals and performances. But he now felt it was a liability. He would have liked to turn it off, like the light before he fell asleep.

The store for Murano glass in the Rughetta was, as he now read on a sign behind the glass door, closed due to the manager's illness, and in his current state of mind he thought of the Archivio di Stato di Venezia, Dr. Dr. Galotti, and the plague documents with their sinister messages.

In the meantime he had to fight the tourist crunch heading toward St. Mark's Square, tons of people also wearing masks who waved to him from time to time. He paid no attention to them. It was better if he avoided the crowd and pushed on ahead, he told himself. He first came to the Frari Church and then to the Scuola Grande di San Rocco with its series of Biblical pictures by the Venetian painter Tintoretto. He immediately disregarded the thought of going inside, because just before he got to the church, he unexpectedly found an antique store that had paperweights. Without taking off his mask he pushed open the door. When he asked about old paperweights, the bejeweled woman who owned the store was suspicious—probably because of his mask—put a small one on the countertop, and as soon as he asked to see something else, she picked up the first one, put it back in the display case, and then looked for a new one. This procedure was repeated several times until, finally, the antique dealer came out of the backroom and asked: "Would you like to see something more expensive?"

Aldrian nodded, and the cordial man came back with a colorful old paperweight in millefiori technique. It looked fantastic. The symmetry of the individual small colorful glass entities in the paperweight's interior and its blue, yellow, green, and white elements simply astonished Aldrian. He couldn't recall having ever seen a more beautiful item, and the price of 980 euros didn't dissuade him. He paid with his 100-euro bills, put the change and his carefully wrapped purchase in the pocket of his windbreaker, and allowed the antique dealer to open the door for him. He automatically headed in the direction of San Pantalon, because he didn't want to run into his sister-in-law or her husband. At one of the mobile market stands for souvenir apparel along the way he bought a black baseball cap with the St. Mark's lion, put it on, and arrived at the church just as it was opening. Altar boys in red-and-white attire escorted the priest in a chasuble amid a small group of people, and when they got outside, the priest stopped and exchanged warm words with the faithful. Aldrian took off his cap and mask and entered the church. He didn't really know what he was doing. He sat down on an empty pew in the nave and, since he was very tired, stretched out his legs and gazed up at the ceiling fresco above his head. Once again, it immediately captured his attention, and when he closed his eyes, he could feel himself floating up and then begining to fall . . .

He finally opened his eyes again. It was quiet and ice cold, and the heaven or hell on the ceiling was still waiting to swallow him up. He got up, established that he was alone, and a glance at his watch— it was 3 in the afternoon—confirmed that he had slept for almost four hours and accidentally must have been locked in the church because they closed it over the lunch hour. He reached for the phone in his pants pocket, silenced it, and decided to do nothing until the portal was opened. Although it was ice cold, he had to laugh at himself. He imagined he was Noah, waiting in his ark for the dove to return with a fresh olive branch in its beak and to announce the end of the Flood. He unconsciously reached for his jacket lapel and felt for the gold pin. Then he went back to the pew and looked up above him. He didn't dare toss in a coin and turn the ceiling into heaven. He felt more like a drop of water that had gotten in the undertow of a drainpipe and was being swept along . . .

When the church was finally open, he remained seated, though he was terribly cold. In the meantime he had lain down on the pew again. He found it strange that the ceiling fresco wouldn't release its hold on him, but he also enjoyed the experience.

He finally put a coin in the apparatus and gazed up at the illuminated heaven.

It was warmer outside. Still freezing, he put the mask and the cap back on and strolled across the piazza. Gazing in the display window of a gourmet food store, he was surprised that he wasn't hungry. From one minute to the next he decided to visit Carlo Fibonacci in his frame and poster shop and ask him about the world's largest beetle that Jakob had painted. Nevertheless he took a circuitous route so he could get warm when he finally arrived at the shop. Without taking off his mask, he went in. The door wasn't locked and the lights were on, but there was no one in the "junk shop," as he secretly called the place. Jakob's beetle picture was hanging in its frame on the wall behind the sales counter. He glanced around, fumbled under the counter and, since there was a key in the small door, opened the little lock. He pulled out two drawers containing pictures that Jakob had painted. He recognized them immediately since he owned several himself, and there were lots more in Jakob's apartment. But not all of them had Jakob's signature. There were others, too, on old paper, and signed with other names. "Maria Sibylla Merian," he read, and "John James Audubon," along with others that he could only skim in his haste. In the second drawer he found two watercolors that portrayed Venice in the style of J.W. Turner, and a marvelously painted small bird. He took the two sheets and the picture of the robin, put them in the nylon bag along with the Pierrot mask that Diego Sarcia had also given him, and pulled out the drawer holding small change, a sharp paperknife, and a smudged frayed notebook. When he opened the notebook, he saw it contained names and telephone numbers. Instinctively he put it in his pocket and then heard a sound. In his magic act he had always been able to make himself disappear, but this time he didn't have the necessary props. So he silently crouched down behind the sales counter. At that moment the shop door was pushed open and he heard Carlo Fibonacci's voice.

"No," he was saying calmly, "I don't have any more pictures."

"I don't believe you," someone forcefully interrupted him.

Fibonacci remained calm.

"Are you questioning my integrity? Eh?"

The other man didn't speak.

"Are you trying to make me out a liar?" Fibonacci went on, now upset.

Someone turned out the lights. He heard a blow, a moan, and the scuffling sound of a body hitting the floor.

Since Aldrian was afraid that they might find him if they went looking for the pictures, he leaped up and pulled the revolver out of his jacket pocket. Immediately the lights came back on and he now could see an unknown younger man with black hair, parted and slicked down with pomade. He was wearing a black coat, a silver-grey necktie with a white shirt, holding brass knuckles in his hand.

"Who are you?" Aldrian shouted at the man. "What are you doing here?"

"Police! Put down your gun and put your hands up," the young man answered callously.

"Show me your ID!" Aldrian barked, and with that the young man took off running. Aldrian leaped over Fibonacci's body, flipped the light switch behind the front door and looked out at the street from the now-darkened shop. Since the piazza was crowded with many pedestrians, he couldn't see where the young man had gone. He was cautiously about to leave the store when he heard a loud moaning. He turned around and instantly realized that Fibonacci was sitting up and starting to call for help.

He instantly headed off in the direction of San Pantalon. Walking at a normal pace, he turned down toward the Fondamenta del Forrer that ran along the Rio della Frescada. Since there were only a few people here, he took off the cap and the mask, and—after first putting the three pictures under his sport coat and slipping on the Pierrot mask—he dropped the other things and the nylon bag into the canal. His dexterity came in handy, because he didn't want to damage the watercolors or be seen putting on the Pierrot mask. He took a deep breath and pondered his next move. He thought it might be best if he called Beatrice. He activated his smartphone and saw that she had already called him five times.

"Where are you?"

She scolded him that in another fifteen minutes she would have called the police. Then she broke off and it was quiet.

I'm on my way to your place, everything's fine," he said, and hung up. As he set off for the Frari Church, thereby avoiding the Scuola Grande di San Rocco and the shop where he had purchased the paperweight, Beatrice called again and asked him to keep talking to her while he was on his way. But a call from Commissario Galli interrupted them and he had to hang up on her.

"Can you talk?" he asked Aldrian without waiting for an answer. "We found the body of your pursuer and identified him, thanks to the ID you provided. However, the name doesn't match. His real name is Vladimir Ivanov, a Russian that we've been after for some time for various crimes. The SIM card you gave us was no help, because Ivanov had all calls transmitted through a number in the Ukraine that no longer exists. Besides, they were only exchanging codes. You were the last person to have seen him alive, and he had all the wounds you specified except for two shots in the face from a gas pistol and a blow to the head from the butt of a pistol that knocked him unconscious. That could have possibly stunned him before they threw him into the sea. In any event he was found at the Campo Nani e Barbaro on La Giudecca island . . . Are you still on the line?"

"Yes. I'm near Campo San Polo."

"What are you doing there?"

"I went out to get some fresh air." He knew he couldn't mention either the shop at the Scuola Grande di San Rocco or San Pantalon or Carlo Fibonacci, but also his stop at Diego Sarcia's mask store. He was just coming to the Campo San Polo when he agreed to meet Commissario Galli in half an hour, and then he hung up. He instantly called Beatrice, but didn't let her get in a single word. "They found the man who followed me. He's dead," he said. "The Commissario is on his way to my place. I've got to hurry." He took off the Pierrot mask, tossed it in a trashcan, and hurried home. He ran the last stretch to the fish market. He hastily opened the door, put the revolver in the wardrobe, and hid the paperweight he had just bought, along with the three watercolors from Fibonacci's frame store in another compartment. But he kept Fibonacci's phone book in his breast pocket. He then realized he still had the white mask that he bought at the Rialto Bridge upon his arrival. To avoid further complications, he stuck it behind some groceries in the kitchen. He had just disposed of the mask, removed all traces, and opened the window when Beatrice rang the doorbell.

She hugged him and whispered in his ear that he was an asshole and kept everything a secret. Then she kissed him, and he realized how much he loved her.

"Where were you?" she asked. But before he could respond, Commissario Galli and a policeman were at the door.

Jakob's apartment wasn't heated anymore, so it was hardly possible to have their conversation there. So Aldrian invited the two of them and Beatrice into his small kitchen where they all sat down at the dinner table.

"I don't want to beat around the bush. You are a suspect in the murder of Vladimir Ivanov."

"It wasn't me, I swear."

"Then who could it have been? Give me something to go on."

"I've told you everything."

"That's not enough."

"There's nothing more to say, unless I make something up."

"And?"

Aldrian knew that the Commissario didn't have much on him, so he wasn't afraid. The whole thing was more like a game of cards where each one only knew his own hand. No one spoke, neither the police nor Beatrice.

"I can take you down to headquarters, if you're not willing to cooperate with us."

Aldrian said nothing.

"You could have been followed by Ivanov and then blackmailed by him."

"I would have told you if that had been the case. And I can't imagine what he would have used to blackmail me."

"I don't believe you."

"Stop. That's ridiculous. You can't even answer any of my questions: Where is my brother? Where is Elena? Why have they both disappeared? Are they still alive? You expect me to solve your riddles by blaming me for a murder, coercing me to invent some story that you would then discover was a lie so you could convict me . . . Take me down to headquarters if you think it's necessary, but you won't get any answers to your questions there either."

Aldrian knew how to unsettle people, that's what he had done when necessary for many years at the Vienna State Opera and because he enjoyed doing so. Even though he knew that the cardboard box with the banknotes and the revolver were here in his apartment, he wasn't afraid. The senselessness that encompassed everything around him freed him from his doubts and fears as soon as he became part and parcel of them.

"Where did you hide the gas pistol?"

"I don't own a gas pistol."

"But you could have had one."

"Oh, sure. When the man started to follow me, I bought in while I was fleeing so I could kill him. But where, please tell me, could I have done that? Where is there a gun store?"

"You can always find a gun. A gas pistol, easily. Or your brother could have had one."

"If my brother even owned one, he could have taken it along when he left the house."

"I know there's something you're not telling me, even though you must know you're in danger!"

"Why would I do that?"

"I don't know. Maybe you've got something going with your brother? In any event, the business must be profitable. Think about his house in Greece. And maybe you killed the Russian for him—"

At that point Beatrice interrupted the Commissario.

"You don't know what you're talking about," she said.

"No?—Apparently you, as a journalist, have better information than I do, Signora Stefanelli," Galli responded with scorn. "Who knows? Maybe you yourself were a witness when Vladimir Ivanov was fatally wounded on La Giudecca?"

"You know it's just as likely that the dead man was killed by his own people, because Michael had taken his ID."

"Very clever, I must admit! But what if Jakob Aldrian himself is a member of the organization? And his brother, too?" The Commissario no longer attempted to hide his disdain.

"And Ivanov? Did he also belong to an organization?"

"And what if he didn't?" Galli made a silly face.

"I can see you only have hunches."

Galli was silent.

"Give me your full address on the Campo San Polo so we can put your house under surveillance," he then said brusquely.

"I think that's a bad idea as long as Michael's pursuers don't know that he's staying at my place."

"Maybe they already know."

"And if they don't?"

"This isn't the first time we've staked out a house and haven't been detected."

She wrote her address on a piece of paper and, together with Aldrian, watched the Commissario and the policeman until they had disappeared in the fish market.

When Beatrice went into the bathroom, Aldrian took the newly acquired paperweight out of the wardrobe, took the wrapping paper off and tossed it into the box under his bed, and put the paperweight, the revolver, and the brain slice in his pocket.

Fifteen minutes later they were hurrying to the Campo San Polo, and after eating lasagna and drinking wine, they went to bed. They embraced passionately several times, Beatrice plying him with questions the whole time. But Aldrian wouldn't admit anything. He disputed everything she surmised and didn't reveal any of his secrets.

Early the next morning he hid the brain slice and the new paperweight behind the collection of paperweights on Beatrice's bookshelf and put the revolver back in the desk drawer. He didn't want to give her the paperweight just yet. It would just make him look vulnerable, he told himself.

He checked to make sure that Beatrice was still asleep.

His biggest headache was the money in the cardboard box. He had been on the verge of telling Commissario Galli about it, but hadn't had the courage. Then he thought about the two watercolors in the style of William Turner that were in his wardrobe. He might be able to identify one of them. He started to search Beatrice's library for an art book when he discovered a framed picture above the sitting area, one he hadn't noticed before. He noticed it was the same size as one of his sheets, but apparently painted on a different aged paper, and he read on the frame: "For Beatrice, from Jakob." He quickly found an edition of William Turner's watercolors of Venice. A plain slip of paper was placed in the book as a bookmark.

He opened it and saw the same picture that was hanging above the sitting area and also was in his wardrobe. Even the format—9.6 by 12.2 inches, as he measured with a ruler—was the same as that mentioned in the art book. It bore the title *S. Giorgio Maggiore and the Zitelle from the Giudecca* and was a sketch of the housing block, the church with its bell tower, and a sailboat. Because the watercolors had been applied sparingly—"a touch of rose and orange," according to the book—it created the impression that there was a dense bright fog. Jakob had reproduced it so accurately that you couldn't tell it from the original. Coincidentally it depicted the spot near where he had overpowered his pursuer with the gas pistol. There were other volumes about the English painter, including a small slim edition from 1988 with the title *Turner at Farnley—the Book of Birds*. He learned from the copyright page that it was a catalog for an exhibition at the Clore Gallery in London and showed precisely the robin that he had in his wardrobe at home. Since Elena was a restorer and knew everything about various types of papers and colors—and in addition was always traveling to Paris and London—he suddenly suspected that Jakob and Elena had forged these pictures together. He also noticed that the bird picture he took from Fibonacci's frame shop had been painted on aged paper. In the slender volume he had in his hands, he read about the twenty birds Turner had created in Farnley Hall for the son of the owner, his friend Sir Walter Fawkes. Young Hawkey had wanted a comprehensive book, but, Aldrian learned, after having painted pheasants, partridges, and grouses, Turned quit. As he put the books back on the shelf, he remembered there had been other illustrations of birds and flowers in the drawer behind the sales counter in Fibonacci's shop—presumably, as he suspected, by Maria Sibylla Merian and the American ornithologist John James Audubon. Jakob told him that Audubon had first killed the birds with fine birdshot or asphyxiated them with fumes, and then mounted them on a wire framework. One of his reports stated that he frequently had to kill more than a hundred birds a day. Aldrian was familiar with the illustrations in *The Birds of America* that Jakob owned, and he knew that his brother could copy them.

But that he had become a forger—Aldrian was now more and more convinced—had presumably become possible only because of Elena. Was that why the two of them had disappeared? And was that why someone had burned down their property in Greece? But why had they followed and attacked him? And why did they give him that huge amount of money to leave Venice? He decided to say nothing and to mull the whole thing over, because he was now certain that he was close to solving the puzzle. And what now? It occurred to him that he still had an appointment with Director Zorzi in the Biblioteca Marciana.

It was obvious that sooner or later he would have to fill in Commissario Galli . . . Galli would turn his apartment upside down, he reflected, so he would have to hide the money somewhere else . . . Maybe in Jakob's store, since the police had already searched it? And if they did find it, they couldn't connect it to him. Whatever he did, it was necessary to swap the box for one of Jakob's suitcases. Who knew anything about his brother's luggage and could prove that one was missing? All that and more now went through his mind.

Since Beatrice was still sleeping, he quietly got dressed and took the key to lock the door. As he stepped out onto the piazza, he briefly glanced around. No one seemed to be watching him. He first hurried down the Rughetta del Ravano to the fish market. Then he went up to his apartment, got the three pictures out of the wardrobe, and made sure they were done on aged paper and perhaps had even been painted with antiquated colors. He now had a strong urge to just get rid of the package, the money, and the pictures. After he had taken the book about chiromancy by Johannes Hartlieb with its illustrations of hands and put it in the wardrobe—since he didn't want to part with it, because of his brother's dedication—he carried the package down to Elena's and Jakob's apartment, set it down in the living room, and went to look for their luggage. As anticipated, he found it in the wardrobe with their clothes and laundry. At that moment he thought he understood why the strangers who attacked him had searched the apartment before or after his arrival. They were probably looking for more of Jakob's paintings, he told himself. Of course they hadn't touched the framed pictures hanging on the walls ... Perhaps because they didn't want the missing pictures to be a clue to the forged ones ... He glanced over at the reproduction of Adalbert Stifter's *View of the Beatrixgasse in Vienna*, still in its wrapping; it now seemed absurd that he had wanted to give it to Jakob upon his arrival and had even left it in his brother's living room. He thought long and hard as he took out a travel bag, stuck the money inside, took the address label off the package and put it in his pocket. As he hid the three watercolors in a suitcase, it occurred to him that his nephew Emilio would be back sometime. The last thing Aldrian wanted to do was put the young man in danger ... So he took the key from the bulletin board, emptied the money from the travel bag into the suitcase with the pictures, and put it in a backroom in the store in an old storage cabinet full of animal skulls, which meant he first had to make room for the suitcase. Then he went back up to his apartment, dropped the address label from the package into a trash bag, picked up a pair of scissors, and went back down to his brother's apartment. He cut up the wrapping with the scissors, tore up the letter, and put the shreds in the trash bag that he then, as was customary in Venice, put out on the street after he had checked to make sure no one was watching him. The only other thing that could incriminate him now, he thought, was the notebook with the telephone numbers that he had taken from Fibonacci's frame store. All of a sudden he also thought he knew why he had been followed, attacked, and beaten up: presumably someone had seen him when he first arrived, carrying the reproduction of the Adalbert Stifter painting into the house, and consequently assumed he must be Elena and his brother's accomplice. But the large amount of money in the package—how did that fit in?

For several minutes he looked through Fibonacci's pocket telephone book. The names and numbers were written in pencil, red marker, blue and black ballpoint ink. He estimated there were roughly a hundred entries. Out of curiosity, he looked first to see if Dr. Dr. Galotti and the diver Sergio Celi were listed, but he didn't find their names. Then he looked up Jakob and Elena Aldrian and, to his surprise, discovered both their names, as well as Margherita's. On the other hand, neither Beatrice nor the souffleur Lorenzo Verra were there. But then he came upon yet another surprise: he found a "Sergio" and a "Vladimir," which made him immediately think of Sergio Celi, the diver, and Vladimir Ivanov, his dead pursuer . . . There was also a "Diego," but the telephone number wasn't the same as that of Diego Sarcia, the mask-maker, that Aldrian had saved in his smartphone. He knew he'd go crazy if he didn't try to talk with Carlo Fibonacci. Nevertheless the telephone book was valuable because other people's names would turn up and he'd have their phone numbers, he told himself. But searching for names among these pages had upset him more than he cared to admit. Every person he met could have had something to do with the disappearance of his brother and his sister-in-law—with the exception of Beatrice and perhaps the souffleur at the Teatro La Fenice.

He put the little telephone book in his breast pocket, gazed out the window, and thought he saw a figure in the shadow of the fish hall, someone observing the house. He decided he'd have to be careful and check if he was being followed again, then locked his apartment door and that of his brother, and in his hurry almost stumbled down the stairs. Once outside, he cautiously locked the front door. On his way to the fish hall, he saw someone run off and tried to follow him. In spite of the crowd he couldn't let the man outrun him, but eventually lost sight of him when the man disappeared beneath the arcade at the Fabbriche Nuove. Aldrian stopped, out of breath, and waited until he got enough air in his lungs. It was either one of Commissario Galli's men on surveillance duty or another pursuer . . . The thought didn't scare him as much as made him angry. He kept looking around, clenched his fists and checked the street, but he didn't see anyone among the tourists who looked suspicious. The bulk of the pedestrians were approaching from the opposite direction, which made it easier for him to check. He didn't regret that he had left the revolver at home, possibly because it would have made everything even more senseless than it already was.

Diego Sarcia was sitting behind his small table, as always.

Aldrian noticed he was in a bad mood, because the man didn't budge and only mumbled a brief greeting.

"Something wrong?"

"No, why?" Diego asked in return.

"Because you're so quiet."

"That's because of you. Why don't you just go back to Vienna? You can come back when everything's over."

"What's supposed to be over?"

"I'm not going to respond to that."

"Tell me what you know, Diego. This whole time I've got a feeling there's something you're not telling me."

Diego raised his head and looked him in the eye.

"You sound like my wife."

Aldrian took it to be a joke, but also an attempt to change the topic.

"Do you know Carlo Fibonacci?"

"Sure . . . Who doesn't? He's got a small shop on the Campo San Tomà. If you want a picture framed, you go to him."

"And what else?"

"What do you mean?"

"Are you in touch with him?"

"Sure . . . He had me build a puppet theater for his grandkids. Why?"

"Because he's a friend of Jakob and Elena."

Diego was silent and wouldn't look at him.

"Are you coming to my mask workshop on Sunday? You've been wanting to see it for a long time now," he then asked.

"Yes. Sunday."

Several people entered the store, laughing and talking non-stop, and as Aldrian was leaving, he took advantage of the opportunity to pocket an eye mask that was lying on a counter as a decoration. Diego had seemed unapproachable . . . or, he wondered, was that just his imagination?

The Campo San Polo was now busy, children in masks were running around, their mothers or fathers were trying to make them happy or were lost in thought or were phoning someone or were talking with each other. He unlocked the front door as quietly as he could, and, after locking the door from the inside, left the key in the lock, and was relieved to see that Beatrice was still asleep. He was even able to undress and slip back in bed without disturbing her. He closed his eyes and went over what he had done in the meantime. He must have fallen asleep because, when he woke up, Beatrice was in the kitchen. She was fixing spaghetti with clams, tossing the clams that wouldn't open into the garbage can. While he was setting the table, he asked her what she was going to do that day.

She wasn't aware that he had left the house earlier that morning.

Beatrice thought he should continue researching for his guidebook, but come home promptly that evening . . . either to her place or to his apartment.

She went into her room and came back with two keys, one for the front door, the other to her apartment. She put them down in front of Aldrian without explanation and dished up his spaghetti.

"Aren't you going to eat?" Aldrian asked, leaning back in his chair.

"No appetite." She rinsed her hands in the sink and continued: "Don't you understand that you're insulting me?"

"I don't know any more what's true and who I am," Aldrian answered.

"Why won't you talk to me about it?"

"Because I don't understand anything. I don't even understand myself."

"You don't want to talk to me about it?"

"That's right."

"Why not?"

He didn't speak. It was the senselessness of his actions that he wanted to explain to her. It was the only possibility of comprehending the matter.

"When you do something that has no meaning—"

"Then you should stop," she interrupted.

"No, because maybe then you can understand what's behind the senselessness."

"Behind senselessness is senselessness, and behind that more senselessness. You'll see."

"How do you know that?"

"Because perhaps I deal with everyday reality and you are more preoccupied with fantasy."

"You mean the fairytale world of the opera?" Aldrian asked with irony.

Beatrice didn't reply.

"I was more like a watchmaker who made sure the precision parts run smoothly . . . On the other hand, you yourself are living here in Venice in a kind of fairytale world."

For a time they didn't speak. Now Beatrice filled her plate with spaghetti after all and began to poke around in it while Aldrian pretended to eat with gusto. He poured a glass of wine for Beatrice and for himself, silently clinked glasses with her, and tried to empty his plate because his thoughts were focused exclusively on what was bothering him.

"Why don't you trust me?" Beatrice asked after a while.

"That's not it."

"What else could it be?"

"Fear."

Burning Money

Beatrice left for Milan the next morning, and they said goodbye affectionately. Aldrian decided to go to his apartment and freshen up before his appointment in the Biblioteca Marciana. But first, for no specific reason, he pulled out the Carpaccio book and studied the two paintings again—the cormorant hunt in the bay and the two women on the terrace—that were, in fact, one. It stimulated his thoughts that the two levels of reality were originally united, then separated, and ultimately rejoined. He had now also found the second level in his brother's life—but there were still many questions left unresolved. Reality and dream. How well he knew these two parts of his own life, reality and the power of imagination. And on the back of *Hunting in the Lagoon*, a letter holder, the third level of reality: memory and the secret thoughts associated with it—hate, desire, longing, confessions, jealousy, deceit, indifference. Truth usually involved just one of the levels . . . But what was the whole picture? Even some parts of Carpaccio's work were still missing, entirely compatible with Aldrian's concept of reality and truth . . . The whole truth? The limitations of language . . .

He had Carpaccio's picture on his mind all the way back to his apartment.

Preparations for the weekend's Carnivalesque "Parade of the Marias" were underway. He was no longer afraid of being watched or followed, perhaps because the crowd of masked people was so large. And at the fish market folks in masks were photographing the flowers and dead marine life. It was peculiar how the centuries mingled, Baroque with Rococo, futurist vision with fantasy, fairytale with utopia. Nevertheless he was amazed that everything seemed normal to him, even though it looked so crazy. After he had unlocked the door, he picked the mail up off the floor as usual. Before he put it down, the front page of the newspaper caught his eye.

"Counterfeit money in circulation," he read. Several businesses in Venice had received payments in false 100-euro bills. Among them was the shop with the paperweights whose owner complained that a masked man had purchased a paperweight with phony 100-euro bills, Aldrian learned.

The only emotion Aldrian felt was rage. If he gave Beatrice the paperweight, she might think he was the culprit. He unlocked the door to Jakob's shop, took the suitcase with the money and the three pictures from the storage cabinet and carried it up to his apartment. He wrapped the bills in two grey trash bags, rolled them together, and stuffed everything into his travel bag that he kept in the wardrobe. Afterwards he tore up the three pictures, the robin and the two Turners—all of them forgeries that must not fall into the hands of the police—and put the shreds with the forged euro bills. Without hesitating, he ran back downstairs and out the door, heading in the direction of Santa Croce. He first wanted to put the two trash bags with the counterfeit money among the other trash bags that were in front of all the houses, but someone always turned up: an old man with his little dog that was just doing its duty, random tourists, a man with a mail cart that he arduously hauled up the steps of a bridge . . . In light of these incidents the only thing he could do was keep walking slowly and wait for a chance to get rid of the bills and the ripped-up pictures. He finally discovered a canal with no one in sight, but when he took the first of the two nylon bags out of his travel bag, two girls ran past and almost stumbled over the piece of luggage. At this point he didn't know where he was. Near the Grand Canal? Near Campo San Polo? He didn't want to end up there, no matter what. He was finally able to get rid of the two bags at a deserted bridge over a narrow canal. The first one sank slowly, but the second floated on the surface and drifted away. Aldrian didn't want to wait around until it sank, so he turned back with the empty travel bag in his hand. When he came to more trash bags, he set the travel bag down with them and, after taking a roundabout route, eventually ended up at the fish market. Relieved by the fact that he was once again part of a crowd, he walked around until his mind was clear. Then he went back to his apartment, showered, changed clothes, and lay down on the bed, exhausted, until Beatrice called. After saying hello, he told her he had gone home to get dressed for his visit to the Biblioteca Marciana.

"Is there any news?"

"Nothing. What kind of news?"

"Counterfeit money is going around Venice."

"Really?"

"100-euro bills. Do you have any in your wallet?"

"No, I don't think so—oh, yes, one . . . but it looks pretty old."

"Be careful, or they'll lock you up," she laughed. "You're the first man I've ever persistently chased."

"And you're the first woman who's ever persistently chased me."

It felt good not to have to be cautious about every word he spoke. She was taking time for him, apparently she wasn't busy just then.

"What are you doing?" she asked, as he was wondering if the trash bag with the rolled-up pack of 100-euro bills and the shreds of the three pictures had sunk or floated on and was perhaps still somewhere in the canal.

"I was just trying to decide whether it makes any sense to keep working on my book," he answered, preoccupied.

"I think you should do it. It distracts you. But it'd be best if you go back to Vienna. I could take a vacation next week and meet you there."

No, Aldrian thought, I'm staying right here . . . Even a souffleur can't leave his post during an opera performance if there are problems. He has to do all he can to save the evening.

And a magician? he asked himself. The best he could do would be to make himself disappear from the stage. Only by some inconceivable magic trick, he thought, could he compensate for a mistake.

"I'll think about it," he replied before she hung up. But in reality he was considering something else entirely. Presumably they had sent him the money so that the police would arrest him as a counterfeiter. So he really never did own the bills. He couldn't even mention them to Beatrice. Moreover they presumably intended to discredit his brother. And the actual crime that Jakob committed—specifically, forging pictures—must remain a secret, and everyone involved as well. That had been a demonic stunt, but now it was his turn. First, he had to get to the Biblioteca Marciana undetected. He still had the eye mask that he would put on as soon as he found something to wear on his head. He had to become someone else quickly and unobtrusively ... and disappear in disguise in the Biblioteca.

As was now his habit, Aldrian gazed out the window at the fish market before he left. When he saw nothing suspicious, he put on his black sport coat that he had in the wardrobe for visits to the Teatro La Fenice or for invitations, and after putting on his windbreaker, left the building by the shop's front door. He reached the Rialto Bridge without incident, people in masks were everywhere. At a mobile stand he discovered a Harlequin cap with little bells similar to the disguise that one of the men had worn when Aldrian was attacked shortly after his arrival. He purchased it and inconspicuously stowed it in the white plastic bag the vendor offered him. He then crossed the Rialto Bridge, turned around on the other side and came back, though he hadn't seen anything out of the ordinary. At the ticket booth of the passenger shelter he bought a new weekly pass, hurried back across the Rialto Bridge and returned yet again, and while lowering his head just a bit, he quickly put on the eye mask and the fool's cap. He did it all so flawlessly that any pursuer—whether from the police or one of his adversaries—would have had to stop, completely baffled, and search for him as he was already hurrying down the Rughetta del Ravano to the Cantina do Mori. He had to fight his way against the surge of masked people who behaved as if they were drunk, laughing at everything they encountered. He was happy that he now fit in with the crowd as a court jester with an eye mask.

The Cantina do Mori was in the Calle dei do Mori—for the first time he read the street number, 429, and his brain immediately calculated: $4 + 2 + 9 = 15$, $1 + 5 = 6$, which made him think of six-sided snowflake crystals and honeycombs and the six legs of insects. His mind continued to produce crazy mutations: instead of "Cantina do More" he got "Cantina d'amore," and then "Cantina della Morte"—a restaurant of love and of death. Out of curiosity he opened the narrow glass double door. The place was bursting at the seams. Copper kettles were hanging from the ceiling, and behind the long dark-brown bar stood Angelo, the bald owner in glasses, and his son Mario, both wearing white aprons. In this room they looked like two psychiatrists or nurses in a madhouse. Behind them, on shelves, the medicine: whiskey, Aperol, vodka, and grappa, to one side a cash register and an open door to a storeroom with racks of bottles. As always, Aldrian felt at home in the dark dining room, even if most of the customers were wearing masks. In a lighted displaycase were the *cicchetti*, the appetizers: tramezzini sandwiches with bacon, creamed salt cod and Parma ham, sliced polenta, fried vegetables, hard-boiled eggs and anchovies, lobster and small octopuses, sandwiches with bonito, skewered onions with tomatoes and pecorino. He was finally able to make his way to the bar. He got a small sample of appetizers on a plate and drank a bottle of beer while leaning against one wall. He grew to appreciate the laughter and the loud talk of the bystanders and was especially glad that Angelo and Mario hadn't recognized him, even though he had had to speak when ordering and paying his bill. To his surprise, he heard a voice behind him that sounded familiar. Who else but his friend, Lorenzo Verra! He pronounced each word distinctly, as he always did, this time quite loudly to be heard over the din, and Aldrian instantly realized that his friend was talking once again about the fire at the Teatro La Fenice.

"You know the unpleasant smell of Venice, Madame," he was just saying. "We Venetians have grown used to it, but you, you don't come here very often, and have most certainly detected the faint odor of decay and salt."

Neither Lorenzo nor the elderly woman in expensive clothing was wearing a mask.

"I shall never forget the 29th of January 1996," Lorenzo continued. "That night the Teatro La Fenice burned down, and the faint odor of decay was replaced by the horrible sharp stench of the fire. I saw the blaze from St. Mark's Square as I was leaving the Caffè Florian around 10 p.m. I immediately heard voices shouting 'La Fenice is burning!' You can understand how that hit me, as if someone close to me had died. I ran as fast as I could through the city and could see and smell and hear the catastrophe already from a distance. The entire roof was burning, but the worst was the water shortage, because the canals, the Rio de Fenice, the Rio dell' Albero, the Rio della Verona, and the Rio Santa Maria del Giglio which all surround the building had been drained because of construction work. Sparks were flying up into the sky, and even the next day the wind was still swirling ashes in the streets. The water to fight the fire had to be dropped by helicopter during the night. More and more curiosity seekers flocked to the theater, it was almost like today at the Rialto Bridge, except people weren't laughing. Many were crying, all of us were crying. I saw a part of my life, my love, go up in flames. And do you know who was responsible? The electrical engineer Enrico Carella and his cousin Massimiliano Marchetti—I knew them both personally—who were working on improvements to the fire alarm system. They set the opera house on fire because Carella was facing a 7500-euro penalty because he hadn't complied with the contractually guaranteed deadlines."

Aldrian had heard the story a thousand times and also knew that Lorenzo would soon begin to cry.

So he left the cantina and was swept along by the "organized insanity," as he called it. Colorful confetti and garlands were tossed in the air and then rained down on the passersby. People hastily took over the Rialto Bridge which made Aldrian think of some sort of crazy sacred ritual. He was barely able to push his way onto a packed vaporetto by shoving aside inattentive waiting passengers, but once on deck he saw himself momentarily surrounded by four plague doctors. They each wore a black three-cornered hat, a black costume and a long coat, cloths to cover both throat and mouth, bird masks with long beaks, glasses, white shirts and gloves, each one holding a long cane that they used to point out just about everything, though they neither spoke nor laughed. Initially the four pointed to him, then at the pallazi, an approaching passenger shelter, or at some other person. Aldrian felt apprehensive, but he gradually overcame the feeling he was being threatened. And when he realized that the four were only entertaining themselves, to his own amazement he actually felt they were somehow protecting him.

The Piazzetta at St. Mark's Square had been transformed into an open stage. It made him think of the masked ball in the novel *The Phantom of the Opera*, and he remembered that he had once performed his magic act for the staff at the closed Vienna State Opera, portraying Red Death, the phantom in the book.

At the entrance to the Biblioteca Marciana he took off the fool's cap, stuffed it in the plastic bag and deposited the eye mask, too. But he still couldn't take his mind off the events of the day—now like a haunting recurring dream.

The Biblioteca Marciana

The woman with glasses at the reception desk looked sleepy, but as soon as he gave his name, she asked him to wait while she telephoned. Aldrian was able to look beyond the reception desk and into the reading room; the silence and calm in the room were like a promise that the second world had displaced the first world in this long and tall building. Light streamed down through the glass roof and fell on the hall, ringed with columns, that was previously the interior courtyard of the mint, the *Zecca*, as Aldrian had learned from his brother. In addition, the reading room was softly lit by table lamps and about one-third full. The receptionist now indicated the impressive broad staircase, and—after checking his nylon bag with the fool's cap and silencing his phone—Aldrian left the first world behind with every stride as he ascended into the second. Waiting at the top of the stairs was the director, Dr. Marino Zorzi, an elegant cordial gentleman, as it turned out, his grey hair parted, his dark-grey suit and tie of the finest material. He graciously invited Aldrian into his office with a magnificent view of the Lagoon, the Grand Canal, and San Giorgio Maggiore island. Outside a second window stood a construction crane, "for years now," as the director explained. To Aldrian's relief he spoke clearly, like a teacher to his pupil. The room was approximately 20 feet high, and the arched windows framed sky, water, and, in haze, the two churches Santa Maria della Salute and San Giorgio Maggiore.

The sky above and the water below, Aldrian thought, clouds and seagulls above, larger ships and gondolas like giant crows below . . . and in fog the entire scene resembled a vision. Aldrian felt that he had arrived in a parallel universe. Leather-bound folios were shelved in a green-paneled cabinet behind the director. The gleaming panel reflected, in reverse, the books, the sea, the sky, the moving cloud formations, the gulls, and the gondolas. Dr. Zorzi was just saying that the library possessed a million volumes, 13,000 manuscripts, 24,000 prints from the 16th century, and 2,300 incunabula, so-called "cradle books," and that their holdings also included the libraries from the monasteries that were disbanded by Napoleon. Apparently he had noticed that Aldrian was still staring at the cabinet panel—for his part, saw Aldrian reflected in the polished wood—but continued without hesitation that the great inspiration for the establishment of the Biblioteca Marciana had been the poet Petrarch who had promised to donate his books if it was built. But in the end he kept them for himself. Still, they did possess several ornate manuscripts, such as the sonnets of *Triumphs* from 1370. At that point he recited from memory what "the master" had written about Venice: "I see ships, as large as my house, with masts taller than its towers. They are like mountains that swim on the water. They cruise every part of the globe and brave immeasurable dangers. They bring wine to England, honey to Russia, saffron, oil and canvas to Assyria, Armenia, Persia, and Arabia, wood to Egypt and Greece, and return fully loaded with products of all kinds that are then sent out to all corners of the world. Beside Petrarch's writings the library also owned first editions and bibliophile rarities," Dr. Zorzi continued, "such as editions of the Palestinian and Babylonian Talmud, a copy of the Quran from the beginning of the 16th century, writings from Giordano Bruno, the heretic who was burned at the stake in Rome, for example *De la causa, principio e uno* and *De l'infinito, universo e mondi,* as well as the first printed edition of Marco Polo's *Book of Marvels*. More than anything else, the unique holdings of Greek manuscripts had made the Biblioteca Marciana the center for humanistic studies as early as the 16th century. Too, the collection of operatic manuscripts from the 17th century was among the treasures of the library," Zorzi added with a smile. "The creator of the library, the famous architect Jacopo Sansovino, not only built the Biblioteca Marciana, but also redesigned and then completed the Old Procuraties on St. Mark's Square—those being the original administrative buildings of the Republic, the Zecca and the Loggetta del Campanile. The architect's contract goes back to 1537. Eight years later the vaulted arch of the existing reading room collapsed and Sansovino was thrown in prison as punishment . . . But Titian the painter and Aretino the writer interceded on his behalf, and he was set free some time later, though he still had to reimburse the city for damages."

Aldrian hadn't been listening very closely. He had already learned the most important things from his brother and from the souffleur Lorenzo Verra, so he kept on staring at the reflective panel and saw, in reverse, how the seagull flocks flew over the lagoon and the ships came and went.

"The library is enormous, you can be here for months and still get lost," Dr. Zorzi concluded, and opened a door in a cabinet on the opposite wall that held hundreds of keys. Aldrian had never before seen such a large number of keys in one place, and they made him think of clefs and the thousands of notes in a musical score. To compose an opera, each of the notes must "fit," like the keys in their locks. As Aldrian glanced at the white reading lamp, the paperweight, a small sculpture of books, and writing utensils, he discovered two hand-bound worn and battered folios, *Periodici Giornali I and II.* As a result of their sustained use, the exterior of the books reminded Aldrian of the brownish-black skin of a lizard. There were only vestiges of the hand-written labels that had been attached to them.

Dr. Zorzi stood up, and what happened next seemed to Aldrian—as he experienced it and when he thought about it later—like a long airplane flight over a mysterious continent. They passed though a door in the director's office to a wood-paneled library room with a balcony that was stuffed with books on shelves, and, below that, desks, computer screens, stacks of paper, and, on the floor, mounds of empty cardboard boxes and opened books . . . along with desk lamps and blue chairs . . . and a man in a black sweater beside a blond woman, the two so engrossed in their work that they didn't look up. Aldrian gazed at the ceiling to study the stucco decorations, then looked down at the terrazzo floor with its varicolored brown, black, and white dots of granite or dolomite, of limestone and marble. Aldrian noticed on the wall—and it now seemed as if he were flying into the past—a calendar with an old date, a sign of the silent advance of time. He told himself, as he often did, that things were alive. This thought had come to him back in his childhood, and without it he might not have become involved with magic. During his magic acts he learned to make things a part of his body, as if they were something like his teeth or auditory ossicles, and that was why they worked automatically in his hands, without being influenced by his thoughts . . . Once again his thoughts wandered to the magic book and his brother's letter in the package that the delivery boy had handed over to him . . .

Director Zorzi led him to the next room, and this time Aldrian thought about a storm that swept everything upside-down, a storm that truly "raged." Apparently no one had tried to clean up the chaos. Very old iron lockers with cleats and rivets, like rusty treasure chests pulled from the sea, underscored the impression of destruction. Ladders leaned against cabinets that gave the impression they had spikes on the inside that would pierce condemned men when you closed their doors like the so-called Iron Maidens. Aldrian was already entering another workspace full of empty cardboard boxes and paper. He was amazed. It looked like the workshop of a magician suffering from Alzheimer's disease.

They climbed a wooden staircase and were on the second-floor balcony, several yards above the heads of the students and several yards beneath the ceiling.

With overcrowded bookshelves at his back, Aldrian initially felt like some type of supervisor. The director led him to the second-floor walkway where he could overlook the large reading room from a bird's-eye perspective. He counted the rows of tables and chairs: in total there were four on each side, and on each of the honey-brown tabletops three reading lamps with white lampshades that made the reading lamps seem to be wearing white gloves, like the students when they handled valuable old books. Bookshelves were set up in the middle of the reading room and between the individual rows of tables, dividing the room in sections so that people could study undisturbed. He discovered in one of the nooks a statue of the poet Petrarch, replete with laurel wreath. He then turned his attention to the students who were moving about the room as if in slow motion. Others sat at the tables, immersed in their books and manuscripts.

They kept going, through functional rooms of the archives, as the director explained, past steel shelving and beneath neon lights, ventilation ducts, and cable conduits. Everywhere they went it smelled of aged paper. Of course Aldrian had no idea where the next door would lead. At one point he came to a small office with several computer monitors, tall crown glass windows and glass cabinets of books. The director opened one of the windows, and Aldrian could look down on the Piazzetta and a herd of masks, the two columns, the Doge's Palace, and St. Mark's Basilica. The wooden benches from the acqua alta were still there. He gazed at the café chairs with their costumed customers, the gondolas, and the sea. It felt like Dr. Zorzi had opened the cover of a gigantic picture book where events took on a life of their own. The director then closed the window and, once again, they went through a seemingly endless series of rooms with copiers, lamps, overstuffed wastebaskets, central heating elements, coat racks, shelves, brown cardboard boxes, neon lights, tables, chairs, and books, books, and more books. They crossed bridges full of books that led to rooms of books and on to more rooms with books. Sometimes wire mesh was put up in front of shelves to prevent theft . . . which made Aldrian think of a prison for books. After a large room packed with more books and glowing computer monitors there was an irregular series of rooms of the same size, or of smaller and larger dimensions, so that you felt as if you were in a mirrored room that projected the feeling of infinity. Here a ceiling fresco portrayed the poets' horse Pagasus that flew to the sun and apparently had its stall in this labyrinth. Last of all they came to a connecting room with one wall covered by a curtain that reminded him of a puppet theater. The director opened the curtain and Aldrian saw the world depicted on the famous map by Fra Mauro from 1459. Aldrian told himself it was the world behind the world. It had become visible like an illusion in a magic trick, and together with the opening of the curtain it gave the former prompter the impression of being the setting for some unknown opera. Here was the boot of Italy in the blue Mediterranean, furrowed by the white lines of waves, inscribed parchment labels unfurled in the water, and small white sailing ships. Aldrian read the appellation for the body of water: "Mare Mediterraneum." It seemed as if language with its alphabet had descended from heaven upon the sea and had formed islands. One of the assistants whom he hadn't noticed before, gave him a magnifying glass that allowed him to study the masterpiece up close and be astonished at all the little details . . . the rivers and cities and mountains, a visionary and yet scientifically accurate painting by an observant artistic spirit, by a Leonardo da Vinci of geography who inherited the fate of physicists of all centuries who had tried to draw a map of the world but either had no access to the smaller world beyond quantum mechanics nor to the macroscopic world of the entire universe. In front of the map stood Fra Mauro's bronze bust, a large head with cunning eyes and a mouth frozen in a perpetual smile. Aldrian had the impression that this man was the artist who invented all the masks in the world.

Beyond this room was the ceremonial room of the Biblioteca Marciana with its geometrically patterned marble floor, ancient sculptures, ceiling frescos by Tiepolo, Titian, and Tintoretto, everything opulently decorated, opulently embellished as if he were now in some treasure chamber of the intellect. Yellow translucent curtains were hanging at the arched windows and showcases with illuminated manuscripts and ancient painted globes stood along the partitions. Aldrian had the feeling that the floor could disappear beneath his feet at any moment. Passing through a black marble doorway he came to the next hall of this dream empire that resembled the first. Aldrian asked himself if the globes were intended to be illustrations of the geography of dreamworlds? Did the documents behind the glass record a world history of dreams? Everything that the human race, since its inception, had dreamed or imagined in its thoughts? Everything unspoken and forgotten? Had these nonexistent worlds on the globes and in the documents been imagined as physically extant? Was he now in a hall of counter-history that also documented a world history of the animal kingdom? Their destinies, their thoughts, their bloody slaughter and extinction? Aldrian continued his fantasy, wondering if here was the key to a different understanding of the world? Was the ornamentation of the marble floor the diagram of a parallel universe with its own stars?

The director had stopped and seemed to have guessed Aldrian's thoughts.

"People have quite often called Venice a fairytale city. That's accurate only insofar as there are both glorious and gruesome fairy tales. The Venetian mind that created and experienced these fairy tales obviously has two sides. One side records historical events and lies—the Archivio di Stato di Venezia and the Doge's Palace—, the other is the realm of lively fantasy, of art, of religion—the Biblioteca Marciana, the museums and the churches. Both halves of the brain communicate with each other, and for that reason it is difficult to gain an objective overview. Venice's enemies have referred to the city as an evil land- and water snake, or as a treacherous Adriatic toad. In writings designated *Antiveneti*, a Frenchman—Claude de Seyssel—describes Venetians as a people who crawled into the swamps, as if neither the sea nor the land wanted them: dominant not through weapons and cunning but through theft and deception, hungry as the lion on their coat of arms, insatiable for land, money, and blood. The Venetian government was portrayed as a tyrannical oligarchy that perpetuated its terrifying dominance with the aid of spies, torture, and poisoning. In contrast, however, are the songs in praise of Venice that have always existed and still are sung today. In them Venice is the epitome of beauty. Just consider the Renaissance paintings, Bellini, Giorgione, from Titian to William Turner's watercolors, the architecture and—what you yourself know better than I—the music

228

from Vivaldi to Luigi Nono, from Monteverdi who composed and performed the first great operas right here, down to Verdi's brilliant works and Igor Stravinsky whose opera *The Rake's Progress*, based on the paintings and etchings by William Hogarth—as you are well aware—had its debut in the Teatro La Fenice . . ."

"On the 11th of September 1951," Aldrian thought to himself—and instantly his head was filled with Stravinsky's music, with its references to various operas, a prayer by the horns that evokes *Fidelio*, or a journey to hell in *Orpheus* . . . Moreover he recollected the life of the libertine Tom Rakewell and his path through casinos, brothels, and madhouses as William Hogarth had depicted him and Georg Christoph Lichtenberg had interpreted him, and as Aldrian himself had prompted at several Salzburg Festivals.

"Writers from Petrarch and Boccaccio to Lord Byron, Casanova, Ruskin, Henry James, Rainer Maria Rilke, Thomas Mann, Ernest Hemingway, and Jean-Paul Sartre have been inspired by Venice. And don't forget the theater: the Commedia dell'arte and Goldoni . . . What I'm trying to say is that it's always a matter of perspective." He abruptly stopped speaking, as if he had forgotten what he was saying, left the hall, hurried ahead of Aldrian, up stairs and then down again, and opened a door to the study hall for manuscripts. Although there were people present, Aldrian couldn't hear a sound and therefore had the impression the room was used only by mutes. Here, too, white translucent curtains covered the windows. Black cords connected to small lamps were growing out of the tables to facilitate the study of the valuable parchments, Aldrian suspected. What would the people here be doing? What images went through their minds? What thoughts? Lecterns in the shape of birds' wings held open books. As Aldrian now realized, the walls were decorated from floor to ceiling with ornamental leaves and other geometrical designs, the ceiling itself resplendent with the St. Mark's lion. Of course there were books on shelves everywhere, and Aldrian imagined that they formed a chorus of assorted voices that sang to him or whispered something, like sirens trying to lure him into staying. Some of the readers were wearing white cotton gloves that contributed to the silence, Aldrian felt. And here, as in most of the rooms, computer monitors glowed. The pointed arches lent the study room a monastic ambiance. A middle-aged man, half-bald with a beard and wearing a sweater, was just quoting from a folio. Aldrian thought: "He's comfortable, he's happy." Aldrian felt the man—in his niche of three bookcases—was safe, as if isolated from everyday cares and woes. On another table stood a lone ventilating fan, unplugged from the wall socket. And there were wooden stepladders everywhere, neon lights on the walls, and a wooden floor with a checked pattern.

"Well?" the director asked before they went further. "Are you finding your way around?" He smiled.

"It's like reading a musical score for the first time. Things don't fit together until you've finished the whole thing," Aldrian replied.

The director nodded and continued to smile before leading Aldrian back down to the reading room. From here you could easily discern the former inner courtyard. When Aldrian again saw the readers immersed in their books and notes, it occurred to him that he had always fought against the impossibility of understanding everything: at best he had noticed tiny fragments, colorful stamps on envelopes, though he would never know what was in the letters themselves. If he looked at it in a certain way, he hadn't really tried to understand more through his studies; instead, he had found a spiritual path. After all, hadn't he regarded his music studies like a sort of meditation? The only way for him to immerse himself in this world was in a magical, almost enchanting way, like a silent child at play. He leaned back and gazed at the ceiling that consisted of a concrete grid and square windows. The six-cornered honeycombs inadvertently came to mind again. But the bees, he thought—though he knew it was crazy—perhaps build six-cornered honeycombs because they have six limbs, while humans only have four . . . like insects with two arms and two legs, and you never know what they are thinking and what they are going to do. White spotlight-shaped lamps hung above the arcade arches and were focused on the floor. Now Aldrian saw up close the powerful statue of the poet Petrarch. He wore a laurel wreath on his head, below that a cowl that Aldrian had seen before on depictions of Dante. It was tied under the poet's chin, as if he had a toothache. In his hands, a book that he clutched to his chest, as if it were something secretive and sacred—Aldrian understood, it was *My Secret Book*. Petrarch's gaze was distant, introverted. A few steps further on, Aldrian and the director were standing before a large brown wood cabinet with numerous drawers that had written labels in alphabetical order. This card catalog reminded him of a medication index in a drugstore that provided information about poisonous and medicinal plants. He enjoyed pulling out the drawers and rummaging around in the card catalogs or thumbing through volumes of indexes kept nearby: "Inventario vol. 16," he read, and below that a long sequence of numbers. Of course there were also computers in the room.

Like a bookworm, Aldrian squeezed his way up a wrought-iron spiral staircase to the next floor. A freezing Signora Luciana with pigtail and sweater was already waiting to guide him through the third level. Before turning Aldrian over to his colleague, the director explained there were a total of 400 storage rooms. "But you won't want to see all of them," he concluded with a touch of irony.

Signora Luciana led him past long rows of steel shelves bursting with books, folios, and brown cardboard boxes to the place on one wall where Fra Mauro's world map had been located, and from there to another window onto the reading room. He concentrated on gazing down from this new perspective at the insects with four extremities in the reading room. Ultimately he couldn't shake the thought that he was observing strange creatures rather than students. Then he was off again, negotiating narrow corridors with neon lights. The further they went, the more unsettling the rooms in their interchangeability: stack of countless books—each one valuable, each one important, each perhaps irreplaceable. He then stumbled upon a low empty bookcase that looked like a prototype of a tile stove, and it was even rusted black. On top, hip-high, was a piece of paper with a drawing that Aldrian recognized, but Signora Luciana took it and put it in her pocket without saying a word. Aldrian thought it looked like graffiti he had seen in urinals. He also saw a dark spot on the wall in the form of a giant insect and was amazed that without a doubt this random shape resembled the imprint of an ant. Then again, he stopped at a city map of Venice in a glass frame that hung on the wall in a forsaken corner. It was in all shades of yellow, the ocean stained amber, as were the Grand Canal, the Canale della Giudecca, and the smaller canals. The parts of the city were in a lighter or darker urine yellow, in some places whitish-yellow, fainter toward the Fondamente Nuove, almost bleached, with green-yellow and egg-yolk blotches. Aldrian loved the color yellow and was fascinated by the strange beauty of this forgotten city map. He thought it could also represent the brain of some unknown being that was discovered dead and dissected like the brains of the madhouse patients on the island of San Servolo. Almost horrified, he realized how closely it resembled the brain slice of the famous conductor that Beatrice had gotten from her ex-husband and then given to him. He also thought that under an electron microscope it might turn out to be the speech center of the unknown being, a memory center that included the city's major museums and churches, the realm of dreams—the sea, the water. That's where the visages of the night come from, he suddenly believed.

Passing by the annals and catalogs bound in parchment and leather that glittered in gold letters, they came to the extensive travel library. Since Signora Luciana was in a hurry, he only had time to read a few of the individual Latin titles: Leonardo da Vinci's *Codex Atlanticus*, Lepsius's descriptions of Egypt and Ethiopia. There were also books packed and bound in wrapping paper with the inscription "Non dare in lettura," which probably meant that you couldn't bring them into the reading room, but it made Aldrian think of the package with the counterfeit money, the book about palmistry, and the letter from his brother.

On their way back, time and time again he saw through various windows the pretty Royal Gardens, the "Giardinetti," down below, and the canal with the three rows of moored boats and gondolas that looked as if they were sleeping in the still waters.

Dr. Zorzi was waiting outside his office to say goodbye to Aldrian, and when Aldrian asked him how long he would continue to run this palace of books, the man only shook his head, saying that he only had two or three years till retirement. Pointing through the open door and the window to the Piazzetta, he added as a melancholic joke: "Then I'll just be one of the many."

Fibonacci's Long Journey

The woman at the cloakroom gave him back his plastic bag, and Aldrian paused at the entrance, put on the eye mask and the fool's cap, and set off through the mob of costumed people to the San Marco Giardinetti station where he had to stand in line. He reactivated his phone and saw that Beatrice had tried to reach him. He dialed her number as quickly as possible in the crush of people.

"Where are you?" she greeted him as she always did.

"In front of the Teatro La Fenice," he lied, because he thought it possible that his phone was being tapped. "I'm going to a restaurant to get something to eat." But Beatrice asked him to come back to her apartment on the Campo San Polo: "You've got my keys."

"Yes."

"Don't go to a restaurant. Buy something on the way, there's wine in the refrigerator."

He didn't respond.

"Do you hear me?" she asked.

"Right now it's so jam-packed . . ."

"I'll probably be back day after tomorrow, I'll call you this evening. I love you." She hung up and Aldrian felt a desire to see the ceiling fresco in the San Pantalon church and possibly visit Margherita and Eugenio, but he knew he was kidding himself, because, to tell the truth, he wanted to pay a visit to the frame dealer Carlo Fibonacci. He waited until he could squeeze his way through the masked people and board the next vaporetto, and he was even able to find a corner seat inside the cabin before he was surrounded. In the colorful confusion he noticed a very short athletic fellow costumed as Pinocchio, and, chattering nearby, two children dressed as the fox and the cat from the storybook, another girl—dressed as a fairy with blue hair—was staring off into space, while a fire-eater and puppeteer with a red beard and hair was looking after them. At the stern of the boat he also recognized the woodcarver Mister Gepetto with the talking cricket, which made Aldrian think it must be a theatrical troupe that performed the play *Pinocchio* on the street. He imagined he was one of the troupe and enjoyed a feeling of security. He reflexively reached into his breast pocket. His fingers grazed Carlo Fibonacci's pocket address book, the one Aldrian had lifted on his last encounter. He decided to examine it closely because he was now convinced that it contained further clues. In any case he now had a key in his hand, if only he could find the right lock. When he concentrated, he could envision rooms, halls, and the reading room of the Biblioteca Marciana. He almost fell asleep, but the Pinocchio troupe was improvising brief scenes from their play and had burst out in loud laughter. The other passengers began to applaud, so the actors sang the ballad of the sea monster, the giant whale that first swallowed Pinocchio's father and then the boy himself. When they had finished the song, another group started singing "Gente di mare," and with the song about the "people from the sea" ringing in his ear, Aldrian got off at the San Tomà station where a large crowd was waiting to board. Levity was everywhere, no drunkards disrupted or fought, most people just strolled along in their masks and costumes like every other day: children with their parents, tourists, individuals, and groups. They appeared and disappeared as if it were the most normal thing, as if it were just a normal day. It seemed to Aldrian that, when dressed as fools, people got along better than they did the rest of the year. The masks in the shop windows seemed like the faces of beings that didn't yet have names. And the instruments in one music store looked like strange animals: snakes, turtles, a black stingray with black and white teeth. Aldrian could see himself in a wetsuit, standing alongside the terrariums and aquariums whose occupants would stare at him motionlessly.

Carlo Fibonacci's store was empty, like most of the shops that day. The proprietor himself was sitting at his desk, absentmindedly thumbing through a newspaper.

Aldrian stuffed the fool's cap and the eye mask in the thin nylon bag that he had taken out of his jacket, and stepped inside.

The frame dealer looked up.

"I've come to buy the drawing of the giant beetle," Aldrian said right off.

Carlo Fibonacci just stared at him, as if Aldrian had died and had now come back as a ghost.

"Weren't you here when I was mugged?" he asked.

Aldrian shook his head.

"You weren't?" Fibonacci pulled himself together and went on the offensive: "Sorry, I don't have it any more."

"You sold it?"

The frame dealer nodded and acted as if he had gone back to reading his newspaper.

"Where did my brother paint the pictures?"

"How am I supposed to know that," Fibonacci replied, without altering his pose.

"At home?"

Fibonacci looked up briefly, cleared his throat, and answered testily: "What are you talking about? I . . ."

"I haven't found anything in his apartment—no paints, no papers, no canvas or brushes," Aldrian interrupted him as if this were an interrogation.

"I already told you, I don't know," Fibonacci responded indignantly.

"Did he work with you? At your apartment?"

"What do you want from me?"

"I want to know what hideout my brother used to forge the paintings."

With a lightning-quick move Aldrian pulled the pocket telephone book from his breast pocket and put it right back.

"So *you* stole it!" Fibonacci gasped in disgust.

"Call the police! I'll wait right here."

"So you *were* there when I was mugged . . . Now I remember. You're a thief!" The frame dealer trembled, enraged. He reached for a pencil and a piece of paper and hastily wrote down an address. Aldrian recognized the handwriting right away since he had glanced at the entries in the little telephone book.

"Who else knows about this?" Aldrian asked unemotionally.

"Give me back my telephone book!"

Aldrian put the slip of paper in his pocket and answered tersely that he would check out the address first.

Fibonacci suddenly leaped over the sales counter and tried to stab Aldrian in the face with a letter opener. Aldrian saw everything in slow-motion, he reached out for the hand with the pointed object and twisted it around, as Fibonacci yanked his hair with the other hand. The letter opener fell to the floor with a clatter, and Aldrian punched the wild man on the chin, knocking him into the clutter behind the sales counter.

Then Aldrian ran out of the store, turned down the first side street, deftly put on the eye mask and the fool's cap, and instinctively hurried to San Pantalon. In that instant it seemed like the perfect hiding place. Near the church he again turned off his phone and put the fool's garments in the plastic bag. It was a habit of his to put everything back in its rightful place, and that was the only reason he had been able to work at the Vienna State Opera as the *Maestro Suggeritore*. And during his magic act, too, it was necessary for him to make his sleight-of-hand and other activities automatic.

As the darkness inside the church enveloped him, his anxiety disappeared with the confidence that he was safe. He saw that he was the only visitor, and that, too, reassured him. First of all he put a coin in the spotlight apparatus, and as the ceiling was illuminated and then darkened, he had the sensation of flying and falling, as he had the first time. He quickly put another coin in the slot, pulled out the little telephone book and the slip of paper with the address. It read "Calle San Domenico" and the number of some building. No name, no other information. He took out the folded Marco Polo map of Venice out of his breast pocket, glanced around and unfolded the map but couldn't find a street or alley by that name. The lights went out and he put the map back in his pocket. Had Fibonacci pulled a fast one? He didn't think so, because the telephone book would reveal all of Fibonacci's shady deals. If he had given Aldrian the correct address, he could warn the unknown gang and make sure Aldrian wouldn't be able to snoop around.

By now it had grown even darker in the church and he could feel the cold, but also the desire to stay and reactivate the spotlights. Suddenly the church door flew open and a throng of masked and somewhat inebriated people swept in.

Most of them grew quieter, giggling cautiously. Someone coughed as Aldrian put in another coin and the ceiling lit up.

It was instantly silent, a few whispered a bit, looking around for a sacristan or a priest. And then they all stumbled back out onto the street, laughing loudly.

Moments later, probably drawn by the voices, the priest did appear, glanced at Aldrian, and then went back into the sacristy.

And the spotlights that had lit up the ceiling went out. Aldrian, too, wanted to leave the church, but he put in another coin and thumbed through the telephone book, baffled. Just before the spotlights went out, he stumbled onto the word "Domenico." He tried to decipher the line, but since he didn't have any more coins, he couldn't activate the spotlights. So he hurried outside and opened the telephone book. "Giovanni Battista Tiepolo, C. Domenico del 1302," he read.

He compared the entry with the slip of paper that Fibonacci had given him, which also read "Calle San Domenico" with the same house number "1302."

Just then he realized that he hadn't put on either the fool's cap or the eye mask. He glanced around, and since no one was watching, he quickly transformed himself back into a stranger.

Tiepolo had been a painter, he reflected, and decided to talk to Fibonacci again. He repeatedly checked to see if he was being followed, but he didn't notice anything out of the ordinary. As he turned the corner to the frame shop, he again was confronted by a horde of masked drunks that he avoided by entering the store, and as he stepped in, he almost tripped over Fibonacci who was laying on the floor in a pool of blood. What happened next was more a result of instinct rather than of conscious reflection. He looked up and saw a door behind the clutter that was slightly ajar. He burrowed his way through an accumulation of junk—a broom, various frames, a chair with three legs—and disappeared into the darkness behind them. In the silence he could hear someone running. He clicked on his smartphone's pocket flashlight, listened, and when he had to swallow, he was afraid that the sound would give him away. So he remained silent and was then aware of someone on the top floor attempting to break into something wooden with a solid object—a pistol grip? Next he heard a shot fired—apparently from a weapon with a silencer—and footsteps hurrying down a stone stairway. Aldrian immediately realized that he, too, must flee. But he first ran upstairs, pushed against a half-open door, and found himself in a room with a leather couch and a TV set. The apartment door, he decided, had been forced open by the gunshot. Without thinking, he hurried down the stone stairway and out onto the busy street.

A crowd had gathered a few steps away in front of Fibonacci's store and was staring through the open entrance at the dead man. They didn't pay any attention to Aldrian, so he was able to get away inconspicuously.

He hadn't really understood what had just happened. The first thing that occurred to him was that he was a fool, a real fool among people who were only playing at being fools and thus experienced it as emancipation. He reprimanded himself that he, on the other hand, was truly a fool since he had gotten himself into mortal danger.

No matter what, he felt he had to get rid of the fool's cap as quickly as possible. He yanked it off his head and, at the first available opportunity, dropped it by some trash bags leaning against a building. He kept the eye mask on. When he activated his phone, he saw on the display several calls, from Commissario Galli, Margherita, and Beatrice ...

Had they found Jakob? Or Elena?

He called Beatrice's number, and she complained that he was driving her mad. Then he learned that Commissario Galli had turned up with a search warrant and Margherita had had to open up his brother's house for the police.

"Where are you?" she asked, incensed.

"I was in St. Mark's, I'm now on my way home in the middle of all the Mardi Gras celebrations."

"You're supposed to call Commissario Galli."

"You call him!" Aldrian answered, and turned off his phone. But he ran to the Campo San Polo, bought an envelope, stuffed the little telephone book inside and sealed it. He tore up the slip of paper on which Fibonacci had jotted down the address and, as he walked, scattered the shreds like confetti. Lastly, he went to see Diego Sarcia in his shop on the Rughetta del Ravano. As he was opening the door to the store, several masked people tumbled out, jesting with each other about their appearance. Diego was sitting in a chair and stared at Aldrian in amazement.

"Can I visit you tomorrow in your studio?"

"Sure."

"When will you be there?"

"Around eight o'clock."

"Please hold on to this envelope for me."

Diego nodded.

"A suicide note?" he asked.

"What do you think?"

"Nothing. I don't think anything and don't want to know anything." He paused briefly as two customers entered the shop. "Apparently the police are at your brother and Elena's house," he whispered cautiously and put the envelope in his pocket.

"Calle San Domenico 1302, Giovanni Battista Tiepolo," Aldrian said to himself as he crossed the Fabbriche Veccie and came to the fish market. He had inconspicuously thrown away the eyeglasses beforehand.

Police boats were docked there, and masked curiosity seekers were milling around in front of the Jurassic Park store, while two policemen encouraged them to move on. Aldrian felt totally calm, but he could tell how fast his heart was pounding when he approached the policemen and said that Commissario Galli was expecting him.

Aldrian had been able to see from a distance that the store lights were all on, and that five or six policemen were in the process of searching the displays.

They promptly took him up to Jakob and Elena's apartment where a teary-eyed Margherita whispered to him that Carlo Fibonacci had been stabbed to death . . . The Commissario had just gotten the word. Aldrian didn't show any reaction to the news.

"Where is Jakob? Where is Elena?" he asked.

Margherita only shook her head, and then he was taken directly to the Commissario.

"We're going over the whole place one more time," Galli explained to him in place of a greeting. "We've been waiting for you to arrive before we search your apartment. May I have your keys?"

Without saying a word Aldrian gave him the keys and sat down on a chair at the living room table. The Commissario also sat down after giving the keys to one of the police officers who were in the process of turning Jakob and Elena's apartment upside down. It was ice cold.

"Why are you searching the place again?" Aldrian asked.

"Do you mind?" Galli waited for a response, and when Aldrian didn't speak, he added: "We're pursuing every lead."

Aldrian considered this briefly.

"Who gave you a lead?"—I'd be interested in hearing that," he answered in a brusque tone.

Galli ignored his question and didn't try to disguise his own displeasure.

"Where were you this afternoon?"

"Why do you want to know?"

"This isn't going to work!" Galli blurted out indignantly.

"Am I a suspect?"

"I'm asking the questions here."

"First I have to know what we're talking about here."

"About your brother and your sister-in-law."

Aldrian was silent.

"Would you rather go down to police headquarters?"

"I won't tell you anything there either, so long as I don't know what we're talking about."

"Up to now we don't have a clue as to the two missing persons! But counterfeit money has turned up, 100-euro bills . . ."

Galli observed him with suspicion.

"And what does that have to do with me?" Aldrian responded.

"You're asking the questions again!"

"Okay, fine. That doesn't have anything to do with me."

"We're investigating if your brother is involved in the matter."

"Why?"

The Commissario was silent . . .

"You've been living in this building from time to time over the course of several years. Didn't you noticed anything? Your brother was frequently on trips, your sister-in-law as well. In the meantime, the Jurassic Park store was run by your sister-in-law's sister, Signora Margherita Bellucci. She clearly doesn't know anything," he added sarcastically. "But you were here from time to time. Didn't you notice anything?"

"No," Aldrian answered.

"Did you know that Signora Bellucci was helping out in the Jurassic Park establishment?"

"Yes, I can remember one or two occasions."

Galli leaned back, as if he were bored, and changed topics.

"To date, the counterfeit money has turned up in seventeen shops."

Now Aldrian understood why someone had sent him the package with the phony 100-euro bills. It had been a trap, to incriminate him to the police.

"Give me your wallet and stand up!" The Commissario continued the interrogation.

Aldrian unwillingly stood up and let them search him. Another policeman put everything he found on Aldrian on the table, and after the Commissario had examined the objects, he gave them back to Aldrian.

"What's the second key for?" he asked in passing, and when Aldrian told him it belonged to Beatrice Stefanelli, Galli continued: "In the meantime we're certain that your brother and his wife couldn't have amassed such a huge amount of money that we found at the bank from the income of their store alone," he now related casually. "And then there's the wholesale pearl trade—but it's unlikely that the couple could have used that to finance everything. The counterfeit money deal would be one solution." He paused, and then asked: "Do you know Carlo Fibonacci?"

"Yes, but not very well."

"When was the last time you saw him?"

"When I visited Margherita, two days ago, I think."

"And?"

"I was walking past his shop. The door was open, so we exchanged a few words . . . nothing out of the ordinary."

"Counterfeit money also turned up in Vienna yesterday," Galli again changed topics.

"What's that got to do with me?"

"Of course your brother illustrates scientific books . . . He's got talent . . . It wouldn't be too difficult for him to forge a banknote, especially since his wife is a restorer and knows her way around various types of paper."

"What am I supposed to say to that? That I saw him copying banknotes all day long?"

"You keep forgetting that I'm the one who asks the questions here."

"That's all so absurd, there's nothing more I can say."

"Where did they get the money for the house in Skala Kallonis?" From among the papers in front of him, Galli pulled out a photograph and shoved it over to Aldrian. "Beautiful property," he went on. "Your brother was planning to erect a large number of beehives. He had them build a station for observing birds. And inside the house there was a library that housed thousands of new and vintage books in several rooms: primarily about plants and animals, but also about paintings, that's what the Greek police report . . . Sadly, most of it burned up."

Aldrian saw that the picture was blurred, probably taken with a smartphone, and didn't actually show anything significant.

"He studied biology, he was an assistant at the university, he was searching for beauty," Aldrian said as he studied the photo.

The paradisiacal, he thought to himself, his brother had wanted to create a Garden of Eden for Elena and himself, with birds, fish, and insects. That corresponded with his religious beliefs and his love for painting and music . . . and he had presumably forged paintings to get it . . . possibly money, too.

"His project must have cost a fortune," Galli continued. "When we analyze his tax returns, it's not possible for him to be able to afford these properties."

"I don't understand tax returns. It isn't illegal for him to earn large amounts of money."

Galli leaned forward and studied Aldrian closely. "We know that. Don't give me the runaround! Where were you this afternoon?"

"In the Biblioteca Marciana."

"How long?"

"You can ask Director Zorzi."

"Give me an estimate," the Commissario insisted, not willing to be distracted.

"I can't say."

"Why not?"

"Because I lost all track of time."

"And then?"

"St. Mark's Basilica."

"What did you do there?"

Aldrian remembered how he and his brother had gazed at the Genesis cupola, and he replied that he had seen the Genesis cupola.

"How long? Or had time dissolved there, too?"

"Yes."

"And then?"

"I watched the goings-on at St. Mark's Square and walked back home."

"And did time dissolve there as well?"

"You already know the answer. Congratulations."

"In the meantime the frame dealer Carlo Fibonacci has been murdered. He was stabbed in the throat."

"That's depressing," Aldrian responded, picturing the corpse and pool of blood.

The Commissario didn't say anything more and turned to his colleagues. After about a half-hour the policeman who had been searching Aldrian's apartment entered the room and, after shaking his head, handed Aldrian his keys at Galli's instigation.

"Why are you staying in Venice?"

"Because I haven't counterfeited any money . . ."

"We've had a tip that your brother—"

"Who?" Aldrian interrupted him. "Who gave you the tip?"

The Commissario just looked at him.

"You don't even realize," Aldrian said, "that you're being tricked."

"And who would benefit from that?" Galli asked arrogantly.

"Not I, at any rate."

"I certainly hope not, for your sake," Galli retorted condescendingly.

Slowly the policemen and Galli himself withdrew, without so much as a goodbye.

Aldrian could tell that he was getting angry again, and when the last man shut the front door behind him, he shouted "Assholes!"

He looked up and saw Margherita standing on the landing.

"Don't ask me anything right now!" Aldrian yelled, furious, and followed her into his brother and sister-in-law's apartment.

In the darkness and cold they didn't say a word. When he turned on the lights, he saw the photo of the house in Skala Kallonis lying on the table. He gave it to Margherita, and she studied the picture silently for a long time.

Finally she asked him: "What are you thinking?"

Aldrian knew that he needed to keep his secrets to himself, and replied: "That I'm going back to my apartment."

She got up, and he walked her to the front door.

"I like you. Eugenio likes you, too. We'd like to have you come and stay at our place," Margherita said suddenly.

They hugged, and Aldrian conscientiously locked the door behind her. It now became clear that he should go back to Vienna. But he also knew that he wouldn't.

Elena and Jakob's apartment was a mess, and—in spite of how cold it was in the place—he began to clean up. He picked up the books from the floor and put them back on their shelves, hung the pictures back on the walls, and put everything else—as best he could recall—back it its proper place. Then he rolled out the carpets, straightened the papers on the desk and put them in various drawers. Last of all he took Jakob's set of keys, hanging at their usual location, put them in his pocket, and went up to his apartment. He put everything in order here, too. It occurred to him that the "Jurassic Park" store had also been searched, but before he could go back downstairs, Beatrice called. She was in Milan, but had to know every step he had taken, every sentence that had been spoken, every thought that had come to him. The thing that concerned her most was why he was still in his apartment and why—as he insisted—he wasn't afraid.

"I don't really know," Aldrian replied.

Later he actually did go downstairs to the store. The soft lighting was still on. He turned it off because, as he told himself, he didn't want to provide a good target.

He couldn't sleep. Even when Beatrice called again and assured him of her love, she couldn't get through to him. He pictured the murdered Carlo Fibonacci in the pool of blood and now knew that Jakob and Elena were dead. When he remembered that the magic book of palmistry with Jakob's dedication had been included in the package with the counterfeit money and the letter, and that all of it was in his wardrobe, he felt anxious. He didn't want to admit it, but he was afraid that some day it could be used against him as evidence, so he got dressed, went back down to his brother's apartment, and put the palmistry book back on the bookshelf before he went back to bed. He had to leave the light on, look around the room, and examine the same furniture and objects over and over again. Then he finally realized that he himself was in a state of absurdity, and that that was now the only thing he could comprehend.

It was dark when Beatrice called again, and he had to promise her he would stay home. She would be back after the weekend, but had then scheduled several days off, she said.

"I can't wait," Aldrian responded.

They would go somewhere together. Maybe to Milan ... "I know you love La Scala, and from there we could go to Assisi. Your brother liked to go there ..."

"He told me about it."

"Sleep tonight at my place on the Campo San Polo. Promise me!"

"Yes."

What he also couldn't get out of his head was the empty space behind the events. Who was behind Fibonacci? he wondered. Apparently Carlo had known too much and that's why he was stabbed. But with whom had his brother been dealing? He dismissed the thought that the business had been run by Fibonacci; the frame dealer had only been an insignificant middleman, he assumed. His death had opened a trap door beneath Aldrian's feet. And after falling, he had landed on another trap door, and so on and so on. In his mind's eye he could see the stage at the Vienna State Opera, the trap room with its passageways and mechanisms and, in the basement, the machines. Above the stage were the galleries of the fly space, and behind the curtains a maze of cables and shafts, and way far back was darkness, and back beyond that, suddenly, ordinary everyday life ... But the stage and the trap door he had fallen through consisted of many stories of trap rooms with trapdoors that let him fall deeper and deeper.

He didn't wake up and get out of bed until noon. It was Saturday.

He glanced out the window. Dense grey fog enveloped the building, and he could only glimpse the merchants putting out their wares—they were like shadows of color in the light of the fish market. Now and then he could tell that some of them were wearing masks. He saw two clowns, a rabbit, and an Oliver Hardy in a toque. He stood at the window for a moment and suddenly felt an unfamiliar desire for normal everyday life. He would be so glad, he told himself, to wander through the fish market, past the stands with fruit and vegetables and the woman who sold flowers, on his way to the Rialto Bridge or to the Ostaria Dai Zemei and have breakfast there and chat with Ettore and Giacomo. He didn't want to think about his brother and Elena right now. He was again overcome with exhaustion, and the next time he woke up, he noticed that the noises from the fish market had subsided. But people with masks were now beginning to take over the city, so he decided to stay home.

At one point he went out just around the corner to get sausage, cheese, bread, and wine, and then fled, as fast as he could, back to his apartment.

The entire time he tried to figure out what he should do next, but he couldn't think of anything.

THIRD BOOK

Dies irae

It was early the next morning. He was still in bed and suddenly realized what he should do next; this often happened immediately after he woke up, so he didn't hesitate to pursue the ideas that had come to him. He looked for his map of Venice, unfolded it, and found the Calle San Domenico in the index. It was across from the park behind the Garibaldi monument that turned into the public garden, the Giardini Publici. He had often strolled past the monuments to Verdi and Wagner, their music in his head, and he would then sit down on a bench and let entire acts from their operas pass before him. He now remembered that he had agreed to meet with Diego Sarcia in his studio, and he put Jakob's key ring in his pocket. After he had gotten dressed, he put his smartphone down on the kitchen table because he was afraid that Beatrice might call or that Commissario Galli might try to trace his phone's location. Then he called Diego Sarcia's number, and when the man answered, Aldrian said: "I'm on my way."

"Okay, I'm almost there."

"And don't forget the envelope."

"How many millions did you put in there?"

You stupid jerk, Aldrian thought, and hung up. What if somebody had tapped his phone! He took his black woolen cap out of the wardrobe, put on gloves, turned out the lights and left.

Out on the street he was invisible in the fog. It had always been his desire to be invisible and to view everything surreptitiously. Perhaps that was why he had become a prompter, he thought. At the San Bartolomeo church, the first mobile market stands surfaced out of the fog, and he bought a new eye mask that he put in the pocket of his windbreaker along with the black woolen cap. Then he made sure that the pin with the gilded dove was still on the back of his lapel before arriving at the Rialto Bridge station. Visibility was so limited that you first heard the labored drone of the vaporetti before they emerged from the fog like large floating lanterns. At one point a gondola appeared out of the grey wall, and at first the only thing you could hear was the cuff of the oar. A group of men and women, dressed as peasants in hats, headscarves, white aprons and shopping bags, materialized at the gangway. Aldrian could see that they were jovial, and though he never would have considered joining the Carnival activities, he envied them. Tourists out of costume photographed the group, the cameras' photoflash eerie in the fog. As far as he could tell, he wasn't being followed. Another gondola appeared, this time with four Chinese or Japanese. At this early morning hour the only people in the passenger shelter were an old woman with a shopping cart and three men smoking cigarettes, wearing gold half-masks with red and black feathers in their hair that gave them the appearance of gamecocks. Everyone was listening and looking in the direction of the approaching vaporetto. At first Aldrian feared—incorrectly—that the masked men were out to get him or were undercover police, but when he realized that they weren't interested in him in the least, he calmed down. Finally he heard the familiar sound of an engine, the deep grumble when the vaporetto geared down, and moments later saw the well-lit white boat approaching out of the void. There were less than a dozen people sitting in the vaporetto, their faces adorned with the white "bauta" mask with no mouth. They had black three-cornered hats on their heads and wore black cloaks. With spastic gestures they pretended as if they were lunatics. They laughed shrilly and emitted bleating sounds. Aldrian still hadn't put on his mask and didn't dare put it on in the vaporetto. Tourists fleeing the Carnival events were standing with their suitcases in the aisle up ahead. "Fugitives from madness," Aldrian thought. The three young men in their gold masks and feathers had also stayed out on deck. It seemed to Aldrian that he was dreaming about some ritualistic funeral. His thoughts were reinforced by seeing the men, now transparent as reflected in the windowpanes, unrecognizable in their white masks and three-cornered hats. Whenever he saw people in masks, their gestures, their shouts and laughter, and the palazzi along the banks of the Grand Canal, he asked himself what message he should derive from all this. Was he supposed to be afraid so that he abandoned his plan? Was he being shown that everyone was ignoring him? Or was he being mocked and taunted? He was relieved when the vaporetto finally docked in San Stae. He reprimanded himself: who was supposed to be sending him a message? He criticized himself: what nonsense are you dredging up? What message are you even talking about? He decided the only thing to think about was his next step, and then the next one, and the one after that, and so on.

He pulled out the city map and checked the route that Diego had described. The workshop was located at Santa Croce 1807. To get there he had to wend his way through narrow alleys that suddenly became dead-ends, so that he again experienced a feeling of disorientation and confusion. It got even worse as new groups of masked individuals appeared, disappeared, approached him, avoided him, briefly drew him into their festivities, but mostly overlooked and ignored him. Meanwhile Aldrian thought he had stumbled into the passageways of gigantic snail shells where plankton organisms, diatoms, bristle worms, rotifers, tunicates, and dinoflagellates frolicked.

At the workshop he encountered a female employee who was making mirrors, masks, and pictures following Sarcia's prototypes. She had on rubber gloves and was in the process of applying paste on a model for a Venetian mirror. The model had the shape and appearance of a huge hoof print, possibly from an elephant-size buffalo. Then Diego came in and took him to a closed-off salesroom displaying different puppet theaters for Commedia-dell'arte figures, accurate to the smallest detail. He showed Aldrian an even larger one made of papier-mâché that depicted a spot under the Procuratie arcades with a view of St. Mark's Square, along with the requisite Commedia-dell'arte figures: the two acrobatic servants, "Arlecchino" in their colorfully checkered patchwork costumes, and "Brighella," the schemer in a nauseous green suit, as well as the glib "Colombina," Diego Sarcia explained. The two male puppets were sitting between columns on the stone floor. The second puppet theater was a stage with red velvet curtains, as Diego remarked, with a plague doctor, the "Dottore," standing front and center—his mask and crooked nose reminded Aldrian of an enraged black-and-white rooster; "to his left, the bearded Pantolone," to the right the funny old woman with her lace blouse and eye mask. In front of the three figures were piles of colorful masks, behind them the Grand Canal and the Santa Maria Salute. Aldrian took off his gloves, and Diego began to lecture:

"As you can see, masks have become my reason for living. For Venetians they have been accepted articles of clothing like hats or shoes. The tradition began back in the 13th century, but attained its peak in the 18th when people wore masks all year long, especially the 'bautas'"—Aldrian had seen them on the faces of the vaporetto passengers shortly before—"with the black veil that covered the hair, ears, and neck. It was even compulsory at the Doge's coronation and receptions for foreign dignitaries. As a rule, you didn't put your mask on until evening, following vespers. Masks blurred class distinctions and helped break down barriers between the sexes. Respected nobles were able to visit brothels and casinos incognito, women had the opportunity to move freely in pants underneath the long cloaks. It wasn't until Napoleon that wearing masks was completely prohibited. He was afraid of subversive powers that could hide behind them."

While Diego spoke, he put on various papier-mâché heads, one consisted of two small faces, another one of a horse, or he provided Aldrian with the mask of a fat sultan, including turban and mustache. In the end the female assistant came—attracted by their laughter—wearing a cat mask on her face that gave her a captivating playfulness. They went back to the workshop, to the paints, pots and jars. Aldrian immediately thought of Jakob and, turning to Diego, asked whether his brother had had a workshop, a studio, or office facilities.

"I've asked myself that same question . . . Honestly, I don't know . . . Jakob made a mystery out of everything, and Elena did as well. The two of them avoided mentioning particular details, never said where they were traveling or where they had been. Mostly they just talked about plants and birds, their family, of course, and about art, about painters and paintings . . . Most of their trips were to Paris and London."

He was now standing in a corner with mirrors on both sides so that Aldrian saw his friend in triplicate, as well as the walls adorned with masks in the background. In passing, Diego told his assistant to open the store and—when they were alone—gave Aldrian back the envelope with Fibonacci's phonebook that Aldrian quickly slipped into his breastpocket.

"This is for you!" he said, and gave Aldrian the mask of a powdered Casanova with a wig. "In case you want to get into the lead chambers."

Aldrian let Diego put the mask on him. If anything, the mask fit into his plans perfectly.

"It's a shame about Elena and Jakob's house in Greece," Diego said, and Aldrian didn't want to ask how he knew about it. It hadn't been mentioned in any of the newspapers or else Aldrian would have heard about it from Beatrice or Margherita.

"Do you have a gun on you?"

Aldrian shook his head, and Diego pulled a key out of his pocket, opened a steel filing cabinet, and put a pistol with silencer in Aldrian's hand. "Six shots," he said. "It's the best I can do."

"I want to pay you for it."

Aldrian put 200 euros on the table, and Diego pocketed the money.

"It's all yours now. Don't bring it back. And you didn't get it from me."

Aldrian was now convinced that his friend was selling guns illegally.

He made his way back to the vaporetto station with the Casanova mask on his face, but he didn't put his gloves on until he reached the

San Stae station, then looked around because he had forgotten to check if anyone was following him. He can't afford to make any mistakes, he told himself. The invisible prompter in the back of his head was still functioning, and he trusted him. Unexpected flashes told him he was being photographed, and although he didn't like it, he remained calm and waited until the packed vaporetto appeared from out of the fog, filled by a class of schoolgirls. As Aldrian suspected, they were Lolitas in fingernail polish, their faces painted for Carnival that communicated, perhaps unintentionally, both innocence and desire. He took a vacant seat among the schoolgirls and, from their giggling and laughter, deduced that they recognized Casanova's face on his mask. The windowpanes rattled and clattered whenever the vaporetto braked and stopped at a passenger shelter. He guessed that a university student and coed sitting beside him—neither of them masked—were reading their lecture notes. Apparently they were memorizing a section. When they got off at the Accademia Bridge, a fat woman who seemed to have stepped right out of a Fellini film sat down next to him. Her hair was dyed red, and she wore two silver thumb rings on one hand, on her wrist an ornate watch with crystal chips that imitated diamonds, and was wearing a red embroidered blazer. Her face had a thick layer of powder, her eyebrows and lips were also heavily made-up. She smiled at him briefly and then gazed straight ahead or through the side window. The white boat docked at St. Mark's Square, and all the passengers ran off into the fog so that, for a moment, Aldrian was sitting all alone on the vaporetto. But seconds later more passengers streamed on board, occupied the seats, and didn't settle down until the vaporetto sailed on. He realized that the cabin was now occupied predominantly by people in everyday clothes. That was disconcerting because he still had his mask on, not wanting to stand out among all the other costumed revelers. He debated whether he should get off at the Giardini station to remain incognito, because there wouldn't be many people strolling in the park in this thick fog. Since the vaporetto was sailing in the direction of the Lido, there were no large crowds at the stations, and few passengers got off. So he got off at the Giardini station, waited until the boat disappeared in the fog, glanced around and tried to get his bearings by looking where he suspected San Servolo might be. But the only thing he saw was grey air. Undecided, he strolled back to the "Donna Partigiana" memorial. It was dedicated to the partisan women who lost their lives in the fight against fascism. The large bronze sculpture depicted a drowned woman who was lying on square and rectangular concrete platforms, surrounded by steps. At high tide it almost completely disappeared beneath the water, at low tide, however, it gave the impression that it had been washed ashore. Aldrian had already seen the powerful woman with her long hair, large hands and feet. She had always been a prominent part of the city, but this time he was so moved that he had to fight back tears because she made him think of Elena and Jakob. It all seemed so eerie in the fog. Moreover, the geometrical platforms and steps in the water reminded him of bee boxes, which only intensified his anguish.

At first he couldn't tear himself away from the sculpture, and he only began to walk on when he felt hate slowly rising within himself, combined with the thought of revenge. In his confusion he went back to the park and entered the Giardini, as if it were a test of his courage. He told himself that as soon as he became afraid, he would go back on the next vaporetto. This time the monuments to Verdi and Wagner didn't elicit their music, and when he looked more closely, he discovered that their noses had been knocked off—which only increased his hatred. He took out the city map and subsequently made his way through the foggy Giardini Garibaldi that was bordered on two sides by old villas and buildings. He noticed that the buildings were in poor condition. He turned to the left after the statue of the Italian freedom fighter and reached the Calle San Domenico. At number 1302 he read on a stone tablet above the doorway with its Roman arch that this was the birthplace of Giovanni Tiepolo. That wouldn't be a very good hideaway, Aldrian thought. He walked a little further and came to a villa with pealing plaster. Red and yellow leaves covered the lawn, and the tops of the tall trees disappeared in the fog. There was no name on the post at the entrance, everything looked dismal. On top of that, there was a red sign with white lettering: "Beware of the Dog!" Aldrian climbed over the wire fence that was partially overgrown with shrubs and found himself in the midst of oleander bushes. There was no movement. Some of the villa's shutters were closed, there wasn't a light in any of the windows. Still wearing the Casanova mask, he approached the building resolutely. As he saw right away, the bell had been torn out, so he used the pale-brass doorknocker, but still no movement. Since he didn't want to make more noise, he tried to open the door, but it was locked. So he studied the lock and searched for the right key on the ring that he had taken from Jakob's apartment until he finally found it. He cautiously entered the house, stopped and listened before closing the door behind him. Of course that might not be such a good idea, because if there were someone in the house and Aldrian had to flee, it could prove to be an obstacle. There wasn't a sound in the hallway, and when he called out Jakob and Elena's names, it echoed in all the rooms as if the large villa were entirely empty. But he was also aware that there were faint sounds that he could no longer perceive due to his hearing loss. Cautiously he opened the first door and was standing in a kitchen where he saw a hot plate, a sink, a table with empty water and wine bottles, two glasses, an empty ashtray, and two chairs. A naked light bulb hung from the ceiling. He called their names again, but everything remained silent. The dust on the floor mingled in his thoughts with the fog outside. Dead flies were piled up between the double windowpanes. In the next room that was unfurnished, dozens of them were stuck to a flytrap that seemed to be a warning. He entered other dusty rooms and then went upstairs. The first door that he cautiously opened led to a workshop with painted curtains depicting the view of a lush garden that extended down to the distant sea. He saw cypress trees, pine trees, and bodies of water that reflected the sky, butterflies and birds, bee boxes, telescopes for bird-watching, and a telescope for the night sky. No doubt this was Jakob and Elena's house, their *paradiso* that they had never mentioned to him. Becoming impatient, he took off the Casanova mask and put it on the floor. In the middle of the room he found a white cardboard model that apparently represented the house and the grounds of this "paradise." Judging from an illustration that was lying on the floor, a rough draft of the prototype was done on the underside of a large folio that was labeled *Victoria Amazonica*, the Latin designation for the giant water lily. At first glance the plant resembled a green spider's web, except it was stronger and, instead of threads, had vein-shaped vascular strands that radiated out from the center and was partitioned by smaller transverse strands to form discrete rhombic and rectangular cells. At the spot in the center where the strands met and the stem of the giant lily joined the leaf is where the old villa with its terrace and the planned additional buildings stood, assuming the shape of an ellipse—following the contours of the lily leaf. The asymmetrical parcels would be filled with water that mirrored the sky or, as he saw, could be planted in water lilies. The symmetrical part was designed to feature beehives, trees, and shrubbery, groves of oranges and lemons and olives, and small wheat fields . . . The two recesses on the opposite sides of the leaf-shaped grounds gave the entire complex the shape of two wings of an enormous bird. Aldrian looked up and gazed through the window at the fog. Since he didn't notice anything suspicious, he opened the next door to a workroom that was chock full of paint cans, chemicals, turpentine, bottles, tubes, jars, palette knives, magnifying glasses, brushes, a drawing board, pencils and colored pens, and an easel. Spread out on the table were pages cut from art books, enlarged illustrations of the works of various painters: William Turner's bird studies from Farnley Hall and his *Venice Watercolors*, Maria Sibylla Merian's pictures of plants and insects, watercolors by Georg Flegel: tulips, irises, carnations, roses, daffodils, marsh marigolds, lilies of the valley, stock flowers, anemones, cyclamen, currents, peapods, nuts, acorns, strawberries, and apples, but also studies with a kingfisher, a blue titmouse, a parrot, a fly, prawns, clams, a silkworm in various stages of development, and a stag beetle. The illustrations of the still lives— watercolors of magical beauty—were stacked to one side like the copies of an etching of Rembrandt's marbled cone shell, the study of a lesser kestrel by Arcimboldo, along with several watercolors by Paul Klee. Aldrian glanced around again, then opened a white cabinet with sliding doors. When he opened the doors he came upon a smaller stack of pictures that Jakob himself must have done. Aldrian took the painted papers from the cabinet and immediately felt the cold on his legs. He would have liked to just run away and leave everything the way it was, but his curiosity was greater than his discomfort. Searching through the cabinets he also found old canvases, rolls of old types of paper, and chemicals to obtain old colors. He put Jakob's pictures on the table and on the floor, searched for the relevant one from the torn-out pages, and could tell that they weren't clumsy forgeries, but skillfully varied representations. It was supposed to look like the artists he had copied had produced one or two variations of a certain motif or left behind previously undiscovered watercolors and paintings. It must have taken Jakob many hours, many nights for his work. Why had he never mentioned it to Aldrian? He then asked himself how everything must have taken place. He hadn't found any traces of counterfeit money—but, of course, that didn't mean anything. There could be a second workshop, a second study . . . In any event, Elena must have acquired chemicals for the colors, the old paper and the old canvases, and Jakob must have gone to the applicable museums and studied the paintings he would eventually forge. Aldrian now knew for certain that even if he didn't run away, he would never see the two of them again . . . If they had been murdered, there must have been a reason. And while Aldrian deliberated in this room full of his brother's forgeries, he realized that presumably Jakob had wanted to part ways with the organization for which he had worked. "Probably," Aldrian thought, "he wanted to sell the forgeries himself . . ." He was now certain that Jakob had wanted to leave everything behind and take off for Greece. And he was also sure that the organization hadn't discovered the location of the workshop. It was possible that Fibonacci had taken over the business end for Jakob; regardless, he had hidden his brother's forged pictures under the sales counter. Aldrian stared at the pictures for a long time. He also thought he heard two strokes from a pendulum clock on the lower floor. He held his breath and waited, but everything was quiet. There must be someone in the neighborhood or in the city who had kidnapped Elena and Jakob, and when they weren't prepared to cooperate, held them captive or had probably even killed them. The only thing he could do, Aldrian told himself, was erase the traces of Elena and Jakob's second life and make the pictures disappear, along with the colors, the old canvases and paper rolls, the curtains, and the model of their Garden of Eden. In order to accomplish that, he would have to set the entire workshop on fire—the thought didn't cause any regret, because he himself was in danger of being dragged into the crime. He then noticed a metal cabinet in one corner. He immediately knew it was Jakob's "Noah's Ark." As he pulled out the drawers and saw the old colored etchings of plants and animals, he forced himself to think of something else as he threw them onto a pile. He added the forged pictures, types of paper, canvases, illustrations from art books, and other combustible materials. In doing so, he again felt rage at the covert organization, but also at his brother. He could see Jakob and Elena's faces before him, and he fought back tears of sorrow and fury as he took shellac, turpentine, and ethanol that was stashed among the paints, poured them on the pile, lit it all, and fled to the adjoining room. The explosion behind him set everything in flames. He closed the door and made preparations to set fire to the workshop, but recoiled at a sound. It was so slight that he almost missed it. He quickly reached for his pistol, switched off the safety, and waited. In the meantime, smoke and a foul smell began to spread from the next room. Someone really had opened and then closed the front door. The sound of rapid footsteps came from the entryway, then someone was climbing the stairs to the second floor, and Aldrian hastily hid behind one of the curtains. A pigeon sat on the windowsill and watched him with a yellow eye. Aldrian concentrated on the footsteps that were close-by, then the door opened and, as Aldrian peeked out from behind the curtain, he saw a male figure frantically looking around, bending down to pick up the Casanova mask on the floor. For a brief instant, before the man put on the mask, he recognized the face of Sergio Celi, the diver who had pretended to be so uninformed. But he didn't have a time to think, because Celi was holding a pistol with a silencer and began to kick the curtains. Suddenly he stopped and glanced in the burning workroom. He quickly turned back and began shooting at the curtains. Aldrian had immediately dropped to the floor, had fallen against the curtain and he tried to hide. As the curtain silently fell to the ground, he saw that Celi in the Casanova mask was pointing his pistol at him. Before Aldrian could pull the trigger, something exploded, and he realized that Celi's mask had a hole below the forehead and blood was streaming out. Celi lost his balance and fell to the floor of the workshop, lifeless. It took a moment for Aldrian to realize that he had been the one who fired the shot. He took the mask off the diver's face, saw the gunshot wound in the man's eye, and confirmed that Celi was dead. What if Celi had only fired because he was afraid? Maybe he had worked with Jakob? And maybe the building even belonged to him? . . . He automatically removed the little logo from the inside of the mask that belonged to Diego Sarcia and tossed it on the pile with the model and the fallen curtains. Then he went through Celi's pockets. He took the man's smartphone, and though he wanted to get away, he removed the SIM card, put it in his pants' pocket, and stuck the cellphone in his jacket. Celi also had a gas cigarette lighter and a pack of 100-euro bills in his wallet that reminded Aldrian of the counterfeit money. Furthermore, Aldrian found IDs and the picture of a woman. He pocketed everything but Celi's driver's license. He cleaned off any possible fingerprints from the license and the wallet and tossed them out the window where the pigeon had been and down into the garden. Meanwhile the pool of blood under Celi's head had spread. Just as he was using Celi's lighter to ignite the curtains, the model of the house in Skala Kallonis, and everything else combustible, he clearly heard other noises from the first floor. He took out the pistol again and didn't move a muscle. As hard as he tried, he couldn't make out any sounds. He cautiously got behind the open door. Somewhere on the ground floor a pendulum clock he must have overlooked began to strike. A second later the black-haired young man whom he had confronted at Fibonaci's and who claimed to be from the police stormed into the room, realized what had happened, and swiveled around, a gun in his hand. But before he could pull the trigger, Aldrian had shot him in the chest. His adversary dropped his gun, and when Aldrian fired two more shots, the man fell to the floor. Once again it was quiet, and Aldrian listened to determine if there was any other movement. He then noticed that the flames from the adjoining room had spread to the studio. Without deliberating, Aldrian took the young man's weapon and put his own in the dead man's hand. Then he searched him and found no smartphone, but he did come up with keys and an ID made out to a Rocco Scarlatti. In addition he found a business card in the man's wallet in the same name with the address of a used bookstore on the Fondamente Nuove and a telephone number. Aldrian put everything back in the dead man's jacket except for the ID and the business card. The smell of smoke was now much stronger, he could hear the fire crackling, so he left the studio, ran down the stairs and opened the front door. The fog was so thick that he could barely see. After he climbed back over the fence, he put on the eye mask and his black wool cap and ran down the Calle San Domenico in the direction of Garibaldi's statue and, from there, over a bridge to the Giardini vaporetto stop. He stopped, out of breath. His throat hurt and he still felt the chill. In a panic attack he threw Sergio Celi's telephone and the pistol from the black-haired Rocco Scarlatti in the Canale di San Marco, then tore up Scarlatti's ID—but not the business card—and only realized later that he hadn't even checked to see if anyone was watching. Making up for his mistake, he dropped the paper shreds into the water, took the key to the villa from his brother's key ring and threw it as hard as he could into the fog bank shrouding the canal. He shouldn't get on a vaporetto just yet, he told himself. He automatically headed in the direction of St. Mark's Square, and with every step the events more and more closely resembled some kind of insanity. He kept on telling himself he wasn't crazy, until he eventually convinced himself. He walked on past the Donna

Partigiana memorial without even glancing at it—it now reminded him even more of Elena and what he had just done. He realized he was acting like some wind-up toy. Every time he crossed one of the stone bridges with their steps he was caught off guard. In the back of his head four words kept repeating themselves: "I am not crazy!" He paused in front of the Museo Storico Navale. As a rule he could mentally recall the rooms with thoughts of Richard Wagner's *Der fliegende Holländer*, "Steuermann! Lass die Wacht!" with its buoyant ending, or "Kein Zweifel! Sieben Meilen fort trieb uns der Sturm vom sichren Port." But the only things he noticed were the silence and the darkness and his 'I am not crazy!" that he continued to whisper. In front of the bridge to the museum an earthmover was at work in the drained bed of the Rio dell'Arsenale; he had heard it a minute ago but not reacted. The earthmover blocked his view of the fog that had swallowed the Isola San Diorgio Maggiore on the other side of the lagoon. He recognized the two large black anchors along the wall at the entrance to the Museo Storico Navale, but this time they were only heavy iron objects. A row of benches stood in front of the anchors, a figure lying on one of them. At first he thought someone had forgotten their overcoat, but pant-legs and shoes were sticking out of the coat, though the head was hidden under the garment. He glanced back at the bridge and saw an invalid whose entire left arm was missing and, when Aldrian looked more closely, his left leg as well. He was wearing a torn jacket and sweatpants that were rolled up to the knee of his prosthesis. Apprehensive, Aldrian turned toward the bundle of humanity on the bench. The stranger just might be dead. He was wearing loafers with perforated tops in the British style, grey socks, grey knickerbockers; the rest was just a bulge under the blue overcoat. The earthmover's motor stuttered and roared to life. Aldrian thought about the two men he had shot, dismissed the thought, climbed the steps to the bridge, and kept telling himself that he wasn't crazy. Perhaps in reality the young man with black hair had been a faster draw, and Aldrian was now the one wandering around in the netherworld. In the meantime he noticed yet another homeless man, this one in a cap and denim jacket. He was leaning on a bench—his face horribly disfigured—staring at Aldrian, who was forced to turn away. The next bridge led to the Riva degli Schiavoni that was more heavily populated, and the more bridges he crossed, the more densely clustered the masked revelers grew. In the netherworld there were no faces, just masks, he told himself. There was confetti on the broad sidewalk, and in the fog all the figures he encountered and joined really did look like ghosts. He didn't want to consider what consequences were awaiting him as a result of his bloody episode. On all sides there was a jumble of voices that laughed, called out, babbled, conversed. He walked on, past the vaporetto station and the souvenir salesmen, the bronze monument to Vittorio Emanuele sitting astride his horse, and the Ponte della Paglia; from there he could see the Bridge of Sighs. At the base of the next set of stairs a beggar woman was waiting. Her face covered with burn marks, she wore a headscarf and was just putting on a Mickey Mouse mask. When he reached the Piazzetta San Marco he thought he had stumbled onto a pitched battle in the fog. It wasn't possible to take one step forward without pushing or shoving someone aside. There was no common purpose, people just wanted to be there. Aldrian worked his way through the shoving and jostling on all sides to the public ballroom without a roof—St. Mark's Square. On a stage the traditional Best Mask Contest had already begun. In the back of his head Aldrian could hear the voice of Commissario Galli, asking him for an alibi: Where were you at such and such a time? So Aldrian redoubled his efforts to get to Caffè Florian, but once there, he saw that everyone was caught in a traffic jam: large and small groups of people were trying to gain entry; in the rooms sat people in elaborate costumes, masks with plumes, gold masks, powdered faces or three-cornered hats sitting next to unmasked Japanese and Europeans. Aldrian assumed the role of a security guard or of an owner who was just doing his duty, and by acting in a purposeful manner was able to finesse a spot by the glass front door that he then shoved open—even though a waiter in a white tuxedo kept shaking his head, indicating that everything was "occupato," "taken." He squeezed inside, took off his cap and eye mask, saw a vacant chair at a table with four Japanese, and sat down in spite of the group's protests. The waiter appeared immediately and, with gestures of denial, insisted that he vacate the chair. Unmoved, Aldrian played a deaf mute, reached for a napkin, and with his ballpoint pen wrote the word "spritz," adding a polite "pronto." The waiter shrugged his shoulders, and a moment later the Japanese man whose seat Aldrian had taken reappeared. While his agitated friends reported what had just taken place, Aldrian gazed out the window at the flattened faces of the passers-by who were staring into the Caffè. The Japanese customer came over and reminded him in English that Aldrian was sitting in the man's chair. Aldrian briefly looked him in the eye, kept a straight face, and placed his open hands over his ears, shook his head, pretending he was deaf. At that, a different waiter appeared with a red cushioned stool, placed it at the table, and the Japanese gentleman, with raised eyebrows, sat down. By now Aldrian was certain that people would remember him being here. In retrospect his idea was ridiculous and his behavior unnecessary. Embarrassed, he attributed these actions to his confusion. He gradually warmed up. As soon as he had drunk the first spritz and ordered a second, in writing, he saw a boy dressed as Zorro, playing with a yo-yo. The child had a black suit, the typical black eye mask and a wide-brimmed Spanish hat. The yo-yo danced up and down, and Aldrian told himself that it would decide whether they would arrest him as a criminal or not. The down movement meant "yes," the upward movement "no." But first the boy would have to start a new game. Aldrian didn't take his eyes off the yo-yo. With total concentration and an intense look in his eyes, the boy once again made the yo-yo bounce down and up, added two tricks, and then quit. Before Aldrian could write down his order for a third spritz, the boy started back up, but apparently the point was to keep Aldrian in suspense, because the boy didn't make any mistakes. All of a sudden Aldrian no longer wanted to watch and didn't care what the yo-yo predicted. With a banknote in his hand, he gestured to a waiter, and didn't even wait for the man to sort out his change. He also didn't look back at the yo-yoing boy and the Japanese at his table, but left the Caffè distraught and, once outside, made himself invisible again with his eye mask and black woolen cap. On the stage in the middle of the square he saw elegantly dressed and masked women in the thick fog, while in the crowd there were similar fantasy characters along with people not in costume. He briefly thought of the ceiling fresco in the San Pantalon church, but was instantly yanked back to reality by unfolding events. Beneath the arcade passageways with their brightly-lit display windows of jewelers, souvenir shops, stores for antiques, fashion, and Murano glassware, photoflashes flickered as if they were exploding fireflies. He let the crowd carry him along, not knowing where he would end up. It gradually sunk in that he had just killed two people. In the meantime a professional troupe was dancing a tango on the stage. The crowds grew, more and more pedestrians with wigs, hats, and costumes in fashions from the 18th century dominated the street scene. Everyone wanted to ogle, admire, and photograph—and be ogled, admired, and photographed. A female vocalist came out and rendered sad Neapolitan songs, but the crowd didn't respond. The make-believe nobles, princes and princesses, sultans, sheiks, and historic figures moved like clouds of late-summer mosquitoes, circling the same spot. In the fog Aldrian noticed a large black poster in green lettering with a square opening the size of a puppet theater. As it so happened, puppets were indeed acting out a melodrama: a magician transformed a barber into a crocodile, then into a mouse, then into an incompetent barber surgeon who couldn't even pull teeth, until the love of a washerwoman returned him to his original self. Aldrian was unintentionally swept along by the crowd, there was no letup. Despite the fog he recognized a mulled wine stand at the campanile. You could smell its fragrance from some distance away. He maneuvered over toward it, bought a drink in a white paper cup, and noticed a man in uniform, his jacket with gold braid and knickerbockers. The fantasy soldier arrived at the black poster with green lettering and the opening for the puppet theater. He climbed in and faced the audience, grinning all the while. He disappeared for a moment—Aldrian assumed he was changing his costume—but through the puppet theater opening he presented his bare ass. For as long as he was there, everyone laughed and photographed him with their photoflashes. Other than that, nothing happened.

Aldrian fought his way back to the arcade passages where a crazy old woman was standing in front of a stationery store with fountain pens of black enamel and amber, speaking with her mirror image in the display window and gesturing. Wearing a cap over her headscarf, she unexpectedly turned to face him, and gave him a combative look . . . He slowly left the piazza that disappeared behind him in the fog; the only thing he could hear was some music and the sounds of jumbled voices. Police regulated the stream of people on the streets. They directed the crowd into certain streets, closed others off—it was pointless to try and swim upstream. Every time Aldrian saw an officer, he became anxious. The flood of masked revelers continued non-stop past display windows of mask shops, shoe stores and gourmet retailers, past restaurants where masked waiters were dressed as clowns or as 18th-century burghers. But when the waiters were wearing their normal clothing, they now seemed to Aldrian as if they were in costume. He also thought some lingering policemen were in disguise, as were two gondoliers with their straw hats and striped T-shirts. He was eventually able to duck into a side street that seemed less crowded, but that turned out to be an illusion. He almost stumbled over a young man sitting on the ground with a cardboard sign: "I am poor, have three brothers. Looking for work." When he got closer, he saw that the young man was a young woman. A little farther on, he stopped in front of an elegant antique store featuring gold Buddhas, ivory objects, a painting of a woman applying makeup, and an old mask with three faces. There were more beggars squatting here, unmoving. They only stared at the tin cups between their legs or gazed at the people passing by. At one point he could hear guitar music coming from somewhere in the fog, then an accordion or singing.

There was a mob scene at the Rialto Bridge similar to the one at St. Mark's Square. People in costumes were backed up on the steps between shops, acting as if they were in an amusement park.

Like a piece of driftwood in a flooded stream, he was swept past Diego Sarcia's mask store, then past the Ostaria Dai Zemei, and though he thought about Sergio Celi the diver, about the pistol and the Casanova mask, about the deserted building in the Giardini Garibaldi, the pools of blood and paradise, the forged paintings, the fire and the fog, he no longer had to convince himself that he wasn't crazy. Everything around him had changed so much that he could no longer come to any conclusions, and what had happened in the old villa where he heard a pendulum clock strike and killed two people had become a component of his reality. He realized how the horrible events had combined with the crazy environment, how the Carnival atmosphere now permeated them so that they had been transformed into something fictional. Though he hadn't intentionally planned it, he really wasn't upset when he arrived at San Polo. The mob from the train station had made it extremely difficult to keep going. Laughing people in masks were throwing confetti, and a popular yellow merry-go-round whirled children dressed as Robin Hood, Harry Potter, butterflies or tigers, while an attractive female mandarin kept things under control. At first Aldrian couldn't tear himself away from the merry-go-round, from the children on seats hanging from chains who appeared out of the fog and then disappeared into the fog, though he would rather have gone on to Beatrice's apartment. Seen from above and in the fog, the activities on the piazza had to look even more incredible, he thought. Four girls in red wigs and heavy makeup were sitting behind a table, painting faces with watercolors and tubes of paint.

Aldrian took off his mask and woolen cap and, surrounded by a gaggle of giggling girls, had a black tattoo-like design painted on his forehead and cheeks. When he was finished, they held up a mirror—he saw he looked like a Maori in street clothes. For quite some time he couldn't take his eyes off a child sitting in a huge teacup on another merry-go-round as it spun on its own axis while completing its circular course. In the meantime teenagers were spraying adults with colorful "spaghetti" from aerosol cans. The goop stuck to the victims' clothes, but they laughed anyway. There was a puppet theater in a large tent with transparent sides of plastic sheeting that was shrouded in fog. Curious, Aldrian approached, imagining he was a white rabbit that a magician was about to pull out of a hat. The theater was set up on a collapsible stage. A dark-haired woman was standing out front, talking with the puppets she held in her hands while explaining the play to the audience. She talked, explained, asked the puppets questions, challenged them to do things, and scolded them. A cart contained paraphernalia and other useful items that added humor to the play, and she would offer them to the puppets. The puppets included three little pigs and a dog, a convict whose ears were rinsed out by the woman. The little pigs farted the whole time, and the children laughed themselves silly. There was also a great deal of yawning, burping, and snoring on the small stage. Aldrian tried follow the plot, as he did every time he went to the theater, opera, or to the movies. A shaky backdrop materialized, depicting a farmhouse with a functional front door and, nearby, an outhouse. Hanging on the front wall of the portable stage was yet another bag containing everything the puppets needed for their show. At the conclusion of the "Play of the Winds," as the performance was called, Aldrian applauded wildly along with the children and then left. He fled into the maze of alleys where he encountered fewer pedestrians, and the images from the large villa once again overwhelmed his thoughts. Once again he was in his brother's workshop before the young black-haired man burst through the door and pointed his gun at him. He saw himself throw Sergio Celi's wallet out the window. He saw the empty rooms and the flytrap on the ceiling, saw himself take the Casanova mask off Sergio Celi, the blood streaming out of his eye and covering his face. As he emerged from the alleys, he came to a brightly-lit piazza, and then to the Campo San Tomà. From a distance he could tell that the shutters in Carlo Fibonacci's store were let down. He didn't stop since he didn't want to meet anyone, not even Margherita and Eugenio. As if out of habit, he headed for the San Pantalon church. In fact he doubted that it would be open today as he shoved the door and it swung open. Two elderly women were kneeling and praying in the front pew. He sat down near the entrance and waited. It wasn't long before the two old women left and he could move to the middle of the nave and insert the proper coin into the spotlight apparatus. He then stretched out on one of the pews and gazed up . . . It now seemed as if the angels were fighting and descending upon him like a swarm of voracious locust that wanted to devour him. Finally the spotlights dimmed and he realized someone was speaking to him.

"Signore . . . Signore!"

Startled, Aldrian sat upright and recognized a priest bending over him. He immediately reassured the priest that he wasn't drunk or sick, he was just admiring the ceiling fresco. He was sorry if he had behaved disrespectfully, he added. The old priest didn't quite believe him, but asked if he wanted to confess. He didn't? Would he rather be left alone?

Aldrian wanted run off, but the priest touched his arm and said: "Go to the Campo San Giacomo dell'Orio, that's where the authentic Venetian Carnival is held, the way the locals celebrate!"— He walked Aldrian out of the church and pointed in one direction, and, after thanking the man, Aldrian went back out into the maze of alleys. At one point he stopped, not knowing where he was. He discovered he had come to a canal along the Fondamenta Minotto, according to his city map. With the map in hand he gradually drew closer and closer to his destination, though he rarely saw anyone else in the fog. Eventually he crossed the Corte Canal and came to the more populated Campo San Giacomo dell'Orio. "From the madhouse, via the wrong road, back into life," he thought. A farmers' market was underway on the Campo when he arrived. Just then a piglet was being cut up, white rye bread was for sale, and folks were drinking ombra, but, aside from the children, very few people were wearing masks around the vendors' stands. On other tables you could find sausages, salami, cheese, and condiments. Just then Aldrian realized that he was hungry. He ordered two sandwiches, purchased a small bottle of wine, and sat down on a bench. Locals in coats and random passersby were relaxing outside the cafés. Acquaintances and neighbors were chatting all around him. It seemed as if they were all enjoying a few pleasant hours—and Aldrian envied them that. He drank a second bottle of wine, waited until the alcohol had taken effect, and then asked one of the farmers where the next vaporetto station was.

"Biasio," the heavy-set man replied, pointed in one direction, and then turned his back on him. Aldrian acted as if he had understood the man, but by the next street corner he had forgotten the name, took his map out again and finally found the passenger shelter.

He boarded the vaporetto, found it half-empty with only a few of the children on board in costume. He assumed that most of the people in masks were in the streets leading from the train station to St. Mark's Square. In any event he found a vacant seat and gazed out the window at the Grand Canal. The dense fog that blended sky and water made him happy. He could barely make out the other bank. The approaching boats first appeared in silhouette, then were suddenly upon them as if someone had conjured them up.

"A journey through a sea of clouds in the sky," he thought. The fog above the water was greyish-green, greyish-white higher up, and grey-gold in the clouds that hid the sun. In the interim he became aware that children were staring at his painted face, but he didn't mind. His brother's key ring pinched in his pants pocket, and it persuaded him to go back to the building with the workshop to see what had happened to the burning building. He had completely lost his sense of time, so he was surprised that it was getting dark and would soon be nighttime. The curtain had fallen in the "movie theater" of Aldrian's thoughts.

From the vaporetto he could see that the festivities on the Piazzetta were in full swing. It seemed as if everyone had just been waiting for the sun to set. Most of the passengers got off, a few others boarded. It didn't seem very smart for him to visit a place where he had killed two men just hours before, but the urge to see the villa or its charred ruins was stronger than his apprehension. He must not put himself in danger, he decided. When the vaporetto docked, he saw that they had now reached the Arsenal, and when they sailed on, he still could see people on the benches in front of the Museo

Storico Navale. The vaporetto finally came to the Giardini station where Aldrian could already begin to smell smoke. Boats from the police and fire departments were tied up underneath the Rio di San Giuseppe bridge, and they were pumping water through hoses. From the Giardini Garibaldi—where he could see a crowd of people and the burned-out building that had presumably collapsed—he moved on to the Calle San Domenico. En route he continually encountered people in masks, so he didn't stand out from the crowd. He forced his way between the curiosity seekers up to the smoking building and determined that the fire was out, though they were still pumping water onto the ruins. The complete upper story was demolished and there was nothing left of the roof.

The police dominated the scene, even more than did the fire department. Men in uniforms were all over the place, conferring, telephoning, and casting indifferent glances at the spectators. Aldrian overheard bystanders saying that two charred corpses had been discovered in the destroyed villa, along with weapons, so the police were treating it as a crime scene. Aldrian couldn't identify with the crime scene, the fence, the garden, or the ruins, or with the event that made these people so upset. He didn't want to admit that he himself was the person who had caused this mob to gather. Even though he was freezing, he couldn't leave until he caught sight of Commissario Galli just coming out of the ruins. He fled as inconspicuously as possible back to the Giardini station and took the next vaporetto to San Silvestro. An inebriated Carnival group in animal masks and paper hats were laughing on the forward deck and eventually disembarked at the Piazzetta di San Marco.

There were even larger crowds all around the Rialto Bridge. "As if the Mother of God had made an appearance," he thought grumpily. Even at the fish market people in masks were dancing in spite of the cold and fog, and without musical accompaniment. At his brother's house he picked up the newspaper and the mail that were lying behind the front door as usual, and dragged himself upstairs. Now he realized just how tired he really was. On the display of his smartphone—that he intentionally had left on the kitchen

273

table—he noticed that Beatrice had tried to contact him, but he didn't activate the phone. He fell on his bed and was instantly out cold.

Yet Another Interrogation

He awoke to the flashes and explosions of fireworks. It seemed as if a war had broken out. It was dark and still foggy outside, and he remembered his brother's stories about fireworks on Sunday being the traditional finale of Carnival in Venice. His mind was still dealing with the remnants of an abandoned dream as he contemplated what he should do next. From the moment he opened his eyes, it was clear to him for the very first time that he had shot two men and set a building on fire. He still couldn't comprehend it, closed his eyes, and dreamed a bit longer. Half-asleep, he saw the faces of the two dead men and Commissario Galli coming out of the ruins, then the mob of masked people at St. Mark's Square, and he was again jolted out of sleep. He could hear that the fireworks were still in progress. In the fog he had the impression he was in the middle of thunderclouds. He estimated that he had come home about 8 or 9 p.m. It occurred to him that his face was still painted, so he got out of bed, undressed, and went into the bathroom where he carefully washed his face and took a shower. After he had thoroughly dried off, he got fresh underwear out of the wardrobe, stuffed his dirty things in a trash bag, and slipped into pajamas and his bathrobe. The flares and booms outside continued unabated. First he removed the small photograph that he had taken from Dr. Dr. Galotti's wallet and called three or four of the phone numbers written on it. All of them were inactive. He couldn't make out the last number. Then he took Sergio Celi's SIM card and replaced his own with it—since his phone was the same brand as that of the diver. Finally he put

275

Carlo Fibonacci's pocket telephone book on the table, compared the stored numbers with the call list, and painstakingly determined that they had only three numbers in common. He repeated the search process, compared the numbers with those in Fibonacci's little phone book, and came to the same conclusion. There were only three numbers that matched up, each with a single letter instead of a name to indicate the contact person: none of the three had an area code, so he concluded that they were all local numbers. Only then did he realize that one of the numbers was for his brother's store. And the other two? He searched his jacket for the business card for Rocco Scarlatti, the black-haired young antique dealer, and compared it with the remaining numbers. As a matter of fact, the number on the business card matched the first one, so there was only one unknown number remaining. The best thing, he thought, would be to call that number sometime during the day. He wrote that number and Scarlatti's in his notebook, crushed the chip with his shoe, and cleared away the pieces. He tore up the remnants of the business card and the small photograph and flushed them down the toilet. Then he put Fibonacci's little address book in one of the folds of his map and put it in the breast pocket of his sport coat. He took the key ring back to his brother's apartment. An hour had gone by, the fireworks were over, and he was amazed that he was no longer afraid and didn't feel he had to run away. For the first time he had the feeling—if only for a brief instant—that he had "everything under control," but he immediately admitted it was an illusion. His fate was not in his hands. Then he was startled by a loud knocking at the front door and someone shouting: "Police!"

Aldrian got up, put the key in his pocket, activated his phone, and put both of them in the pocket of his bathrobe before he carefully went downstairs without turning on any lights. It suddenly occurred to him that something must have given away his presence. He hesitated to enter the hallway to the front door because he instinctively thought it was possible that someone might shoot through the door, so he paused and listened. Someone shouted "Police!" yet again. Otherwise the only sounds were the muted Carnival noises from the fish market. He hesitantly edged his way along the wall to the front door and waited. Since nothing happened, he peeked out the peephole, but the only thing he could see were darkness, fog, and occasionally people in masks. As quietly as possible, he put the key in the lock, quickly turned it and opened the door angrily, but there was no one there. He noticed there was a package at his feet. It was addressed to him with the inscription: "You're next!" He recognized the threat— his name and the cross—from the slip of paper they had put under his bed after he was attacked. At first he wanted to kick the package and run back into the building, but in spite of his misgivings he bent down, grabbed it, stepped back into the building, and locked the front door behind him. In the dark he put the package on the table and then turned on a light. He stood there for a moment, lost in thought, then went up to his apartment and came back down with a knife and scissors. Was it some kind of explosive? A picture or some news from Jakob and Elena? He opened the package and found two objects wrapped in aluminum foil. Without hesitation he pulled out the smaller of the two. It was solid and cool, like something frozen solid, and when he unwrapped the foil there was a severed hand that he recognized immediately. It was Elena's! There was also a hand in the second foil wrapping, and he wasn't surprised to see that it was Jakob's. There was a 100-lira banknote, presumably counterfeit, in each hand. And when he took the money, he saw that both palms had painted symbols in black ink that ran up to the fingers, and he immediately recalled the illustrations in the book about palmistry that had been in the first package as a Christmas present from his brother. He tore up the two banknotes, ran back up to his apartment and flushed them down the toilet also. When he came back to the stairwell, the phone in the pocket of his bathrobe rang. He picked it up and, after confirming that it was Beatrice, answered.

"Where are you?" she asked urgently.

"In my apartment."

"Why aren't you at the Campo San Polo?"

"It was too noisy. I'm sorry, but you woke me up."

"I called you several times yesterday."

"Yes. I forgot and left the phone in the kitchen."

After a long pause Beatrice asked impatiently: "Did you get home late?"

"Around midnight."

"But why didn't you call me back?"

"Because I fell asleep."

She didn't respond, and he apologized again.

"I was at St. Mark's Square, in Caffè Florian, then at Campo San Polo . . ." he added. "I didn't want to be thinking about things the whole time. I love you."

While he was talking on the phone, he envisioned the two men he had shot and the severed hands of Jakob and Elena. He didn't want to explain everything to Beatrice over the phone, just the thought of doing so made him even more miserable.

"I can't wait until you get back," he added.

"You don't make things easy," Beatrice answered. "I hope there haven't been any new developments in the meantime."

"Yes, I hope so, too."

"Did you forget that I'm taking vacation starting Friday?"

"No. I can't wait."

As soon as he finished their conversation, he ran downstairs to the hallway and began to cry.

It hadn't been his brother who tried to best him as a magician by sending him the first package with the counterfeit money. It was the same people who were now humiliating and taunting him.

The police came half-an-hour later, and fifteen minutes after that, a drowsy Commissario Galli appeared.

He walked over to the package and asked: "Is there a ransom note?"

"No," one of the policemen answered.

Then Galli turned to Aldrian. He noticed that he had been crying and shook his hand.

"I'm very sorry," he said.

Aldrian led the way and sat down at the kitchen table. The

Commissario regretted that he had to ask him some questions.

Aldrian wondered if Galli had seen him or if someone had recognized him at the burned-out building. He had to be careful what he said, so he didn't say anything until Commissario Galli addressed him.

"How did you get the package?"

Aldrian haltingly reported what had happened, and had to struggle against the images in his mind.

Then the Commissario quizzed him about every detail, wanting to know how Aldrian had spent the day before, what time it had been when he had been here or there, and what had been going on, and who could verify his story. Aldrian didn't mention that he had been masked and had changed clothes. He also didn't mention anything that could tie him to the two dead men and the burning building. And he didn't tell about his visit to San Pantalon church because he assumed the old priest would remember his painted face. He also said nothing about his trip to the farmers' market at Campo San Giacomo dell'Orio. If he wasn't sure what to say, he would cover his face with both hands, emit an exhausted sigh, and think until he came up with something. The longer the interrogation lasted, the more he understood that the Commissario connected everything to the counterfeit money and suspected his brother. Aldrian disagreed with Galli's suspicions and allegations, and the Commissario now wanted to know how he interpreted the severed hands, insisting that Elena, his brother's wife, was also involved in the "events" and in this "case," as he put it. After an hour and a half—with Aldrian on the verge of tears several times—they had reached a dead end.

The Commissario changed topics and now told him that two men had been found shot to death and burned to a crisp in a burned-out building near the Giardini Garibaldi. The police assume that one of them was Sergio Celi whose mother had bequeathed him the building; witnesses attest that was there light in the studio usually only at night. The police had also recovered remnants of paint cans and equipment for producing graphics—all of which pointed to the conclusion that this might have been the forgers' workshop. But the most remarkable discovery was Sergio Celi's wallet that turned up in the garden. It had no fingerprints, which pointed to a third suspect. To top it off, it contained counterfeit 100-euro bills. "It's also remarkable that we couldn't find any telephones that might have contained information about the recent crimes—especially regarding the murder of Carlo Fibonacci. And as in the case with the two dead men, we didn't find Fibonacci's telephone or records," he continued. "We only have the SIM card that you took from Ivanov and passed on to us. Does that make any sense to you?"

Aldrian shook his head. "I haven't thought about it. I've got other problems."

"If nothing else, we've recovered two pistols. Apparently it was supposed to look like the two men shot each other. If you haven't already made plans, I strongly urge you to leave the city. I've already told you that several times. We just need to know where you're staying."

Aldrian felt miserable and asked the Commissario if he could lie down.

"I understand," the Commissario replied. "We'll be downstairs in the hallway." And he left the apartment.

Aldrian knew the risk he was taking, but he was so desperate and filled with hate that he was willing to take the chance. He turned off the ringer on his smartphone and briefly listened to hear if anyone was coming up the stairs. He paused for a moment, closed his eyes, and tried not to think about anything, and then called the numbers that he had found on Sergio Celi's SIM card and written down.

He let it ring four times, and just as he was about to hang up, an angry woman's voice answered.

"Boscolo!"

"Sergio," Aldrian whispered.

"Sergio?" the voice asked, expressing both aggravation and amazement.

"Yes."

"We thought you were . . ."

"No."

The woman quickly recovered her composure and flew into a rage: "This trouble was all your fault. You worked together with Jakob even though you knew Rudolfo would have no other choice than to . . ." Aldrian now heard an angry man's voice in the background.

"You shouldn't have called us in Chioggia!" the woman blurted out and hung up without saying goodbye.

He didn't waste any time thinking it over, and called Beatrice's number.

"They sent me Elena and Jakob's hands," he heard himself saying.

Beatrice didn't answer, and Aldrian waited until their connection was cut off.

As he was lying on the bed, he thought about the mask maker Diego Sarcia. He was now convinced that Diego was mixed up in this. Then he imagined the severed hands again. To distract himself, he recalled the photograph that he had taken from Dr. Dr. Galotti's wallet and the three men in the picture: Jakob, Galotti, and, on the periphery, a fisherman whose face he would never forget. Was the archivist involved? Or the fisherman? Maybe he was the man in the house in Chioggia? And maybe his name was Boscolo? If so, then he, too, would have been aware of his brother's talents. And if he worked in tandem with Dr. Dr. Galotti, that would explain some things. He had to speak with Diego, then look for Boscolo in Chioggia, and, lastly, consult the medical historian. He shouldn't trust anyone, he thought, and he had to remove any evidence that might lead to the art forgeries—he owed that to Elena and Jakob.

There was a knock at the door, and Aldrian unlocked it.

"You lock yourself in?" the Commissario asked, irritated.

Aldrian said nothing and looked past the man.

"Do you need any help?"

"No."

"I mean, are you all alone?"

"No. Signora Stefanelli is coming over this morning."

"We're leaving now, but we'll be in touch."

Aldrian followed him to the door, and then watched as Galli and the policemen walked through the fish market and off into the foggy night. One of the officers was carrying the white plastic box with Jakob and Elena's hands to the police boat. It seemed to Aldrian that policemen were accustomed to horror, as if they were working on an assembly line and had done the same thing thousands of times.

Exhausted, he locked the front door again, laid down on the bed, fell into a deep sleep, so he didn't hear Beatrice knocking. It wasn't until she phoned that he slowly came to. She hugged him, sobbing, in the hallway and put her head on his chest. Up in his apartment she explained that she had become nauseous when she heard the news. And even now she couldn't hear any of the details without crying. She begged him to leave the building as soon as possible, no matter what, and go off somewhere with her.

"To Chioggia," Aldrian said, also numb from grief, and he could hear Boscolo's wife: "You shouldn't have called us in Chioggia!"

"Chioggia? Why Chioggia?"

"Because I've never been there. Whenever I suggested going there, Jakob always refused or found an excuse."

"Did you know that I grew up in Chioggia Sottomarina? Not far from the beach," she replied, astonished.

She took her cellphone out of her down jacket and entered a number. "I've got to call the editorial office," she explained. She stepped out onto the landing and closed the door behind her.

In the meantime Aldrian packed his suitcase, took his passport and everything he needed from the wardrobe, destroyed his own SIM card so he couldn't be traced, and when he stepped out onto the landing, she was still on the phone. It looked as if she'd been crying again.

As they were leaving the building, they saw a stranger not far from the front door who was watching them intently. But of course that could also have just been their imagination.

Chioggia Sottomarina

Looking back, he couldn't remember their early-morning journey. He only knew that he had almost forgotten his brother's key ring in the house and that they had traveled in the fog to St. Mark's Square and then on to the Lido where, for the first time, he felt some relief. After leaving San Silvestro he had fled to the vaporetto cabin, on the side with a view of San Giorgio Maggiore so that he didn't have to see the sculpture of the drowned partisan woman, the "Monumento alla Partigiana," and the Giardini Garibaldi—both on the other side. During the entire trip he wasn't able to find any answers to his many questions.

It occurred to him that the Lido was dead this time of year. There was a cool breeze. They took the #11 bus to Chioggia, traveling over the flat and narrow island of Pellestrina with its wall of marble blocks along the coastal side; he could see cyclists progressing along the top of the wall as if they were riding through the fog on a tightrope above the sea. The wall had originally served as a defensive fortification; it now protected the island from flooding. Without believing that he would ever write his tour guide, he tried to remember all the things that Beatrice told him, but he was haunted by his thoughts the entire time. It seemed as if he was being transported in an ambulance from a trench into the hinterlands, and he couldn't wait to get out of the bus and go hide someplace where no one could follow him. The bus stopped at a cemetery and they transferred to the #11 ferry. At a point where no one would notice, he tossed the remains of the damaged SIM cards—Sergio Celi's and his own—into the water.

It wasn't until he saw the colorful fishing boats, the nets and the rigging, and smelled the air that he was able to escape his brooding thoughts.

Chioggia Sottomarina was a large seaside resort. Beatrice's aunt owned an old villa not far from the beach that was closed off in winter. Beatrice told him that as a child she had stayed there with her mother. She had the keys in her purse—she always carried them "out of habit," she explained.

Beatrice stopped first at a grocery store, then, in the house, it was as cold as a block of ice, but, with Aldrian's help, she was able to turn on the heating. She said that the rooms had seen better days. Each of the rooms had flowery wallpaper. There was a blue iris room, a yellow jonquil room with a piano, and a red tulip room; there were thick layers of old wallpaper underneath. Beatrice was astonished when he tried to see the older layers by peeling back the edges at the doorjambs and windowsills, and peeking beneath them. He first saw a bit of black wallpaper with silver flowers, then a small piece of green with white seagulls, and finally yet another layer with a butterfly pattern.

Since they were still cold, they took blankets from the beds and wrapped themselves up in them. Later Aldrian sat down at the out-of-tune piano and played arias from *Cosi fan tutte*, *Le nozze di Figaro*, and *Don Giovanni*, though he could still see the severed hands in the box. Beatrice was grateful, and he could tell how proud she was of him. To make her happy, he went on playing from Vincenzo Bellini's *I Puritani*, *Norma*, and *La Somnambula*.

When they finally warmed up, they ate fruit, dried tomatoes, bread, and drank Soave wine from the grocery store. As it got dark, they became restless and felt the need to get out of the house, first in a taxi over the 2,300-foot-long *Translagunare* bridge, and then on foot through the old town. They strolled in the fog, first up and down the Corso del Popolo and then the Fondamenta della Canale Vena, past closed cafés and businesses, and finally crossed two bridges while Beatrice told him stories from her childhood. On the way he asked her to buy him a new SIM card with a new phone number in her name, since he was afraid that Commissario Galli would track him down. She didn't quite understand, but did it nevertheless. Back in the old villa, Aldrian inserted the SIM card and played the piano until they went to bed in the iris room and cuddled.

They were up half the night and could finally talk to one another. But Aldrian defended himself, as usual, against her assumptions, and Beatrice gradually began to doubt her own conviction that he was continually lying to her.

The next morning, while she was out buying fresh fruit, wine, and coffee cake, Aldrian sat at the piano, reflecting. He blocked his new telephone number and called Diego Sarcia at his mask store.

Diego was in a bad mood, business wasn't what he hoped it to be, and Aldrian also got the impression that Diego didn't trust him. But then why had he given Aldrian the gun without the slightest hesitation? Did he himself belong to the organization, or was he a middleman who did business under the table? Or both? Moreover Aldrian was convinced that Diego knew all about the house fire in Greece and the two dead men in the building in Garibaldi Park.

"Why did you help me?" Aldrian asked, after they had said hello.

Diego didn't give an answer. He was silent.

When Aldrian didn't speak, both of them waited in vain for the other to resume the conversation. To mollify him, Aldrian eventually thanked Diego for his help.

"What help?" Diego asked irritably, giving Aldrian the impression that Diego didn't want to say any more. Of course Aldrian understood that Diego didn't want to discuss the matter over the phone—he, too, was afraid of someone listening in, and he now wondered why he had even called Diego in the first place . . . The actual reason was his own distrust, the questions for which he had no answers. And Diego had immediately understood his problem. He also could have hung up, Aldrian told himself, but he hadn't, and Aldrian interpreted this as a bond of friendship.

In that instant Diego ended the conversation, and at first Aldrian was mad at himself, but then he became furious. The only one he could think of to vent his anger on was Dr. Dr. Galotti, but he didn't want to risk some new rejection. Besides, Aldrian had stolen that photograph from him. The archivist must have realized it in the meantime and considered where he might have lost it. At their last encounter in the vaporetto, Aldrian recalled, the man had fallen asleep . . . But that a pickpocket had taken his wallet and only kept the photograph before he escaped unnoticed—that was the stuff of dreams. Dr. Dr. Galotti also knew about Aldrian's magic tricks. Then, all of a sudden, he realized what he could do.

He phoned information, asked for the phone number of the Archivio di Stato di Venezia, and waited for the main office to connect him.

"Pronto," Dr. Dr. Galotti responded, seemingly out of boredom.

"Sergio," Aldrian said in a guarded tone.

"Who?"

"Sergio Celi."

"And?"

"Sergio Celi," Aldrian repeated.

"I don't know you."

"Greetings from Rudolfo."

"Rudolfo? Which Rudolfo?"

"Boscolo."

"The fish dealer?"

"Yes."

"Did you meet him?"

"Yes."

"I haven't seen him in a long time . . . How is he?"

"Fine. You should come to Chioggia!"

"Me?"

"Yes."

"He should call me himself if he wants to extend an invitation!"

The conversation was interrupted, and for some strange reason Aldrian was pleased with what he had done. He now knew for certain that Boscolo was the fisherman who was with his brother and Galotti in the photograph from Galotti's wallet. But a moment later he doubted everything. In any case he wasn't convinced that they were not involved. He instinctively turned and saw Beatrice standing in the doorway.

"I was just about to go shopping," she said. "You said you were Sergio Celi. I called the Ostaria Dai Zemei trying to reach him."

"Celi's dead."

"Where did you hear that?"

"From Diego Sarcia who owns the mask store. I called him just now and he told me. I suspected that Galotti had something to do with it."

"With what?" She sat down on a chair.

Aldrian didn't answer and began to plunk around absentmindedly on the piano. The random tinkling slowly took shape and became a furious staccato. He imagined that the yellow jonquils were falling from the wallpaper like rain, the tulips and irises in the other rooms too, and when he looked up, Beatrice was gone. There was a note on the table, as if hastily thrown there. Aldrian abruptly got up and read it: "I've been working with the police." It had apparently been written in a hurry.

It was quiet until Aldrian finally dialed Beatrice's number.

"Did you read what I wrote you?" she asked without even saying hello. Her voice was impersonal.

"Let's talk it over."

"You don't talk. You cover up everything you've been doing."

"There's nothing to cover up. I'm just overwhelmed." He could hear the sound of a motor and asked: "Where are you?"

"The vaporetto's coming. I've got to hang up."

"Don't leave!"

It wasn't a good day for Aldrian.

The house was still cool.

He found a bottle of grappa, slugged down two half-full waterglasses—the only thing he wanted was to get drunk quickly, blank out time, turn it off in his mind, and erase his thoughts and the image of the severed hands. From time to time he would gaze out the kitchen window into the fog and drink some more. The flowers in the three rooms had resumed their original places on the wallpaper and formed a pattern. He imagined the rooms were cabins on a ship, though he knew in his heart of hearts that they really weren't. He was in the old villa that belonged to Beatrice's aunt. But it was more enjoyable to imagine that he was alone on a ship. And he was relieved to think that something was wrong with reality. It wasn't as all-encompassing as it seemed, he told himself. It wasn't as complicated as people assumed. It existed only so people could prove they were alive. He now believed every thought that came into his head. Reality hides in the reality behind reality, his head formulated. He had finally begun to understand the mystery of life.

Even though the heating was turned on, he was still freezing. And he now realized he had to go to the bathroom. His brain was injured, his circulation malfunctioned, and he almost fell down. He didn't revive until he was sitting on the toilet. Beatrice immediately came to mind and he commanded his thoughts to "Stop!" as he stared at the pattern of the terrazzo floor. "Time is a wildfire," he suddenly thought. "Or a brushfire." And he saw the burning building in the Giardini Garibaldi, and himself as he ran from the fire. When the image of the severed hands appeared, he stumbled into the kitchen and drank some water. The bottle of grappa on the table was almost empty. And the immutability of the flower patterns on the wallpaper was proof of the simplicity of reality. He knew that was contradictory—that was the greatest insight that came to mind.

He woke up at six in the evening. It was dark outside. Aldrian was still woozy, and the more he thought about the past few days, the more he was ashamed of himself.

Still dazed, he called Beatrice's number, but she didn't answer. He didn't care that she had supposedly been working with the police or even was working for them, he realized with amazement. He keyed the words "I love you" into his phone and sent the text message. He had the feeling that things couldn't be any worse than they were right now.

He dressed in warm clothes, went outside, and could hear the sea somewhere in the darkness and fog. A caffè was open not far away where—as he had discovered earlier from his window—men and women of various ages were eating small portions of fish and drinking. Not all the tables were taken, so he stepped inside, found a window seat, and ordered, sardines, white bread, and a bottle of beer. On a nearby chair he found a newspaper with a photo of Elena and Jakob and the burned-out house on the front page. It hit him like a ton of bricks, but the worst was—at first he didn't know why—that it didn't affect anything around him. He had been confronted with his innermost secrets, yet no one here was remotely interested. The waitress put the dead sardines down on the table and didn't even look at him, because people at the next table were joking with her and she was involved in that lively conversation. He was just an insignificant organism in the midst of the external reality, of the darkness, of the fog, of a café or a restaurant. If that's the way it was, he would be able to look through the newspaper without anyone noticing. Though it made him nauseous, he ate the "children's portion of fish," as he called it, with slices of bread and drank his beer. The newspaper article, he learned, assumed that it had been a war between two gangs of counterfeiters that had flooded Venice with 100-euro banknotes. Phony 100-euro bills were also in circulation in Milan, Genoa, Florence, and Rome. They were even afraid that it could be one of the greatest swindles in recent years. Jakob and Elena were suspected of having been involved in the crime. But there was no mention of their severed hands, only that they were missing and that the police had been trying to locate them for some time. The burned-out building in Venice, they suspected, could have been the counterfeiters' workshop. In addition, they assumed that the two dead men had shot each other or been killed by a third party who had also set the fire to cover his tracks. One of the men, Sergio Celi, a professional diver, had been the owner of the building. Aldrian put the newspaper back down on the chair and noticed that it was the paper that Beatrice worked for. He instantly realized that his situation was hopeless. After his initial shock he came to the realization that Beatrice must have known everything the evening before she left him. She had only waited to confront him, but that night they had become so intimate as if they would stay together forever. For her the decisive factor was definitely that he lied to her. Just the thought gave him a bad feeling. No, he had altogether a horrible feeling about their future together. He ate the headless sardines, while the tiny heads with their large eyes lay on the plate before him; they seemed like parts of little toy puppets. He ordered another beer and asked for the telephone book. There were several pages of Boscolos and two Rodolfos. One was a plumber, the other a fish wholesaler. The phone number he had called pretending to be Sergio Celi was that of the fish wholesaler and shipyard owner, and he made a note of the office address and the man's residence in the Calle Manzoni. Aldrian was convinced there was some connection with the photograph. He also presumed that Rodolfo Boscolo and Jakob knew each other in the past. "Had known each other," he thought, before he corrected himself. After he paid his bill, he bought two more bottles of Soave wine that he drank occasionally in his younger days. Back then, of course, he could rarely afford a bottle.

He realized he must have left the lights on in the villa, though he secretly hoped that Beatrice had come back. But the place was dead, and the electric heating still gave out too little warmth, so he went right to bed. "I'm lying in bed," he thought, "like a sick man." The pillow smelled of Beatrice's hair and the sheets of her perfume. He got up, opened one of the two bottles of wine, guzzled two glasses, one right after the other, and went back to bed. He put the glass and the bottle down on the floor beside the bed. Then he turned off the light and his smartphone, because all he could think of was whether Beatrice might call. His insides were in turmoil and he insisted that he mustn't lose perspective. He emptied the entire bottle in the dark and brooded over what he could do, until he finally fell asleep.

While brushing his teeth early the next morning he saw in the mirror that he had the beginnings of a beard since he had quit shaving a couple of days ago. He didn't care. As he slipped into his shoes, he thought it was probably best if he continued to ignore his phone since it just kept him from concentrating on the issues at hand. He thought about the prompter's box where he had been sealed off and isolated from the outside world. Although invisible, he had been able to influence everything. During the opera performances he was a sort of "guardian angel" who kept watch over the singers, over every note, over every word. And even though he was wrapped up in the moment, he had to think ahead—several beats, several phrases of the score and the libretto—so that he was prepared for anything that might go wrong. Last but not least, he was on his own and remained anonymous. The conductor Leonard Bernstein had once called him a "guardian angel"—Aldrian thought it sounded too dramatic, because he saw himself only as the instinct of a complicated organism, much like a human brain.

He then understood that none of these comparisons helped, they were like scaffolding without a building. From now on he was alone, but in a different way than before.

It was still dark as he crossed the long well-lit Ponte Translagunare, from the netherworld into the real world, as he told himself. The sea below him was black, and there was heavy traffic on the Isola Cantieri. Numerous fishing boats were docked beside several factory-type buildings while delivery trucks pulled up or were being loaded.

He finally came to the old city and the Canal Vena that he knew from a walk with Beatrice; he admired its pilings and colorfully painted boats that lay on the smooth reflecting water. The streetlights were on, so everything looked like the backdrop for an outdoor opera, except that a car was parked in front of one of the houses. The Calle Manzoni, he now saw, was a cross street. It connected the two large canals, the Canal Vena and the Canal San Domenico; one side dead-ended into the water, the other ran into a road with traffic. So, Aldrian thought, there were two possibilities of getting to the building, by boat or by car. But he couldn't find a nameplate on any of the houses. Back up by the water on the Canal San Domenico he discovered a dense row of medium-sized shipyards. From a sign he determined that the largest one belonged to Boscolo. The white yachts between the cranes impressed him with their elegance. On the opposite side, smaller open and enclosed motorboats. The canal was calm, there were no lights in any of the offices. He crossed the Canal Vena, just as on his walk with Beatrice, and came to the Corso del Popolo where he had seen an Internet café that was just opening. It was 8 o'clock in the morning and he increasingly encountered people and vehicles, mostly delivery vans and bicycles. The Internet café wasn't heated, the air was stale, so the young man who was running the place left the front door wide open. Aldrian rented a desktop computer, found the fish wholesaler Rodolfo Boscolo who owned another shipyard near the harbor in addition to the shipyard on the Canale San Domenico. He immediately recognized Boscolo from the photograph that he had taken from Dr. Dr. Galotti, even though the photo was more than twenty years old. Boscolo had always been a powerful man, but now he was fat, his hair had lost its former luster, and there was a scar across his forehead. So he had known Jakob and Elena for a long time and yet still taken their lives. Aldrian refused to consider that thought, but something made him certain of its validity.

In front of a kiosk a few houses further on, he saw a brochure from the Hotel Grande Italia with a city map of Chioggia. He bent down and picked one up. At the same time he glanced at the front pages of two morning papers and saw the photographs of Sergio Celi and the young black-haired Rocco Scarlatti. He bought the two papers and sat in the café across the street where first he examined the photographs and then studied the articles. From the articles he concluded that they hadn't found out much more beyond the identification of the two dead men. They were still focusing on the workshop of some counterfeit gang in Celi's house, along with the suspicion that Jakob and Elena were somehow involved. Aldrian wasn't mentioned at all. He ate breakfast, unfolded the brochure with the city map, and found the harbor, the shipyards, and how to get there. He now felt the way he wanted to feel: empty inside.

There were more and more fishing boats tied up at the dock. The shipyards were, of course, extensive, and he doubted that he would be able to confront Boscolo there. Besides, he didn't have a weapon. That fact gave him a certain amount of relief, but he didn't trust it. He knew that when he had recovered, he could better handle the situation. But at the moment he had the feeling of being only one note in an entire operatic score.

The fog over the Ponte Translagunare was so thick that the traffic mysteriously appeared like flying saucers and then disappeared again. He couldn't recognize any of the drivers. He was also so miserably cold that, for a brief moment on the bridge, he imagined he was an alien, hovering in mid-air.

In Sottomarina di Chioggia he bought bread, cheese, fruit, wine, and a bottle of grappa. The fog receded a bit, and once back at the apartment, he read the newspaper articles once more and considered giving up and going back to Vienna.

Who Is Beatrice?

That same day, on a small black shelf in the tulip room, he found Beatrice's children's books and her schoolbooks—she had written her name in some of them—and, among them, two notebooks with the heading "Diary 1" and "Diary 2" and the corresponding years. There was also a photo album that contained a letter. He sat down on the couch, first glanced through the photo album that showed Beatrice as a thirteen-year-old in a bathing suit at the beach together with her mother, her aunt, and a dog. A few pages further on were devoted to her girlfriends—and a young man, a childhood sweetheart, he concluded. On another dozen small black-and-white and color photographs he saw her with another man, apparently the subsequent pathologist Ludovico. Finally, Beatrice with her mother at the wedding. He then read the letter that contained congratulations on her fourteenth birthday. It was written on a typewriter and signed "Your Dad." Aldrian opened the bottle of grappa, took a swig, and set it down in front of him. He thumbed through the photograph album several times, studied each picture, and gradually felt he could see the youthful Beatrice in front of him. He finally began to read her diaries. They were written in a terse style, describing her daily routine in Chioggia. At the beginning it was all about her dog, Joke, and his behavior that she described in brief episodes, then about her mother whom she obviously loved very much, about her aunt Julia whose "admirer" she couldn't stand, and finally about her father, a journalist who had moved to Rome to be with another woman and subsequently pursued his career there. The more he read, the more clearly he saw the family take shape: the father was a smoker, drank too much, wrote news stories, and was on the road most of the time. She loved him and hated him, sometimes more the one than the other. He was of medium height, dark-haired, needed reading glasses, and had given her the dog Joke. He only wore his glasses in one of the photographs, a posed photo that showed him at work on his typewriter.

Her mother was often the focus of Beatrice's criticism. Since her husband didn't regularly contribute alimony payments, she worked as a secretary for an accountant in Chioggia and summer evenings in the beach café owned by her sister who helped out during the rest of the year in the city tourist information office. There was "always something to do," as Beatrice phrased it. Her first friend, Augusto, lived in Mestre and spent his summer vacations in Chioggia Sottomarina. In spite of her youth and although spoiled, but also "controlled" by her aunt whom she loved and by her mother, Beatrice was a self-reliant and independent girl who—against the wishes of the two women—went by herself to be with Augusto and even traveled to see her father in Rome. Prior to her trip, she lied that she was going to Mestre, but in reality she had borrowed money so she could go to the capital where her father reimbursed her for her travel expenses and introduced her to his girlfriend. Her name was Leonora and she worked in the advertising department at the newspaper. Beatrice didn't like her. She described her as insincere and dishonest, her father as superficial and unreliable . . . Aldrian learned about her girlfriends, and especially of her love for movies and the actresses Frances McDormand and Laura Dern, and of her crush on Brad Pitt. Pop music heroes also played a role, and she had a preference for the political left wing. But most of all she had been a member of an amateur theatrical troupe in Chioggia that performed Goldoni and even Brecht's *Threepenny Opera* where she played the part of "Jenny." And she wrote articles for her school paper about cultural topics. She was especially committed to her first boyfriend Augusto. Back then he was in senior high school in Mestre and loved science fiction novels, especially those written by Philip K.

Dick that he would read at the beach and then tell Beatrice about them.

Beatrice—Aldrian felt—made a mystery of her life. Instead she focused her attention in high school on her surroundings, on teachers, a bad grade, her mother's influenza that she described in great detail, or a trick that she taught her dog Joke.

Aldrian had emptied half the bottle of grappa by the time he started the second diary.

On 12 June 1992 she had noted: "Yesterday my father was found in his car, shot to death. He was in Sicily, near Palermo, researching the murder of Giovanni Falcone who had been killed, along with his wife, Signora Francesca Morvillo, and three bodyguards on 23 May by a Mafia bomb on the way to his vacation house."

She related that the car had been left on a country road and was found by a shepherd who was herding a flock of sheep out to pasture. Beatrice wrote page after page about her father and her divorced but grieving mother. The funeral was in Rome, she went alone, and then stayed overnight with the girlfriend. Beatrice made no entries for the next four months, but she had glued newspaper articles about the murders of Falcone and her father in the diary. In the fall she had split up with Augusto and had gone kayaking through the lagoon with her new boyfriend Ludovico. They went to almost all the islands. Beatrice described their excursions and attached photographs of Ludovico and herself. The entries concluded with their return trip from Sant'Erasmo, the "vegetable island," where they toured the Torre Massimiliana, an old fortress from the days of the Austro-Hungarian Monarchy. For a long time Aldrian debated whether he should call Beatrice, but decided not to, and kept drinking until he passed out.

Searching for Rodolfo Boscolo

The next morning Aldrian took a shower, brushed his teeth, but didn't shave. He discovered an old woman's bicycle in the vestibule that he hadn't noticed till now. After a light meal he went back to the tulip room, skimmed through the two diaries and the photo album once more, then put them back on the shelf. He opened all the doors in the house, went down to the cellar and up to the attic where he found a hammer in a toolbox and took it with him. He got ready to leave and, after filling the tires with a rusty hand pump, rode across the Ponte Translagunare to the old town where he bought a lock for the bike, leather gloves, a black coat, and Timberland shoes that he promptly put on. He tossed the old shoes into the next trash can and put the jacket into the plastic bag from the department store, but not before he took the pin with the small gold dove and fastened it to the inside of his coat lapel. He parked the bike, glanced around, and with the plastic bag in hand, strolled over to the fish market, past the stands with vegetables and fruit, along the Canale Vena, to the red tent of the fish wholesaler Rodolfo Boscolo on the Corso del Popolo. Parked in front was a white delivery van bearing the company name. The seafood on display was the same as the crabs, octopi, clams, rays, sardines or sea bass at the Pescheria di Venezia, even the canvas awnings and drapes were the same color. Above the booths hung orange and black round lampshades with electric bulbs that shone down upon the dead creatures as if someone was going to do a magic trick with them. He left the fish market after fifteen minutes, went looking for the white delivery van with the red lettering and—when he found it—saw the name "Rodolfo Boscolo," and below that: "Mercato Ittico all'Ingrosso." He took out the city map and found the main market on the island of Cantieri between the old town and Chioggia Sottomarina. It must be the well-lit building with the delivery trucks coming and going that he had seen the day before from the Ponte Translagunare. Without hesitation he decided to go find it.

He took the turnoff from the bridge and felt like he was riding into a motion picture. The entrance to the district was bordered by three factory-style buildings with signs indicating government offices and those of a security firm, in addition to some veterinary clinics. Also a shipping company, a savings bank, and a bar. The canopied fish hall behind them took up almost half the space, numerous fishing boats docked to the right and left of it. Cars were parked between the government buildings, and in front of the fish hall men were loading the merchandise in white Styrofoam boxes. Aldrian leaned the bike against a wall, secured it with the new lock, and took the plastic bag from the luggage rack. He wasn't allowed in the fish hall, the stalls had been closed for some time now, only the cold pungent smell was reminiscent of the dead animals that were delivered day after day. A worker told him that the wholesale trade started at 6 a.m. and by 9 a.m. everything was all over. And there wasn't a lot of noise, the worker insisted, generally the customer spoke with the seller by whispering as they stood beside each other, an ear turned to the other's mouth. "The largest fish wholesaler? Boscolo, of course!" a nearby fellow in an olive-green rubber apron replied to Aldrian's question. He went on to explain that Boscolo only came here once or twice a week, to check that everything was okay, otherwise he had more important things to do. Aldrian went back out to the piazza and found the building with the bar. Everything reminded him of a factory, only the colorful fishing boats gave the impression of a small harbor.

The bar had fish sandwiches and spritz, and Aldrian—the plastic bag between his knees—wolfed it down in an attempt to satisfy his hunger and thirst. Two workers at the bar were just talking about the two dead men in Venice in the building near the Giardini Garibaldi. They had differing opinions of whether the two had shot each other or a third party had been involved.

"Why a third man?" the older of the two asked, displaying two gold teeth.

"Why not?" The short fat man with a mustache and wearing overalls snorted as he stuck a sandwich in his mouth.

"Haven't you seen the newspaper?" It was all about phony money. It was printed in Venice, wasn't it?"

There was a brief pause as both men chewed.

"Those weren't beginners, they weren't clueless. We know who they're talking about. Anyway, there haven't been any bogus bills around here."

"We can thank Boscolo for that," the other man said quietly.

They changed the topic, as Aldrian paid and hurried to get back to Sottomarina.

After he had crossed the Ponte Translagunare and the fog had lifted, it seemed like everything was obscured by billboards, one right after the other. Again he had the feeling of having strayed into a movie. The camera had filmed what he saw—a dog peeing on an advertisement for a well-known suntan lotion and then silently trotting along beside him, a teenager on roller skates who, it turned out, was the owner of the dog, a beverage truck approaching with its lights on high beam, a woman pushing a baby carriage with a sleeping child bundled up inside, several shuttered snack bars, people on bicycles who dodged him, and a pretty young woman smoking a cigarette in a doorway. Everyday impressions that, individually, contained a secret. Other people didn't see his secrets either, he thought, nor Beatrice's secrets, and Jakob and Elena had never given the impression that they had a second formidable world. "Money rhymes with honey," he thought, even though it was meaningless, or perhaps for that very reason. Between the billboards he could see the beach that disappeared into the fog. The sea beyond was completely hidden by the fog. A huge billboard for Coca Cola reminded him of this past summer as if there would be no summers in the future. A couple of old men, leaning against their bicycles, were standing side-by-side, smoking and chatting. And a child, partially in the fog, was running across the meadow, a paper kite trailing behind. He was startled by the thought that it would soon be nighttime and he didn't have any schnapps in the house. This time he wanted something else to drink . . . He tolerated vodka better than other kinds of liquor, but he liked raspberry brandy best of all. Jakob and Elena were always glad when he brought a bottle from the Wachau valley, and they would empty it while reminiscing about their childhood. Or about how Jakob and Elena had met. But Aldrian had never spoken about the fact that he himself had been in love with Elena and still had some lingering feelings toward her . . .

He didn't wake up until it was dark outside. He no longer knew if he had only dreamed about seeing those billboards.

He got out of bed, put on the new Timberland shoes, a sweater, and got back on the bike en route to the old city. He had put on his windbreaker because it made it easier to pedal. And he put the pin with the golden dove back on.

The fog had gotten thicker. On the Ponte Translagunare he had the impression of floating along in a raincloud. Conversely, the narrow alleys and canals seemed dreary.

Aldrian parked the bike in a side street off the Corso del Popolo, then walked up one side of the street and back down the other, peering in the bars and cafés, in the ostarias and ristoranti, secretly hoping to find Rodolfo Boscolo. He crossed the Canale Vena and went as far as the Calle San Domenico. He went into the church and stood in one corner for a long time, studying the votive panels. There were forty or fifty of them, each one illustrating a tragedy—fishing boats in a stormy sea, dying people in their beds, a child falling out of a window or a man who lost his hat falling from a rooftop and saw the Blessed Virgin Mary and the dead Christ, a sailor falling from the mast, a burning house, again and again ships in distress on an angry sea. Those who had been rescued have been dead for a long time now, as he learned from the dates, but they had been allowed to extend their lifespan a bit longer. His sentimentality was transformed into curiosity when he observed the small paintings as illustrations of a magic trick. By the time he had studied all the votive panels it was obvious that he had had much more good fortune than all the rescued people together, and he understood that his plan to kill a man was disgraceful. Nevertheless, he didn't reject the idea.

After he had walked up and down the Corso del Popolo again, he took a narrow alley back to the Canal Vena and suddenly saw, to his amazement, Boscolo who had sat down at a window seat in an ostaria with two other men dressed like fishermen. At first Aldrian couldn't believe it. Unlike in the photograph, Boscolo now had a mustache, dark suit and tie, but the nose and eyes were unmistakable. The two strong men in jeans and sweaters, one with an earring, the other with a tattoo on the back of his hand, were eating roast beef. He wasn't completely sure it really was Boscolo—he had wanted this to happen too much to be sure—and at the same time a coincidence like this seemed unlikely. He crossed the canal at the next bridge, since he had found a bar across from the ostaria where he could sit at a window and watch Boscolo from there. It was a little after eight o'clock, so Aldrian ordered spaghetti Bolognese, a glass of red wine, and asked for a newspaper. As he ate, he frequently glanced across the canal. Just then three people went into the ostaria, but no one came out. He ordered another glass of red wine and began to read the paper when two men came into the bar and sat down at the next table.

"He's over there with his chauffeur and a bodyguard," one of the men mumbled, and they both stared across at the ostaria. "I'm curious how he's going to get out of this mess with the funny money," the other whispered.

Aldrian raised the newspaper higher and hid behind it while noticing that the crime in Venice had disappeared from the front page. He could only find a report in the local news, telling that the police had staked out several suspects but without concrete leads.

"We're working with all available means," Commissario Galli had cautiously remarked.

In the meantime the two men had also begun to read their papers, as he saw reflected in the window.

"It's a scandal," the younger one began in a muted tone as he drank his beer. "Everyone knows about it, and we just stand around and watch."

"Your father was on the police force . . . you think it was any different back then?" the older man said in a low voice.

They drank, and after a while the younger fellow whispered: "Since his family's in Venice, he goes to the Calle Fabris every night . . . And doesn't go home again till around midnight."

"I know."

"Everybody knows he's got a mistress, his wife's the only one who's in the dark." He suppressed a laugh.

"She deserves it. Anybody who gets involved with Boscolo knows what to expect," the older one whispered.

Aldrian understood that these men must be policemen. He emptied his glass, paid, and waited in the next side street where he could still see the ostaria and Boscolo. Then he pulled out his city map, found the Calle Fabris, and determined that it ran parallel to the Calle Manzoni. So, Aldrian reflected, Boscolo was having an affair with one of his neighbors. Fewer and fewer people and cyclists appeared and then disappeared in the fog. The two policemen in civilian clothes left the bar after half an hour and went off in the opposite direction. Aldrian was freezing and afraid of catching a cold, so he would take a couple of steps and then slip back into the shadows.

Boscolo finally came out. He said goodbye to the two men on the street and came directly toward Aldrian. Without waiting, Aldrian turned and walked ahead of Boscolo. He soon heard the man's footsteps on the cobblestone street, apparently he was wearing handmade hobnail boots, Aldrian thought, and: "This is how I'll follow you, except without a sound." Boscolo changed to the other side of the street, passed Aldrian, and briefly turned to see his face. With that, Aldrian slowed down, increasing the gap between himself and Boscolo. After all, he knew where his enemy was going. Of course he couldn't let the distance between them get too great, he thought, because he needed to find out which one was the mistress's house. As he walked by the Calle Fabris and glanced down the street, he was able to see Boscolo just opening a door and disappearing inside a building. He rushed over to the house, made a mental note of the front door, and then went on to the Fondamenta San Domenico, the coast road parallel to the canal where the boats were asleep on the water. For just a moment, in spite of the cold and damp or possibly because of them, he would have liked to stay right here, it was so nice. He calmly made his way back to the Canale Vena and from there to the Corso del Popolo to look for the bicycle. He also enjoyed the trip into the gathering darkness, and it was also pleasant that he saw or was passed by few vehicles. He was amazed at himself. He asked himself why he was feeling so good, and he had no response. He reflected that Boscolo hadn't been condemned to death, there were still other options ... He could return to Venice, go home to Vienna, he could kill Boscolo without any witnesses, or he could wait until Beatrice turned up, but that seemed to be the least likely of all the possibilities.

On the long street into Sottomarina there were two illuminated billboards, and in the dark Aldrian had the feeling of flying through space. The billboards were now just artifacts from a gigantic explosion that had demolished a space station. They hovered in the darkness like remnants. As he passed a parked car, he noticed there was a young couple inside, making love. The topless woman was sitting astride the man, or had he only imagined it?

Back at the villa he realized he'd forgotten to buy a bottle of vodka, but he still had some Soave wine, so he drank a glass and ate some ham and cheese until he became tired.

This time he went on foot past the billboards that now seemed larger and menacing. He imagined making a pilgrimage route from billboard to billboard over the sandy ground, from one shrine to the next, from the sacred Rolex wristwatch to the blessed lipstick and nail polish, from there to the hallowed Mountain Bike, and then on to the venerable ice cream cone and the holy Vespa, from one sacred hotel to a sanctified roller rink . . . From then on he only looked at the pilings that held up the billboards, like pilgrims adoring an effigy of the Madonna. At his feet lay the relics of the holy things: empty beer cans, soft drink bottles, pages from newspapers, tin cans, cigarette butts, plastic bags, a condom—gradually he drew closer, and could hear . . . the ocean. When he came to the beach, the things changed. Although there were still sacred relics lying around, washed ashore, faded, polished by the water and the ocean floor, he collected various seashells and mollusks—pointed, round, spiral-shaped—compared them, and thought about Jakob. At this point he and Elena were probably lying at the bottom of the sea. He was completely calm as he considered the possibility. There was no other explanation. He put the seashells in his pocket and trudged through the damp sand until his feet were cold and wet. Even in the fog, the ocean had lost nothing of its attraction. It reawakened his childhood, his youth, hugs and kisses, the taste of salt in his mouth, and was populated by angelic and demonic creatures that seemed enchanted. Standing on the shore, he wasn't surprised by the recent thought of his prompter's box that had afforded him a vantage point to life on the stage. Since the fog didn't permit a long-range view, the waves seemed like theater curtains that opened and closed. And he could hear the music of Claude Debussy that he had played over and over throughout his youth: *La Mer.* Though it irritated him now, it kept ringing in his ears like from some dilapidated hurdy-gurdy. He bent down, moistened his forehead, and the cold ocean water gave him some relief. He then awoke from his dream.

His eyes focused on the hammer that he had put beside his bed that afternoon. He automatically got out of bed, got dressed in the Timberland shoes and the new black coat, tucked the hammer under his shirt, and rode off on the bicycle into the old town. On the way he realized that he had forgotten to fasten on the pin with the gold dove. But maybe it was better this way. Throughout the whole ride he could feel the heavy hammer pressing against his stomach, constantly seeming to signal him that he was crazy. His bout of nerves prompted him to consider that he was making this whole thing up. In reality he was in Vienna and was just thinking of jumping out the window, he thought. Or in a psychiatric ward where he'd been admitted and sedated after an unsuccessful suicide attempt. In this fog he felt as if he were in a giant cocoon. Today Chioggia seemed like a deserted suburb of Venice, it was similar to the region around Sant'Elena and the island of San Pietro that he liked. When it was warm, washing hung from the windows or on a long line from one building to another, sometimes even over a canal or an alley.

There was evening rush hour on the Corso del Popolo, and he only realized just now that it was much too early. He cussed himself, called himself an idiot because now he had to hang around for several hours with the hammer under his shirt. So he rode back, and the further he got from center city the more unlikely it seemed that he would try to kill Rodolfo Boscolo later. On the way he bought a bottle of vodka in a store and put it in his coat pocket. It was 8 o'clock when he reached the villa, carried the bike into the hallway, and put the hammer down on the table. He would definitely do it tomorrow, he resolved. He ate a little, but the silence got to him. No, he protested, he wouldn't wait till tomorrow! Was he going to be forever underway in this dream between billboards on down to the sea, collecting seashells on the beach until the damp and cold told him he was on his way to the underworld? He did everything he could to block out the overture by Gluck. He wasn't Orpheus, and Beatrice wasn't Eurydice.

An hour later he stuck the hammer back under his shirt, slugged down two glasses of vodka, and got on the bike. Struggling with the intention of killing the man who had his brother and his wife on his conscience, he could think of nothing else than getting it over with.

He would wait for him in the darkened Calle Fabris, because he hated the idea of watching some ostaria and then following Rodolfo Boscolo, uncertain whether he might be noticed. Besides, Aldrian didn't want to sit in the tratoria across the street out of concern he might be identified later on. So, arriving at the house of Boscolo's mistress, he leaned the bike against a wall, stood in a darkened basement stairwell, and waited. He waited for the empty feeling to come and make it easier for him to hammer Boscolo to death. He had to think about his brother and Elena the whole time, and how someone had chopped off their hands and tortured them.

He waited for more than an hour, feeling the hammer against his stomach, and remembering his youth together with Jakob, the encounter with Karl von Frisch, and later their planned paradise in Skala Kallonis, the counterfeit money, the two dead men in the deserted villa, the Giadini Garibaldi, and Beatrice, not even knowing where she was. But he was unable to create the anticipated feeling of emptiness—just the opposite, his anxiety grew until he left and, counter to his original plan, rode to the ostaria on the Canale Vena where he parked the bike. The hammer under his shirt began to hurt, and his rage grew with every step until he reached the ostaria and peeked inside. The only customers were a young couple and an old man. So he ran back to the bike and rode to Sottomarina as fast as he could. The Ponte Translagunare seemed like the home stretch of a bicycle race and, already out of breath, he pedaled as fast as he was able.

It wasn't until he opened the refrigerator that he admitted he was relieved. After he had finally caught his breath, he filled a drinking glass with vodka and downed it in one swig.

Funiculì, Funiculà

There was still fog the following evening, and the street was wet from rain as a car drove by now and then. Ever since he woke up that morning with a bad hangover and while waiting for the headache to wear off, he balked at the thought of using the hammer. Should he take a file? A screwdriver? A rock he could throw? Then he decided after all on the hammer. But this time he would take a shopping bag where he could hide it. He found a tin of tea, brewed some, drank two cups, ate bread with some butter, and gradually felt better.

It was seven o'clock that evening when he loaded the shopping bag with the hammer in the luggage rack and, wearing a sweater and windbreaker, rode off. In the dark he barely saw the billboards, the few he did recognize renewed his feeling of futility and lonliness. As in Venice during Carnival, he could hear the voice of Umberto Tozzi singing "Gente di Mare" from some bar, but there was no one in sight. The rain fell silently and in fine droplets. This time on the Ponte Translagunare he thought about tabletennis, he himself being the ping-pong ball.

At first he didn't know what he should do in Chioggia. He parked the bike, took the shopping bag with the hammer, and went down the Corso del Popolo between black and colorful umbrellas until he came to a narrow cross canal and a bridge over the Canale Vena. On the other side, in the Calle Don Bosco, he discovered a movie theater with the same name. Don Bosco and Boscolo—that couldn't be a coincidence, he told himself. He felt moisture on his face and in his hair, and an unknown conductor in his head pointed an invisible baton at the poster for the movie *The Wolf of Wall Street* with Leonardo DiCaprio. A group of people with umbrellas was cheerfully conversing in the street in front of the movie theater. Aldrian considered it a good omen and remembered certain cinemas and that he and Jakob would discuss the movies long after the show. He bought a ticket and couldn't understand why he was suddenly so nervous. Perhaps it was the people who irritated him. He went to the restroom, found a discarded newspaper in the wastebasket beneath the sink, and took it back out in the lobby. There weren't any more articles about the incidents in the local news, there was only one comment in the letters to the editor and it was critical of the police.

When the door to the small auditorium was open, he waited until it became dark, put down the newspaper, and sat down in the back row. There weren't many people present. While a trailer was shown, someone came in and sat down exceedingly slowly in the row in front of Aldrian. That was strange because there were vacant seats all around. As the dark images on the screen were replaced by brighter ones, he suddenly thought he recognized Boscolo. Aldrian automatically thought about killing him. He had the shopping bag with the hammer at his feet and was mentally prepared to strike. He decided he could escape through the side door with the lighted sign reading "Uscita di sicurezza," "Emergency Exit." The action on the screen was coming fast and furious, and if you didn't pay attention, you only saw a compilation of endless film trailers. Aldrian also couldn't understand most of the spoken words, because either the sound track was too loud or the actors were shouting at each other. Boscolo sat motionless in front of him: the man didn't bend down, didn't change his sitting position, didn't laugh, didn't cough. Aldrian felt in the dark for the shopping bag, lifted the hammer a bit and felt its weight. But he put it back in the bag, because he intuitively realized the impossibility of his plan. For a time he just stared at the back of Boscolo's head, the small bald spot in the middle of his thinning hair that he could recognize when there were bright pictures on the screen. Or, when the flickering images permitted, he studied the man's bare neck, his shirt collar and sportcoat with a few fine hairs on the shoulders. At times he intermittently followed the action and tried to distract himself with the half-naked women and the absurd plot. At one point, time seemed to stand still, but a glance at his watch told him an hour had already passed. The next time he stared at the back of Boscolo's head, he told himself that blood and brain matter would soon be oozing out. He even imagined a page from a forensic medical textbook where the corpse was shown with a clinical description. The lights went up. Aldrian pulled himself together, grabbed the shopping bag, pulled up his collar, and inconspicuously left the theater. Once outside he realized that he had been mistaken. The man in front of him wasn't Boscolo, but an older gentleman with a birthmark on his temple. He was overcome with despair and anger. He ran across the bridge to the other side of the canal and on toward the sea. It was obvious that he had lost his nerve, so he stopped and told himself to go to the Calle Fabris and wait for Boscolo in the dark basement stairwell. He had to stick to his plan and not react to every little thing, he admonished himself as he crossed the Canale Vena. Before he entered the Calle Fabris, he put on the leather gloves, and only then went to the basement stairwell. A car drove by. Startled, Aldrian turned his head aside to hide his face, but the car stopped, the headlights were turned off, someone opened the front door to the house and stepped into the briefly lighted hallway. While he was waiting, Aldrian noticed a small cobblestone, picked it up and put it in the shopping bag. A moment later he saw Boscolo coming down the street. He could hear his enemy's footsteps and that he was whistling. Resolute, he took out the hammer, prayed that no cars would come along, and backed up against the wall.

"Funiculì funiculà." Aldrian was familiar with the song from the symphonic poem *Aus Italien* by Richard Strauss. "Cable car up, cable car down," Boscolo kept whistling as he unlocked the front door. In the song "Funiculì funiculà," the singer has just persuaded his beloved "Giovanna" to ride the cable car with him to the top of Vesuvius to enjoy the view into France and Spain where he wants to propose marriage, when Aldrian, in a panic, struck with his hammer, and Boscolo went silent. Even before he fell to the cobblestone street, Aldrian hit him again in the face, and a third time on his temple. He heard an ugly cracking sound, dark blood spraying onto his gloves. He quickly put them and the hammer into his bag and ran off on the Fondamenta San Domenico.

The traffic with its noise, lights, and the boats at the dock brought him back to his accustomed reality, but now he felt threatened by everything: by the reflections of the fishing boats and houses in the water, by the passing cars and cyclists, the glances of pedestrians, the event notices and advertisements on the walls that seemed like wanted posters to him, or by a man who was lighting a cigarette. He didn't calm down until he saw seagulls sleeping on a ship's mast. He didn't have the strength to look around and check out the situation, the only thing he could do was to keep moving. At the busy Calle San Giacomo he started off in the direction of Sottomarina before he realized that he had parked the bike on the Corso del Popolo. How could he have forgotten that! He felt the cobblestone and the hammer in the shopping bag and an inner voice told him not to get the bike if he didn't want to be arrested. In spite of the threat, he ignored it. On the contrary, he decided he had to silence the voice! But the voice wouldn't stay silent. He found the bike, rode frantically across the Calle San Giacomo toward Sottomarina, but it wasn't until the Ponte Translagunare that he felt some relief and the desired emptiness. From the world back into the hereafter, he told himself. He pulled over, listened to the sound of the waves beneath him, reached for the shopping bag on the luggage rack, dropped the hammer into the deep and heard it hit the water with a splash. The only light from Boscolo's factory came from the fish hall, beyond that were only shadows of the other buildings. Then he also tossed the bag with the cobblestone and the gloves into the sea where it made a splash in the water. He looked back at Boscolo's fish hall and tried to picture how the owner's death would be received tomorrow morning.

The closer he came to the beach, the more the emptiness expanded inside him, until he didn't notice it anymore.

He automatically pedaled and steered. He was surprised that there were no billboards. In retrospect he couldn't actually say what it was he had seen beyond the bridge in Sottomarina.

He washed his hands in the bathroom and looked at himself in the mirror. Fortunately his jacket wasn't soiled, but he still wanted to dispose of it along with his jeans. He took off the pin with the dove, stuffed the clothing in a trash bag, cleaned his shoes, then washed down the bike and the tableware, and—after showering and washing his hair—he changed his underwear. Finally he dumped the empty bottles and the packaging from his purchases into the trash bag, and, last of all, checked every room until he felt confident he had destroyed all the evidence. Then he packed his suitcase and drank the rest of the vodka, until he was out like a light . . .

At some point he awoke with a start. He felt a human body. Disoriented, he sat upright.

"It's me." He heard Beatrice's voice and couldn't believe it. It wasn't until she turned on the floor lamp that he gradually began to understand, but it took some time before he realized where he was, what he had done, and why Beatrice had come. He mind was a jumble of images from his memory that appeared out of context and then disappeared again. It took a great deal of concentration to break free from the chaotic reality in his head and to realize that Beatrice was asking him to run away with her.

He saw the hammer coming down on Boscolo's temple, heard the man fall, and in the back of his head saw himself fleeing on the bike across the long bridge as fast as he could go. Without a word, they fell into each other's arms. Beatrice cried, and he held back his own tears.

"You've got to get out of here!" she whispered.

"Yes."

"As quickly as possible."

"Has something happened? he asked, confused and guilt-ridden.

"They found Elena tonight . . ."

It took her some time to calm down.

"Her body washed ashore on the beach in Grado, wrapped in the remains of a plastic bag . . . Her right hand was cut off. The plastic bag had been weighted down with rocks, and her corpse was probably torn from the canvas by some obstruction underwater."

As Aldrian listened to her, he was thinking about how he himself had thrown the hammer and the shopping bag with the cobblestone from the bridge. He had thought about Jakob and Elena and their fate so often that now he was numb and completely without motivation. After the two of them had checked one more time that there were no traces of his presence, they left the villa, put his suitcase and the trash bag in the trunk, and looked back at the now dark and deserted house.

For the first several minutes they rode in silence along the beach road. They rarely saw a light in any of the houses. It was three o'clock in the morning.

"There is one more thing . . ." Beatrice began. "Rodolfo Boscolo . . . Do you know him?"

"No."

"Someone beat in his skull with a solid object in Chioggia. He's in poor condition, the injury to his brain is so severe that he won't recover or die from it either. The police suspect that he is responsible for the counterfeit money and the victims Ivanov, Fibonacci, Celi, Scarlatti, and Elena . . ."

"And Jakob?"

Beatrice was silent. And Aldrian didn't say anything either.

After a while, Beatrice pulled over to the curb and stopped the car.

"You can't go back to Venice now," she said. "We were never in Chioggia. You were in Milan. I'll confirm that . . . I won't ask you any more questions, because I don't want you to lie to me."

She waited for him to say something, but he couldn't think of anything to say but just stared out the windshield into the darkness.

Half-asleep during the drive, he saw the events unwind in an unchronological sequence and similar to the votive panels that he had seen in the San Domenico church: Fibonacci, dead in his frame store; the two hands of Jakob and Elena in the box; the burning building with the two dead men; and his attempted murder of Rodolfo Boscolo. They were the most amazing magic tricks that he could have ever imagined, he thought as he opened his eyes and distanced himself from them. But he hadn't been the magician, he realized, more like the white rabbit that had fled—before he was pulled out of the hat.

He didn't straighten up until it became light.

"Where are we?"

"Twenty miles from Milan," he heard Beatrice say.

She turned on the radio.

"And where are the things?" he asked, after a pause.

"I got rid of the clothes at a garbage dump."

Before Aldrian could ask any more questions, Mario Lanza began to sing "Funiculì funiculà" on the radio.

FOURTH BOOK

The End of a
Journey Is the Beginning of a Journey

In Milan

1

Aldrian didn't leave the apartment in Milan for eleven days and had time to think everything through. Over and over again it was the same memories and thoughts that distracted and moved him. Was his brother still alive? Sometimes he truly believed so, but other times he was convinced that they had murdered him and thrown his body in the ocean. The coroner had determined that Elena had been executed with a bullet to the head, but her hand had been severed while she was still alive. The police presumed that Jakob had met the same fate as his wife. According to the newspapers that Beatrice regularly brought him, the criminal organization behind the counterfeit money had ostensibly tagged them as "potential" snitches and traitors. But there was no evidence to support the supposition that Jakob and Elena were part of the counterfeiting affair. And what then? In the meantime the paper had reconstructed the "timeline" of events. The killers must have forced their way into the house at night, dragged his relatives onto a boat at the fish market, and then presumably taken them to a ship where they were tortured. Eventually they hacked off a hand from each of them, according to the article, and shot Jakob and Elena that same night. In the end they had thrown the bodies overboard. Due to some fluke, Elena's body had washed ashore, while "the sea," as the newspaper described it, "had not released Jakob's body." There was no mention of art forgeries nor of the couple's plan to create a Garden of Eden in Greece, though there was something about a future "summer home" in Skala Kallonis. Like all puzzles, this case also aroused the wildest rumors and speculation: Jakob and Elena had possibly wanted to set up a workshop and a printing press in Skala Kallonis for a "major project of international counterfeiting." Of course not only the sister-in-law Margherita denied that, but also Elena and Jakob's son Emilio. In Beatrice's weekly magazine they wrote that he, Michael Aldrian, the victims' brother and brother-in-law, had "disappeared without a trace," was "lying low" or in hiding, and was wanted by the police. He knew that Beatrice, too, was interrogated by the police in Milan but had insisted she knew nothing. From that point on, Aldrian was certain that she hadn't collaborated with the police. A different newspaper connected the assault on Rodolfo Boscolo with the murder of Fibonacci and the two dead men in the villa on Garibaldi Park. They referred to their "sources." The word "Mafia" was frequently cited, and the medical condition of the fish wholesaler was described as "in critical condition" or "in a vegetative state." It seemed safe to say that he would "never be the same again." No specific person was a suspect, instead journalists wrote about a "gang war."

The News

2

The night train that Aldrian and Beatrice had boarded to attend Elena's funeral in Venice traveled through the darkness as if it were flying through the universe on its way to the moon.

While they were still in Milan, Aldrian had torn up and burned Fibonacci's pocket telephone book and wondered what he should do with the paperweight he had bought for Beatrice and then hidden on the shelf in her apartment. At least he would pack the expensive item in his suitcase and give it to Beatrice later. They had agreed that Beatrice would return the brain section from the famous conductor in the plastic cube—along with the pistol—to her ex-husband.

There should be nothing that could indicate what had happened. As with his magic tricks, every movement, every decision must be carefully planned and observed. The most important thing was to avoid anything that could reveal the "trick." But he one thing he couldn't make disappear up his sleeve was his conscience, along with various scenes in the back of his head, dreams, spontaneous memories, astonishment, and a distinct loathing of himself. He tried to gloss over the irritations, to withdraw, to work on the computer, listen to music, read the paper or watch TV, but each of these activities only made him more aware of what he had done. At first he had been surprised that he found no satisfaction in avenging his brother and sister-in-law, but the further his deeds receded into the past, the dumber they seemed . . . In the empty train compartment he held Beatrice's hand and told her he loved her. She nodded, but he noticed that she still didn't completely trust him because he didn't tell her what had really happened. On the other hand he was afraid that if she knew the truth, she would leave him. He told himself that once he began to confess, he was lost, so he would have to deny everything or not tell her anything, and he preferred the latter. But it was more difficult than he first imagined. He badly wanted to confide in her. He had stopped drinking large amounts of alcohol because it had become much easier for him to talk about himself, and he was in danger of telling her everything. At the same time he wondered what was going through her mind. Did she know more than she let on? In anger she told him she had collaborated with the police, but he was convinced that wasn't true. He could only assume she had learned a few things at those times when, as a journalist, she had had contact with Commissario Galli who was leading the investigation. But she denied knowing any of the details and usually concluded their discussions with the thought: "If it's the way you say it is, you've got nothing to worry about." He grew to hate this sentence. At night they embraced, and the next morning when they had breakfast together Beatrice was still affectionate, but in the evening, as soon as she came back from her editorial work, she started back in with her questions that generally ended in a quarrel and ultimately silence. Nevertheless he loved her and, deep down inside, believed she loved him, too.

He was just wondering what would have become of him if Beatrice hadn't accepted Margherita's invitation and they hadn't become lovers—when Beatrice's phone rang in the train compartment. She leaped up, answered "Yes, yes," several times, and sat back down. Before Aldrian could ask her what had happened, she blurted out: "They've found Jakob." She calmed down and then went on: "About a half-mile from where they found Elena." At first Aldrian felt a strange sense of relief because the uncertainty had come to an end. And he could also feel that his guilty feelings had subsided. He suddenly had the certainty that he had acted correctly.

All doubt had vanished, he no longer had any regrets. And now he would be able to deal with Commissario Galli differently than just two minutes ago. Then he saw his brother's face before him, his questioning expression, and his unruly hair that he could never tame.

When they came down the steps from the train station to the Grand Canal, the darkness was illuminated by only a few lampposts and floodlights. It looked like a photograph taken at night with a flash. Then a vaporetto came along. It looked like a lighted white coffin that floated over to them, growling. He had the impression that it didn't belong to his reality. It was simply there, like the water at night. The cobblestone street wasn't a part of his real world, neither were the people who approached them individually and then disappeared as if they were extras in some movie. In Beatrice's apartment he became a lifeless object, he briefly thought about the section of the conductor's brain on the shelf and his present for Beatrice until his exhaustion turned him into another dead man on the bottom of the ocean.

Beatrice's Farewell

3

Beatrice was still asleep.

It was dark, and he thought it must be the middle of the night. Then he saw that it was evening, so he got up, went into the next room and phoned Margherita. She answered in a monotone and sobbed as soon as she heard his voice.

"You poor thing, you've lost your brother!"

"How do you know that?"

"It's on the news and Commissario Galli told me. He's looking for you . . . Where are you?"

"I've just arrived in Venice."

She sobbed again, and then continued in a calmer voice: "Emilio is here. He has no idea what to do now."

Aldrian thought for a moment. There was no doubt in his mind that he would help Emilio.

"We've put off Elena's funeral," Margherita went on. "They should be buried together."

"Yes."

"What have you been doing all this time?" Margherita asked. And when he didn't respond: "All of a sudden you weren't there anymore and you didn't call . . . We've been terribly worried about you . . . The Commissario suspected that you were working together with your brother."

"Did they interrogate you?"

"Yes, twice, at police headquarters."

"They think they are on the trail of a counterfeiting gang and that Jakob and Elena were working for them. They supposedly made the banknotes, and you at least would have known something about that," Aldrian said.

"That's absurd."

"What did they want from you?"

"That I would confirm their suspicions. They haven't found anything, because there's nothing to find. I only know a little about the house and garden in Lesbos that have since been destroyed."

Aldrian pictured the model of the house in Lesbos that burned down, the replica in the shape of a huge artificial water lily, the backdrop with the panoramic view, and the fire that destroyed all traces of the house and the building itself. The model in the secret workshop had suffered the same fate as the Garden of Eden in Lesbos. He was convinced that Jakob had made his fortune by forging pictures. But then there were some unresolved issues . . . Had they possibly forced his brother to draw a counterfeit copy of the 100-euro bill? And was Elena pressed to provide the paper and the ink?

"What are you thinking?" he heard Margherita ask.

And when he didn't respond, she continued: "They talked about the plants and animals, the lizards, birds and bees, the greenhouses and preserves, the fish pond and the swimming pool that they wanted to build there."

Aldrian knew their plans better than anyone. The self-centeredness of his brother and sister-in-law that had presumably motivated the project still made him angry. For that reason he wanted to end the conversation, and said that someone was waiting for him. But Margherita asked if he didn't want to stay with them?

"No," Aldrian answered, "it's better this way."

"When will you come and visit?"

"Tomorrow."

"Definitely?"

"Yes, definitely."

Meanwhile Beatrice was now awake and came out of the bedroom, cell phone in her hand, so he finished the conversation.

"Commissario Galli," she said out of the blue, "just called and wants you to come down to police headquarters. But before you go, I want to tell you what I know. I've kept you out of all the deliberations and speculation. I've given them your statements as my own. I've made it clear that I consider you innocent, and the whole time we were in Milan I didn't betray you in my telephone conversations with Galli. But I can't do it anymore . . ."

Aldrian told himself it was better if he didn't react. He sat down at the table and Beatrice, pacing back and forth, recited point for point what the police knew, what they suspected, and what they couldn't explain.

There were several recent developments: Rodolfo Boscolo was so severly injured that he would remain an invalid. Who did it was still a mystery. Rocco Scarlatti, the black-haired used-book dealer, had belonged to Boscolo's organization, as had Sergio Celi and Carlo Fibonacci. Due to Jakob's extraordinary artistic abilities they thought art forgery was possible, though they had no proof. Celi had baled out at the right time, and just before he left the organization he had rented the study to Jakob. However there was no sign of a printing press. In any event, there was a reason why Jakob would have rented the study: inquiries revealed that he had received a contract from a British publisher to illustrate a bird guide.

But then why were he and his wife killed? According to Beatrice, Galli assumed that Celi had had the idea of counterfeiting money. In some way or other—perhaps through blackmail—he was able to force Jakob to work for him. Boscolo must have tried to locate the workshop. Everything else was unclear, since the police knew so little about the structure and ramifications of the organization.

"So, where have you been this whole time? I'll confirm that you've been staying in Milan because you wanted to lay low, and I'll confess to Galli that I lied to him."

The good magicians against the evil magicians, Aldrian thought. Each one tried to decimate the other. And, to top it off, the police were also involved.

After Beatrice told him everything she knew, she asked him to leave.

"I'll bring your suitcase over to Margherita's," she added.

Aldrian's thoughts were already with the police interrogation and he didn't answer. He shaved off the beard that he had grown and got dressed. Beatrice had left him alone, but when it was time for him to leave the apartment, she suddenly asked if she could accompany him.

Aldrian declined the offer, and she unexpectedly flung her arms around his neck.

They stood like that for some time.

At Police Headquarters

4

It was already midnight. Commissario Galli had gone off-duty and the grumpy Inspectore Bruno Gabbiato had tried to entangle him in contradictory statements. It was a kind of linguistic chessgame that Gabbiato—in mock naiveté, as Aldrian soon realized—ingeniously dominated. At one point he would confront Aldrian with phony evidence, then seemed to ignore his response, but later came back to the same point, or he seemed to believe Aldrian but then would challenge him at the next opportunity. The entire time Aldrian stuck to his story that, following his last conversation with Commissario Galli, he had gone into hiding at Beatrice's apartment in Milan; it turned out that Inspectore Gabbiato hadn't been informed. He immediately called Beatrice who confirmed Aldrian's statement. When Commissario Galli reappeared two hours later, having grown restless, he nodded his assent that Beatrice had told the truth, but accused the two of them of misleading the police and threatened them with possible consequences. In conclusion he apologized, to Aldrian's surprise, that they had interrogated him for such a long time, but it was now possible for them to conclude that he was no longer under suspicion. He then asked Aldrian to identify his brother's body that was being "studied" at the Forensic Institute in Padua.

Reunion with Jakob

5

During the entire trip to Padua he couldn't think of anything but the face of his dead brother. Aldrian was afraid that it could be disfigured, the eyes and mouth wide open, or that it had been mutilated by the gunshot and bloated by the ocean water. He had so often seen on TV what would now take place that it bored him. But this time it was his own brother whom he hadn't seen for over a year and who would lie, naked and dead, before him.

The room stunk from something that made him nauseous, and the interrogation had worn him out so that he was dizzy. His brother's body had been prepared for identification. A young woman in white scrubs pulled back the sheet covering Jakob, and Aldrian saw a pale bloated grimasse and a bullet hole in the middle of his forehead. He knew that this sight would destroy the memory of his brother forever. And the stitches on Jakob's waxy chest from the autopsy were imprinted on his mind. He nodded and turned away.

Alone

6

They brought him back to the Campo San Polo, stressed how sorry they were, and apologized for the lengthy interrogation. Then they let him go.

"Shit on you! Shit on all of you!" Aldrian cursed silently.

Beatrice wasn't home, but his suitcase was still in her bedroom and he still had the keys to the building and to her apartment. He thought of the paperweight that he had bought with counterfeit money and was going to give to Beatrice. In any event he couldn't leave it in Beatrice's apartment.

He looked in the refrigerator for grappa, found a half-empty bottle, and drank it all. Still, the mask-like face of his dead brother stayed with him—until he finally fell asleep.

A Final Conversation

7

The next morning he found a note on the kitchen table: "Will be back this evening, love, Beatrice."

He quickly dressed and headed for the Piazza San Tomà. He wanted to visit the Chiesa di San Pantalon, not his sister-in-law. On his way he noticed that the masks had disappeared. As usual, he basically encountered tourists. The locals he saw were mostly old folks with dogs, rollators and walking canes, a few spry men were hanging around in the bars. The church was just opening as he arrived. He sat down in a pew and gazed up at the ceiling painting that portrayed the fall of the angels and their transformation into demons. He was familiar with the phenomenon: when he stared at it for an extended period of time, he fell with them into the fiery depths. After a few minutes he put a coin into the spotlight apparatus and went back to his pew. This time he flew with the host of angels up toward the throne and the demons were incinerated in the divine light. It was a strange rollercoaster ride that he repeated several times until he left the Chiesa di San Pantalon and returned to the Campo San Polo. On the way he had decided to visted his maskdealer friend, and saw him through the display window, characteristically sitting at his desk, painting a mask.

"We've got to talk," Aldrian said, without even saying hello.

"We do?" Diego got up, hung the "chiuso"/"closed" sign on the front door, turned out the lights, and waited.

"What do you want?" he asked reluctantly.

"You have to ask?"

"When I heard that your brother and his wife had disappeared, I knew that they had been killed," Diego replied. "I know the whole story. Jakob and Elena forged pictures—by Turner, Flegl, Sibylla Merian—"

"I know," Aldrian interrupted.

"You do? That amazes me."

"I saw the paintings at Fibonacci's when I arrived in Venice."

"Fine, let's cut to the chase," Diego said calmly. "I'll deny everything if you go to the police." He paused and then went on unemotionally: "As a boy I was a member of the organization, you know what I mean . . . At 25, I was the manager at one of the most famous Ventian hotels. After ten years I wanted out, but they threatened to kill me. That lasted almost a whole year—then they gave me the two stores so I wouldn't forget who owned me. In the beginning I only had permission to make and sell Pinocchio figures. It was a form of humiliation: you know, the long nose because of the lies. Pinocchio was also changed into a jackass and swallowed by a sea monster. That means that I was to always remember what had happened and what could happen to me. It took another five years before I got permission to make and sell masks . . . I'm not going to tell you more than that . . . I was still in contact with my friends from back then: with Fibonacci, Scarlatti, later with Celi. They checked on me day and night and treated me like shit . . . Rodolfo Boscolo no longer spoke to me. But I was still at his mercy, because he humiliated me in front of everyone whenever he felt like it . . . So I started to think how I could extricate and avenge myself. I first persuaded Jakob to work with Fibonacci and then talked the two of them into breaking away from Boscolo and his people—murderers and thieves. When Jakob and Elena were kidnapped, out of revenge I sicced Scarlatti, the used-book dealer from the Fondamenta Nuove, on Fibonacci, and then the diver Sergio Celi on Scarlatti. I eventually succeeded in creating suspicion between them, each felt threatened and cheated by the other. A year before Jakob disappeared I brought Sergio Celi together with Fibonacci—Celi was supposed to find a workshop for Jakob and Fibonacci could then sell the forged pictures. Most of them were sent to Russia and China, to Canada and America. Jakob was brilliant and Boscolo earned a ton from his work. My major concern was Boscolo. When you showed up, it put me in a bind, because you're different than Jakob. I had already sicced Rocco Scarlatti on Fibonacci and Celi and vice versa, so that they'd put each other away. But you took your own revenge. I warned you not to stay in Venice and, when you insisted on staying, I gave you guns. As you can imagine, I'm also involved in the illegal arms trade. It's small potatoes, but it helps keep my business afloat. I really wanted you to clear out. Boscolo's people set a trap for you—the counterfeit money—so that you would become a suspect. And the more unfazed you were, the more ruthlessly they went after you. The severed hands were supposed to make you panic and run away. Then you suddenly disappeared. Not long after, Rodolfo Boscolo was permanently taken out by a hammer. To be honest, I don't think you're capable of a cold-blooded killing—but who knows? In any case, one arm of the organization has been amputated. I admire you: you were in danger, but you didn't lose focus and stray from your plans. But I think it's time for our friendship to end. We'll forget about each other as if we'd never met."

Diego went to the door, turned the lights on, removed the "closed" sign, and sat back down at the table. But Aldrian wasn't to be dismissed so easily. "I've got one more question," he said.

"I'm not going to say anything more," Diego emphasized.

"I want to know if Galotti had anything to do with this."

Diego went on painting a mask, and Aldrian asked impatiently: "Yes or no!"

Without glancing up, Diego shook his head and gestured with his hand that he was finished with the whole affair.

Back on the street, Aldrian was shaken, and he now hated Diego. But they were still bound together by their shared knowledge. If one of them talked, the other would be in the soup, Aldrian thought. Of course that would be lovely if you were a soup connoisseur. To be dissolved in soup, he thought, so that only your spirit was left in the bowl. The soup spirit that lives on. He wondered why he was even thinking about soup.

The Ostaria Dai Zemei was packed, as always. Ettore rushed past, expressed his sympathy, seated him at a small table in the restaurant, and Giacomo automatically brought a spritz and gave his condolences, too.

"Do you want something to eat?"

"Thank you."

Five minutes later Ettore came back with a plate of tramezzini and placed it in front of Aldrian.

They asked no questions, and he said nothing. He sat there silently, drank, ate a bit, and when he left the restaurant at dark, the two refused to let him pay.

"Come back again," Ettore said in passing.

"And bring Beatrice with you," Giacomo added.

Lost in thought, Aldrian went back to the Campo San Polo. Beatrice wasn't home yet, and the empty apartment only intensified the terrible lonliness that enveloped him.

When the telephone rang and Margherita asked why had hadn't come to visit, he told her about the interrogation at police headquarters and his trip to Padua.

Ca' d'Oro

8

He had stayed awake for a long time trying to reach Beatrice.

The next morning he found a note on Beatrice's rumpled half of the bed that read: "I got back very late and had to be up early. I didn't want to wake you. Love, Beatrice."

To combat his sadness, he got dressed and left the apartment. It was already noon, the sun was shining, and the streets were full of people. Where should he go? Without any particular reason he headed toward his brother's house and the fish market. At Diego Sarcia's mask store he kept his head down and looked at the pavement so that he didn't look in the store window as he usually did. Sarcia was the crank in the meatgrinder he'd just been put through, Aldrian imagined. That Diego had only used him was a depressing thought.

Out of habit he turned down the narrow street with the small shops and then on to the fish market. The Jurassic Park store and the front door were sealed off, and it was obvious that he would never again set foot in his studio apartment. Too many things would bother him. As he stood before the display window, he had to think of his brother and Elena, realizing that the two of them had been surprised during the night, pulled out of bed, and hauled to the Pescaria.

"Aren't you the brother? Aren't you Michael Aldrian?" someone said to him and—when he turned around—photographed him with a smartphone.

Aldrian automatically fled to the fishhall that was not as busy now and realized, when he turned around, that the stranger was still following him. He was sure it was a member of Boscolo's organization, but he couldn't tell if the man was armed or was just tailing him. So he hurried past the flowerstand and between the rows of fruit and vegetable booths to the Grand Canal, saw that the packed traghetto "Sofia" was docking, and got there just as it was about to leave. Most of the passengers were standing in the gondola ferry, a young mother with her baby carriage was just in front of him. The seats were all taken so that he also had to stand the whole trip across the Grand Canal. To distract himself, he first studied the gondolier who stood at the prow and rowed on the lefthand side, then the second man at the stern who did the same from the righthand side. At that point he saw that his tail was standing between tall pilings back at the fish market, still trying to photograph him with his smartphone. Aldrian turned back, lost his balance and would have fallen if a man behind him hadn't reached out and steadied him. When Aldrian had righted himself, the other passengers smiled at him as if he had just made a funny joke, and a child got up and offered him his seat. He now sat on the narrow bench, squeezed between a tiny senior citizen with a walking cane and an equally fragile woman or nurse with neon-blue hair. Somebody called out: "Falling into the Grand Canal brings good luck!" and everybody laughed.

They abruptly docked at Campo Santa Sofia, and Aldrian—still on the run—sprinted around the block and then across the Strada Nova to the narrow Calle di Ca' d'Oro. He hurried along beside a brick wall and back toward the main canal. After a few steps he recognized the richly decorated wooden door with its rectangular peephole and the palace, previously painted a golden color. Ahead was the garden with a white stone fountain. He realized he had missed the entrance to the museum, returned to the street and back to the two glass doors that led to the lobby with the ticket office. Since he had always seen the Ca' d'Oro from the fish market, he immediately recognized the delicate enhancements that looked as if they had been created by a goldsmith. His brother had told him that the "House of Gold," a late-Gothic pallazo from the 15th century, was built of polychrome marble, painted ultramarine, and embellished with gilt stonemasonry on the side facing the Grand Canal. It had arcade galleries on two floors.

Aldrian first went up to the balcony on the third floor and gazed out over the Grand Canal to the fish market and also to his brother's building, just to make sure that the stranger hadn't followed him. Cautiously he scanned the opposite bank, the gondola ferry landing, and then even the passengers in the traghetto, but without spotting the man. Still restless, he went down a floor and again checked the immediate premises and the boat. Only then did he sit down on a marble bench along the wall and close his eyes. He was at the right place, he thought. When he opened his eyes, he saw that the sun was shining on the mosaic floor, forming fantastic geometric shadow patterns. Everything of architectural beauty that the exterior facade had to offer was a silent immaterial mystery on the mosaic floor. There was, in addition, the play of light from the crown glass in the side windows that covered the wall with a softly glowing pattern of bluish and pale golden Newton's rings.

After a while he stood up and walked on. Every time he had been here his impressions were more intense than anywhere else, and each time after his first visit it was a déjà-vu experience. Two fragments from the exterior frescos that were originally located at the Fondaco dei Tedeschi, the former settlement of German merchants in Venice—Titian's barely recognizable Judith and a portion of a nude by Giorgione—were now in wood frames and embellished the interior walls of the Ca' d'Oro. Aldrian had frequently passed by the Fondaco dei Tedeschi that later served for many years as the main postoffice in Venice because it was right on the Rialto Bridge. He also knew that there was a brisk trade in cloves, nutmeg, ginger, saffron, cinnamon, sugar, and pepper beneath the arcades and in the rooms. He was familiar with the fragrances of oriental bazaars and his nose detected a fine trace of them when he just thought about the place. There were also lemons and oranges for sale, along with wine and olive oil, almonds and figs. His brother told him that pearls and gems were also bought and sold there, glassware from Murano, fabrics of silk, cotton and damask cloth, velvet, brocade and gold thread, not to mention paper and books.

The play of shadows on the floor had changed, moved on, become longer or shorter, faded and been replaced by new shapes. He now wandered through several halls with archeological finds in display cases: smaller and larger remnants of jugs, goblets, and plates from the 15th and 16th centuries, according to the descriptions They seemed to him like revelations. Here and there he tried to expand the patterns in his head, but they all disintegrated into oblivion. He had always been fascinated by archeological finds, by shards and splinters. When he listened to music it became clear that he had to acknowledge the mysterious, the inexplicable that attracted him if he wanted to truly comprehend it. He shouldn't consider the musical scores as a type of mechanical philosophy, but rather as molecules, atoms, and quantum particles of a language that would become visible and audible only through the musical notation. Aldrian loved to reproduce the insights of science and the arts—as far as he understood them. They, too, were splinters of a whole that was loosely constructed from the available fragments. The sight of the shards in the display cases also brought him back to the universe of the prompter's box where tones, notes, melodies aroused certain feelings in him that he was not really able to explain afterwards—especially when a performance was truly successful. But he did realize that the mysterious, the irrelevant, contained a type of shorthand message that he could only appreciate through his emotions. He was able to comprehend everything, thanks to his deceptions as a magician, because each of his slight-of-hand movements came from an enormous bag of tricks. Without his having noticed, his musical sensitivity for the mysterious had grown until he finally understood that it was more important for him than all the logical explanations that could be found in the musical score. The creative work, he thought, seemed to revolve around the question of whether you took the fragments that resulted from your work and unified them into an entity or left them unresolved—regardless of what you were undertaking—because there were no answers. As he pondered this, he couldn't get enough of the patterns of the shards.

This time he avoided viewing Andrea Mantegna's painting of St. Sebastian pierced by numerous arrows, because just the thought of seeing it brought his dead brother to mind.

He left the Ca' d'Oro when the shadow formations gradually dissipated. As soon as he stepped out onto the street, the impressions and ideas were gone, and he kept an eye out for the man who had taken his picture. At the traghetto landing he saw that it had just left, so he stood there and watched it cross the Grand Canal. It went back and forth all day long. Always the same route.

The traghetto—after loading passengers—came back across the choppy water, rowed by the gondoliers in their black jackets and blue-and-white-striped jerseys. Meanwhile more passengers had gathered at the landing. After the boat had docked and the travelers had come shore, the new passengers boarded—among them a man with a large dog—and they moved off. The trip was without incident and Aldrian, who first checked the opposite bank but didn't see the man, occasionally watched the dog as it stared at the water. As he disembarked, Aldrian noticed that the gondoliers' lodge was decorated with a picture of the Virgin Mary. He didn't go past his brother's house, but made a detour to the Campo San Polo and watched to make sure he wasn't being followed.

Beatrice Returns

9

He sat down at the table in Beatrice's apartment and knew that he had long since given up on his project to write a guidebook.

Beatrice finally called and said she wanted to spend a lovely evening with him.

They cooked together, ate and drank, and hugged in the dark room. They talked the rest of the evening about what had happened, and Aldrian described for her what he had discussed with Commissario Galli. She suddenly smiled, shook her head, and said: "Everything you've told me is so improbable that I believe you."

Beatrice, Aldrian, and Emilio

10

Aldrian didn't leave the apartment again until the day of the funeral. There was only one exception. First he became interested in Jakob and Elena's Garden of Eden, googled it on the Internet and discovered that the location on the bay at Lesbos was truly fantastic. He didn't tell Beatrice about the stranger who had photographed him—he didn't want to upset her—and lied to her that he was staying inside as a precautionary measure. He also didn't talk about the island of Lesbos and Jakob and his wife's paradise. Instead, between phone conversations with Beatrice, several times he called the mostly silent Emilio who was staying at Margherita's and told him stories about his parents' everyday lives, his own health, and of old times. However he didn't allow his nephew to come visit him and—with the same advisory that it might be too dangerous—he also declined the invitation to come to Margherita's or even move into her apartment. On the other hand, his memories of the workshop and Sergio Celi's house, of the two dead men and the fire, as well as the architectural model and the backdrops came into sharper focus. Gradually his daydreams merged with Jakob and Elena's dreams of paradise. His own paradise was a construct of letters, notes, and colors, from music, books, paintings and costumes—it was illusory, he told himself. Jakob and Elena, however, had wanted an actual, a "real" paradise. Still, in Aldrian's imagination he had frequently been an imaginary figure, so that now—after he himself had acted like a fictional character—he didn't mind taking excursions into reality instead of becoming a completely fictional character. When he had gained this insight into his situation, he called Emilio back and suggested, first in the form of hints, that they take a trip to Lesbos together. He knew that, as far as possible, his nephew had to get over his loss, and that he and Beatrice could help him in that regard. But first, Emilio had to want it himself and be interested in making the trip, which, following Aldrian's initial suggestion, turned out to be precisely the case. When he eventually told Beatrice about his idea, it didn't take her long to agree.

This was how Aldrian tried to distance himself from his grief, and when he couldn't entirely forget what had happened and felt the painful absence of Jakob and Elena, he did experience the desire to escape from his personal nightmare.

The following day he informed Margherita of his plan, and she was enthusiastic because she was very worried about Emilio. Time and time again she cried on his shoulder, and each time her complaints turned into rage and then into expletives directed at the police and journalists.

Beatrice booked the plane tickets, read the reports in the paper about the tragedy, and told Aldrian everything she thought was important. The newspaper articles had become shorter and relegated to the section on local news, though reporters were waiting for the funeral. As Beatrice already knew, people still suspected that the murders had to do with the counterfeit money. But there was no proof that Jakob and Elena had been involved in any crime, and the family—especially Margherita and Emilio, but Aldrian, too, supported by Beatrice—spoke about deliberate character assassination of the two victims.

The Final Chapter

11

On the day of the funeral their grief, repressed by everyday affairs, returned with a vengeance. A few days earlier, Beatrice had convinced him to attend the Teatro La Fenice and hear George Frederick Handel's oratorio *Il trionfo del tempo e del disinganno*, "The Triumph of Time and Disillusion." They had reserved two box seats so people wouldn't recognize him. Till now, Aldrian hadn't been interested in this oratorio and, since his hearing loss, he had been reluctant to listen to anything new. But his curiosity finally became so great that he overcame his objections and went to his beloved opera house. This time the name *Fenice*, "Phoenix," affected him as never before.

Aldrian had discovered on Beatrice's laptop that "The Triumph of Time and Disillusion" was an allegory where the figures of Time and Beauty were in conflict with Pleasure and Disillusion. Time and Beauty had become estranged because they saw that they had aged. Beauty threw herself in the arms of Pleasure, while Time grew closer to Disillusion. Eventually the latter gained the upper hand. At the last moment Time and Beauty found their way back together, naked and cleansed with the ashes of Regret and Sorrow. The music of the oratorio that he heard for the first time understood him. It wasn't he who understood what it meant, but rather the music that recognized what was happening within him. It remained in his head as he sat between Beatrice and Emilio during the funeral in the Santa Maria Formosa church and saw the two flower-covered coffins before him. At the reunion with his nephew Emilio outside the church, the young man—an umbrella in hand—threw his arms around Aldrian's neck and asked that he be allowed to keep his arm around Aldrian's shoulders. And they remained standing like that in the fog. It was the same place where, on the day of his arrival during the acqua alta, an African had sold him the small golden dove that he still wore under his lapel and now called "Fenice." Back then he had subsequently witnessed a baptism.

Because of the rain they didn't stay long outside on the forecourt where a growing crowd of people was gathering under umbrellas. There were many motorboats on the Rio de Santa Maria Formosa. Two imposing gondolas, decorated with large gilded seahorses and an equally gold angel emerging from a seashell, were moored on the embankment at a stone bridge. The two gondoliers in raincoats and hoods were standing nearby with their arms crossed. And inside the church the pews quickly filled, so that remote friends and acquaintances and especially curiosity seekers had to line up in the middle section.

Aside from the Zemei brothers, Dr. Dr. Galotti, and Diego Sarcia, Aldrian suddenly recognized among the mourners the man who had photographed him in front of his brother's house. This time the fellow wore black so as not to attract attention. The stranger glanced at Aldrian and nodded briefly, which Aldrian found odd. He bent over to Beatrice, pointed out the man, and asked her if she knew him.

"Yes, he's a colleague," she whispered, "from *Il Gazzettino*. Why?" Aldrian only replied that the man had nodded to him.

He could barely follow the Mass and the priest's eulogy—Handel's music was still stuck in his head and he surrendered to it. Time and time again brief memories of Jakob and Elena interrupted the oratorio that only he could hear and confused him to the extent that he had to repeat entire sections in his thoughts. At one point he placed his arm on Emilio's shoulders, though the young man didn't seem to notice. As best Aldrian could tell, Emilio was following the proceedings with an unresponsive expression.

The coffins were decorated with Jakob and Elena's favorite flowers, white lilies and yellow roses, each lid adorned with one type of flower. At the end of the Mass, Aldrian followed the coffins out onto the piazza that was crowded with the mourners' umbrellas all the way to the silver-grey coffinboats "San Michele 2" and "San Michele 3." They resembled limousines but had no canopy at the stern so the coffins could be mounted on the rear platform. On the short walk from the church down to the boats he could hear the rain beating loudly on his umbrella, and, as if he were accustomed to doing so, he climbed down the steps and into the boat with the yellow roses, while one of the black-suited morticians steadied him by holding his arm. Beatrice and Emilio sat down next to him a few moments later. Emilio stared at the deck. The young man first thought he was in his mother's funeral boat, until he realized that the flowers accompanying the coffin were those of her beloved spouse. As for Aldrian, he gazed—as if from a prompter's box—through the side window up at the people with their umbrellas who had gathered as a silent chorus. He was back with his own thoughts and heard Handel's oratorio from the point where it had been interrupted. But right after their departure they got caught in a traffic jam by the stone bridge. Aldrian saw that there were motorboats on both sides of the canal, and two more large ones were approaching from under the bridge, so the first funeral boat and then the second had to travel in reverse back to the landing by the church. While this was happening, Aldrian noticed tourists taking pictures from the bridge. Individual flashes penetrated the grey atmosphere of fog and rain. When the motorboats had passed, the first and then the second funeral boat started all over again, but in the same instant, on the other side of the canal, a large gondola appeared, carrying tourists in rain gear and hoods. Undeterred, the "San Michele 2" steered toward the bridge, slowed, and gave the gondola a gentle bump that briefly knocked the passengers off balance, and the gondolier reversed, cursing the whole time. Following the "San Michele 2," they came to the broader Rio de Santa Marina, as Aldrian now gazed through the windshield at the funeral boat ahead of them in the fog, at the coffin and the white lilies.

They docked at the San Michele cemetery, and he tried to be attentive. Waiting for them here beyond the vaporetto station was a large crowd, including several photographers who were uninhibited. The reporter from *Il Gazzettino* arrived in the next boat. He surprised Aldrian by handing him his business card and apologizing. Aldrian realized that he hadn't left Beatrice's apartment for over a week because of this man.

The coffins were transported through the cemetery gate, and the mourners, flowers in hand, respectfully stood back and let them pass, following Jakob and Elena through a second gate. On the ledge of a wall adjoining a monastery building Aldrian noticed tiny figures of Jesus and Mary, a statue of St. Joseph holding the baby Jesus, two ceramic jars, and a large bottle with artificial lilies.

The funeral cortege proceeded past row after row of ten unit-high columbarium walls and seemingly endless rows of children's graves. Of course Aldrian was familiar with the cemetery, he had made several pilgrimages to the graves of Stravinsky and Luigi Nono, but this time he primarily noticed the seagulls scurrying in the grass between the headstones or standing on the slab gravestones as they cleaned their feathers. In the fog and rain the procession passed a wreath of stone rose blossoms that hung on a stone cross, past stone eagles on columns, and stately cypress and pine trees.

A double grave had been dug for Elena and Jakob. Since Margherita had requested that there be no eulogy, the coffins quickly disappeared into the ground, and Emilio, who was clinging to Aldrian's arm, began to cry, so Aldrian led him off to one side. From there they watched the mourners toss bouquets into the pit. They also recognized Elena's relatives who had arranged themselves at the gravesite and, as some sobbed, thanked each individual for his or her condolences.

In the meantime Aldrian used his phone to order a watertaxi, walked the mute Emilio back to the vaporetto station, and waited with him to get away from the San Michele cemetery. There was no one else around when the Commissario unexpectedly came through the gate and straight for them. Aldrian excused himself, gave Emilio the umbrella for a moment, and went to meet Galli. The Commissario, wearing a hat and raincoat, expressed his condolences by silently shaking Aldrian's hand with his head bowed.

"I must admit that I'm relieved there are no charges against you at the moment. We've not been able to locate the printing press and your brother's blueprints. Perhaps everything was done in Naples or in Sicily, who knows?"

Aldrian nodded, and Commissario Galli returned to the cemetery without turning around.

Shortly thereafter, a group of curiosity seekers in intense discussions came through the gate. Aldrian heard the watertaxi coming and again saw his nephew Emilio silently weeping and staring at the ground.

Emilio had packed his suitcase two days earlier. He still cried for a time on the trip with the watertaxi, which made Aldrian wonder if it was such a good idea to take him along on the journey to Greece. He wasn't able to console the young man. Emilio didn't calm down until his closest relatives eventually arrived at Margherita's apartment.

Margherita and Beatrice were dishing out the pre-cooked food. The guests silently sat down at their places, a glass of wine in hand.

It was now noon. Margherita didn't eat a thing. Aldrian could see how exhausted she was, and was now convinced she would be relieved when they left on their trip. He had paid for the entire funeral, but he steadfastly refused to mention it.

It wasn't until they reached the airport that Emilio revived. He suddenly seemed more composed and was even curious about what he was going to see. And Aldrian could tell that he wasn't alone. Beatrice had taken a year's sabbatical, he now learned, and although sad, she was secretly full of expectations. He remembered that he had signed a contract to give a magic show at the fantastic Hotel

Miramar in Opatija. But first he had to see what paradise looked like. Even if it was destroyed, there was still the land, the sea and the river, the birds, bees and salamanders, the fish, rocks and stars.

The paperweight he had bought for Beatrice was in his luggage, along with the brain section of the famous conductor that he wanted to bury at the spot where Jakob and Elena had planned to build their house.

"At some point," Beatrice said to him as they had taken their seats on the plane, "we'll be able to get some peace and quiet. And then," she paused briefly, "you can tell me what really happened."

#

AFTERWORD

"Michael Aldrian—Avenging Angel or Fictional Puppet?"

Over the course of four decades Gerhard Roth has built a well-deserved reputation as a prolific writer, known primarily for his 7-volume cycle *Archive des Schweigens* (Archives of Silence) and his more recent 8-volume series *Orkus* (Orcus, Hades); the current novel, *Die Irrfahrt des Michael Aldrian*, is the first in a projected three-volume cycle, set in Venice.

Gerhard Roth was long considered a controversial writer, often sharply critical of Austria, past and present—a brilliant pariah, a *Nestbeschmutzer*, literally a bird that befouls its own nest. His many awards finally culminated in the Grand Austrian State Prize in 2016, considered an act of official forgiveness, and certainly long overdue.

Roth has been fascinated to the point of obsession with his country's history, of its collusion with National Socialism as well as actual recent incidents: the disappearance of a Mozart fragment, the murder of three Chechen refugees, a gas explosion in his own Viennese neighborhood, among others. More recently he has occupied himself with riddles, puzzles, and labyrinths; alongside the earlier novels, *Der Plan* (1998), *Das Labyrinth* (2004) and *Grundriss eines Rätsels* (2014), Michael Aldrian's Venetian odyssey consists of wandering the maze of narrow streets and waterways, encountering the enigmatic "insanity" around him.

THE BREADTH AND DEPTH OF EXISTENCE

Gerhard Roth has a predilection for portraying the variety and abundance of experiences that broadly constitute life in its myriad forms. For example, in *Grundriss eines Rätsels* the writer Philipp Artner creates a stunning (if outrageous!) construct that could be considered an alphabet of life—animal, vegetable, and mineral; animate and inanimate; the significant and the trivial; the good, bad, and the ugly—highlighting the diversity and profusion of life's contents:

Draft 2

a = coal, coal heap, coal spots, coal dust
b = fat masturbating imbecile
c = nest and eggs of a duck
d = lost hatbox
e = the 70th Surah of the Quran in the Cyrillic script
f = the face of Mayakovsky
g = soldier
h = man in socks with a large penis
i = first menstruation
j = priest at the altar, reading
k = kitchen towel with dead flies
l = language of the birds
m = mathematical formula for the universe
n = farewell note from a suicide
o = peeling onions
p = hunter with rifle

q = fat floating on soup
r = language of goldfish
s = a severed nose
t = naked hairdresser, naked dental assistant
u = broken eyeglasses on a paved road
v = open cadaver of a slaughtered lamb
w = leather suitcase full of pocketknives
x = croaking frogs
y = painful infection of the buttocks
z = cooking applesauce with cloves and cinnamon
ä = seagulls crying above Amsterdam's canal
ö = agaves
ü = gasoline spill on water [1]

Obviously, thousands of other examples could be substituted for the above, further expanding the magnitude of the content.

As a complement to his writing, Roth is an avid photographer, having published several volumes of photos from his travels.[2] Many of his pictures have served as visual stimuli for scenes in corresponding novels.[3] His descriptions of actual historical locales and structures—including their dimensions, architectural features, and even their color—provide an existing and verifiable reality for his fictional characters.

But whether writing or taking pictures, Roth's approach is similar:

---

1 Gerhard Roth, *Grundriss eines Rätsels*, (S. Fischer Verlag: Frankfurt, 2014), 505–506 (my translation).

2 Photo volumes include *Grenzland*, 1981; *Die Photo-Notizbücher*, 1995; *Atlas der Stille*, 2007; *Im unsichtbaren Wien*, 2010; *Über Land und Meer*, 2011; *Im Irrgarten der Bilder*, 2012; and *Spuren*, 2017.

3 For example, in *Der See, Der Plan, Der Berg, Der Strom, Das Labyrinth*, and *Die Stadt*. See Daniela Bartens and Gerhard Meltzer, eds., Gerhard Roth, *Orkus: Im Schattenreich der Zeichen*, (Springer: Wien, 2003). For a glimpse at six of Roth's pictures of Venice, see: Stefan Zavernik, "Irrfahrt durch Venedig: Gerhard Roth im Interview," 80 *Kulturzeitung*, 13 March 2018.

"Reality is infinitely large for the human eye and the human mind, it encompasses not only the microscopically small but also the macroscopically huge universe. Thus a photographer has infinite possibilities, from the near-at-hand to the most distant. But things that are invisible to the senses also belong to reality, for example, thoughts in your mind .... Pictures and work on the photographs are also an attempt to make 'the insignificant' visible."[4]

In his fiction, Roth has also provoked the insight that every microcosm can be a macrocosm: for example, even a small rural town, such as the Styrian village of Wies in *Grundriss eines Rätsels*, can contain a wealth of experiences, both good and bad, as any major city in the world, encounters that we would normally expect in metropolises such as Vienna or Venice.

VENICE

And now Roth depicts Venice, continuing the infatuation that Northern Europeans (Thomas Mann, Goethe, Proust, Nietzsche, Alfred Andersch, et al.) have had for the water city. A primary attraction is its climate and geography as "La Serenissima,"—the unique water city, typified by its historical significance, wealth, charm, and grandeur of the arts.

The attractions of Venice for a land-locked Austrian like Aldrian (and Roth!) are a vibrant history, impressive palaces

4 Gerhard Roth: *Spuren*, herausgegeben von Daniela Bartens und Martin Behr: "Die Wirklichkeit ist für Menschenaugen und Menschengehirne unendlich groß, sie umfasst nicht nur das mikroskopisch kleine, sondern auch das makroskopisch große Universum. Ein Fotograf hat daher unendliche Auswahlmöglichkeiten, vom Naheliegendsten bis zum Entferntesten. Zur Wirklichkeit gehört aber auch das für die Wahrnehmung Unsichtbare, z. B. Gedanken im Kopf .... Die Aufnahmen und die Arbeit an den Fotografien sind auch der Versuch, 'Unbedeutendes' sichtbar zu machen.'"

and villas, official buildings and tony restaurants populated with romantic Italians and exotic foreigners, canals that serve as the main thoroughfares with vaporettos and gondolas for transportation, a maze of narrow streets and alleys requiring a map for orientation with remarkable but out-of-the-way sites such as museums, libraries, bookstores . . . and even a madhouse!

Much of the novel fulfills Aldrian's initial impulse to create his own unique guidebook to Venice with its monumental beauty and coexisting reminders of its storied brutality.[5]

> Roth employs popular Venetian subjects, such as the costumes and masks, museums and churches, the pedantically repeated regional cuisine, the everyday adventures of shopping at the fish market, the attraction of the Doge's Palace. On the other hand, there are the counter-histories, the brutal side of this fairytale city, discoveries that are found in no guidebook—such as the cemetery on San Servolo.[6]

Aldrian covers the usual tourist haunts—St. Mark's Square, the Doge's Palace, and the Bridge of Sighs, for example—but is more intrigued by lesser-known sites, such as churches, archives, markets and unique shops, vaporetto routes to the outer islands, and legends such as that of Casanova and Matteo Lovat, the fanatic who crucified himself. Though Aldrian's research is complicated by the *acqua alta* and annual Carnival celebration, music from his favorite operas

---

5 Reminiscent of Roth's own 1991 non-fiction guide to Vienna, *Eine Reise in das Innere von Wien* (A Journey into the Bowels of Vienna).

6 Sven Hanuschek, *Frankfurter Rundschau*, 18 October 2017: "Roth benutzt gängige Venedig-Topoi wie die Verkleidungen und Masken, die Museen und Kirchen, das pedantisch wiedergegebene regionale Essen, das Alltagsabenteuer eines Einkaufens am Fischmarkt, die ,Schauseite' des Dogenpalasts. Auf der anderen Seite gibt es die Gegengeschichte, die grausamen Seiten dieser Märchenstadt mit Entdeckungen, die in der Tat in keinem Reiseführer stehen – wie der Friedhof auf San Servolo."

serves as spiritual inspiration, again underscoring the profusion of life's experiences in this unique environment.

THE CHARACTERS

Roth's recent fiction has featured individuals who are forced out of their professional and everyday routines and must deal with new, unusual, and even life-threatening situations. Their previous training and lifestyle do not prepare them for these encounters, so they must adapt as best they can, often facing defeat or even death: the librarian Konrad Feldt in *Der Plan;* the five narrators in *Das Labyrinth;* Vertlieb Swinden in *Grundriss eines Rätsels,* and, of course, the titular figure in *Die Irrfahrt des Michael Aldrian* exemplify this concept. Instead of "prompting" the action, as he has done throughout his professional career as *Maestro Suggeritore,* Aldrian is reduced to the role of spectator—he is rarely able to plan and must struggle to react to the unexpected. Venice, its environment and events become puzzling, even for an experienced visitor like Aldrian.

In this context, one observer has emphasized the mutability of such figures:

> His [Roth's] works deal with the boundary between normality and insanity, with the relationship of criminals to victims, but most of all with the question of human capabilities. And in this regard, Roth is very clear: mankind doesn't stem from the apes, but from chameleons . . . .[7]

---

7 Oliver Pfohlmann, "Das Chamäleonhafte des Menschen," *literaturkritik,* 6 June 2018: "Seine Werke beschäftigen sich mit der Grenze von Normalität und Wahnsinn, mit der Verfasstheit von Tätern und Opfern, vor allem aber mit der Frage, wozu der Mensch fähig ist. Und was das angeht, so ist für Roth ausgemacht: Der Mensch stammt nicht vom Affen ab, sondern vom Chamäleon . . . ."

Roth emphasizes the transitory and transitional nature of life—and thus that of his characters—in our current novel's marvelous opening sentence: "I was a child prodigy, now I am a nobody." Roth's latest gambit originates from a fascinating premise: What happens when child prodigies mature? Jakob and Michael were gifted children: the older brother, Jakob, could draw, while Michael had a musical ear. Since neither could create original works, Jakob becomes an illustrator and Michael an opera prompter. Jakob ultimately uses his talent to forge artworks in order to afford his version of "paradise," a villa in Greece. Meanwhile, Michael loses his hearing and thus his occupation—without his gift, he is basically a normal human being with impaired hearing who can seemingly do little more than slight-of-hand and magic tricks.

ATTACKS, PURSUITS, ENCOUNTERS, MURDERS

The beauty in Aldrian's life—the music, the paintings, the "magic"—are unexpectedly replaced by isolation, abandonment, and despair. How should he react? In the critical moment after he was first attacked, his immediate thoughts were:

> Something had happened that had wiped out his past . . . . It struck him that he was acting like a criminal, but he also didn't feel like a victim—more like a witness or, rather, like a future perpetrator. He decided he would put up a fight. (56)

In an attempt to protect himself and later to avenge his brother and sister-in-law, Aldrian shoots three people—wounding his initial pursuer, killing the diver Sergio Celi and the used-book dealer Rocco Scarlatti—and ultimately bludgeons Rodolfo Boscolo with a hammer. Somehow he is able to prevail against these violent criminals, against all odds. He has proven to be more resilient, more aggressive, more courageous, more deadly than he could have imagined.

DIES IRAE—FALL FROM GRACE, REDEMPTION, OR SIMPLY ESCAPE?

One critic has observed a duality at work:
Like two voices of a duet, like the left and right halves of the brain, the two levels of reality are placed in opposition—the Carnivalesque-nightmarish and the logical-rational—to the point that the each and every point of reality becomes suspect. The entire text is structured as a dichotomy: heaven and earth, paradise and hell, angels and demons (both worldly and religious), power and impotence, reality and dream, memory and oblivion, fiction and reality, interior and exterior, high and low, light and darkness, metamorphosis and mimicry, and so much more can be extrapolated from this one original schism, as the Christian iconography of Judgment Day differentiates with its separation corresponding to the ascendance into Heaven and the fall into hell. That the hope for an actual 'real' earthly paradise can cast mankind into hell, that heaven and hell are thus closely associated, we recognize as one of Roth's lifelong themes.[8]

---

8 In an insightful summation of the novel, Daniela Bartens writes on the Literaturhaus Wien website from 10 January 2018: "Wie zwei Stimmen eines Musikstücks, wie rechte und linke Hirnhälfte, werden die beiden Realitätsebenen gegeneinander geführt – das Karnevalesk-Alptraumhafte und das Logisch-Rationale –, bis der Realitätsstatus von allem und jedem fragwürdig wird. Der ganze Text ist dichotomisch strukturiert: Diesseits und Jenseits, Paradies und Hölle, Engel und Dämonen, (weltliche und kirchliche) Macht und Ohnmacht, Wirklichkeit und Traum, Erinnern und Vergessen, Fiktion und Realität, Innen und Außen, Oben und Unten, Licht und Dunkel, Metamorphose und Mimikry und viele mehr lassen sich aus der einen, ursprünglichen Spaltung, wie sie der christlichen Weltgerichtsikonographie mit ihrer Trennung von Aufstieg in den Himmel und Höllensturz entspricht, ableiten. Dass die Hoffnung auf ein diesseitiges, sozusagen verwirklichtes, 'echtes' Paradies die Menschen in die Hölle stürzen kann, Himmel und Hölle also nah beieinander liegen, kennt man als eines der Lebensthemen Roths."

Indeed, the provisional working title of the novel, *Dies Irae—A Venetian Nightmare*, focused on the search for paradise on earth.[9] Clearly, the title was modified, and the focus of the novel as well: the search for paradise was that of Jakob and his wife Elena. until their dream home in Greece was destroyed as they themselves forfeited their lives in their criminal endeavor.

Michael Aldrian, however, is only trying to deal with the insanity around him. Five times he visits the Chiesa di San Pantalon with Gian Antonio Fumiani's immense ceiling fresco depicting *The Martyrdom and Apotheosis of St. Pantalon*—the descent of angels into hell and their return to heaven, all illuminated by spotlights, thus summarizing and emphasizing his own loss of profession, the loss of his brother and sister-in-law, his loss of innocence through his deeds and murders, and the possible loss of Beatrice. Aldrian perhaps interprets Fumiani's ceiling painting as confirmation that he, too, is part of this human tapestry of good and evil, of fall and possible redemption.

TO BE, OR NOT TO BE

Aldrian is not able to solve the case. At the conclusion of Aldrian's sluthing, Diego Sarcia confesses the details and structure of his own "organized" crime in the chapter "A final Conversation." As a mask and puppet maker, Sarcia uses his livelihood to further heighten Venice's dichotomy of appearance and reality, and, as the "puppeteer," has controlled the murderous action. Sarcia reveals that he himself is ultimately responsible and that Michael has *merely* killed two men and seriously injured two others who were all at the

---

9 Roth, in an interview with Bernd Melichar, "Die Sprache, mein gordischer Knoten," in *Neue Vorarlberger Tageszeitung*, 9 March 2016: ROTH: "Aber ich arbeite natürlich an meinem nächsten Roman. Er spielt in Venedig und erscheint 2017. Der vorläufige Titel lautet: 'Dies Irae—Ein venezianischer Albtraum.' Es geht um die Suche nach dem Paradies auf Erden."

periphery of the plot. Michael, however, does not regret his actions, feel guilt or remorse.

> He suddenly had the certainty that he had acted correctly. All doubt had vanished, he no longer had any regrets."(325)

In the end, he hasn't avenged his brother's and Elena's deaths—Sarcia is responsible and yet goes unpunished. As Aldrian leaves Venice for Greece, he must ponder if his work is done, his revenge complete, or is he simply walking away, escaping, until his scheduled magic performance at the Hotel Miramar in Opatija, Croatia? One critic concludes: "Michael Aldrian becomes involved in conflict and accepts the fight, however not heroically, but rather with disguises and deceptions, resulting in physical and mental pain."[10]

Regardless of our conclusion as to Michael's culpability, the entire story is complicated by a brief paragraph at the beginning of the novel. While still in Vienna, Aldrian encounters his neighbor, the writer Philipp Artner (the wily manipulator and riddler behind the *Grundriss eines Rätsels*) who mentions that he is writing a novel:

> "Are you off to Venice again?" Artner had asked, and when Aldrian replied "Yes," the writer added: "I'm working on a novel that is set in Venice, and you are in it." (5)

Is the book we have just read the novel Artner had promised? If so, then Aldrian's actions are not real, but fictional, his "sins" only literary illusions, his despair and revenge merely the writer's invention. We've seen such authorial tricks before, committed by the

---

10 Almut Oetjen, "Was versteckt sich hinter der Sinnlosigkeit?", Belletristik-Couch, *October* 2017. "Michael Aldrian gerät in einen Konflikt und nimmt einen Kampf an, aber nicht heldenhaft, sondern mit Verhüllungen und Täuschungen, durch Ertragen von körperlichem und seelischem Schmerz."

"writers" in both *Labyrinth* (where the writer creates other parallel characters to carry the narration, à la Fernando Pessoa) and *Grundriss eines Rätsels* (where Philipp Artner himself writes both his own death and his reincarnation); both "writers" are truly omniscient and omnipotent authors who can write whatever they please. That, and repeated references to Pinocchio, reinforce the puppeteer/puppet relationship and succinctly paraphrase the ultimate correlation between author and character. Such authorial legerdemain colors all that follows, forcing the reader to consider—much like Aldrian in Venice—what is reality and what is fiction.

#

The Author

Gerhard Roth (1942–2022) was born in Graz, the son of a medical doctor and a nurse. He originally intended to study medicine, but soon discontinued his studies. For ten years Roth worked as a computer programmer to support his growing family, but since the mid-1970s he was exclusively a writer. His major works consist of a cycle of seven novels, *Die Archive des Schweigens* (The Archives of Silence), and another novel cycle, *Orkus* (Hades). His work has earned extensive critical acclaim over the years, including the Döblin Prize (1983), the Kreisky Prize (2002), and the Grand Austrian State Prize (2016), among many others.

The Translator

Todd C. Hanlin (1941–2022) was Emeritus Professor of German at the University of Arkansas. He authored a book on Franz Kafka, edited Charles Sealsfield's *Austria as it is,* and a collection of essays entitled *Beyond Vienna: Contemporary Literature from the Austrian Provinces*; he wrote on numerous Austrian authors, translated a dozen novels and a similar number of plays, as well as a volume on *The Best of Austrian Science Fiction.* Hanlin translated six novels by Gerhard Roth, including the Venice trilogy, all for Ariadne Press.